Selection Day

Aravind Adiga was born in 1974 in Madras and grew up in Mangalore. He was educated at Columbia University in New York and Magdalen College, University of Oxford. His articles have appeared in publications such as the *New Yorker*, the *Sunday Times*, *Financial Times* and the *Times of India*. His first novel, *The White Tiger*, won the Man Booker Prize in 2008. His second novel, *Last Man in Tower*, was published in 2011.

Praise for *Selection Day*

'When a Booker Prize winner decides to put cricket at the centre of his new novel, it almost seems as if the game must jump to its feet, button up, zip it and stand to attention. *Selection Day* is bound to grab the attention of the cricket-playing-novel-reading parts of the world and be quickly checked out for any familiar faces, in-jokes or suchlike. It's got some and a potshot or two.'

– *The Indian Express*

'Aravind Adiga bats against a country "phixed and phucked" – like a white tiger. Adiga's mastery lies in his ability to unpack cities. His detailing of the urban landscape is never superfluous, never mere literary bluster. It is through the minutiae that he conjures inequalities.'

– Nandini Nair, *Open*

'Like Balram Halwai (*The White Tiger*) and Dharmen Shah (*Last Man in Tower*), there are some characters in *Selection Day* – Mohan Kumar, Anand Mehta and even Tommy Sir to an extent – whose vision of life is limited. It's as if they have no shame or guilt in running after whatever they are pursuing in this new social framework of greed and grab. But unlike *The White Tiger* – for which there were whispers that Adiga's voice was sometimes inauthentic – little rings false in *Selection Day*. Yes, Mehta's satirical haranguing of the Indian way of life may be a bit too much – "Indians are basically a sentimental race with high cholesterol levels" – but what is an innings without a few daring shots? Adiga scores big with his third novel.'

– *Financial Express*

'[*Selection Day*] goes back to an old theme – the pursuit of social mobility, this time through cricket. The very first chapter shows us

Adiga at his best: Here is humour that the writer doesn't have to work hard at, as well as a superb characterization.'

– Elizabeth Kuruvilla, *Mint*

'Aravind Adiga's new novel looks at India's cricket obsession ... [It] follows the lives of two talented, budding cricketers from a Mumbai slum who seek to find a way out of poverty by making it big in the game.'

– *Hindustan Times*

'*Selection Day*, Adiga's third novel, supplies further proof that his Booker Prize, won for *The White Tiger* in 2008, was no fluke. He is not merely a confident storyteller but also a thinker, a sceptic, a wily entertainer, a thorn in the side of orthodoxy and cant ... Powerful ... Soulful ... What this novel offers is the sound of a serious and nervy writer working at near the top of his form. Like a star cricket batter, Adiga stands and delivers, as if for days.'

– Dwight Garner, *The New York Times*

'Adiga seems boundlessly gifted once again. He makes beautiful sentences; creates wonderfully eccentric, original characters; and moves his plot along at a brisk pace. There's energy and wit on every page ... Adiga superbly captures the intimacy between the two brothers, as they bicker, tease and protect each other ... as Adiga explores themes of ambition, failure, homophobia and threats to freedom – whether on a personal or national level – he has produced a nearly flawless novel, and further proof that he is among our finest contemporary novelists.'

– Carmela Ciuraru, *San Francisco Chronicle*

'The best novel I read this year ... In its primal triangle of rival brothers and a maniacal father, hell-bent on success in cricket in India, Adiga grips the passions while painting an extraordinary panorama of contemporary sports, greed, celebrity and mundanity.

As a literary master, Adiga has only advanced in his art since his Booker Prize-winning *The White Tiger*.'

– Mark Greif, *The Atlantic*

'Adiga is an exceptionally talented novelist and the subtlety with which he presents the battle between India's aspirants and its left-behind poor is exceptional.'

– *Richmond Times-Dispatch*

'An engrossing and nuanced coming-of-age novel ... Adiga has succeeded in composing a powerful individual story that, at the same time, does justice to life's (and India's) great indeterminacies.'

– *The Sunday Times* (UK)

'Sensually told and unpredictably plotted ... Adiga's prose has a bustling energy that makes it highly readable.'

– *Financial Times* (UK)

'A captivating and sensitive coming-of-age story that tackles various new themes: the confounding nature of sexuality; the darkness that accompanies excellence and achievement ... Adiga's characters, like his settings, are getting more complex with each book and this complexity makes his indictment of the contemporary world all the more urgent and convincing.'

– *The Times Literary Supplement* (UK)

'A master class in integrating character and landscape ... Peppered with dashes of humor, this dark and unflinching story is an unqualified triumph.'

– Booklist Starred Review

'Brilliant, raw energy ricocheting off every line.'

– *Publishers Weekly* Starred Review

'Captivating.'

– *Harper's Bazaar*

'A great read, even if you're not a fan of cricket.'

– *Bustle*

'Adiga writes a prose of crazed energy, bright color and acrobatic logic ... comical and searing ... *Selection Day* brings a family, a city and an entire country to scabrous and antic life.'

– Michael Upchurch, *Chicago Tribune*

'Ambitious ... filled with smart, spot-on observations about the perils of growing up.'

– Mike Fisher, *The Milwaukee Journal Sentinel*

'Spirited ... the elements of *Selection Day* are strong throughout: a dramatic, readable arc; satire glinting with hints of tragedy; a witty, vibrant voice.'

– Hamilton Cain, *StarTribune* (Minneapolis)

'Wonderfully original.'

– Ru Freeman, *The Boston Globe*

'Exuberant and incisive ... Each sentence flickers like a match with life. Adiga swoops in and out of his characters' inner voices with frightening precision and speed, laying out the paranoia, obsessions, tokens, idols and self-made prisons of each man in a few bright, laser-like sentences ... Richness and rot, decadence and decay, cricket and corruption: These make up Adiga's Mumbai. *Selection Day* asks: Amidst all this, is there any such thing as freedom?'

– Annalisa Quinn, *NPR (National Public Radio)*

'Many novelists are called Dickensian, but Adiga comes closer than most, albeit with every last speck of Victorian sentimentality suctioned out. His characters are brightly and sharply drawn and animated with great energy; reading about his Mumbai is like taking a double shot of espresso ... You need not know anything about cricket in any of its variations to savor *Selection Day*. In fact, you don't need to have any interest in sports at all. Cricket serves Adiga as a marvelously flexible metaphor: for the (lost) dream of civic integrity, for tradition and authority, for the contest that is life in a rapidly evolving economy ... Class is Adiga's great theme, and his depiction of its workings in India ranges from the fondly comical to the savage ...[a] ferociously brilliant novel.'

– Laura Miller, *Slate*

'Adiga writes with customary acerbity and astuteness. Class resentment is the gasoline that fuels the brothers' ambitions and gives this novel its noisy volatility. The gritty urban realism that animated *The White Tiger* and *Last Man in Tower* is again on display ... *Selection Day* churns with the same propulsive energy.'

– Sam Sacks, *The Wall Street Journal*

'This is a novel with a broad sweep, accomplished with commendable economy and humor, in a sinewy, compact prose that has the grace and power of a gifted athlete. And it pulses with affection for Mumbai itself; the effortless sociological dissection recalls Katherine Boo's *Behind the Beautiful Forevers* ... *Selection Day* transcends sport. This is a book about choice and destiny, smothering family ambition and the pull of a young person's nascent identity. You're just going to have to trust me that the cricket is worth it.'

– Marcel Theroux, *The New York Times Book Review*

By the Man Booker Prize-winning author of *The White Tiger*

ARAVIND ADIGA

Selection Day

FOURTH ESTATE • *New Delhi*

First published in hardback in India in 2016 by Fourth Estate
An imprint of HarperCollins *Publishers*

First published in paperback in India in 2017 by Fourth Estate
An imprint of HarperCollins *Publishers*

HarperCollins Publishers India, Cyber City, Building 10-A, Gurugram, Haryana-122002, India
www.harpercollins.co.in

2 4 6 8 10 9 7 5 3 1

P-ISBN: 978-93-5277-020-5
E-ISBN: 978-93-5177-828-8

Typeset in 10.5/14.2 Stempel Garamond
By Saanvi Graphics Noida

Printed and bound at
MicroPrints India, New Delhi

MIX
Paper
FSC
FSC™ C218906

This product is made of FSC®-certified and other controlled material.

HarperCollins Publishers, Macken House, 39/40 Mayor Street Upper, Dublin 1, D01 C9W8, Ireland

My Mother, Usha Mohan Rau

‘My heritage is … like a lion in the forest;
it cries out against me.’

Jeremiah 12:8

I, too, have a secret.

Pebbles and pen-tops; the gold tin-foil wrappers of chocolates; battered coins and the leather handles of cricket bats; cracked green buttons and two-inch needles full of rust: I understand them all.

Pen-tops, you are really lemons. Pebbles are sweeter. Rusty needles are vinegary. The floors of rooms are buttery. Good paper is milky and cheap paper becomes bitter. Orange rinds are tastier than oranges. Only one thing in this world is tasteless.

Plastic!

He was four years old. Every evening at five thirty his father would take Radha Krishna out for cricket practice, and then he would be alone in the room all three of them lived in; he was in *Kattale*.

Kattale is darkness in Kannada, his mother tongue: and so much darker than any English-language darkness.

In *Kattale*, his nose pressed against the mirror; he breathed on glass. His tongue grew: and he began understanding and reunderstanding.

You, glass, are just salt. The bindis that go on a woman's forehead taste like Kissan mixed-fruit jam. Wool is burnt starch. Cotton is cooler than wool, and better at keeping scents.

People came next. When he sniffed Radha Krishna's white cricket T-shirt, even before he began licking, it smelled of one of the seven kinds of sweat. The kind produced when a boy is scared. Then he knew Radha had been at cricket practice with their father.

This was his secret world. His tongue was a white sail and when it grew big he could go from one end of the world to the other. Alone, in *Kattale*, like Sindbad, he explored. Then when he was seven or eight years old, the lights came on one evening, and his father caught him licking the mirror. A blow fell on the boy's back; blow followed blow until his stomach vomited out everything it had tasted, and he became like Radha Krishna, and like everyone else.

No more secrets.

There's usually no one in the school corridor in the evenings so I go there after practice with my cricket bag on my shoulder, to wash my face and hands with the antiseptic soap. But that evening I saw a boy standing alone in the corridor: he had a nose like a beak. In his left hand he held a little round mirror and he was looking at himself in it. Suddenly I remembered something I'd forgotten for years. That evening when I was still a boy, and pushed open the door to the women's toilet by mistake, and saw my mother inside, examining the kajol around her eyes in the mirror, I began sweating, and my heart beat faster and faster. That is when he looked up from his mirror and noticed me.

Six years later, Manjunath had just opened the door to another hidden world.

PART ONE

Three years before Selection Day

Eighth Standard

'I've got news for you, Tommy Sir.'

'And I've got news for *you*, Pramod. You see, when I was twenty-one years old, which is to say before you were even born, I began working on a history of the Maratha campaign at the third battle of Panipat. It had a title: "1761: the soul breaks out of its encirclement". Because I felt that no truthful account of this battle had ever been written. All the histories say we Marathas lost to the Afghans at Panipat on 14 January 1761. *Not* true. I mean, it may be *true*, we lost, but it's not the true *story*.'

'Tommy Sir, there is a younger brother, too. He also plays cricket. That's my news.'

'Pramod. I am *sick* of cricket. Talk to me about battles, onions, Narendra Modi, *anything* else. Don't you understand?'

'Tommy Sir. You should have *seen* the younger brother bat today at the Oval Maidan. You *should* have. He's nearly as good as his big brother.'

Darkness, Mumbai. The bargaining goes on and on.

'And you know just how good the elder brother is, Tommy Sir.

You said Radha Krishna Kumar was the best young batsman you've seen in fifty years.'

'Fifty? Pramod: there hasn't been a best young batsman in fifty years in the past fifty years. I said best in *fifteen* years. Don't just stand there, help me clean up. Bend a bit, Pramod. You're growing fat.'

Behind glass and steel, behind banks and towers, behind the blue monstrosity of the Bharat Diamond Bourse is a patch of living green: the Mumbai Cricket Association (MCA) Club in the heart of the Bandra-Kurla Financial Centre. Floodlights expose the club's lawns, on which two men scavenge.

'I ask you, Pramod, since you insist on talking about cricket, what is the chance of elder and younger brother from the same family becoming great cricketers? It is against Nature.'

'You distrust sporting brothers, Tommy Sir. Why?'

'*Mistrust*, Pramod. Pick up that plastic for me, please.'

'A master of English cricket and grammar alike, Tommy Sir. You should be writing for the *Times of Great Britain*.'

'Of *London*.'

'Sorry, Tommy Sir.'

Sucking in his paunch, Pramod Sawant bent down, and lifted a plastic wrapper by its torn edge.

'The younger brother is called Manjunath Kumar. He's the *biggest* secret in Mumbai cricket today, I tell you. The boy is the real thing.'

Chubby, moustached Pramod Sawant, now in his early forties, was a man of some importance in Bombay cricket – head coach at the Ali Weinberg International School, runner-up in last year's Harris Shield. Head Coach Sawant was, in other words, a fat pipe in the filtration system that sucks in strong wrists, quick reflexes and supple limbs from every part of the city, channels them through school teams, club championships, and friendly matches for years and years, and then one sudden morning pours them out into an open field where two or maybe three new players will be picked for the Mumbai Ranji Trophy team.

But he is nothing if he can't get Tommy Sir's attention tonight.

'No one knows what the real thing looks like, Pramod. I've never seen it. How can *you* tell?'

'This Manju is a real son of a bitch, I tell you. He's got this way of deflecting everything off his pads: lots of runs on the leg side. Bit of Sandeep Patil, bit of Sachin, bit of Sobers, but mostly, he's *khadoos*. Cricket sponsorship is a brilliant, brilliant, brilliant idea: now you can make it *twice* as brilliant.'

Grey-haired Tommy Sir, taller and wiser than Coach Sawant, kept his eyes on the lawn.

'After thirty-nine years of service to Bombay cricket, they make me clean up like a servant, Pramod. After thirty-nine years.'

'You don't *have* to clean up, Tommy Sir. You know it. The peon will do it in the morning. See, I know Manju, the younger brother, is the real thing, because if he's not, then what is he? A fake. And this boy is not a fake, I promise you.'

Having completed a round of the cricket ground, Tommy Sir had started on a second trash-hunting circle within the previous one.

'Pramod, the idea that the boy has to be …' he bent down, examined a stone, and let it drop, 'either real or a fake is a very Western piece of logic.'

He moved on.

'Do you know what the Jains say, Pramod? *Seven* varieties of truth exist. Seven. One, this younger brother might in fact be the real thing. Two, he might be a fake. Three, the boy might simultaneously be the real thing *and* a fake. Four, he might exist in some state beyond reality and fraudulence that we humans cannot hope to comprehend. Five, he might in fact be the real thing *and* yet exist in a state beyond our poor human capacity to comprehend. Six—'

'Tommy Sir. Please. I know what I felt in my heart when that boy was batting. I know.'

'My dear Pramod. Hockey is India's national game, chess best suits our body type, and football is the future.'

Two old stumps lay in their path. Tommy Sir picked up one and Sawant pretended to pick up the other.

'Football has been the future for fifty years, Tommy Sir. Nothing will replace cricket.'

The two men walked the rest of the circle in silence, and then Tommy Sir, holding the stump against his chest, started a third tour of the ground.

He spoke at last.

'Pramod, the great George Bernard Shaw said: they haven't spoken English in America in decades. And I say about Indians: we haven't played cricket in decades. At least since 1978. Go home now. I am very tired, I want to hike near Mahabaleshwar this weekend. I dream of mountains, Pramod.'

Sawant, fighting for breath, could see only one piece of uncollected rubbish: a white glove lying in the very centre of the ground. Clenching his fists, he raced Tommy Sir to the glove, and picked it up first.

'A bit of Sandeep Patil meets a bit of Ricky Ponting. You should have seen the boy today.'

'Are you deaf?' Tense muscles extended Tommy Sir's high forehead. 'In 1978, Sunny Gavaskar lost the ability to leave the ball outside the off-stump, and since then we've been playing baseball and calling it cricket. Go home.'

He snatched the glove from Sawant.

Walking to a corner of the ground, he let the rubbish spill from his hands: in the morning, the peon would move all of it into the storeroom.

As Sawant watched, Tommy Sir got into an autorickshaw, which began to move. Then, as if in a silent movie, the auto stopped, and a man's palm shot out and beckoned.

Loaded now with both men, the auto left the Bandra-Kurla Complex for the highway, and then turned into Kalanagar, where it stopped outside a mildew-stained housing society.

Suffering Sawant to pay the driver, Tommy Sir got out of the autorickshaw; he looked up at the fourth floor of the building to see if his daughter Lata had left the lights on in the kitchen despite his telling her, for twenty-two years, that this was against every principle of Home Science, a wonderful subject which they once used to teach young women in every college in this country.

Tommy Sir pointed at the sky over his housing society: the full moon was balanced on a water tank.

'Pramod, on a night like this, you know the young people in Bandra just go crazy. Out in the Bandstand, those boys and girls walk all the way out onto the rocks, sit down, start kissing. They forget that the ocean exists. Slowly the tide comes in. Higher and higher.' The old man raised his fingers to his collarbones. 'All at once, the young people stop kissing, because they find themselves sitting in the middle of the ocean, and they start screaming for their lives.'

He paused.

'Pramod – what is the younger one's name? Manju?'

'I knew you'd agree, Tommy Sir. You believe in the future of this country. I'll tell the visionary. I mean the *other* visionary.'

'Pramod Sawant: now listen to me. One, this visionary of yours is probably just a bootlegger. Second, I like Radha Kumar, but I don't like his father. The Chutney Raja is mad. I met him six month ago, remember? Now I have to deal with him twice over?'

'That's the only negative point, I agree. The father *is* mad.'

Tommy Sir blamed the full moon over the watertank for what he said next.

'How *much* Sandeep Patil?'

•

For nearly forty years now, a tall, grey-haired man with small eyes had been seen at maidans, school compounds, gymkhanas, members-only clubs, and any other place where boys in white uniforms had gathered. All through the cricket season, either at the Bombay Gymkhana, or at Shivaji Park, or at the Oval Maidan, Tommy Sir would be watching (hands on hips, brows corrugated) and yelling: 'Greatshot!' 'Bowling!' 'Duffer!' When he was angry, his jaw shifted.

A boy scores a century in the sun, comes back to the school tent expecting an *attaboy* from the great Tommy Sir, but instead a thick hand smacks the back of his head: 'What's wrong with a *double* century?' He had broken many a young cricketer's heart with a sentence or two: 'Not good enough for this game, son. Try hockey instead.' Blunt. Tommy Sir was given to the truth as some men are to drink. Once or twice in the season he would take a batsman, after a long and productive innings, to the sugar-cane stand; on such occasions, the boys stood together and watched with open mouths: *Mogambo Khush Hua. Tommy Sir is pleased.*

Not his real name, obviously. Because Narayanrao Sadashivrao Kulkarni was too long, his friends called him Tommy; and because that was too short, his protégés called him Tommy Sir. Like a Labrador that had been knighted by Her Majesty Queen of England. Ridiculous.

He hated the name.

Naturally, it stuck.

On the day before his marriage in July 1974, he told his wife-to-be, who had arrived by overnight train from a village near Nashik, six salient points about himself. One, this is my salary statement. Read it and understand I am not a man meant to be rich in life. Two, I don't believe in God. Three, I don't watch movies, whether Hindi, Hollywood or Marathi. Four, likewise for live theatrical productions. Five, every Sunday when Ranji, Harris, Giles, Vijay Merchant, Kanga or *any* type of cricket is being played in the city of Bombay, I will not be at home from breakfast to dinner. Six, one weekend a year I go to the Western Ghats near Pune and I have to be absolutely alone that weekend, and Six Point Two, because seven points are too many for any woman to remember, before I die, I want to discover a new Vivian Richards, Hanif Mohammed or Don Bradman. Think about these six points and marry me tomorrow if you want. Afterward don't regret: I won't give divorce.

Educated man, literary man, man of many allusions: his column on the traditions of Mumbai cricket was syndicated in sixteen newspapers around India. Artistic man, cultured man, self-taught painter: his watercolour interpretations of black-and-white photos of classic Test matches had been exhibited to universal acclaim at the Jehangir Art Gallery a few years ago. Said to be working in secret on a history of the Maratha army in the eighteenth century. Possibly the best talent scout ever seen in India. Thirteen of his discoveries had made the city's Ranji Trophy team, including 'Speed Demon' T.O. Shenoy, bowler of the fastest ball in the city's history; plus, during a six-month stint in Chennai in the 1990s, he had uncovered two genuine rubies in the South Indian mud who went on to scintillate for Tamil Nadu cricket. On his desktop computer were testimonials from nine current, six retired and two semi-retired Ranji Trophy players; also signed letters of appreciation from the cricket boards of seventeen nations.

And all these people, whether in Mumbai, Tamil Nadu or anywhere else, know the same thing Head Coach Pramod Sawant knows: somewhere out there is the new Sachin Tendulkar, the new Don Bradman, the one boy he has still not found in thirty-nine years – and Tommy Sir wants that boy more than he wants a glass of water on a hot day.

•

There – opposite Victoria Terminus. Disappearing.

Manjunath Kumar ran down the steps towards a tunnel, the black handle of a cricket bat jutting like an abbreviated kendo stick from the kitbag on his left shoulder. Three more steps before he reached the tunnel. *Fact Stranger than Fiction: place a glass of boiling water in your freezer next to a glass of lukewarm water. The glass of boiling water turns into ice before the lukewarm water. How does one explain this paradox?* The eyes bulged in his dark face, suggesting independence and defiance, but the chin was small and pointy, as if made to please the viewer; a first pimple had erupted on his cheek; and the prominent stitching on the side of his red cricket kitbag stated: 'Property M.K. – s/o Mr Mohan Kumar, Dahisar'. In his pocket he had fifteen rupees, the exact amount required to buy peanuts and bottled water after the cricket, and a folded page of newspaper. *Fact Stranger than Fiction: place a glass of boiling water in your freezer ...* The smelly, cacophonic tunnel was filled, even on a Sunday morning, with humanity, hunting in the raw fluorescent light for sports shoes, colourful shirts, and things that could entertain children. *Fact Stranger than ...* Manju worked his way through the crowd. Mechanical toys attempted somersaults over his shoes. To catch his attention, two men stood side by side and slapped green tennis rackets against tin foil, setting off sparks. Electronic mosquito-killers. Only fifty rupees for you, son. *How does one explain this paradox ...* Only forty rupees for you, son. In the distance, Manju saw the flight of steps leading up to Victoria Terminus. One half of the steps lay in twilight. There must be a lunette over the entrance of the tunnel, clouded over with one hundred years of Bombay grime. Thirty rupees is as low as I'll go, even for you, son.

But the upper half of the steps glittered like Christmas tinsel.

Emerging from the tunnel, and about to cross the road to Azad Maidan, he stopped. Manju had spotted him – the boy he saw every Sunday, but who wore a different face each time.

The average cricketer.

Today, it was that fellow staring at the footpath as he dragged his bag behind him. Wearing a green cap and stained white clothes. Fourteen years old or so. Talking to himself.

'... missed. Missed by this much. But the umpire ... blind. And mad, too ...'

From his side of the road, Manjunath grinned.

Hello, average cricketer.

This was the wreckage of the first match at Azad Maidan – this fellow who was half a foot shorter than he had been at 7 a.m., who was blinking and arguing with the air, cursing the umpire and the bowler and his captain and their captain, and growing shorter every minute, because he knew in his heart that he had never been meant for greatness in cricket.

Hauling his kitbag off his shoulders and lowering it to the pavement, Manju unzipped the bag and extracted his new bat: he held the black handle in both hands, and gripped tight.

And waited.

The average cricketer removed his green cap and raised his head, and the eyes of the two boys met.

Manjunath Kumar showed him how to drive through the covers. He showed him how to attack, defend, and master the red cricket ball.

After which, like W.G. Grace, he stood with his weight on the bat handle. And then stuck his tongue out and rolled his eyeballs.

Across the road, the green cap fell onto the pavement. Goodbye to you, Prince Manju waved to the average cricketer, and goodbye – Prince Manju turned to his left, then to his right – to all average things.

I am the second-best batsman in the whole world.

•

'Stop right there. We were talking about you last night. I said, stop.'

The silhouettes of the Municipal Building and the spiked dome of the Victoria Terminus struggled against the morning smog, and the air in between them was scored by cable wires. Blue smoke rose from the garbage burning in a corner.

Between the buildings and the burning garbage stood a fat man, trying to catch Manjunath like a football goalie.

'Come back, boy. Come back at once.'

With a grin, Manjunath surrendered, and walked back to where Head Coach Sawant stood.

'Did you hear what I was saying? I said, we were talking about you last night. "We" means two people. So, who was the other man talking about your future? Ask me.'

Instead of which, Manju, drawing a hand from his cricket bag, showed the coach something.

'What is this?' Sawant asked, as the boy handed him a disturbingly large page of the Sunday newspaper.

'Please, sir. What is the answer?'

Sawant took the Paradox in both hands. His brain struggled with High School physics and his lips with Newspaper English.

... place a glass of boiling water in ...

'I have no idea, Manju. No idea at all. Take it back. Manju,' the coach said, 'why have you brought this to cricket? Is there no one at home you can show this to? What about your—'

'My mother is away on a long holiday, sir.'

As Manju folded his precious piece of newspaper and tucked it into his cricket kitbag, Sawant studied him from head to toe, like a man wondering if he has made a bad decision.

'Tommy Sir was the other man talking about you. You know what it means if he takes an interest in a boy.'

But Manju had flown.

'Hey, Manjuboy! Come over here!'

Twenty other young cricketers stood around a red stone-roller with 'Tiger' written twice on it. They had been waiting for him.

'Chutneyboy! Look at the chutneyboy come running.'

'Chutneyboy who wants to be a Young Lion. Come here!'

It was a court martial: a boy was holding up one of those new phones that were also tiny television sets, and Manju was told to stand on the stone-roller, while the circle tightened around him.

As Manju rose above the circle of white, Sawant, hands on his hips, walked around the stone-roller for a better view.

The boys were making Manju watch, as a woman reporter aimed a mike at a tall teenager, handsome enough in every other way too, but whose eyes, cool grey clouds, were like a snow leopard's.

'Chutney Raja! That's what they call your father, Manju. Chutney Raja!'

'You heard them on TV. My big brother is a Young Lion.'

'Chutney Raja SubJunior! All you're good for is your science textbooks. What do you know about batting?'

'Thomas, today I'll hit you for three fours one after the other. Then, I'll hit you for three sixes. What did you say about my father?'

'He's a Chutney Raja.'

'And what is *your* father then?'

'Your brother is Chutney Raja Junior. That makes you—'

YOUNG LIONS

'Join us in the quest to find the next generation of sporting legends!'

You can see from these images that Radha Krishna Kumar has grown up in what some would consider less than ideal conditions, at the very edge of Mumbai. His father is a variety-chutney salesman, whose main business is his sons. In his own words:

'We have a family secret which makes us superior to every other cricketing family in the city of Mumbai. There is a secret blessing given to my son Radha by the Lord Subramanya, who is our family deity ...'

(Secret from God? Shit. Your father really is mad.)

(Ashwin. I heard that. Two fours!)

'Mr Mohan, is it really true that your son got Sachin Tendulkar out in a practice match or is that just a story?'

'There is a saying in our language: he who steals a peanut is a thief. He who steals an elephant is also a thief. This means we do not lie in matters big or small. Radha Krishna clean bowled Sachin Tendulkar with his fourth ball.'

(This is true! This really happened!)

(Shut up, Chutney Raja SubJunior! And why is your brother called Radha? Isn't that a girl's name?)

Radha Kumar has the status of a superstar in his neighbourhood. We spoke to his neighbour, Mr Ramnath, seen here in front of his ironing stand.

'Dahisar was famous, they used to shoot films here before the river became dirty. The moment I saw Radha, when his father brought him here over ten years ago, I told my wife, this boy will make Dahisar famous again.'

YOUNG LIONS
MONDAY 6.30 P.M. REPEATED ON WEDNESDAY

Follow us on Twitter

•

Enough! Flailing his arms, Manju scattered his tormentors from the stone-roller: time for real cricket, at last.

'... SubJunior! Get ready to bat!'

'Oh Champion of Champions!'

A drum-beat had begun at the far end of the maidan. Padded up, helmeted, and swinging his bat in circles over his head, Manju walked up to the crease.

At noon, he was still batting. Manju Kumar had kept his word to the bowlers, punishing each one of them in a different way for what they had said about his father (and about his brother having a girl's name), lofting Thomas over mid-wicket, driving Ashwin twice through the covers, and cutting, pulling and flicking the others.

Pramod Sawant stood, arms folded across his chest, and watched Manju: passing over the boy's dark, eye-heavy face, pointy chin and solitary pimple, and then over his shoulders and biceps, to settle on the crucial part of a batsman's body. In Australia they bat with their footwork. In India we do it with our wrists. Manjunath Kumar's forearms in action made his coach's mouth water. Dark and defined cunning, those forearms were broader than the biceps; they were a twenty-five-year-old man's forearms grafted onto the body of a four-foot ten-inch child; they were forearms which, as they petted, coaxed, and occasionally bludgeoned the hard red ball to the boundary, made Head Coach Sawant remember, with a shiver, the muscular man in black shorts who had come to his village with the travelling circus three decades ago.

•

There – shirtless, on the floor of a 320-square-foot box of brick. Home. Manjunath was back in the one-room brick shed, divided by a green curtain, where he had lived since his father brought him and his brother to Mumbai, nine years ago. Pressing his palms against his cheeks, the boy went over the newspaper once again:

One theory relies on the 'Lake Effect', which is seen in the cold countries of northern America …

His cricket gear lay around him, and he was stripped to his waist.

Manju saw shadows moving in the blade of light beneath the closed metal door of his home. His father was outside, answering the neighbours' questions. When is Radha Krishna coming back? Does he think he is too big now to talk to his own neighbours?

On the table there was dinner made by his aunt (or possibly great-aunt) Sharadha. The world was in order, except for one Scientific Paradox.

A quick crust of ice forms over the lake, keeping the water underneath it liquid all through winter. Similarly, when lukewarm water freezes, a thin crust forms on top. In a glass of boiling water, in contrast, evaporating steam stops the …

A clattering noise made him look up: a vermin cavalry went galloping over the corrugated tin roof. Rats, rushing towards the flour-mill in the centre of the slum. Manju turned on the television, and increased the volume.

Reaching far behind the television set, he picked up an instant-noodle cup filled with dark mud in which two horsegram beans, planted forty-eight hours ago, had sprouted. New life, fathered by Master Manjunath. He looked at the tender shoots paternally, spilled big drops of water from a glass into the pot, and then returned the life-bearing cup to its hiding place behind the TV.

The final image of the day's episode flashed on television: the cadaver of an American man lying naked on a green dissecting table under a cone of hard white light, before the screen went black and the credits rolled.

Manju looked down at his own body: that thing had started again – he was hard. It was happening all the time now, sometimes even when his father or brother were in the same room. He lay down and pressed himself against the floor.

He wondered what colour his cock had become under the pressure of his own body: and then he felt that it was liquefying under the weight, and spreading, an icy liquid, all around him.

Now he found himself on a frozen lake. He was not alone here. Beamed from the CSI inspection table, the foreigner's cadaver now lay in the middle of the lake.

Promoted to the elite squad of *CSI Las Vegas*, Agent Manjunath Kumar-Grissom crawls, scraping the surface of the ice with his right toenail, inching nearer and nearer to the naked dead body that he must retrieve; but when he is almost there, *click*, *crack*, the surface of the lake starts to break under him.

Whistles and cheers explode all around – Ra-dha! Ra-dha! – for a Young Lion has just returned to the slum, but Manju, who must now go out and smile for the neighbours, is still on the floor, trying to crush his hard-on.

•

An egret flew in from the river and watched the boy, who lay above a well, watching a turtle.

It was an open well, the kind that still exists in a suburb like Dahisar, raised three inches from the ground and covered by a rusty iron grille: and as he lay face down on it Manju watched something beneath the water's skin.

His legs made a 'V' on the chequerwork of the grid, which

creaked as he shifted his weight. Through its interstices, he shone a pen-torch down on the black water.

He lanced his beam of light around the well. There! Splashing out of the black water, it came curiously to the light, a dark and domed creature, its limbs paddling fast.

Manju turned his pen-torch off, and put his face to the cold grille. His heart beat hard against his ribcage which beat in turn against the metal of the grid. In a few hours he would have his chemistry class. He *knew* a surprise test was coming.

Which of the following is used to make bleach?

A. Hydrogen

B. Hydrochloric Acid

C. Sodium Phosphate

D. Chlorine

Please, please, help me: O God of Cricket and also of Chemistry.

From the depths of the well, a cool draught tickled his cheek; the boy's imagination transformed it into a breath from a range of blue mountains. He felt his hair blowing in the breeze: the mountain air of the Western Ghats.

Each summer, the family went back to their village. Taking the train from Mumbai to Mangalore, they then got on a bus that carried them over the hills and towards the shrine of the God of Cricket, their family deity, Kukke Subramanya; past trees with red leaves, and little streams that skipped a heartbeat when a schoolboy leapt into them, past waterfalls shrouded in waterfalls, until they reached a temple hidden deep inside the Western Ghats, where, leaving the bus, and standing in line for hours, moving past burning camphor and sharp temple bells, past a nine-headed painted snake, the protector Vasuki, they finally came to the silver doorframes, beyond which, lit by oil lamps, waited the thousand-year-old God of Cricket, Subramanya.

'Remind Him, my sons. We can't offer Him much money. So remind Him, monkeys.'

'One of us should become the best batsman in the world, and the other the second best.'

Mohan Kumar had his own way of reminding God. As he did each year, he rolled barechested over the hard granite floor of the temple, rolled from one side of the wall to the other, and then back again, until his torso was lacerated, and the secret contract was renewed in his blood.

'Are you licking yourself again?'

'No,' Manju said. 'Just watching.'

'Get up.'

Manju didn't.

And now Radha lowered himself beside Manju, and there were two bodies lying on the old metal grid over the well.

'Let's go. He must have woken by now,' Radha said.

Manju pointed the pen-torch to a spot below them.

'It's that turtle again. She's the mother.'

'Maybe. Let's go home. He may hit you again if he's in a bad mood, Manju.'

'It is the mother. I'm not going till you agree that it is the mother.'

'I can't see it from here, Manju.'

'I'm showing you, I'm showing you.'

Radha, the Young Lion, was square-jawed, tall and muscular, and was sometimes mistaken for Manju's uncle, though there was just a year and a month between them. He strained to see through the grating to where his younger brother was directing the pen-torch beam.

'See. The mother. Do you agree? Then we can go.'

'Wait, Manju. Point the light over there. I think there's one more.'

The pen-torch moved: a second turtle was discovered. It raised its head towards its two human observers. How fascinating, it seemed to be saying, to see the turtles that live in that bigger darkness up there. Done, it lost interest in the boys, and sank back into the water.

'Do you agree? That's the mother. Then we can go.'

Manjunath Kumar pressed against his brother's body; the warmth sharpened his senses.

Suddenly a new turtle came into view: its body angled towards the light, jaw wide open, a rim of gold glistening around its shell.

'Manju, you're wrong. That's the mother. It's bigger.'

'I've hidden it behind the TV,' Manju whispered.

'What?'

'My biology experiment. I want full marks in class this time.'

Two months ago, his model fighter jet plane, a project for his physics class, left on the dining table, had mysteriously vanished after he had put four days of work into it.

'He's going to find it anyway, and then he'll throw it out, Manju. Come. We have to go. He's woken up by now.'

'I want to watch the turtle.'

'Manju, it's not *that* morning.'

'I want to watch the turtle.'

'Manju, it's *not* a check-up morning,' his brother said. 'Don't be afraid.' Radha poked his brother in the ribs. 'And if you don't come now, I'll show him where you've hidden your science experiment.'

The brothers looked at each other for a moment: then both bodies sprang from the well and ran.

Their father had already folded up their cots and propped them against the wall, forming two isosceles triangles; his own cot was on the other side of the green curtain. Next to the dining table stood a metal almirah, which complained of its years of ill treatment in a rash of rusty patches and livid scars; leaning on three of its sides were seven cricket bats.

Old Sharadha, relative of some kind, aunt or great-aunt, polyglot remonstrator in Kannada, Hindi and English, the only woman to have entered their home for a decade, perhaps longer (neither boy can remember exactly when She left), was cleaning the stove and last night's dishes.

Standing before the mirror on his side of the green curtain, Mohan Kumar was painting his moustache, a grooming procedure that could take a quarter of an hour. He turned around with his dye-brush and looked at his sons.

'Were you looking at girls again? Naked girls bathing in the morning?'

'No, Appa. We were looking at turtles.'

'Boys,' Mohan Kumar said, closing his eyes and restraining his anger. 'If you are looking at naked girls, half-naked bathing girls, tell me. I will not punish. But don't lie. What were you two looking at?'

Emerging with a pitch-black moustache, Mohan called his second son to him, held his chin, and turned his face from side to side.

'There's blood in your cheeks, Manju. That comes from hormones. You were looking at girls, weren't you?'

'No, Appa.'

When Mohan Kumar raised his hand, his palm rotated ninety degrees to the left and vibrated, like a man having a fit just as he was saluting; Manju cringed and readied himself; the blow fell on the right side of his face.

In ten minutes, the boys were in school uniform and had packed their cricket bags: they stood at attention while Mohan slid his fingers into the bags to check their contents.

And then, closing the door of their home behind them, the family Kumar left for cricket practice.

When they passed the tyre-repair place with the sign saying PUNCHER SHOP, Manju stopped, and shouted, 'Wrong, that's wrong!'

'Quiet,' Radha said.

But when he looked at his father, Manju knew that he wanted him to continue: he was proud of his son, smarter than everyone else his age in the slum.

'Do You Want Pan Card!' Manju raised his voice. 'Pumpkin Carrot Banana Shapes Fruit and Vegetable Salad Decorators! Pandal, Marriage, Birthday Experts! Everything in English is written the wrong way and I alone know!'

But Manjunath Kumar, world's second-best batsman, knew something much more important than how to spell English correctly: Manju knew how to read other people's minds. It had come to him like one of those special things that some children can do; like being able to move your ears without touching them or curling your tongue up as if it were a dried leaf or flexing your thumb all the way back. If he let himself be still, Manju could tell what other people wanted from him. And he could complete their sentences for them.

He knew that this secret gift, this mind-reading power, had come to him from his mother. Her long, elegant nose; her ravishing smile; her way of looking at him sideways – he remembered all this about his mother. This, too: her sitting on a sofa, fixing her beautiful smile on her visitors, all the time rubbing the silver coin embossed with the image of Lord Subramanya that hung from her marriage-necklace as if it were an amulet that read minds for her. She could always say what her guests wanted to hear, and she pampered them with flattery after flattery, till they left her with their egos refreshed and glowing, as if they had just stepped out of a *hammam*; and then one day, she read his father's mind and vanished. That is what saved her from being killed by Mohan Kumar. Manju was sure of it. That is why their mother had never come back to see Radha or him, even though she must have heard they were famous. She was so scared of her husband she had forgotten her sons.

Right now, reading his father's mind, knowing what he had to do to give him satisfaction and pleasure, Manjunath kept shouting in English, while Radha (who did not have his brother's secret gift) protested:

'Didn't you hear him? Shut up, Manju.'

Manju did shut up: but only because of the grinding noise and a cloud of particulated flour produced by the wheat-mill. It was a tyrant of blue pipes and funnels, the most famous object in the slum, which brought even people from good buildings to Shastrinagar every morning. The noise and choking white dust temporarily pacified the youngest Kumar, but then he began again:

'Internet Gaming Cyber Mahesh Cafe!'

'Manju, shut up, I told you. I know English too, but *I'm* not showing off.'

Following their father, the boys had passed the shuttered shops of their slum, and through a cardboard WELCOME TO OUR HOME arch. The gift of a political party, it was painted blue, and covered by the beaming, disembodied faces of city, statewide and national leaders, at least two of whom were serving jail sentences, a fact which only heightened the impression that they were so many medieval criminals whose grinning heads had been hoisted up above a city gate. An observer from a distance, however, might well judge that the faces on the blue arch were so many genies gathered there to perform friendly magic: for family Kumar now appeared to be walking on water.

The slum had grown at the very edge of Mumbai's municipal limits. For most of the year, the Dahisar river was a rock-filled sewer, lit up by egrets and the flutter of a paddy-bird returning to its nest of twigs. A series of bricks, spaced two feet apart in the water, formed a makeshift bridge: their father had hoisted his cycle over his head, and the boys followed him step by step, as they crossed over the river and into the rest of Mumbai.

At the station – get in, get in – Mohan pushed the slow cricketers and their bags into the fast train. Hurry, hurry. Miss this train and there won't be space on the next one. It'll be rush hour. Yes, I know there's an empty seat, but you can't sit down, Manju. All three of us will stand. I don't want anyone sleeping in the train and yawning during practice.

A thin, tall gap-toothed child went about the first-class carriage, offering or threatening to polish shoes for five rupees each. Mohan Kumar's shoes were polished for free. As he worked, the gap-toothed child looked up at the father of cricketers.

'Young Lions? Young Lions. Young Lions? Young Lions. Young Lions?'

'I sell unique chutneys,' Mohan told one passenger after the other. 'Twenty-four chutneys for each hour of the day. You like Mint? We have Mint. Garlic? We have *Extra* Garlic. Chilli, Hot Chilli, Green Chilli, Sweet Chilli, Mango, Rainbow, 100 per cent vegetarian.'

Manju leaned his face to his brother's shirt and dozed against his body.

At Bandra, the family Kumar got off and walked along the pedestrian bridge, a grid of inverted 'V's, that zigged and zagged, yellow and metallic, over the swamps and green vacant fields of east Bandra. The sun burned, the wet earth reflected, and the two brothers knew they had to run. Down the yellow bridge, in the direction of the Kalanagar Traffic Signal. Radha surged. Yee-haah. Manju wanted to touch his brother – I've caught you, I've … But to his right (he surrendered a yard to his brother) he saw fields of water lilies, and right beside them newly rutted mud roads on which men fought to move their motorbikes. He caught up with Radha and they ran past security guards playing with their lathis, and a cluster of Muslim youth with their feet dangling down the bridge. Because their father was now invisible behind them, Radha turned to his brother and—

'Sofia.'

At once both of them skidded to a halt.

'Spotty Neck Sofia.'

Putting his hands on his hips, Manju turned his lower lip inside out; while Radha, just a year older but so much wiser, smiled.

'Everyone saw *Young Lions* on TV.' He touched his brother on the shoulder. 'You're the brother of a Young Lion. Which girl in school do *you* like?'

By way of reply, Manju said, 'Shut up,' because their father was coming up behind them.

The three walked down from the bridge and went into the suburb of Kalanagar.

An armoured car painted in camouflage drove past them; they had reached the Matoshree compound, home to the most important man in Mumbai. Surrounded by sandbags, a machine-gun unit guarded the home of Bal Thackeray, Permanent Boss of the city. They passed the guns, and roadside canteens serving hot breakfast, and then the Kumars stood before the Middle Income Group (MIG) Cricket Club.

Making his sons wait by the gate, Mohan Kumar negotiated with the security guard:

'We were on the TV. *Young Lions*. We're here to see ...'

'Tommy Sir doesn't come until ten o'clock.'

'He told us nine o'clock. We came all the way for him. My boys shouldn't miss a day's cricket practice.'

'Can't practise here,' the guard said. 'Down the road.'

Where they found a rubbish dump, and a patch of ragged green beyond it.

Radha and his father took the ragged green. Manju strapped on his pads near the rubbish, one eye on the big holes in the ground. Ratholes. Tightening his calf-muscle, Manju raised his right foot on a low brick wall to doublecheck that his pads were fastened. Going down on his haunches, Manju now launched himself over the ratholes. Master Kumar, Rat-Tamer, jumped up and down; underground, rodents shivered. While doing his jumps, Manju turned himself 180 degrees, to see his father lecturing Radha.

'The bat is touching your toes, Radha. You won't be able to drive cleanly.'

Manju saw the irritation on his brother's face.

But the Man had to be obeyed, and Radha readjusted his stance. From a distance, Manju gripped his bat and waited. Radha Kumar attacked; Manjunath Kumar imitated.

The ball had flown from Radha's bat to a distant corner of the wasteland, and Manju took off, until his father announced: 'He who hit it will retrieve it. That is the rule.'

So Radha raised his bat, sucked his teeth, and ran after the ball.

Radha Krishna Kumar meant to honour his end of his father's contract with God. Two years ago, God sent his living viceroy, Sachin Tendulkar, to meet Radha at a practice match at the MCA grounds: Sachin stood at the wicket, and Radha was tossed the ball by Tommy Sir. The boy, who had let his hair grow long, like Sachin's, and had watched Sachin's videos, especially Perth 1992 and Sydney 2004, at least 120 times each, spun the ball right past Sachin's forward defensive stroke and into his stumps. 'Well done, sir,' God's viceroy said and, as everyone clapped, made Radha the gift of his own batting gloves.

At the age of fourteen and a half, Radha was now conscious that his father's rules, which had framed the world around him since he could remember, were prison bars. He saw the red cricket ball inside a thicket of wild grass and thorns. Getting down on his knees he put his hand into the thorns.

Why must a boy not shave till he's twenty-one?

Because the cut of a razor makes hormones run faster in his blood.

And why must a boy not drive a car till his father allows him to?

Because indiscipline will destroy anything, even a secret contract with God.

Drenched in sweat and his father's mad theories, Radha seized the ball and threw it back at Mohan, who had already started stepping back to catch it. Radha admired the method, the textbook correctness of his father's pose. Before teaching his boys, Mohan Kumar had taught himself the science of cricket. But when the ball landed in his palms, it hit the flesh and bounced out, and Radha smiled, and became a year older.

'I told you *not* to come! He hates fathers!'

Radha and Manju saw Pramod Sawant, their head school coach, half walking and half running towards them, pumping his arms.

Mohan Kumar summoned his boys to his side and put his arms on their shoulders, as if posing for a group photo.

'They're my children, I made them,' he shouted back, 'and neither you nor your Tommy Sir is going to steal them from me.'

Coach Sawant clacked his tongue.

'Steal them? This boy loves you, Mohan. If anyone says a bad word about his father, Manju will murder them. But for their sake, you must leave now. Tommy Sir's plan is *visionary*.'

Mohan Kumar pulled both his restless sons into his body.

'Why must I leave? My sons always play better when I am watching them. I've never heard of a cricket scout who doesn't like fathers.'

But Coach Sawant reached over and squeezed Mohan Kumar's right shoulder.

'Do it for your sons, Mohan ...'

After a moment, Kumar let go of Radha. Part of any Bombay school coach's job is to declaw the parent and gently prise from his grip the boys who will contribute to the greater glory of Bombay cricket. Sawant smiled, pointed at Manju, and made ingratiating contractions with his eyes.

'... both your sons, Mohan. And you must go *now*.'

•

More of Mohan Kumar's rules for his sons

Cricket Rules

Same as Life Rules. Keep your head absolutely still. Play straight. Do not loft or hit across the line before the time is right. Hoard. Hoard runs on top of hoarded runs.

Food Rules

No Chinese, noodles, potatoes, fried or otherwise, or junk food. No oil, no ghee, no sugar. Green, bright vegetables, rich in antioxidants. If I ever catch you, Radha, eating dosa at that dirty stall near your school, I'll wake-your-skin-up.

Golden Proverbs

Learn your proverbs, boys. For instance: 'A thousand maggots in the cow-dung patty, but they're all dead by sunset.' Interpretation? Whatever your worries, they're gone by six o'clock. That's not a very true proverb, by the way. Here's one more: 'On its way into town, the king's white horse turned into a donkey.' Think about the meaning of that, my boys. If both of you fail in cricket, boys, the three of us will have to sit outside Dahisar station and beg for our food. But if you really want to understand the life that waits for you as adults, this is the only proverb you need: 'Big thief walks free. Small thief gets caught.'

How to talk about your father with strangers

There is a Chutney Mafia in this city, run by men called Shetty: and they are determined to crush your father's life. Do not discuss any aspect of his past, or what happened to your mother, with anyone.

•

Twilight was her favourite hour.

Manju remembered coming home screaming *Amma! Amma!* only to find their hut empty because his mother was outside, in the strange light, walking in circles by herself. Thinking by herself. Planning something by herself. Perhaps planning to leave him and his brother and run away. Manju breathed slowly. Brilliant sunlight all around – but he was sitting next to his brother, and shaded and protected by Radha Krishna's bulk, he was free to dream. He kept his eyelids half closed, until Radha said: 'Manju, this is all bullshit. Total bullshit.'

Manju opened his eyes wide, looked around, and nodded, before he knew what his brother was talking about.

'That man is never going to give us any money, Manju. It's a waste of time. Let's go. What do you say, scientist?'

Forty minutes had passed since Head Coach Pramod Sawant had brought them over to the club, so that they could be shown to the 'visionary'. Who was apparently the man in the red T-shirt, with the logo that said, Manchester United Gold Key Challenge Supporter.

A dozen boys from Ali Weinberg's cricket team had been summoned to the MIG club, and were sitting in a circle on the lawn; and they watched Tommy Sir and the man in the red T-shirt describe languid circles around them. That was all the two men had done for three-quarters of an hour.

Leaning back to eavesdrop on the two men as they passed, Manju instead heard his brother's voice say, 'Scientist, you know what I'm thinking of right now? She's got a spotty neck.'

Manju elbowed him away, but his brother kept whispering, 'Spotty Neck, Spotty Neck.'

All at once, in both boredom and desire, Radha stood up and began dancing as he sang, *Spotty Neck*, *Spotty Neck*. Radha was the leader of this group of boys; one day he would be captain of their cricket team. The other cricketers joined him: 'Spotty Neck, Spotty Neck, she's got a spotty neck.' Tommy Sir and the rich man in the red T-shirt took no notice. The boys became louder and louder, as Radha swished his hands like a bandmaster before the swaying, singing cricketers.

Only one boy, Manju observed, was not obeying Radha.

While the other cricketers wore regulation school caps, this fellow had his own cap, monogrammed in gold thread with the initials 'J.A.' He had small alert eyes, and a beautiful nose, hooked and swooped, which looked as if it had been made to order. Full black sleeves worn under his cricketer's white T-shirt rendered his arms sleek, pantherlike; and he was rubbing them in alternation, as if getting ready.

The moment he smiled, sickle-shaped dimples would cut into his cheeks. Manju was sure he would see the dimples today, because the last time he and this Mister 'J.A.' had been close together, the rich Muslim boy had not smiled. That was after their match with Anjuman-i-Islam. Dusty and sweaty, the cricketers had waited in a queue by the sugar-cane stand, a reward from Coach Sawant for winning the match. Manju had stood right behind Javed. The Muslim boy's neck, glossy with sweat, was shaved bright below the hairline. When seen from behind, his thick neck conveyed an impression of hidden strength as it expanded into his shoulders. The queue had moved in starts, and the sugar-cane machine had made a tinkling noise as it crushed cane. Before drinking his juice, Javed had lifted his ice-cold glass to the sunlight in an exaggerated flourish that Manju thought might have been meant for his benefit; then, as Manju observed, the powerful throat pulsed and swallowed the juice in one continuous motion.

Now, from opposite points of the circle of white, their eyes met.

'Enough of this shit.'

Manju started, and then realized *he* had not said it. Javed Ansari, the Muslim with the majestic nose, had risen up to his feet, making his black-panther limbs even longer.

'Enough of this shit,' he repeated.

Radha Kumar stopped singing, took a step back, and sat down.

Now the fellow with the commanding nose was, in a very deep voice, chuckling.

U-ha, U-ha, U-ha.

Manju drew closer to his big brother. Radha was not doing much better. With an open mouth he saw the black-panther limbs come closer and closer to him and his brother.

Choosing a route between the Kumars on his way out, 'J.A.' put a hand on Radha's shoulder and nearly kicked Manju in the face as he raised one huge shoe after the other, and left the circle of passive white.

'Ansari!' Tommy Sir shouted. 'Come back. You sit and wait with the others.'

But the boy had left the circle, and was not returning: he kept walking to a car, its door already opened for him by the driver. *Slam.* Engine on, car gone. *He* didn't need any rich man's sponsorship.

•

A magician came thirty years ago to a village in the Western Ghats with an elephant. Not an elephant that did normal work like moving logs with its trunk or pulling down trees, no. It had a secret power, the magician said. He left the creature in the village square and walked a hundred feet away from it – too far for it to hear him. People gathered around the magician. Young Mohan Kumar was one of them. 'Whisper a command for the animal into my ear,' the sorcerer said, 'any command.' Mohan Kumar went up to his ear and whispered: 'Roll on the ground like a baby.' And then – without a word – the sorcerer just looked at his elephant: which got down on its knees, and thrashed about the ground, kicking up dust everywhere. 'Raise your trunk and roar three times.' Again, without a word, the magician forced his elephant to roar. Three times. Mohan watched with his mouth open. That massive beast, with all its muscles, was helpless: it obeyed the brain-waves of its master, it suffered the enchantments of his black magic. When he went back to work, Mohan, a thinking boy, had looked around at the other farmers toiling in the wheat fields, and realized: We are no more unmanacled than that elephant.

This was a truth about life he had never forgotten, even after he had left the village and come by train to the big city. Only recently, Ramnath, his neighbour in the slum, observing that poor Muslims were becoming revolutionaries in Egypt and Syria and kicking out their governments and presidents, had whispered: 'Maybe the same thing will happen in India, eh?' Mohan Kumar had smirked. 'Here, we can't even *see* our chains.'

After being forced by Coach Sawant to leave his sons at the MIG Cricket Club, Mohan had returned to Dahisar, mounted his bicycle, tied two stainless-steel containers of chutneys to its side, and visited a Mysore Sweets, an Anand Bhuvan and a National Hindu Restaurant, before cycling down to Deepa, the Restaurant-Bar near the Dahisar train station. No one bought a thing from him. Heaving his bicycle over his head, he walked over the Dahisar river on the all-but-submerged bridge of bricks, then slammed the bike down, and cycled through the cardboard WELCOME TO OUR HOME arch (shielding his eyes from the gaze of the grinning politicians), past the broken homes and little shops, until he got to his own, where the sight of his neighbour Ramnath pressing white shirts with a stupid industriousness was so unbearable that he went to a teashop for relief.

He squatted by his bicycle and blew on the hot tea. He seethed. Tommy Sir thinks he can cut me out of my own sons' future. I know what he is telling that visionary investor about me. He is calling me a chutney salesman. A thug. A peasant. An idiot.

When he got angry, Mohan Kumar's right eyebrow rose up rakishly, which highlighted the comic element in his small and moustached face.

Looking at his glass of tea, he delivered the speech he wanted to give Tommy Sir (but had had to desist for the sake of his sons):

'Other parents pay tens of thousands of rupees for cricket coaches, but I, a penniless migrant to Mumbai, am the pro-gen-i-tor of pro-di-gies. Mr Tommy Sir, I say these words slowly, why? So that even a man of your mental capacities may understand them. Here are two more words pronounced slowly for you. Amoxycillin. Azithromycin. Do you know what they are? Do you know how to prescribe them? I do. I have taught myself medicine and pharmacology. Mr Tommy allegedly Sir: where were you when my sons fell ill? Where were you when they needed someone to sit by their side and record their temperature every half hour? Mr Tommy: when my Radha becomes famous and glorious, I'll call the reporters to the MIG Cricket Club. To the very place where you humiliated me. And I'll have my press conference right there.'

Even in tea, there is no peace today. The moment Mohan Kumar began sipping, the legless man had to make noise on his flute in a corner of the shop. This legless fellow performed every morning in the train station, and came here afterwards. Holding up his glass of tea, Mohan Kumar looked at the flautist.

Brother. Have pity on me. Think how much I have suffered in life. Please stop.

The flour-mill began its rumbling, giving off pungent fumes – it ground red chillies in the second shift, adding burning eyes to its customary noise pollution.

Mohan Kumar kept looking. The legless flautist kept playing.

Until the father put his glass down, walked over, slapped the flute out of the man's hand, and returned to his spot to pick up his glass, only to find that his phone was ringing.

It was the boys' cricket coach, and he said: 'It's payday, Mohan. Congratulations.'

•

'But where is Coach Sawant?'

Three-quarters of an hour had passed, and Mohan Kumar, an aureole of sweat on his back, had pushed through the crowds around Bandra train station, and returned to Kalanagar, walking past Matoshree for the second time that day, to find a tall grey-haired man, whom he recognized from his one previous meeting nearly six months earlier as the man who hated all sporting fathers, Tommy Sir, waiting at the entrance of the MIG club, along with a stocky middle-aged man wearing a wonderful red T-shirt.

'Gone with the other boys to school,' said Tommy Sir, without smiling at Mohan Kumar.

'I'm Anand Mehta.' The man in the T-shirt, who smelled of cologne, stuck his hand out. 'Just seen your boy bat. Very impressed.'

When he smelled the rich man's hand, Mohan Kumar was overcome by shame. He almost cried.

'Forgive me,' he said, refusing to touch the perfumed flesh. 'For my wet state, forgive me. For my lateness, forgive me.'

'No problem, mate,' the rich man said, slapping Mohan on his wet back. 'My wife Asha says, if people sweat it means they're honest. Can you read my T-shirt? Manchester United Gold Key Supporter. I have a cricket academy near Azad Maidan, did Tommy Sir tell you? Last year, I was happy to escort, at my own expense, seventy-six of the brightest young cricketing bodies in this country under the age of fifteen to Bowral, New South Wales, home of the one, the only, the eternal, the infinite, Sir Donald Bradman, where, in addition to a master class conducted in the Don's own town, the boys also enjoyed a sumptuous meal of Aussie lamb wrapped in brown pitta bread. Australia is the reality principle in cricket, Tommy Sir: otherwise we Indians would think we were good at this game. Am I right, or am I right? Come in, come in, let's eat and do business.'

They sat in the cafeteria of the MIG club, and a waiter came for their order.

'Nothing for me,' Tommy Sir said.

'Order,' Anand Mehta retaliated. 'Order samosas.'

Like many others of his class in Mumbai, Mehta gave an impression of dogged and uncerebral strength. A small square forehead, held tight by close-cropped hair, expanded into a powerful black brush moustache over a stonecrusher jaw; a white fold of fat at the back of his skull broadened down a thick neck into a wide chest and wider paunch whose width he exaggerated by letting his shirt hang loose. His fleshy palms had clearly done no hard work, and yet seemed to sweat a lot. His English was international; he drew his phrases equally from the American, British and Indian dialects, and had acquired the democratic Australian habit of calling everyone around him 'mate'. Halfway through each sentence came a pause in which he stared at a corner of the ceiling with an open mouth, as if just then realizing what he had begun to say; and he had the child's habit of raising his voice when he repeated himself.

'This man,' Tommy Sir said, pointing a finger at the investor, 'is a visionary. He wants to start the world's first cricket sponsorship programme, and of all the boys in Mumbai he has picked yours as his first candidates. You are a lucky man, Mohan Kumar.'

'No, sir,' the chutney salesman replied. '*No*, sir.'

'No?'

'*He* is a lucky man.' He took a breath, and turned to the investor: 'Mr Anand, sir, I was not allowed to be present when my own sons were exhibited to you like goods at the market' – an angry glance at Tommy Sir – 'so I could not present a full picture of their talents. Let me share with you the whole A–Z of Future Champion-Making. Now, sir—'

Everyone stopped talking. Like a gangster introducing a gun into the discussions, Mohan Kumar suddenly placed a white cotton handkerchief on the table. Within the handkerchief was something black and heavy; he unwrapped the white layers to reveal a very large cell phone, which he proceeded to squint at.

'Just checking if any customer has asked for a new batch of chutneys,' he said, re-wrapping his phone in the handkerchief. 'To keep germs away,' he explained.

'Excellent idea.' Anand Mehta grinned. 'Does look a bit odd – but then who cares what they think? There is a wonderful European philosopher named Mister Nietzsche who said, the man who doesn't care about what other men think becomes a superman. I congratulate you on shedding all inhibitions. Now, relaaaaaax. Don't bore me with details. Has Tommy Sir told you the arrangement I am proposing?' Mohan indicated with his head that, no, the arrangement and its details were *not* known to him. Since he was *not* allowed to be present when his sons were exhibited like buffalo at a weekly fair.

'Simple. I'll give you a *certain* sum a month. You can pay all your son's expenses using this certain sum. In return, I negotiate for him in the future with Adidas or Nike or whoever wants him when he joins the Indian Premier League. And I'll take a *certain* interest, by which I mean a fair percentage, in his marketing revenues. Fair enough?'

'No, sir,' Mohan said, clearing his throat. 'No. It is not fair in the least.' He joined his thumb and index finger in the manner of a maestro. 'My sons are not *sportsmen*. They will grow into the Bhimsen Joshi and Ravi Shankar of cricket. Sir—'

Tommy Sir slapped his hand on the table. 'You know where these two boys are from, Mr Anand? Dahisar. From a slum. Hungry Lions.'

'Sir, let me finish.'

'Angry Lion, I think, was what the television people said,' Anand Mehta suggested. 'The boy Radha has these very … film-star eyes. And long hair, like Sachin's. Pepsi, Coke will love those eyes and hair. He will act in films one day, I say.'

Mohan Kumar found himself still sweating from his bicycling, which put him at a disadvantage in the negotiations.

'Sir, I will finish. Returning to the process by which I created two geniuses of will-power, sir, it must be noted that the first principle of my system is diet—'

Tommy Sir turned to Mohan Kumar and indicated, with 'down, boy' motions of his palm, that it was time for silence.

The investor proposed terms.

'I am being asked, to invest, in a highly speculative manner, in a young person, whom we shall call Person X.'

Anand Mehta smiled at the Cricket Scout, and then drew a square with his fingers.

'Is there a *guarantee* that said Person X will get into the IPL team? Can *you* give me this' – he drew a smaller square inside the first – 'guarantee?'

'Sir, a growing body, scientifically speaking, needs three things, known as the triangle of—'

'Shut up,' Tommy Sir told the father, 'right now.' He turned to the investor. 'Radha Kumar is the best batsman I've seen in ten, maybe fifteen years. And he has the right background. Because a middle-class boy can no longer make the Bombay team. You saw for yourself what that Javed Ansari did today. He has everything, money, background, pedigree, but he will never make the team. He comes to practise in an air-conditioned car, with nurse and driver. Can't sit in the sun for five minutes. This boy, on the other hand, this Radha—'

'Maybe you didn't hear me, Mr Tommy.'

The investor drew that magic square again.

It was one of those moments when Tommy Sir realized his age: a decade ago, he would have got up and walked out at this point.

Having taken up painting many years ago as a way to calm himself when cricket-related tension grew unbearable, Tommy Sir now thought about his own watercolour copy of Vincent Van Gogh's *Starry Night*, a reproduction which in some ways improved on the original, and which he had framed and hung in his living room so that its stimulation, direct or recollected, would regulate his heartbeat and lower his blood pressure at moments precisely like this one.

'If you want guarantees, play carrom. And if you don't want the boys,' Tommy Sir looked the investor in the eye, 'we will go to Reliance and Nike and the Big Boys. Directly.'

'Relaaaaaaaax.' Anand Mehta smiled at the old scout. 'I make an offer of … four thousand rupees a month. Four thousand. Done? Are we done?'

'Eight thousand,' Mohan Kumar said. 'For one boy. And fifteen thousand for both.'

'Two?' The investor broke into an incredulous smile. 'Two? I've done plenty of charity in my time, mate, but I did not come here to make a donation.'

'Two. Two is the *opportunity.*' Tommy Sir bunched his fingers together. 'Two is the *visionary* aspect. Listen. Sport alone isn't enough today. People want sport *and* a story. I know, because I am also a writer. Two brothers from the slums making it big. One of them looks like a film-star. It's a story.'

Anand Mehta rubbed his moustache.

'Maybe you're right,' he said. 'As I often ask my wife, Asha: what are Indians? To which I give the answer: Indians, my dear, are basically a sentimental race with high cholesterol levels. Now that its hunger for social realist melodrama is no longer satisfied by the Hindi cinema, the Indian public is turning to cricket. Brothers X *and* Y from the slums. Playing cricket for Bombay. I can see the potential. I once donated a lakh of rupees to a school in the slum near Cuffe Parade, back when I had just returned from New York. You know what the *Mumbai Sun* did? Called me a hero, and printed my photo. Page four. But Brother Y is too young. Voice hasn't broken yet.'

'Manju is almost fourteen,' Tommy Sir said. 'In this city we throw boys out of the women's compartment of the train when they are seven, and tell them, go to the men's compartment. Push and survive. In sport there is not always a difference between a boy and a man. What is cricket, anyway, Mr Mehta? Game of chance. Take two, one may win.'

Anand Mehta looked at the ceiling so sadly.

'What *is* cricket?'

Meaning, no. He was not taking two boys.

He pointed at one man, and then at the other, and asked:

'Done?'

So the scout put his large palms on the table and got to the point.

'Doing well in Mumbai is nothing: being *noticed* while you do well is everything. There are competitions, shields, trophies, prizes I have to get these boys into. There's a fine art to getting a boy selected in this city. No *guarantee*, but ... if I support a boy, he is *well* supported.'

Anand Mehta did not smile.

'For all this work that I will do for the boys, I don't want any money, Mr Mehta. Not one rupee. But I have a simple question, Mr Mehta: tell me, what makes a great batsman great? Hard Work? Sacrifice? Mother's Prayers? Each is necessary, yet all together are still insufficient. Even I don't know. It is a shroud before my eyes. Believe me when I say I could be running a very profitable coaching academy for fat and rich mummy's boys, instead of which I am out here day after day, in the field, in the sun, trying to solve this mystery of mysteries and find a great, I mean *great* batsman. The shroud must part, and that is the only reason I—'

Anand Mehta had other things to do with his life.

'I'll compensate you a thousand a month for your time, Tommy Sir. Done deal?'

The scout looked away.

'Two thousand. Final offer.'

'Plus I want a T-shirt,' Tommy Sir said.

'T-shirt?' Anand Mehta frowned.

'Yes. Like the one you're wearing. Manchester United Gold. For Lata, my daughter.'

Everyone shook hands with everyone else; they bought South Indian paans, rich with clove and pulverized sugar, and placed them on their tongues to close the deal; before the sugar had melted, Tommy Sir had disappeared.

At once, Mohan Kumar caught the rich man by his wrist and said: 'Finally, I can open *my* mouth.'

•

Revenge is the capitalism of the poor: conserve the original wound, defer immediate gratification, fatten the first insult with new insults, invest and reinvest spite, and keep waiting for the perfect moment to strike back. Because every mocking remark that Mohan Kumar had heard about his plan to produce champions had been stored away in his keen memory, he knew only one way of telling his sons he had secured their future for them:

'I've screwed a rich man, my boys,' he said, even though he had taken a liking to Anand Mehta. He clapped his hands. 'A man in a red foreign T-shirt. I flipped him over and screwed him royally. Come and see.'

His boys gathered around; Mohan Kumar showed them a paper napkin from the MIG club, which was covered with writing in a blue ballpoint pen. A contract.

Until mountains fall and rivers dry this contract will be honoured by Mohandas Kumar of Alur Taluka and Anand Mehta of Mumbai. One-third of all future earnings of my two sons Master Radha Krishna and Master Manjunath will be the legal property of Shri Mehta, in return for his commitment to sponsorship. May God fill our mouths with worms if either breaks this contract.

'Isn't it beautiful, boys? Words are magic, remember this: words are magic. There is a man who comes to our village and with a spell and a secret poem he makes an elephant dance for him. Today, I made a rich Gujarati man dance for me. At first he said, No, no, I don't want Manju, his voice hasn't broken, but I said, you will take Manju, because I made two champions! Yes, he said, and he's giving us five thousand rupees each month! But I wasn't done. Made him sit down and bought him a samosa and told him about this flour-mill and how it pollutes the air, until he said, oh, terrible, how terrible, and then I said, there are rats and stupid neighbours, how can I raise champions here – so he gave us a loan, interest-free of 50,000 rupees, so we can get out of this hole, boys! To a more "hygienic location". His words! Screwed him.'

Manju and Radha looked at the contract that guaranteed their future, and the older boy asked: 'But *where* are we moving to? And when?'

Mohan Kumar rubbed his hands, and pointed one of his warmed palms at Radha: 'Get ready for a check-up. Manju, stand outside. Stand at attention.'

Radha began removing his shirt. Manju closed the tin door behind him and stood outside with his arms pressed to his sides like a soldier at a drill. It was evening in the Shastrinagar slum, and men were returning to their homes after work; their faces, dark from fatigue, glowed with the anticipation of seeing their children again. There are times when only a sick man knows how warm and bright the rest of the world is. Manju watched his neighbour, Ramnath, showing his daughter how to stack up a pile of fresh shirts and cover them in newspaper, so that they could be delivered in the morning.

He strained his ears: from inside the hut, his father's voice rose.

'Are you thinking of shaving? I can see in your eyes that you are thinking of shaving.'

'No, Appa.'

'A boy mustn't shave until he's …'

'Twenty-one.'

'Why must a boy not shave till he's … ?'

'Hormones.'

'Which are not good for …'

'Cricketers.'

Tap, tap, tap. On a coconut tree beside their hut, Manju saw a woodpecker hammering away. He thought at once of Mr 'J.A.' with his beak nose. Working with his beak – *tap, tap, tap* – the woodpecker raised his enormous profile, which looked like a tribal mask, and disappeared, only to reappear half a foot higher on the coconut stem – *tap, tap, tap* – before his dark face again vanished, to rematerialize another foot higher: as if he were ascending via masks. In school, Javed had invented a new 'look' for himself these days by wearing his blue monogrammed cap backwards, like an actor in an American film. Watching the woodpecker, and thinking of Javed, Manju smiled until he heard Radha pull up his trousers, and promise to take more scientific care of his cricketer's body.

The tin door opened; one brother came out, and so the other had to go in.

Now safe, Radha buttoned up his shirt, looking at the dark sky; he whistled. He put his hands on his thighs, spread his legs, and walked like a duck. To build strength on the insides of his thighs. Mohan Kumar, after minutely analysing his older son's body, had pronounced the quadriceps as the problematic area of Radha's athletic anatomy.

The brothers had exchanged their roles; inside the closed tin door, Manju was now the one making noises – outside, Radha eavesdropped.

'Didn't you take off your shirt and *chaddi* out there, while I was looking at your brother?'

'Sorry, Appa.'

'Don't move. Manju. What are you doing? Stay still. You think you'll insult me now? You think you'll treat me like Tommy Sir or Coach Sawant?'

'Sorry. Sorry. Sorry. Sorry.'

The boy shrieked from inside the closed tin door. Outside, Radha kept walking with his arms on his legs like a duck, as his father had taught him, conscious with every step of the need to build up his weak inner thighs and overcome the flaw in his otherwise perfect body.

Inside, done with the teeth, tongue, forehead, neck, chest and stomach, Mohan Kumar was checking his second son's particular area of recalcitrance: his failure, his refusal to take proper care of a sportsman's penis.

'Pull the foreskin back, each and every time you do number one, each and every time you bathe – pull it all the way back, otherwise it will become filthy, and filth will become septic, and we'll need to operate on it. Which your father doesn't have money for.'

Manju stood with arched back: his father had moved his foreskin back scientifically and now touched him with a finger. Manju felt his body splitting in two where his father touched. He said something.

'What did you say?' Mohan stared at his son. 'Did you say "Enough of this shit?" Did you?'

Manju shook his head. Certainly he had not said that. So his father zipped him up: weekly inspection done.

Leaning against the wall as his sons did their pre-sleep stretching exercises, Mohan Kumar made a call to his village in Alur, to check on the status of a piece of ancestral land that was tangled in litigation; the boys saw their father use his cell phone as if it were two parts of a walkie-talkie, placing it in front of his mouth when he spoke, and transferring it back to his ear to listen.

Already in bed, waiting for his father to turn the lights out, Manju watched his elder brother dry himself, and lie down in the bed next to his. He watched his father stand by Radha's skull and whisper into it: 'Go to sleep with one thought, son. What is that one thought?'

'That I should be the world's best batsman.'

Manju knew it was coming. He stiffened his body; then his father whispered into his skull:

'And your turn, Manju. Quickly, so I can turn the lights off.'

When the boy said nothing, his father's voice changed, turning high-pitched and whining.

'... fighting with his own father. Complex boy. Fighting with his own ...'

And he tickled Manju in the stomach until the boy gave in and said, '... second-best batsman ...' and 'I love you, I love you.'

Manju's legs were still thrashing and his big powerful eyes were shining. Because his father's expert fingers were warming his tummy.

'Angry with me?' Mohan said.

'Stop. Stop!'

'You're angry with me, Manju. I look into your heart and see the truth. No one has loved your poor old father in his life but you, Manju, and now even you fight with him. Listening? Yes, I know you are. The one thing I never had in life was a friend, Manju. A friend is someone who sees the best in you when everyone else sees the worst. I never had that. I only had you, my second son, to talk to.'

At last the man was gone to his side of the green curtain, and the world was quiet and dark, but beneath their closed eyelids both boys were awake.

'Did he touch your balls this time?' Radha said to the dark, as his brother sniffled in his bed.

'Yes.'

'Anything else?'

'No. That's all he ever does with me. With you?'

'The same. Just examines my balls and cock. And lets me go. But I hate it.'

'I hate it too.'

'Manju,' Radha said. 'We're going to be rich soon. You know this, right?'

He reached over and shook his brother. Radha had been, since the start of time, chief consoler and psychiatrist to the world's second-best, but most intelligent, and most complex, young cricketer.

'Manju, you know the first thing I'm going to do with the money? Buy you a bat. And you know from where? You know from where?'

Radha gave his little brother a good shake.

'You *do* know from where.'

Every Sunday Radha took his brother to Dhobi Talao, the city's sporting equipment district, full of shops glutted with fresh willow and lipstick-red match-quality balls covered in crackly cellophane. There the two boys went window-shopping from Metro Cinema all the way to a back lane, where, below a balcony with a red paper star from last Christmas and in between a store that sold golden sporting trophies and another that sold hard liquor in 180ml 'quarters', like the starting and finishing points of the average Indian male's trajectory in life, was an open door that exhaled fragrant Kashmiri and English willow: *Alfredo Athletic Centre*. Some men are hand-made by God, Manju felt, and some are machine-made – Mr Alfredo, for sure, was machine-cut. With waxed moustache, black bowtie, and the halogen lights shining off his bald head, Mr Alfredo would kindly open a glass case to show the brothers a row of his best imported bats; kindly let them gaze at the best imported bats and discuss the best imported bats, and on some days, when in the kindliest of kindly moods, even let them touch the best imported bats. The moment they got that sponsorship cash, Radha Krishna Kumar and the world's second-best batsman would wrap it in a handkerchief and run to Dhobi Talao and – and –?

'SG Sunny Tonny.' Radha tickled his brother. 'Genuine English Willow! Wombat Select! World Cup Edition Yuvraj Singh Signature Edition! I'm taking your best imported, Kindly Alfredo – or your moustache!'

•

Closing the door of his home behind him so his sons could sleep, Mohan Kumar looked around, made sure he was alone, and then, by the light of a fluorescent streetlamp, slit open an envelope he had brought from the bank. The first instalment of the sponsorship money. Five thousand rupees in fresh cash. Rubbing the crisp notes between his fingers, he mentally divided them into three piles. One for the boys' present (cricket equipment), one for the boys' future (savings bank), and one pile (for this was a man who honours his contracts) for God, to be dropped into His collection box at the Chheda Nagar temple. He put the cash back in its envelope, leaned against the door of his home, and looked up at the night sky. He dialled on a phantom phone, waited till Lord Subramanya picked up in heaven, and then, both imitating and mocking the way in which the Indian elite speak English, told the God of Cricket: 'Thank you sooooooo much, thaaaaaaaaank you s'much, Thank you soooo …'

•

Just inside the forest stood an old arch made of red laterite. No one knew who built this arch; but this kind of stone was not found anywhere nearby, and some people remembered that there was once a statue of a king on top of it. After sunset, people avoided this arch, because elephants and wild boar were known to sleep under it; but one boy was brave enough to go near it at night, and he found the spot loud with bullfrogs and louder with the twinkling of the millions of stars against which the arch etched its black shape. Sitting down on the forest floor, he looked up at all the stars, and felt himself a boy apart from all other boys in the world, resplendent, an uncrowned Adam.

Mohan Kumar had grown up in the poorest end of a poor taluk: Ratnagirihalli in Alur, in the foothills of the Western Ghats. As a boy, each morning at four, he stood on the back of an open lorry that took him to a coffee estate. There he signed his name in a long green register. Then he cleared twigs, dropped sunna from his forefingers in white circles around the plants, and watered the bushes, taking more care of the Arabica, and less care of the Robusta. At ten o'clock, the man supervising the estate paid him three and a half rupees, and he climbed back onto the open lorry. There was school for the rest of the day. He learnt to read and write. This was something new for his family. His dowry went up. Sex: with a prostitute out in the fields; marriage: to a girl from his own caste; employment: to the landowner who had hired his father; pilgrimage: to Kukke Subramanya, in the mountains of the Western Ghats, as soon as his wife fell pregnant. All this was as it had been for generations in his family.

But one morning a neighbour yelled, 'Who is going to pay for the window?'

The window that had been broken by Mohan Kumar's son in the most recent game of cricket.

Mohan looked at the broken glass and remembered what a boy in Mumbai had done to the windows in *his* neighbourhood. A boy named Sachin Tendulkar.

Now Mohan Kumar stood by passing trains and trucks and saw them in a different light. He observed highways and mighty things in a different light. He saw the sun, high over the peaks of the Western Ghats, charge from cloud to cloud like a soul in transmigration.

Mohan, Mohan – how people laughed. Why Mumbai? Take your son to Bangalore to learn cricket – it's closer, cheaper!

Bombay it had to be. Mohan Kumar put his wife and Radha and his second son Manju into a bus and then into two trains before they descended into VT station in Mumbai to take a third train to his cousin's small tin-roofed hut in a slum in Dahisar that was famous for its mechanical flour-mill, which ground wheat early morning and red chillies late morning. 'Anything I touch in Mumbai turns into powder like that flour-mill makes,' Mohan wrote to his brother Revanna back in the village. He had tried photocopying books, binding them, and selling them near the station; the police arrested him and kept him in lockup for a night. Ten lakh books are sold in black in Mumbai every day and he has to be put in lockup! Big Thief Walks Free. Small Thief Gets Caught. A year later he discovered his wife was fucking a Christian man near the train station. He waited for her, and bolted the door behind her. *Never tell your mother lies, never tell your wife secrets.* That was a golden proverb, why had he ever forgotten it? He made up for it with his hands. Nothing more than a man's natural right, but next morning the social workers – *six* of them – barged in and told him to stop hitting his wife, or else go to jail again. Can you *believe* what they do to a man in this city? One night he returned home, and found that she had run away with his money and his honour. So he had nothing left; he lay in bed, and stared at the ceiling, and thought, I should just kill myself.

'Get up, Mohan,' a voice said. Though there was no one else in the room, he heard fingers snapping in the dark.

'Why?' he asked.

The invisible fingers snapped a second time: 'Because I say so. Don't you know who I am?'

Destiny, I suppose, he thought, and rose, and breathed in the crisp, energizing air of crisis.

Taking the bus all the way to a spot in Bandra where one could observe the new skyscrapers of Prabhadevi and Lower Parel, Mohan Kumar clenched a fist and held it over the kingdoms of Mumbai; after closing an eye to perfect the illusion, he brought his fist down on the city.

Except to grow a thin black moustache – a 'statement', he declared, of protest against his ill luck with women – he never complained; he never again looked back; he simply transferred all his hopes in life onto young Radha Kumar.

Old Sharadha came in every day to do the cooking. She made chutneys from green mango, lemon and raw guava, and Mohan

Kumar tried to sell them. This meant that every day he cycled around Mumbai swallowing insults more pungent than any chutney he took with him; yet every night when he lay down to bed, he could say: 'Today my son has become a stronger and better batsman.' Mohan made Radha hold the cricket bat low down on the handle, exactly as Sachin had done. At the age of five he made Radha grow his hair long and pose with the bat for a black-and-white photo exactly as Sachin, Bacchus-haired, had posed at that age. At the age of seven he took Radha by train to Shivaji Park to listen to Ramakant Achrekar, exactly as seven-year-old Sachin had been taken to sit at the great Achrekar's feet to learn the science of batsmanship.

Around this time, his second son also began to break windows when he was playing cricket.

•

'Did you see how much money he had with him?'

'Are you awake? You were snoring.'

'I was pretending to be asleep. Just like you. Did you see the money?'

'No. I didn't see.'

'Manju, you know what I did find on his cot the other day?'

'What?'

'Dirty magazines, Manju. You never saw these magazines?'

'Don't lie. Appa has no dirty magazines.'

'You're an innocent, Manju.'

Radha sat up in bed; his younger brother was turned away from him.

'Whatever you're thinking about, scientist, don't keep it to yourself. Only girls do that ...'

When Manju faced him, his eyes were narrowed, and a furrow cut into his brow, dark and slanting noticeably to the left. Radha remembered that the same flame-like furrow had appeared on their mother's forehead when *she* was thinking: it was like a bookmark left there by the woman.

Manju looked at Radha. 'When you become a famous cricketer and I'm your manager, do I have to give him all your money?'

'I'll kill you if you give him my money. It's just for you and me.'

Radha kicked the body beside him, which kicked back; and each knew what the other meant to say. Let their father become old: they would make him beg for every rupee they gave him.

Every. Single. Rupee!

Both of Mohan Kumar's sons, too, were becoming entrepreneurs of revenge.

Two years before Selection Day

Ninth Standard begins

A fork-tailed black kite wheeled over the wet trees: a rainbow arched over the city. Beneath the circling kite stretched miles and miles of wet trees – banyans, neems, mangoes, gulmohars and palms – whose leaves glistened like ripples in a dark ocean. Rejecting raintrees, palmyrahs and coconut palms, the kite settled on an incongruous wonder, a Christmas pine planted at the highest point in south Mumbai: perched on its crown, the hunter surveyed the city, from Marine Drive to the new towers beyond Pedder Road.

Through ceiling-to-floor windows, Anand Mehta gazed down at the Hanging Gardens of Malabar Hill. Beside him stood a childhood friend, the owner of the windows and the view. Even the bad blood occasioned by their morning meeting, and his friend's point-blank refusal to join in Anand Mehta's latest business venture – cricket, two spectacularly talented slumboys, what could go wrong? – was dissolved by the spectacle before the two men. They remembered being young.

Assuring his friend, 'No worries, mate,' and inviting him over for dinner – Asha's home-made strawberry ice-cream! – Mehta left to make the same pitch to another investor in Nariman Point.

He drove down to Chowpatty.

One hand on the steering wheel, he removed his cell phone from his trouser pocket to find that all six new text messages were from Mohan Kumar.

Pls call must talk sons

He scrolled down to the next, which read:

Must talk sons

Before he could read the third, the phone began ringing.

'I keep sending you updates on my sons, but you never respond, Mr Mehta. There is something I must say …'

'Mohan Kumar, I am driving. The police are cracking down on cell phones. Please.'

'No, you must listen to me, Mr Mehta. It is now one year since we started.'

'As honoured as I am by your involvement in my scheme,' Anand Mehta looked at the roof of his car, and raised his voice, 'I cannot pay more. We haven't seen results yet. Goodbye.'

The first time he met the father of the boys, Anand Mehta was sure he could place the man: an Indian version of that Manhattan bartender you meet sometimes – Mexican, shaved headed, bushy eyebrows, just a touch of Spanish in his accent, who asks if your MacBook Air is thirteen-inch or eleven-inch, and how much memory it has, two gig or four, and who has an expert opinion on every cocktail but will confide with a quiet grin, '*I* never drink, sir,' and who secretly aspires, one day, to run the Gringo establishment he is now a servant of. Yes, that was this chap, this Mohan Kumar: a Mumbai incarnation of that Mephistophelean Mexican bartender. But guess who owned the bar? Ha Ha. And that is why the deal happened.

But now, as the father's text messages kept coming, and coming, irritating Anand Mehta so much he had to stop at Chowpatty on the way back, at Café Ideal, to order a beer, he had to fight the feeling that this cricket venture might just possibly be a very stupid idea.

Mehta was not one of those Parsi gentlemen whose Uncle Freddy or Firdaus would any day now be found cold by the nurse inside Cusrow Baug, leaving his nephew a million in the will. If he lost money he bled.

Anand Mehta thought of a friend, the managing director of the Indian branch of a German bank, who knew someone at the construction firm that built the Bandra–Worli Sea Link. This contact had given him a free pass for the Sea Link – lifetime validity. The banker had millions of dollars in his accounts, three homes in Mumbai, a slim mistress in Pali Naka, yet he hoarded one more privilege. Fortune favours those already fortunate.

Mehta's father had been a stockbroker. There had been a family tradition, handed down from generation to generation, of gently ripping off loyal customers. But Anand had quit that racket: the one known as A Normal Life. Thousands of his generation and social class were still living that normal life: for eight hours a day they sat in their air-conditioned offices in Nariman Point and spoke English to their clients, after which they sat in their air-conditioned cars and spoke Hindi to their drivers, after which they sat at their air-conditioned dinner tables and spoke Gujarati to their mothers. Anand Mehta had been a communist for a semester and a half; but then, changing his politics, he had read Kahlil Gibran and Friedrich Nietzsche; had gone to New York to study business and have an affair with a black New Yorker; had enjoyed life in that meritocratic metropolis, a coliseum of competing nationalities and races (but of all these pulsing ethnicities, one stood out: driven, Anglophone, numerate, and freed by post-colonial entitlement from almost all forms of liberal guilt or introspection – and of this privileged group, Anand Mehta intended to be the most privileged, because he was the one Indian financial analyst who had read Nietzsche); until finally, one long night, he had consumed marijuana in three different forms and stood on a rock by a lake in Central Park and decided to resign his mid-town desk job and confront human potentiality face-to-face in its locus of maximum remaining concentration, which is to say, East, South East, and

South Asia. Anand Mehta was going home. The disappointments that await a young Indian in America, alas, are minor compared to the disappointments that await him on his return to India. It hurt Mehta that not a soul in Mumbai – not even his mother, and certainly not his wife – knew what a sacrifice there had been, Manhattan and Central Park given up for Chowpatty and Shitty Park. He summed up his predicament in a recurring mid-morning fantasy: 'Nuclear war has broken out, Anand. You can save only one city on earth. Choose.' Anand Mehta saved Mumbai, home of his family and culture, of course – but then flew to New York and unbuttoned his shirt to die with everyone there.

Fine, he told his mother, I've given up mid-town Manhattan for you – but don't expect me, please, to settle for just another stockbroker's life. And so, for over a decade now, while his ageing father continued to sell securities from his Nariman Point office, Anand Mehta, from a large annexe in that office filled with computers, far-sighted business journals, and sacred piles of *The Economist* magazine, had been scheming, speculating, and squandering his family's money. He bought big in Thane and Navi Mumbai and sold small; he had been cheated by an Englishman in Dubai and two Lithuanians in Abu Dhabi; and he had dabbled in and been dabbled out of Bollywood.

He licked his wounds; he recovered.

With a childless man's passion for the crucial battles of World War Two, Mehta opened a *Reader's Digest Illustrated History* and read again about Operation Barbarossa. He drank Scotch, and drove down to a two-star hotel near Gamdevi that was melodious with moonlighting college girls. In the mornings he washed his face and made new plans.

Movies gone, real estate gone: so what the fuck is left in Mumbai?

Two years ago, over a long breakfast at the Willingdon Club, Anand Mehta had heard from a 'top' friend, a member of the Board of Control for Cricket in India, a close analysis of a celebrated India versus Sri Lanka one-dayer from the 1990s. It was a fixed match, the BCCI man said. 'You remember that ludicrous last over, don't you? Now you understand why the two of them batted the way they did. I don't know if you noticed back then, but there were endless stoppages in the final overs. Why? Simple. To let one of the physiotherapists take messages to the batsmen, warning them what would happen if they didn't throw the game, as they had agreed to do – because the physio, you see, is the person no one *ever* suspects.'

'So the match really *was* fixed?'

'*Phixed.* Which is to say, it was done in our dismal, derivative, scatterbrained South Asian way, which leaves everything to the last minute and makes life so much more exciting.'

'Wow. This is brilliant. Fucking brilliant. *This* is cricket!'

Flushed with this 'inside' look into the game everyone else in India only thought they knew, Mehta suggested that the Board of Control for Cricket in India (*seriously* North Korean name, that) start retailing a DVD box-set: *Golden Moments of Match-Fixing*, only 1,999 rupees, for Diwali, so that Indians could finally learn the truth about their most cherished national memories.

One day Anand Mehta wanted to do it himself – 'phix' a match – an *international* match.

In the bar, Mehta drank beer after beer, savouring the ocean breeze, the camaraderie of the students with their college badges around their necks, and the hint, which grew stronger with every sip, that a good life could still be lived in Mumbai.

After a couple of hours, he drove to his home on the eleventh floor of Maker Tower 'J' Block at nine thirty that evening. His parents were asleep.

The windows in the living room were open, and the sea breeze was divine – every one of the six rooms in the flat that his father had bought, even the bathrooms, enjoyed an unimpeded ocean view – but Asha, his wife, had to ruin the effect by insisting that they review 'this business of cricket sponsorship' on its one-year anniversary.

Madness. That was what *she* thought. Giving all this money to boys from the slums. Had he forgotten the cricket academy racket he was running in Azad Maidan, wasn't that earning them a steady income every summer?

'These two are sensational, you should see them,' Mehta protested. 'Only fat rich boys came to the academy.'

Over dessert Asha's mood always became worse.

What if the two sensations ran away from Mumbai with the money and went back to their village? Did Anand take any guarantee? This was exactly the kind of trusting and neurotic nature that had ruined every one of her husband's business deals.

And Asha hardly had to remind him of the time – *before* their marriage – when he actually gave money to a school for slum children, did she? Neurotic Man.

When Madame Mehta finally allowed him a chance to speak, Anand – with a *Gotcha* smile – pointed his dirty ice-cream spoon at her.

'You know what it means in India when a woman calls her husband neurotic?'

Although she knew better, his wife asked, 'What?'

'"My husband's neurotic" means, he doesn't like my mother. "He's psychotic" means, he doesn't like *me*. Am I right or am I usual right? Listen: this is why I've made a good deal this time. In fact it's a great deal. Because they're honest.'

As he did when excited, he smoothed out his moustache with his left hand.

'Mumbai is a dying city, true. But there is one thing that it will *always* have. One beautiful thing. Integrity. The integrity of the Bombay common man, known and celebrated throughout India, deeper than granite, the true bedrock of the city. True?'

Perhaps, Asha nodded, with her mouth full of ice-cream. Perhaps.

'One thing I knew, the moment I saw the chutney salesman. He'll sell his sons if he has to, but he'll pay me back.' Using his spoon, Anand drew a rectangle in the air. 'Guaranteed.'

'Why do you think people in Mumbai are honest?' Asha, still non-committal, scraped the bottom of the bowl with her spoon.

She answered her own question.

'It must be the Parsi influence. We had lots of Parsis once upon a time, and they're a straightforward people.'

'No, no, no.' Anand scraped his own bowl faster, knowing that he was drawing close to the moment of Memsaab's consent for his continued sponsorship of the two slum boys.

'It's the Gujarati influence. We're an *even more* straightforward people.'

And now the whole family, even the domestic help busy with the dishes in the kitchen, laughed.

•

From their bedroom, Asha Mehta looked down on the rows of fishing boats buzzing with blue and red electric lights, docked right outside the Maker Towers compound for the 4 a.m. launch into the ocean to gather fish and prawns; as she lay in bed, she heard boisterous male laughter, battery-operated radios playing film songs, bodies splashing in the water, and the *tk-tk* of wooden prows knocking into one another. Beyond the water, Nariman Point, and beyond it, all of south Mumbai coruscated. Then Anand walked in, a smile on his lips and the future under his armpit: a rolled-up A4 sheet, covered with calculations, which he brought into bed and unfurled against the light. There. He showed Asha the figures for one year's investment in cricket sponsorship. He had made payments worth 60,000 rupees to the two boys, plus a loan of 50,000 rupees to the father, plus 24,000 rupees to the old scout. In this same period of twelve months, he knew for a fact that the typical marketing contract of a player on the Indian national team had gone up, according to his 'inside' connection in the Cricket Board, to between 45,00,000 and 60,00,000 rupees. Radha Kumar had gained two inches in height, four kilos of weight (pure dark muscle); the younger fellow, Manju, had gained only an inch and a half, and three kilos of weight, of which half appeared to have accumulated as pimples. All that was on the positive side of the ledger.

On the negative side – Mehta sighed, and turned the lights off – whereas, a year ago, the father of these two geniuses was crazy in a basically good way, now he was becoming crazy in basically the other way.

'What's wrong?' Asha asked, squinting. Turning the lights on in the bedroom, her husband had gone to stand by the window and watch the happy boats below them. The truth was, Anand Mehta also had his doubts about the visionary cricket sponsorship programme—doubts which were rekindled on the first of each month, when Mohan Kumar turned up at his office and looked at the white envelope in Mehta's hand which held that month's cheque. Because Kumar's eyes had in them what Anand Mehta called a 'pre-liberalization stare', an intensity of gaze common in people of the lower class before 1991, when the old socialist economy was in place, and which you found these days only in communists, terrorists, and Naxalites: the wrathful gaze of those who could not possess things, but only waste them. What he saw in that mad father's eyes was not milk and honey for his sons: it was fire.

•

My Appa is once again a magician! – and I want the whole world to know this. If he promises something, *anything*, that thing will come true! Can your father do that? Or *your* father?

The anticipation began well before the last day of the month, when Manju would start tugging on his father's shirt and ask, 'Is it time? Is it time?' And then, on the first day of the new month, the Younger Asset went with Mohan Kumar to Mr Anand Mehta's office in Nariman Point, waiting in the lobby while a clerk brought the money in a white envelope and counted it out; then the Younger Asset returned with his father by train to Dahisar and walked with him to the bank and eavesdropped as he expounded to the branch manager on developments in the gold and real-estate markets.

The truth was, Mohan Kumar's magic seemed to be growing more powerful by the day. Calling the two boys in for their medical check-up one morning – Radha, as usual, quiescent; Manju, as usual, squirming and complaining as his father examined his genitals – Mohan said:

'Neither of my sons loves me anymore. Even when I give them a new home to live in.'

New home? Manju gaped. He ran to his father and embraced him.

Mohan Kumar had finally been able to sell that piece of family land in Alur, and Anand Mehta's loan of 50,000 rupees was in a fixed deposit in Canara Bank, and they had been saving two thousand rupees, month after month, for over a year. All of which meant, 'my two sons who have always doubted your own father, that ...'

•

Manju ran screaming at the black Dahisar river. He went bullocking down the bridge. There was always a group of unemployed young men lounging about here, listening to a cell-phone radio. They smoked and watched the crazy boy.

'Boy!'

'Mad boy, come here. Why are you shouting up and down the bridge?'

With a sweet smile, hands behind his back, Manju walked up to them. 'I'm not mad, I'm Radha Kumar's brother. My father has made lots of money and now we're going to leave third-class people like you and move to a first-class place like Chembur.'

They chased; he ran.

And two mornings later, it all came true.

Mohan Kumar, breeder of champions, had walked over the river, and through the WELCOME TO OUR HOME arch, holding three chrome-plated keys upright, displaying them first to the politicians of the arch, to let them know he was escaping their clutches for good, and then to his neighbours, one by one, while he said: 'Did you laugh at me when I said I'd be famous, Ramnath? I think you did. *You* definitely did – didn't you, Girish?'

Done with such taunts, Mohan Kumar offered a few words of valedictory wisdom to the inhabitants of the Shastrinagar slum.

'Age sixteen to eighteen is the danger zone. Kambli and Sachin, *both* were talented. But only one became a legend. Why? Everything is falling to pieces in this country. Everything. Boys are taking drugs. Boys are driving cars. Boys are *shaving*.'

Some of the neighbours had brought along their sons and their cricket bats for Mohan Kumar to bless: perhaps God's grace was contagious.

Only old Ramnath's mood was sour. Standing in the window of his hut, apart from the rest of the crowd, pressing clothes with his coal-fired iron, he grumbled:

'Gulli-Danda is the real game of skill. Cricket? Cricket was brought here by the Britishers to entrap us.'

Mohan Kumar smiled.

Ramnath continued. 'Indians should play Indian sports. Kho-Kho, Kabbadi, buffalo-racing in the monsoons.'

Mohan Kumar began to laugh: it was the loudest laugh he had had since getting on the train to Mumbai.

'Pack up,' he told his boys.

Old Sharadha was not told to pack up. They would have a domestic servant in the new place. They were that kind of people now, the kind of people who hired other people.

Chheda Nagar was not just any suburb: in its heart stood a Subramanya temple, a satellite of the shrine of the thousand-year-old God of Cricket in the Western Ghats, and for a decade the three Kumars had gone there by local train to pray and to consecrate new bats, gloves and pads. Once they moved to Chheda Nagar, they could visit the God of Cricket, or at least a reflection of Him, every morning.

Nor was the Tattvamasi Housing Society, Chheda Nagar, just any housing society.

Only when their father held open the wooden door bearing the nameplate 'B.B. Balasubramaniam' (the landlord who had sucked

40,000 rupees out of them as a security deposit), and told them to go in, Radha first, did the boys start to believe it. Manju entered, touching the wall with both hands. Can this really be our new home? Overnight, they had become the kind of people who had a working air-conditioner, a big grey fridge, and a largely automatic washing machine. A wooden cupboard just for cricketing gear, equipment, food supplements and antibiotics. Attached to it, a full-length mirror, so they could rehearse their strokes at any time of day or night.

'This is the reason I picked the Tattvamasi Building.' Mohan Kumar opened a window, and pointed to something down below. Standing on either side of their father, the boys saw a little courtyard in between the concrete back wall of their housing society and the brick front wall of the neighbouring building. 'Find your bats, pray, and go. First practice in our new home.'

So, ten minutes after they had taken possession of their new flat, the two boys were ordered out of it. From the window, Mohan Kumar waited for his sons to start using that beautiful brick wall.

But life, of course, can never be perfect. For four nights after they had moved in to the new home, when Mohan turned on their television, he and his sons found themselves witnessing the birth of a new Young Lion.

> A star rises on the horizon: not in the city, the traditional nursery of cricketing wizardry, but across the creek, in the suburb of Navi Mumbai. Here, in Vashi, they gather every evening inside the Adil Housing Society to see a handsome young man practise while his father bowls at him. Is this youngster, as some believe, the best batsman Mumbai has produced in the last fifty years?
>
> A stylish left-hander in the David Gower mould, Javed Ansari, a fifteen-year-old student of the Ali Weinberg School in Bandra, has got Mumbai's sporting cognoscenti excited by his graceful strokeplay. He has already scored four centuries,

six half centuries and two double centuries this year. Cricket is in his blood: Javed is a nephew of Ranji Trophy middle-order star Imtiaz Ansari, who now represents Yorkshire county in England. In addition, his father, a textbook importer in Vashi, once donned the flannels for Aligarh University and has been a cricket commentator for the BBC Hindi service.

Young Lions spoke to Mr Ansari and found he does not approve of his offspring's single-minded devotion to the gentleman's game. 'Ninth Standard is the hardest year in school. Now is when you have to start studying for the Board Exams.'

'So you would like to see him do something other than cricket?'

'Do you think youngsters today will listen to anyone, even their fathers? Javed is hell-bent on playing for Mumbai, and then for India, and no one on earth will stop him.'

YOUNG LIONS
MONDAY 6.30 P.M. REPEATED ON WEDNESDAY
Follow us on Twitter

•

Turning off the television, Mohan Kumar spat on the floor of his new home.

'Go down there,' he told his sons, 'and start practising right now.'

No more long train rides for Manju and Radha; they were now living on the school bus route. Sitting at the back, they startled pedestrians with rude gestures, and fought with their classmates, as the bus wound its way from Chembur towards Carter Road, and into the lane known as 'Ali's Education Corner', slowing as it went past the Karim Ali College of Law, the Karim Ali College of Arts and Sciences, the Karim Ali College of Dental Science, and the Karim

Ali College of Medical and Alternative Medical Sciences, before it stopped at the Ali Weinberg International School.

But the moment the Kumars got down from the bus, they found a Honda City parked outside the school, as if it had been waiting just for them. A pair of legs emerged from the open door, while the rest of the body, visible in silhouette behind the dark window, reclined on the seat and composed a message on a cell phone.

Mr 'J.A.', the new 'Young Lion'.

The previous evening, as Radha and Manju lay in their new beds, Mohan Kumar, while reintroducing his sons to the three principal dangers on their path to glory – premature shaving, pornography and car-driving – had added one more. This Mohammedan (a left-hander!) had every advantage that Mohan's two sons lacked: *his* father had FDs and online stock-trading accounts; *his* father had probably built a home-gym for his son; and he had that thing you needed more than a rich father in Mumbai – he had a *god*father. Wasn't his uncle Imtiaz Ansari a Ranji Trophy man, and wouldn't the combination of money and influence (which is how things work in this world, my sons) make this left-handed boy irresistible on Selection Day, which was coming, which *was* coming?

When Radha saw that silhouette inside the car, his heart contracted: he felt again that suspicion which now gnawed at him that despite everything his father said, his contract with God was not fool-proof, and he might not prove to be the best batsman in the world – and so he sweated; but what went through Manju at the sight of that dim body inside the car was a buzz – the same charge of electricity an ornithologist feels when he catches sight of a rare migratory species of bird.

Open-mouthed, the brothers stared at the silhouette inside the Honda City, until Radha said 'Manju', and Manju said 'Radha Krishna', and the spell was broken, and the two were free to walk again.

•

It was on the morning that Javed Ansari tried to steal Sofia from them that the brothers Kumar finally did something about him.

Sofia, the spotty-necked one, the girl with the car and driver, the girl whose father owned a big chemical plant in Thane, had come to Thambi's that morning with the two brothers.

Thambi's Fast Food Hut, just a few feet away from the Ali Weinberg School, served exactly the kind of food that teachers at the school warned their students against. Cooking in the open near piles of cowdung and buzzing garbage, the food doled out on plates freshly dipped in bilgewater – all of which meant, in addition to their dosa and idli, young people who ate here were likely to receive a complementary side-order of jaundice or typhoid.

Thambi's, inevitably, had become *the* great place for romance at the Ali Weinberg International School.

That morning, Sofia sat on a bench with a textbook pressed against her chest, and a bag slung across her shoulder. Her long black hair was brushed down over her left eye, and she smelled like a large foreign flower. The blood-coloured spots, a birthmark, lay on either side of her fair neck.

'I gave a presentation in class today, on women in today's India. Do you want to know what I said?'

The little outdoor shop was an excitement of garlic and onions; two Tamilians transmitted Radha's orders to a third behind the counter, who sizzled the hot-plate with water, scraped it dry with a truncated broomstick, put a hand on his hip and yelled, 'Dosa?'

'Dosa.'

'Cheese?' asked the man behind the counter, scraping the tawa.

Naturally. 'Double Cheese. Double Double Cheese.' Always impresses the girls.

Pointing his short broom at Manju, the man asked:

'And if I see your father, am I to yell, like last time?'

'Louder this time,' Radha pleaded.

'Getting back to what I said in class about women,' Sofia continued, 'I said, in India today, a woman is either a sucker or a bitch. My dad has taught me that. Do you know what it means? No?

You must be good for cricket only. It means, if you're a woman in a job in marketing or sales, for instance, men will treat you like you don't know what you are doing, and they will try to cheat you. So you have to put your foot down, and get angry and shout at them, and then they'll call you a – a …'

She turned from the elder Kumar to the younger one. She covered the spots on her neck and asked Radha:

'Why is your brother staring at me like that?'

Manju wasn't staring at her: only at the silver 'H' on her sequinned handbag.

The Tamilian arrived with a cheese dosa on a cellophane-covered metal plate. Chutney dripped down the side of the plate.

'Are you *really* eating that?' Sofia asked.

Oh, Radha certainly was. He tore into his food.

Sofia winced. Stroking her handbag with the 'H', she said:

'I'm *also* a sportsman, by the way, so don't think you're special. My Mummy says we get 3.5 per cent added to our final SSC marks if we play sports at the state level, and that will help me get into a good junior college, so she made me join state-level badminton. I go every day after class. My knees hurt, but Mummy says, get into college, and become rich, and you can go to hospital and pay for shiny new knees. Isn't that crazy?'

Radha smiled: 'Let's see the knees.'

Sofia lifted up her school skirt and showed. But when Radha grinned at her naked knees, she grew angry with herself.

'Cricketers!' She covered her knees with her skirt. 'As a matter of fact, I don't know *anyone* who respects cricket. *Lunch-break!* Nothing that stops for lunch can be called a sport. Everybody I know follows Arsenal or Manchester United. Although I hope you're not into Barcelona because I hate their guts. Are you listening to me?'

Of course he was. Done with his food, Radha wiped his lips with the back of his palm, and then began whispering to Sofia about something that was *this* big (he showed her with his hands exactly how big), until she screamed: 'Seven colours! Seven?'

It was true: Manju had seen his brother do it. Radha's thing was enormous, and when he held it tight, after going to the toilet, and squeezed it so that the blood stopped flowing into it, he could make it any colour he wanted. It was all true.

But Sofia just pushed Radha away, and laughed hysterically.

'You cricketers,' the girl said, 'are too funny. You're even worse than J.A.'

'Than who?'

While Radha frowned, Sofia explained that both Young Lions had been trying to impress her, because earlier in the morning, she had been given *this* by Mr Javed Ansari. A piece of fragrant white paper. Radha read it, while Manju, putting his chin on his brother's shoulder, spied.

> *Miss Sofia:*
>
> *You walk in beauty, like the night of*
> *cloudless climes and starry skies.*
>
> *J.A.*

'What the fuck is this?' Radha asked.

Sofia said it was Javed's love poem, written just for her, and that she found it 'touching'.

'He likes me. You cricketers are all *too* funny.'

When Radha saw Manju reading the love poem with a frown, as if he was trying hard to understand it, he couldn't take it anymore.

'Scientist,' he said. 'Give that back to her.'

That Saturday, when no one was looking, the two brothers broke into the school changing rooms, found a green cricket bag embroidered in gold with the initials 'J.A.', and unzipped it. Radha had brought the pen. He examined Javed's gear – his thigh pad, his box, his gloves – before settling on the chest-guard. Placing it on his knee, he wrote something on it. 'Done,' Radha chuckled, and asked Manju to read what he had written on the chest-guard – but what was his younger brother up to? His mouth open, Manju had slid his whole forearm up to the elbow into Javed's green kitbag. The arm was trembling. And *more* of it was still going into the bag!

'That's filthy.' Radha slapped Manju on the head. The younger boy withdrew his forearm at once. Radha held the pen out to him. 'Now *you* write something on his chest-guard.'

Afterwards the two brothers howled and screamed all the way up and down Carter Road in celebration of their victory over Mr 'J.A.'.

•

During the monsoons, the maidans in the heart of south Mumbai – Azad, Oval, Cross – are overrun by weeds. By Independence Day, with rain still falling, dark nylon nets have cordoned off parts of the maidans, and rectangular patches of reddish earth are taking shape inside those protected areas. Similar rectangles turn up at the Police Gymkhana and the Islam Gymkhana along Marine Drive, puzzling the black kites, which fly circles over them, balancing their wings on the sea breeze.

In September, stone-rollers are applied over these patches, levelling out the earth. At the Oval, the rectangles of stubble are now russet, the colour of some of the tiles in the Bombay High Court building, which towers over the maidan. Mounds of cut turf are stacked up; men in khaki shorts sit by the turf; mynahs land and take off, and pigeons roost on the pitches. Two white sight-screens are moved into place against the fence, just beyond which the bronze statue of Sir Jamsetjee Jejeebhoy, first Baronet of Bombay, sits with his hands on his lap and his back to the Oval, disdaining the common pleasures of sport. Then one morning, a bare-chested man materializes on the cricket pitch at the Oval and starts meditating. His palms are folded by his chest and his eyes are shut; only his lips move. A stone-roller waits beside him. Raising his palms over his head, the half-naked man claps once – twice – three times, and opens his eyes.

It is October, and the cricket season has begun.

Ninth Standard continues: cricket season

Was she really *really* dead? Radha seemed to think so. Maybe someone had murdered her and hidden her body in the Dahisar river. No – she had to be alive: Manju was sure of it. Because he remembered the last evening he had ever seen her: he had come home early from cricket practice, and she had been sleeping on the bed. Manju had watched her and thought, when his father slept, his lips thickened, and his face became coarse; but how radiant his mother looked in her sleep. Her lips twitched. Her eyelids pulsed. And as Manju drew nearer to her sleeping body, her lips began moving silently, as if intoning something, some prayer, some secret Sanskrit, some message meant for her son.

'Tommy Sir is here: stop dreaming!'

Manjunath opened his eyes. Through a colourful umbrella overhead he saw the sun; and then dark grinning faces and white shirts all around. He was sitting on a plastic chair in the Ali Weinberg tent at one end of the Oval Maidan.

As if it had fallen from a coconut tree above, he was holding a bat in his hands.

Manju looked around. Holding on to the black bars that ran

around the maidan, men watched the cricket; the lucky ones, day labourers with a morning off, sat on the trunk of a palm tree, sipping tea, silenced at the moment a ball hit a bat. In the middle of the Oval, a Young Lion hunted for runs: Radha Kumar was on fire this morning.

But Tommy Sir was nowhere to be seen.

Showing his middle finger to the other cricketers – they responded with a squeal of delight – Manju closed his eyes and exercised his right to dream.

What *was* she trying to say, lying in bed like that with her eyes closed and her lips moving? Manju had brought his ear to her lips, and he could almost hear the words she was struggling to form: 'Manju, let us find Radha and run away from here before it's too late.'

'Stop bloody dreaming, and get up from that chair, Subjunior!'

This time it *was* Tommy Sir, striding up to the Ali Weinberg tent, along with a middle-aged man. Manju stood to attention with the other boys.

'Boys, this man is the most important man in Mumbai. He will determine your fates one day. Who is he?'

The middle-aged man smiled. 'Please don't embarrass me, Tommy Sir. I'm just a selector.'

'That's exactly what I said, Srinivas, and in plain English. Now, boys, this very important man will tell the story of how he knew Ravi Shastri would play for India just by looking at him. Tell them, Srinivas.'

'That was years ago, Tommy Sir. Ten years ago, we could say, this boy, from his stance, from the way he grips the bat, will make the team. Today, it's all different. Today, it's all a mystery, even to the selectors, who will make it and who …'

The workers sitting on the fallen log cheered. A Young Lion had just roared: twisting his torso, Radha Kumar had pulled a long hop past the mid-wicket fielder, and through the boundary, which was marked with white flags.

•

'Just look at him bat, Srinivas. Do you know his scores in the Pepsi tournament?'

'How can I *not* know his scores, when you text them to me three times a day? It's a rich crop, his batch. There's Javed Ansari, Kumar, and I'm hearing a lot about T.E. Sarfraz too.'

Manju stood close to the two men to overhear.

'Kill it like Yuvraj!' All around their school tent, the cricketers had begun clapping in rhythm.

'Kill it?'

Tommy Sir pointed to Rajabai Tower.

'You heard the story? That Yuvraj Singh hit the clock tower with a six during trials?'

The selector looked at Rajabai Tower.

'It's seventy-five metres to the boundary wall – then thirty more over the coconut trees. Bullshit. No one's ever hit the tower from here.'

Tommy Sir, who had written about Yuvraj's Rajabai Tower-shaking sixer in a newspaper column two years ago ('Some Boys Rise, Some Boys Fall: Legends of Bombay Cricket and My Role in Shaping Them Part 16 – How I Made Yuvraj a Young Prince of Cricket'), looked to his right, where he found little Manju.

'This is the brother, Srinivas. Scientist by nature. If I ask him, he'll recite your life story. Shall I ask him?'

But right about then Tommy Sir saw a man pushing a bicycle into the Oval Maidan.

And Manju wished he could seal his ears. It was happening once again: Tommy Sir was talking about his father as he stood in hearing range.

'You see that creature coming in, Srinivas? Comes and watches every match his boys play. Control freak. Keeps asking me, are they talking to women, are they boozing beer, are they watching blue films? Between us ...' Tommy Sir called the selector in closer, '... has a police record.'

Manju gritted his teeth.

Almost at once, there was a loud crack from the pitch: Radha Kumar, as if competing with the ghost of Yuvraj Singh, had lofted the ball in the direction of the Rajabai clock tower. The sound of his bat commanded the maidan into silence. Two boys almost ran into each other: then one of them stepped back, and the other, with cupped palms, caught the ball.

'The moment I praise him, he gets out. You're next, Manju. Yes, I'm changing the batting order. I want the selector to see Manjunath Kumar. Quick, quick.'

•

Helmeted, padded, centre-padded, chest-padded, thigh-padded, Manjunath Kumar came out to bat; his left thumb throbbed.

All batting – all *good* batting – starts with superstition. Manju already had a personal treasury of superstitions associated with his game – some held in common with all other batsmen (never to wipe the red ballmarks off the face of his bat, for instance) – and some which were peculiarly his own. This one was unique: when he got to the crease, Manju first walked in a circle all around the stumps, and only then stood where he was meant to, in front of them. Next he uttered a little Kannada poem his mother had taught him in his childhood:

Obbane Obbane
Kattale Kattale

Alone, Alone
Darkness, Darkness.

Not *yet* ready to bat. Next, Manju scratched around the dust with his bat, as if he were searching for something, though he had found it already, in his own thumb: a spark of hurt. Next, he took a leg-stump guard, because he felt like scoring on the off-side today, and began tapping his bat.

Now.

Mynahs and sparrows flew into stacks of cut grass each time Manju tapped his bat; the umpire's face darkened by degrees; the fielders crouched. The bowler turned into a small, stupid animal. He pursed his lips and sucked on his teeth, and emitted squirrel-like noises with which he instructed his fielders exactly where to position themselves. Pointing at Manjunath, he yelled: 'This boy is not a cricketer. This boy is just his brother's shadow. This boy reads books! This boy is not going to last *two* balls.'

Manju turned to where the sun was shining over the buildings. It was something his father had taught him to do: when there is pain or distraction, when the sun is in your eyes, lift your palm till it blocks the light. You are now in control of the most powerful force in the universe.

Now look at the bowler, the one who taunted you. And look at the three fielders on the off-side who laughed in response. You will all share in my pain.

Manju's nostrils are dilated; forearms tense. Around him, Mohan Kumar's second son sees the city's landmarks – the Eros cinema, the big blue UFO in Colaba owned by the Taj Hotel, Rajabai Tower, Churchgate station – joining up into a crown whose rim can touch his head if he wants it to. If he bats well enough today.

The first ball he hits right through the covers, humiliating the pair of fielders who had laughed the loudest.

Their punishment has begun.

On a coconut tree nearby, a woodpecker, in a frenzy, rams into wood with its beak; in the middle of the cricket pitch, a boy digs his bat into the pitch, again and again.

•

Over an hour later, having stripped his left glove to give his thumb a good shake – he had just overtaken his brother's score – Manju glanced at the cricketers' tent. Radha wasn't there: but behind the Ali Weinberg pavilion, he saw a man urinating by a coconut tree.

Mohan Kumar was leaning back as far as he could to ensure he didn't miss a single second of his son's batting, even as he relieved himself. What a buffoon my father is, Manjunath thought. How ashamed he makes me of him sometimes. The other spectators would see him peeing in public – whistle at him – perhaps throw things and chase him from the maidan – unless the next ball … was hit high in the air. A tremendous six.

Manju was now batting to protect his father.

•

What is cricket?

A face: Eknath Solkar's face. Right before the 1968–69 Bombay–Bengal Ranji final, his father dies. 'We know your father is dead, you don't have to come to bat,' his Bombay teammates tell him. But it's a grim situation for Bombay, we're losing wickets fast. Solkar performs the rites for his father in the morning, gets into a train, and arrives, stoically, at Brabourne stadium. 'I am here to do my duty,' he says. Pads up, goes in to bat. Bombay takes the lead in the first innings thanks to him: and wins the Ranji Trophy. On a day of supreme personal pain, on a day rich with excuses not to do his job, he does his job.

Or, to put it another way, as Tommy Sir had, in an essay published three years ago in the *Mumbai Sun*: cricket is the triumph of civilization over instinct. As he left the showers by the swimming pool, and dried his hair with his towel, Tommy Sir remembered that wonderful little essay of his. American sports, baseball or basketball, make crude measurements of athletic endowments: height, shoulder strength, bat speed, anaerobic capacity. Cricket, on the other hand, measures the extent to which you can harness these raw endowments. You have to curb your right hand, the bottom hand, the animal hand, giving sovereignity to your left, the elegant, restrained, top hand. When the short-pitched ball comes screaming, and every instinct of panic tells you, close your eyes and turn your face, you must do what does not come naturally to you or to any man: stay calm. Master your nature, play cricket. Because a man's body, when all is said and done, is a loathsome thing – Tommy Sir slapped his underarms with Johnson and Johnson Baby Powder, his favourite deodorant – loathsome, loathsome, loathsome. More Baby Powder, much more. Mumbai is a hot city even at night.

Tommy Sir inspected himself in the mirror. He checked the smell of his underarms.

Civilized and fragrant, the old man emerged from the changing room, and looked for young Manjunath Kumar.

Tommy Sir was one of those who 'lived' in the Middle Income Group Cricket Club of Kalanagar, which is to say, he did his daily six laps in the pool, consumed international cricket and local whisky in the bar, and had tea every evening in the cafeteria towards which he was now walking.

Inside, the waiters stood by a television set watching England play South Africa, either right now or perhaps several years ago.

It was as if a ray of morning light had entered. *Manjooo*. Tommy Sir had not come alone. The waiters smiled at the boy; and then came to him bearing gifts – sit, *Manjooo*. Sit, sit. Little Manju they treated as de facto club mascot. Free snacks. Free Coca-Cola? Don't worry, eat. Your father? He'll never know. The trains would be packed till nine: the three Kumars were allowed to stay on within the MIG club premises till late, but only one was pampered so.

'Look at me, Manju. I have something important to say.'

Though he had been expecting to discuss Radha Kumar with the selector, Tommy Sir had gone silent as Manjunath Kumar began to hit the ball. Standing beside him, the selector, Srinivasan Sir, had watched Manju's batting with his mouth open, as if he too wanted to ask out loud – what is cricket? Because, like Tommy Sir, he could answer the question only in English. But the boy batting before them was answering it in the language of cricket.

'Did I ever tell you my story about Eknath Solkar, Manju?' Tommy Sir asked.

But Manju, biting into a free samosa from the canteen of the MIG club, was concentrating on the pages of his textbook.

'What's the moral of Eknath Solkar's story? Tell me. Every story has a moral. Stop reading that book.'

Like many middle-class Indians of his age, Tommy Sir could be curious only by being hostile.

Seizing the book, he turned it towards him, and read out loud from its contents.'… Lesson 1: Linear Equations; Lesson 2: Highest Common Factor and Least Common Multiple of Polynom … Polynomin …'

Tommy Sir angled the book back towards Manju.

'Every cricketer in Tamil Nadu now has a degree in engineering. At nineteen, they say, let's assess the risk and reward in cricket, too much risk, so let's go to America for college. Manju, you mustn't do that. Did Sachin go to America? Did he finish Year 12? Manju: tell me one thing. When you bat does your science and mathematics help you?'

Chewing samosa, his cheeks full, the boy looked up from the textbook and examined Tommy Sir.

'Yes,' he said. And then, 'No.'

'Yes or no?' Tommy Sir demanded.

But the boy meant, Yes is the answer, and No is the answer you want from me.

'Once during a match with Cathedral I tried to calculate the angle of an extra-cover drive – 35 degrees from the wicket, and a cover drive – 45 degrees.'

'Did that help bisect the fielders?'

'Next ball I was bowled.' Tommy Sir exhaled.

'So you don't think as you bat?'

'I just let my mind go dark before I bat. If I think I always get out next ball.'

Tommy Sir placed a palm on the boy's textbook.

'Manju, look at me. Tell me: which club did Vijay Merchant play for?'

'Fort Vijay.'

'How many sixes did C.K. Nayadu hit against the MCC at the Gymkhana?'

'Too many.'

'Good answer.' Tommy Sir raised his palm from the book – and lowered it again. 'Who is going to break that record?'

Manju chewed his samosa.

'My brother.'

'Is your left thumb hurting?'

Manju stopped chewing: he looked at Tommy Sir.

'You know that is what Javed Ansari told me after the match? He could see you were holding the bat with the right hand only. He thought you might have hurt your left thumb.'

'That Javed is a liar!' Manju stood up. 'I scored faster than him today, so he hates me.'

'Then show me your left thumb,' Tommy Sir said. 'And why were you turning the page of your book with only one hand?'

The boy slid both his hands under the table.

Outside, Mohan Kumar, who stood clapping as his elder son jogged backwards to build up his hamstrings, turned – 'Misssster Moooohan!' – to see Tommy Sir charging out of the club, and dragging Manju along with him.

Holding Manju's left hand up as evidence, he explained everything to the father.

'Boy has a hairline. Still went out there and batted today. *Why?* Because he's so scared of *someone* in his family.'

Manju saw Tommy Sir push his father back.

'Shall I go to the police and tell them what you do to him? Shall I tell the social workers?'

And when the scout threatened to show Manju's broken thumb to his friends in the *Mumbai Sun*, which would certainly result in a negative article about the father, which would certainly be seen by all the neighbours in the Tattvamasi Housing Society, and probably even by the general public of Chheda Nagar, Mohan Kumar folded his palms and begged Tommy Sir, reminding him he was just a poor man, a villager in the big city, victim of the chutney mafia, who had nothing, not even a friend in the world, and even agreed to leave the club at once, with the result that when Tommy Sir put the boy (along with his elder brother) into the auto that would take him express to Lilavati Hospital, he patted Manju's cheeks and whispered into his ear: 'Best fracture in human history.'

•

Lying in bed, Manju watched *CSI Las Vegas*. His brother was holding up an iPad to make it easy for him. In this episode, which he had seen three times before, an old woman was eaten alive by her own cats.

'Is your thumb still hurting?'

'No.'

Radha smiled, but as Manju watched the iPad, he watched Manju.

'Why did you bat if your thumb was broken?'

Manju looked at the closed door. There was a man behind that door. He was the reason Manju did everything.

Radha knew this: yet he watched his brother.

'Was there another reason? Did you also bat with the broken thumb just to impress Srinivasan Sir? He's a selector, I'm the one who should impress him. After I got out, you should have got out. That's your duty. Especially when a selector—'

From outside their bedroom, a voice shouted: 'Complex boy!'

From the living room, seated on the sofa so he could observe his boys' beds, Mohan Kumar said: 'And he has to tell Tommy Sir a lie, that I bowled the ball in practice that broke his thumb. Would I do that to my own son? My own Robusta?'

Radha put the iPad down on the bed and smiled at Manju. And as his younger brother watched, he walked to the door of their bedroom, and slammed it shut.

There was a moment's silence and then:

'Radha, open this door at once.'

Before picking up the iPad, Radha leaned back and stuck out his middle finger at the closed door. When the banging began he shouted:

'I'll call Tommy Sir.'

The banging stopped. And then:

'Are you two watching blue films in that computer that I bought for you which was meant only for cricket?' From the other side of the door, his father's high-pitched, almost hysterical voice continued to accuse his sons:

'Blue films? Foreign films? Foreign women in foreign films?'

•

In the morning, when Radha shook him awake with news that their father had locked himself in the bathroom and was refusing to come out, Manju thought it was all his fault.

'Appa, what happened?' Radha stood outside and shouted at the bathroom door, trying to interpret the noises from within. 'Who has gone to the police?'

Their father slipped the newspaper from under the bathroom door and shouted: 'Javed Ansari has gone to the police. Read, read.'

Once or twice a month, their father became a woman. The boys studied the newspaper article together.

Our readers feed a Young Lion a few questions:

> Q: What are your extracurricular activities?
> *(Soumya M., Navi Mumbai)*
> Javed Ansari: I am reading Peter Roebuck's columns and George Orwell. I also write poetry, both with rhymes and the kind called free verse.
>
> Q: Do you play sports other than cricket?
> *(Joseph, Dhobi Talao)*
> Javed Ansari: Balance is crucial. Every Sunday, I practise football in Priyadarshini Park with my friends. I have imbibed

from my father, who is a freelance cricket commentator, a passion for fine words and poetry. 'With a sword you can cut off the head of one man at a time, but with a pen in your hand you can cut off the noses of a hundred men at a time,' says my father. My interests extend to music where my heroes are Freddie Mercury, Tupac Shakur and Eminem.

Q: How important is the big Selection Day? Does your whole life depend on being picked for the IPL or Ranji team?
(F. Jeevan and Ms Jyoti, Jacob Circle)
Javed Ansari: Success does not mean hurting myself or letting others hurt me. For instance, if someone breaks my thumb saying it is for the sake of cricket, I will take him to the police at once.

'That son of a bitch,' Radha said. 'He must have spies in the MIG club. They told him everything.'

Manju, reading his father's mind, shouted at the closed door: 'I'll never go to the police, Appa. And if they ask me why is my thumb broken I'll say that you are the best father in the world.'

And only then did the bathroom door begin to open.

Ten minutes later, all the world saw Mohan and his boys, hand in hand, one happy family on their way to the temple.

•

Camphor, crushed marigold, wet stone and stale coconut combine to produce the body odour of a South Indian god, an odour not always pleasant, but always divine: and this is the smell which exuded from the closed wooden doors of the Subramanya temple at Chheda Nagar, Chembur. Finding the temple not yet open, the three Kumars bowed to the lord's golden spear, the *vel*, embedded into the side-wall. Radha closed his eyes and prayed audibly: 'Please keep us safe from the police and neighbours and most of all from our rivals in cricket.'

Mohan saw Manju looking at the parakeets on the roof of the temple. He reached over and slapped him on the head.

Sending Radha off to a cricket match – and Manju with his broken thumb to school – Mohan Kumar walked back into the Subramanya temple compound, which was now open, and fragrant with jasmine and good silk, and prayed for the moral improvement of his sons. He sat in the temple courtyard, removed his sandals and looked at the cracks on the balls of his feet.

The thing you do not realize when you are a young father is that they will *never* grow up to be as smart as you. Even if they love you (and Manju *certainly* did), they still provide your enemies with new opportunities. Expand the circumference of your vulnerability. Best if he kept away from Manju and Radha. At least for now.

This meant that for the first time in years, Mohan Kumar was free on a weekday morning.

Might go to Deepa Bar, he thought. Just to sit at one of those dark air-conditioned tables and talk to someone. Even Mr Shetty, the manager.

Having started his bike, Mohan Kumar looked up at the trees. He caught sight of a bulbul – a dash of red among the green – which reminded him of his village near the mountains. Fly home, he prayed to the bird, and tell them *nothing* has gone wrong. Mohan Kumar's plan is just beginning. Because his sons will soon have sons, and they too will bat: a dynasty of cricketers is rising in Mumbai from two drops of Kumar semen.

•

Three Poems about Manju

1. Why I am watching M.
Up on the 4th floor of Ali Weinberg School
In the full classroom that is taking the exam
everyone else has failed already.
I see only one face that is not a slave.

2. The little flame
Has no one else seen
the dark line that cuts into his forehead
when he is thinking?
It leans to the left.

3. M. is a cheater at heart
He wants to cheat in the exam
But he is not bold.
He wants to be free
But he is scared of his father.
He knows the colour of my cap
And my initials.
But he won't talk to me.
He knows
I am watching him right now.

4. Fourth poem (because Javed does what he
wants and breaks all rules)
A star fell to the earth
When no one was watching.
The name of the star is love.
Turn round; for it fell right behind you.

'There are still twenty minutes left, Manjunath.' Mr Lasrado, the physics teacher, returned from the window to his desk to collect the exam paper. 'What is the hurry to leave?'

All the other boys in the classroom were watching. On the blackboard were written the formidable words:

Physics Practice Exam
Number 2: Periodic Table and Atomic Particles.

But Manju insisted: 'Done, sir.'

Mr Lasrado sat at his desk and studied his paper.

'You haven't finished one question. Name five man-made elements. You have only bohrium and plutonium here. What is the hurry? Sit and finish.'

Manju held up his bandaged left thumb. Mr Lasrado lowered his nose and studied the bandage around the sporting finger.

'Cricket?'

'Cricket,' Manju agreed.

Outside in the hall, the peon was pasting a hand-made poster in the hallway: *Ten Easy Ways to Fight Tension during the Exam Period.*

Manju went down the steps, to an empty bench with a view of the parked school buses; he groaned. *Name five man-made elements. Bohrium, plutonium* ... There was a new edge to these surprise tests, monthly tests, half-annual and annual exams. For eight years, the students knew they could not fail. Now all that had changed. Now they could be thrown out of Ali Weinberg if their grades even threatened to lower the school's average in the Board Exams. Five man-made elements. Manju *knew* they were going to ask this question in the surprise test: he *should* have been able to name at least five.

He had lied to Mr Lasrado; the broken thumb had nothing to do with his not preparing properly for the exam, and the *CSI Las Vegas* back-to-back special on AXN had a lot to do with it. But he had read Mr Lasrado's mind, and knew that he wanted to hear about the famous cricket thumb, and not about *CSI Las Vegas*.

What was the point anyway of studying? He, like Radha, would have to drop out after the SSC exams to concentrate on cricket. Their father had already decided. Tommy Sir, for once, agreed with their father. He had seen so many young cricketers in Tamil Nadu say, I have to go to America, have to concentrate on my studies, sorry, Tommy Sir: no more cricket. There was no chance of either Manju or Radha failing at cricket. And if they did fail, Tommy Sir said, so what? Could always go back and finish college one or two years later.

Einsteinium. Is that man-made? Manju played with a lock of his hair.

Then someone whistled – the air filled with perfume – and a boy in a blue cap passed right by him. Farewell at once to both man-made and natural elements. Tucking his textbook under his arm, Manju followed Javed Ansari.

He walked over maroon-and-grey bricks, and through a makeshift cardboard arch painted with images of Mother Mary, to a place where he saw Javed leaning against a coconut tree to give himself a view, through a variety of mildewed structures, of the ocean. Manju saw a flame being struck.

Javed removed his blue cap and tossed it on the ground. Standing against the tree, looking at the waves, and running a hand through his hair, he smoked. Ten feet behind him, Manju struck the same pose with his hand and his hair. He too exhaled.

Describe your interests in life other than cricket, Manju.

Science. Chemistry. CSI Las Vegas.

How boring. What about driving a motorbike?

No. I can't.

Manju, can you please use fine English words in your answers?

Suddenly Manju saw that the figure leaning against the coconut tree had disappeared; and he already knew, as if in a horror movie, where Javed now was. Manju turned around slowly and there he stood, grinning: Mr 'J.A.', cigarette still in hand.

'Why did you and your brother write on my chest-guard?' he asked. 'Do you even know what it means, that thing you wrote?'

How Manju ran. He ran, under the makeshift arch, over the coloured bricks, through the school gate, and back to his classroom, Class 9, Section A, where he waited for his English class to start. Even in class, there was no safety, because a few minutes after the lunch-break, a peon turned up at his desk to summon him with a crooked finger: 'Patricia Principal wants to see you. Now.'

Two Powers ran the Ali Weinberg International School. One Power was seen. In her air-conditioned office, Patricia D'Mello sat beneath a framed black-and-white photograph of M.K. Gandhi, father of India, and a colour photograph of the Unseen Power, Karim Ali, father of modern education in the suburb of Bandra. (The students, naturally, assumed there had been 'hot stuff' between the Seen and Unseen Powers at some point in ancient history.)

Expecting to find Javed Ansari already in the Principal's office, Manju discovered that only he had been summoned. Moreover, Principal Patricia looked pleased. She was a plump woman with jowls, whom the students saw in the assembly hall on Independence and Republic Day, when she delivered solemn forty-minute speeches about patriotism and universal love that often turned sentimental and ended with references to herself as the 'mother of all those gathered here'; but in the privacy of her office she assumed a paternal, punitive avatar.

'Good afternoon, Principal Patricia.'

He held his broken thumb against his chest for her to see.

The Principal lowered her glasses and smiled at him, several times.

'Manjunath,' she said, dragging the final vowel wide. 'Do you know something about me?'

She smiled at him.

Shit, the boy thought, imagining that this was the start of some particularly baroque punishment.

'I too once had a future, Manju.' Removing her glasses, the Principal looked at a corner of the ceiling and smiled.

'People thought I had a future as a writer, Manju. I wanted to write a great novel about Mumbai,' the Principal said, playing with her glasses. 'But then … then I began, and I could not write it. The only thing I could write about, in fact, was that I couldn't write about the city.

'*The sun, which I can't describe like Homer, rises over Mumbai, which I can't describe like Salman Rushdie, creating new moral dilemmas for all of us, which I won't be able to describe like Amitav Ghosh.*

'The sun, which I can't describe like Akira Kurosawa, rises over Mumbai, which I can't describe like Raj Kapoor, creating new moral dilemmas for all of us, which I won't be able to describe like Satyajit Ray.

'I filled five hundred pages like this, Manju. Five hundred. I called it *Phraud*. In the end I gave up writing and thought, let me do some good to society, let me teach young boys.'

Realizing that his broken thumb would not be needed as an excuse, Manju lowered it from sight. He understood that some extraordinary and unknown event had ushered him and Principal Patricia into an unprecedented intimacy.

She placed her glasses back on her nose and smiled.

'You and your brother Radha Krishna – you two are not *phrauds*. What Radha did today in the Oval Maidan, that was remarkable. Founder Ali himself called to tell me, Manju. The Founder called! He was so proud of you two Kumars – and of me. A new city-wide cricket record!'

She put her glasses back on and smiled, so Manju felt he had to say something.

'Yes, Principal Patricia.'

'Global cricket record. Isn't it?'

Manju tried to read the Seen Power's mind, as she kept smiling.

'You *do* know what your elder brother did today, don't you, Manju?'

•

On his way home to Chheda Nagar, Manju had the sweetest experience a younger brother can: a woman stopped him to ask for directions to the Tattvamasi Building. 'Where that boy lives – you know, the one who broke the batting record, you know, the chutney-seller's son.'

'My father,' Manju announced, 'is a businessman in gold and real estate. Radha Kumar, the global-record breaker, is my brother. You may walk behind me.'

When they reached the building, they found the living room already full of people; some of them saw Manju and cheered, Hero! Hero! – 'Not this one, not this one,' Mohan Kumar corrected them, 'this is *tomorrow's* hero'; and on the television, a news reader was announcing,

'Not only is this the highest score ever recorded by a batsman under the age of sixteen in Mumbai, this is also the first time in the history of our inter-school Elite Division cricket that 300 runs have been scored by a batsman in one day's play. The young magician of the cricket bat, Radha Kumar, of Ali Weinberg High School, spoke to our correspondent ...'

More guests came, and more after them; and at 9 p.m. Anand Mehta himself turned up.

'This man,' Mehta told the people gathered around Mohan Kumar, 'is the only other man in Mumbai who has no inhibitions. He is the only other man creating new value in a dead city.'

While Manju brought him white bread to snack on, Anand Mehta talked superman-to-superman with Mohan Kumar, suffering the others, mere humans, to stand around them eavesdropping. 'Entrepreneurship. Most of what we hear about it in the media is absolute bullshit, Mr Mohan. Don't invest in a new business in India. That's some shit we feed the Yanks and Japs. Real money is in turning around old businesses, because the heartland of this country is a Disneyland of industrial disasters: thousands of socialist factories, sick, or semi-sick or partially shut down.

'See, Mr Mohan, Mumbai is finished. Proof. Other night, I'm visiting my aunt. Lives in the ground floor of Pallonji Mansion. You have to do these things, go see these bores once a month, to make sure the maid hasn't murdered them. Usually, all you get from these ladies is the usual South Bombay talk: Haan, girl is looking for a husband in Carmichael Road, maybe even Altamount Road, but certainly not beyond Pedder Road. But this time – this time, I go there, and my old auntie is talking politics. First time in her life. She looks at me and says, "Anand, Anand, did you know

Bal Thackeray is slowly dying?" So what? I say. Indian politicians always die slowly, unless they're Gandhis. And she says, "Anand, Anand, when the Permanent Boss is gone, who will take care of the city?" And then it hits me. My God, it hits me, Mr Mohan. What is Bombay? Shit scared. Deep down no one is *khadoos*. They're all waiting for a Daddy Figure to hold 'em and protect 'em and maybe even hump 'em. That's why I say, we in the city of Mumbai know the future is in distressed assets because we're living in one. Get it? It hurts – but it's the truth, right? That's why, I said, Goodbye, Mumbai. I've got an inside man in north India, an IAS officer's son, and we're going about the city of Dhanbad looking for old industrial plants to turn around.'

Chewing a lump of white bread, Mehta sprayed his host with hard truths and moist starch, and asked periodically that Mohan Kumar's cell phone be extracted from its handkerchief cover (his own phone had broken down, he explained). As Mehta made calls, and told people that 'his investment' had broken a global record, he kept chewing, seemingly bent on devouring all the bread in the Kumar home.

At nine thirty, Mohan Kumar, scratching his ankle with one hand, raised the other and gestured, like a statesman, for the people to behave themselves and quieten down, and confirmed the buzzing rumour.

'Please keep it to yourself, but it is true: Shah Rukh Khan has asked to see Radha. It is true.'

That is why the boy wasn't home: he had gone straight from the cricket grounds to the Bandra Bandstand to meet the world's most famous film-star. The crowd sighed.

Later, they saw him on television. Master Radha Kumar, holder of the record for the highest score in Mumbai school cricket, still in his soiled cricket whites, which the TV people had insisted on for authenticity, and whose shabby state only heightened the power of his grey eyes, stood before Shah Rukh Khan's mansion in the Bandra Bandstand, answering questions from a TV reporter:

'Shah Rukh Khan called me a teenage human skyscraper, because I made so many runs, and he said two things in Mumbai keep going up and up, skyscrapers and school cricket scores, then he asked how does a young man like you have the concentration to become a teenage human skyscraper, and I said, my father has trained me in willpower, and then he said, which part of the innings was the hardest, and I said, for me, no part of the innings was hard, because my father told me first become a centurion, and then become a double centurion, and then become a triple centurion, and then …'

'Hopeless,' his father said, slapping his forehead in front of all the visitors. 'Stammers when he's asked a simple question.' He and the remaining visitors discussed and dissected Radha Kumar's performance, and though they identified a few good things in it (Radha's snow-leopard eyes could never lose their glamour), they awarded it, on the whole, very poor marks; with the result that when Radha Kumar finally returned to his home, he was, to his surprise, received as a failure.

He and Manju would have to wait till the next day for their first taste of cricketing stardom: which is to say, their first real chance to do some fucking.

•

'What is Shah Rukh Khan's bungalow like? How many Ferraris does he have? Is it true that two German fans, both blonde girls, wait all day long outside his house for autographs? Did you get to meet Gauri?'

It was after class, and Radha and Manju, who were supposed to report for cricket practice at the MCA, had instead been 'picked up' by Sofia, and were being driven by her chauffeur to the city, for a bit of 'shopping'. Manju, assuming he had been brought along for the sake of appearances – to provide some cover while his brother and the girl got up to some serious 'shopping' – sat stiffly in the back of the car, while Sofia, from the front seat, fired questions at Radha.

'But don't get a big head, okay? You're bad enough as it is.'

Sofia's thatch was even more pronounced now, and Manju wondered how she managed to see through the hair covering her eye.

'We have a *dictatorship* of cricket in this country,' the girl said, opening her handbag with the silver 'H' and rummaging about in it till she found a mirror. 'Everyone in school was trying to talk to you today, it was crazy. But they're bringing Lionel Messi to Mumbai, and that will be the end of your stupid cricket.'

Leaning forward from his waist, Manju saw a large cell phone, lipstick, a round mirror, some hundred-rupee notes, some change.

While she checked her lipstick, Sofia watched the younger boy in her round mirror, but addressed the older:

'What happened to your brother's thumb?'

Sofia frowned, and, as they passed Mahalaxmi temple, reached over to touch Manju's bandaged thumb – 'poor thing' – leaving him confused.

'Have you seen this road before, Bandage Boy?' she asked, letting go of his thumb.

'No.'

She laughed a little.

'It's Pedder Road. You must have heard of it?'

Manju said, 'No,' because that was what she wanted him to say.

Maybe he should have done a namaste when they passed the temple. She would have enjoyed that.

Radha intervened: 'One thing you must know if you are going to be with me – never tease my younger brother. He's a bit shy. Don't bully.'

'I'm not bullying him,' Sofia said. 'I am strictly opposed to all forms of harassment. Hey, Manju,' she turned around to him again, 'you know I have this project for class that fights discrimination against women? My dad gave me the idea. I am calling up chemical companies everywhere in India and finding out where it is safe for a woman to work in sales and marketing. You know, because she has to go by herself in buses and rickshaws selling the company's chemicals to strange men, right? My dad is helping me, and together, we're going to make this map of India, which will show where it is perfectly safe for a woman to work in sales and marketing. Like South India is safe. But not Andhra Pradesh, because my dad says that Andhra men have a chicken-eating and macho culture. We have drawn a big map at home and we're filling it in blue, for woman-safe, and red, for not-so-woman-safe places, where the men eat too much chicken. Manju boy, are you listening? I'm not bullying you. Okay?'

'Okay,' Manju said.

Half an hour later, he was open-mouthed, gazing at a magic horse that lived among handkerchiefs, perfumes and jewels. He was standing outside the Hermès luxury store in Horniman Circle, gazing through the windows.

Radha and Sofia were inside, 'shopping'.

His nose pressed against the glass, Manju gaped at the torso of the horse, which was composed of tiny, multicoloured enamel bricks, and was split into three parts, to fit the three display windows. A real kitten examined Manju as he examined the jewelled horse.

The most valuable thing we have in our family, Manju wanted to tell the kitten, is wrapped in cellophane and kept inside the almirah: Sachin Tendulkar's own glove, given to my brother Radha. But the kitten grew bored and licked its paws.

The door opened, releasing scent, golden light, and Sofia. Radha had his arm around her waist, and said: 'They don't have anything good here. We're going to another place to shop.' The top button on Sofia's shirt was undone, exposing more of the dark spots on her cream-coloured neck.

Manju followed them in the direction of Ballard Estate, until his brother turned around and made a rude gesture.

So he went back to his magic horse. Inch by inch, Manju brought his nose closer to the glass.

The kitten meowed: Manju looked at its open mouth, at its little teeth.

His heart began to beat.

Two evenings ago, he had been watching the history channel, as a tall thin European man stood by an exposed stone arch and talked about the Mughals, and about Emperor Akbar the Great, how he liked paintings of wild leopards and wild peacocks and wild ducks and hunting dogs. Watching the European man's chiselled nose, his soft hair, his powerful Adam's apple and tense lips, against the backdrop of all that raw Islamic stone, Manju felt the need to hide beneath the sofa (settling instead for turning the TV off and picking up a new bat and standing in front of the full-length mirror to practise his extra-cover drive); and now, as he thought about that European with the chiselled nose – bang, it had happened, even as the kitten was watching: his cock was stiff, and he had to walk with his feet wide apart to hide behind the safety of a pillar.

The kitten followed him, meowing.

As he wiped his sweat with one hand, and then with the other, Manju saw his father, driving a red Bajaj Pulsar right past him: and the nightmare was complete.

Mounted on his bike, the Progenitor of Prodigies had followed his two sons all the way to Horniman Circle. Now instinct was leading him straight to Ballard Estate. He knew exactly where his son had gone with that girl.

He's going to kill Radha when he finds him with a girl, Manju thought. He sprinted behind the red bike, shouting, 'Appa! Don't hurt Radha! He's your son, remember!'

•

What made you go 'Wow, that's crazy!' about Anand Mehta was not that he had had a Negro girlfriend in America, or that he was loudly contemptuous of his own class, or that he drank too much at the Yacht Club and declared that he could fix all of Mumbai's problems in five minutes 'with a guillotine'– no, what *really* disturbed members of his own class was the horrible but true rumour that Mehta had donated ten or fifteen lakh rupees to a school for slum children in Cuffe Parade. A donation! To a school in the slums! He could have done the decent thing, and given five hundred rupees to the Malabar Hill Lions Club, but no – a *donation*! To slum children!

Nevertheless, out of respect for his father, his years in New York, and his entertainment value, most of his classmates generally agreed to listen to his next big idea.

'Imagine an *Economist* article. A real *Economist* article. That only the two of us can read, a whole year before it is printed.'

A TV showed an old cricket match at one end of the bar; at the other, a wide window gave a view of trees swaying on Marine Drive. Anand Mehta sat on a sofa with a bottle of Foster's, and nibbled on two bowls of fried snacks.

His visitor, who had just wiped his face with a white handkerchief, said: 'I'm sorry I am late, Anand. Really, I am. See, I thought we were meeting at the Taj President.'

The man who had arrived late was Rahul 'Jo-Jo' Mistry, whose father, like Mehta's, was a stockbroker; unlike Anand, he still worked with Daddy in Cuffe Parade. When Anand had sent around a mass email about Radha's triple century, inviting potential investors to purchase equity in his unique cricket sponsorship programme, Mistry was the last man he had expected to reply. Old Money types, unless liberated by an instinct for debauchery, which 'Jo-Jo' seemed unlikely to possess, rarely took risks.

Refusing Mehta's offer of the fried snacks, 'Jo-Jo' Mistry, heir to a 200-crore brokerage fortune, insisted on further explaining his tardiness.

'When you said the Trident I thought you wanted me at the President. I always thought this hotel was just called the Oberoi. Isn't that funny?'

Anand Mehta took 'Jo-Jo' Mistry's small cold hands in his and pumped some life into them.

'Relaaaaaaax, Jo-Jo. Relaaaaaaax.'

How, Anand Mehta thought, as he reached for more deep-fried starch, could you live all your fucking life in South Bombay and still mix up the Trident and the Taj President? Only if, like old friend 'Jo-Jo' here, you were not required to think in order to survive, because Grandpa Mistry had bought big fat plots in Worli and Chembur in 1955 at eighteen rupees an acre and shoved the title deeds up your baby bum, which you have kept tightly clenched ever since. Reaching for a few more fried rings, Mehta looked at 'Jo-Jo' Mistry and licked his lips.

(But his eyes looked up at the ceiling when he was lying, and this had tipped off his friends for years.)

'Now, I would like to make you the exclusive gift of an *Economist* article, one year in advance.'

Here they were interrupted again, because 'Jo-Jo' had brought another potential cricket investor with him, an old white man in a beige suit. Mehta shook hands with him, and discovered he was American.

'Are you in sports management?'

The old American smiled and said, 'I am the one man who is despised on every country on earth.'

Mehta thought about it. 'Are you a plastic surgeon?'

Which made everyone laugh.

'Let's try this,' the American said, enjoying the game, 'I like my prose paratactic, my women flexible, and my governments libertarian. Who am I?'

'Chinese communist.'

'Close enough. I'm an investment banker,' the American confessed, and Anand told him of the three years he had spent in New York – and of his intimate knowledge of Central Park, especially the pond area called Hernshead, towards the south – and of his knowledge also of Peter Luger, Scalini, Wolfgang's Strip House, Bouley, Daniel (Lithuanian waitresses!), Union Square Grill (the *things* you can do in that Men's Room of theirs!), Gramercy Tavern, Grimaldi's, Lombar—

'You know, Anand,' 'Jo-Jo' Mistry interrupted him, 'I actually played cricket.'

'I remember, mate.' Anand Mehta smiled. 'I remember. You were a keeper, weren't you?'

'Substitute wicket-keeper. Being ambidextrous, I was good at collections with my left hand too, which most Indians are not.' Mistry demonstrated how he gathered the ball this way and that, this way and that. 'Coach never gave me a chance. Even now it hurts.'

'Like the first time you wanted a girl. Can't be forgotten. Ah, cricket. We had to get rid of the English, I always say, in order to enjoy the benefits of English civilization. You will keep hearing,' Mehta turned to the American, 'that other sports are becoming popular in India, like tennis or volleyball, but the thing to understand about cricket, sir, is that our government has no option but to enforce the *mandatory* playing of this game in India. You see, we are sitting on a time-bomb: we're missing about ten million women from our population, due to female infanticide. This extraordinary fact is known to you, I assume? Do not make *any* business decision in India until you familiarize yourself with our male-to-female sex ratio, the result of decades of selective abortion. I predict that young Indian males, lacking women to marry or even to mate with, are likely to become progressively more deranged. This is already visible. Now, only one thing on earth can save us from all this rogue Hindu testosterone. Cricket. Have you ever tried to kill someone with a cricket bat? All but impossible. The deep and intrinsic silliness of cricket, I think, all that fair play and honourable draw stuff, makes it ideally suited for male social control in India. Can you imagine what will happen to crime and rape in Delhi and Mumbai if boys here start playing, say, American football? I believe that in the years to come, to pacify hundreds of millions of desperately horny young Indians of the lower social classes, our government has only three real policy options: to legalize prostitution, which it won't do; to make liquor significantly cheaper than it currently is, which it can't afford to do; or else, to supply us with a never-ending stream of narcotizing cricket-based entertainments. Bread and Tendulkar. Televised cricket in India is essentially state-sponsored lobotomy (you *must* hear our cricket commentators) – and we'll be getting a *lot* more of it soon. What do you think, Jo-Jo? Am I right or am I as usual right?'

But 'Jo-Jo' Mistry was still demonstrating his ambidextrous wicket-keeping skills along the table's surface. Anand Mehta knew exactly why Jo-Jo was acting like an idiot, the same reason he had so cunningly brought an American along: because any moment he could say, Oh, *Cricket*, we thought you meant High-Yield Corporate Debt, and leave.

Mehta excused himself for a minute.

Out in the lobby of the Trident, dipping his finger in a brass bowl filled with rose petals, he answered his phone.

'Tommy Sir, I'm in a business meeting. You keep texting and calling.'

'Mr Anand. Can you come to St George Hospital at once?'

'Absolutely not. What a question. I'm in a meeting.'

When Tommy Sir explained the situation, Anand Mehta put his palm on his forehead and wished the game of cricket a speedy extinction.

•

Although he was that rare cricket lover who was not also an Anglophile – kept safe from that lunacy by his knowledge of what the British had done to India in the twentieth century (Partition, the Bengal famine, the Gandhi–Nehru family) and the greater horror they had deposited here in the nineteenth century, the Indian Penal Code, which was *still* in force (like the mad grandfather everyone knows should be locked up in the attic, but who sits in the living room with a cane in his hands) – Tommy Sir had, nevertheless, developed a grudging respect for the rascals, freebooters and thugs who had carved out the Raj in the eighteenth century. James Grant Duff writing the history of the Marathas with one hand while discharging his flintlocks at the Marathas with the other. That takes balls. French call it sangfroid. And of that eighteenth-century legacy of balls, more respectably termed sangfroid, the sole surviving shard we possess in India is the game of Test cricket.

Which was exactly why Tommy Sir smiled at young Radha Krishna Kumar, that living manifestation of sangfroid, as he stood at the head of an outpatient bed in the St George Hospital, Mumbai, even as Anand Mehta entered the hospital ward, asking, 'Where is this Holocaust situation, please?'

Raising himself up in his bed, Mohan Kumar folded his hands as his benefactor arrived.

'My own son has done this to me, sir, my own Radha …' His two boys stood on either side of the wounded Mohan, like a better and a worse angel. He pointed a finger at one, and then at the other. 'My right leg is broken. My own two sons did this. Radha struck the blow. Radha did it. Please tell the police: please tell them who has hurt who, who is guilty and who is innocent here.'

As they left the hospital, Tommy Sir told Anand Mehta a different version of events. This monster without a name from the mountains of South India, this chutney-seller, was in competition with the two penises he had created.

'He follows Radha on his red bike all the way to Ballard Estate, and then goes running up and bangs on the door where Radha is with his girlfriend, saying he will murder everyone inside. I told you he has a police record. They say he tried to finish off his wife. To protect his girlfriend, Radha, brave boy, pushes his father, who falls down the stairs and breaks his leg. We need a licence in this country to buy a gas cylinder or open a tea shop, but there is no licence required to have children.'

'My God,' Anand Mehta said, slapping his forehead. He had just parted with a five-hundred-rupee note, transferred via Tommy Sir to the wounded paterfamilias.

'The more money I give them, the more money they suck up. It's a disaster.'

'No,' Tommy Sir said. 'No, no, no.'

He made a small space between his fingers, and smiled.

'It's wonderful. The more money you give them ...'

He brought his fingers together.

'... the *less* freedom they have.'

As his chauffeur drove him away from the hospital, Anand Mehta looked at the one-inch gap he was holding captive between his thumb and index finger, and the street lights on Marine Drive cast a golden furrow over his car.

•

After being helped by his sons into a black taxi, Mohan Kumar used his crutches to chastise them in alternation, all the way back to Chembur. Both boys silently ate their father's blows, but each time Radha's eyes met Manju's, they relayed the same message: *Next time he tries to do this to me, I'll break his neck instead.* When the taxi reached their building, Mohan paid the driver with Mehta's five-hundred-rupee note. But after Radha and Manju got out, he continued to sit in the taxi and said, feebly, 'Wait. We need a better story to tell.'

The boys stared at him through the window.

'The neighbours will ask,' Mohan Kumar explained, 'how I broke my right leg.' •

'In the old days they used to say, let Bombay field two sides in the Ranji Trophy and the final will be Bombay versus Bombay. Today look at us. Have we produced one major batsman in this city since Sachin? Small towns all across India are producing hungry batsmen. Things are not going to be easy for you Bombay boys. So don't make them any harder by dropping catches. Now get the bloody hell into a circle around me. Time for catching practice. Time for pain. The ball is going to fly at your faces. Ready, boys?'

'Yes, sir, Tommy Sir!'

Manju's face had been smeared with white war-paint: zinc cream to protect his skin. He stamped on the wild grass at the centre of Azad Maidan; dragonflies fled his brand-new spikes. A Pepsi bottle and a decaying canvas shoe lying in the grass each got a kick. He bent low; he watched the stone-roller.

Six boys were watching that roller. Tommy Sir had the red ball in his hands. He threw it at the curved stone; deflecting off the edge, the shiny new cricket ball flew straight at one boy's eyes.

Radha caught the ball, fumbled with it, slipped, and dropped it.

Manju winced; he rubbed the back of his thighs. That was where Radha was going to get it. Under-arming the ball to Tommy Sir, Radha turned and waited.

First, the speech:

'You know how many batsmen fit into a cricket team? Just six. So why, duffers, do you make things harder for yourself by dropping catches?'

Now for the punishment.

Manju closed his eyes. He heard it. Tommy Sir had thrown the ball straight into his brother's back. When he opened his eyes, Radha, his elbow bent, was rubbing the spot where the ball had hit.

The six boys crouched once more in front of the roller.

Radha loved everything to do with the game: the three rounds of jogging around the maidan to warm up, the jumping jacks, the stretches, even the chastisement that followed a dropped catch. With hard work he had made himself a good fielder. Manju did not practise half as hard. But Manju caught with his left hand as well as with his right, and could hit with just one stump to aim at. On the run.

Now that he had been punished, Radha knew that Tommy Sir, serial humiliator, would aim the ball at Manju next. Lowering his eyes, feeling strange in the stomach, Radha realized he couldn't say if he wanted Manju to catch the ball or drop it.

He crouched, his fingers tense.

But no ball came.

Tommy Sir was walking over to a banyan tree that stood just outside the maidan. From behind it, the boys now saw a pair of crutches poking out. The man who had been hiding behind the tree now came into view and the yelling began.

'They're my sons!'

'We had an agreement! Out. Out.'

Radha turned to Manju, who was looking at him. The boys saw Tommy Sir arguing with the man on the crutches, then forcing him to get into a black taxi, and slamming the roof as it drove away.

Manju looked at his brother again.

Don't look at me, idiot, Radha shouted, loud enough for all the boys to hear, because he didn't know that his brother had already read his mind.

Don't let all three members of our family be disgraced today. Look at the ball.

The Harris Shield begins

Early morning at Cross Maidan. The shops of Fashion Street are closed. The concrete tower of the Tata Communications building rises in one corner; the domes of the Western Railway headquarters and a flame-shaped Zoroastrian fire-temple are visible on the other side of the maidan. Boys in white have gathered in a semi-circle at the centre of the maidan, and they are looking at an old man; the old man is looking at an electronic mike in front of his nose.

The old man's name is J.B. Adhikari; he might have played for Bombay, though no one was sure when; and he was spending his retirement writing a history of one hundred and fifty years of Bombay cricket in the library of the CCI, where he was so often seen snoring over a newspaper it was generally felt his history would take one hundred and fifty years to write.

'Gharana.'

The old man spoke at first to the mike, and then, as if gaining in confidence, to the boys.

'We call it the Mumbai Gharana. A School of Music. A school of music of cricket. You know the names. Ajit Wadekar, who led us to our first series win in England in 1971; Farokh Engineer and Vinoo

Mankad; Eknath Solkar, the finest close-in fielder this country has seen; the two gems of Indian batsmanship, Sachin and Sunny; and the two Dilips, Sardesai and Vengsarkar. All of them were local boys like you; they learnt to play at the Oval and the Azad Maidan. Like you they took the trains and buses; like you they batted in the Kanga League in the rain and in the Gymkhana in the heat. Now what are the characteristics of this Mumbai school of music expressed as cricket? All-round defensive and attacking play; a strong back foot; the skill to survive the moving and turning ball alike. When he stands at the wicket, a young batsman must bring to his technique all the toughness of our city. He must bat selfishly. Must humiliate the other side, particularly if it is Delhi. He must hoard runs for himself. But he must also bat selflessly. Sacrifice himself when the team needs it. Scoring a century or double century is not enough: it has to be the *right* century or double century. It takes more than just success to join the hundred-and-fifty-year-old gharana of Bombay batsmanship. So, boys: Play hard. But play within the rules. And may the spirit of Vijay Merchant and Vijay Manjrekar shine upon you.'

First day

0–131 runs

By 11 a.m., Manju, his muscles warmed, his face striped with zinc cream, was swinging his bat in big circles with his left arm.

Grim, grim: all was grim. Put in to bat by Dadar Bhadra School, Ali Weinberg had lost its openers in the first few overs, and then – Khallas! – its star batsman, Radha Kumar, record-holder, was bowled around his legs.

One Kumar out, another in: Manju observed his superstitions. Even as the fielders cried, 'The crazy boy is doing it again,' he circumambulated the stumps. 'Obbane, Obbane/Kattale, Kattale.' Wait. Wait. Not yet ready. He looked all around.

In one corner, he saw the Dadar Bhadra coach, seated on a white chair under blossoms of white and pink bougainvillea and shouting nonstop at his boys – *Dil se khelo! Avinash, Aisa mauka aur nahi ayega! Shall I tell your father that you are no good? You. I want minimum two wickets and two catches from you. Let's at least make an effort, guys? If you believe we can win, boys.*

'I said not yet ready!' Manju held his arm up to tell the bowler to wait.

He had to find his rhythm. Scraping the crease with his bat, he began hunting for the rhythm. Tap, tap, tap. Before he could find the right rhythm, another bat's tapping interrupted his, and he had to hold his hand up once again and shout: 'Wait.' At the non-striker's end, wearing a blue helmet with the initials 'J.A.' in gold lettering, Javed Ansari stood tapping *his* bat, imitating Manju, beat for beat.

Fascinating, Tommy Sir thought, an hour later. He was standing as far away as his eyes would let him. Both Ansari and Kumar were playing better than they had ever done before: and this partnership of theirs, which had already accumulated 90 runs, might well make tomorrow's newspapers, if it continued like this. The two boys were perfect contrasts. Long-sleeved, elegant, Javed's footwork was basic, but his southpaw strokeplay had the intricacy of exquisite filigree-work; Manju's batting was direct, simple, iron. As they played together, they did not speak, and barely even acknowledged each other's existence: yet Tommy Sir saw the two styles blend.

•

As the papers reported the next day:

> Batting for the Ali Weinberg School of Bandra, the combination of Manjunath Kumar and Javed Ansari had added 260 runs at the Karnatak Sporting Association pitch of the Cross Maidan; both batsmen had become centurions.
>
> 'The bowlers have given up; the fielders have given up. The real contest now appears to be between the two batsmen themselves.'

Second day

132–150 runs

On the morning of the second day, the coach of Dadar Bhadra School, now straddling his white plastic chair under the bougainvillea blossoms, had *not* given up: he continued to yell at his underachieving bowlers with unflagging energy – *Pyaar se fielding karo, Ramesh – What is this nonsense, Avinash? – Adi, let's see some spirit, young man. What will I tell your father otherwise?*

By 11 a.m., both Manju and Javed had changed bats, opting for heavier versions of their SGs, an indication that the real hitting was just beginning.

Second day: after lunch

151–256 runs

Manju and Javed's partnership had broken at least seven known Mumbai school records. One of them had made 212. The other was four runs behind.

The post-lunch session began. As Javed, rubbing the black rubber handle of his cricket bat, watched from the non-striker's end, Manju, bending low and orientalizing his style with baroque wristwork, flicked the first ball from outside off-stump to the square-leg boundary.

Each time either of them hit a four, the two boys solemnly walked down to the middle of the pitch and touched their gloves, then turned and walked back.

Suddenly, in the middle of the pitch, as their gloves met, Javed asked:

'Does your father tell you only one of us can be Tendulkar and the other has to be Kambli?'

Manju's mouth opened.

Javed repeated his question. Manju moved back to take strike. He saw the golden 'J.A.' initials on the blue helmet, and thought: It's a mind-game.

In the next over, Javed hit a four off the back foot. The boys walked down the pitch, and touched gloves again.

'Same thing my father says,' Javed said.

Manju looked around.

'Does your father tell you things will be easy for me because I'm a left-hander?'

Manju ran back to his crease. But the next time they walked to the middle of the pitch and touched gloves, he said:

'I've given the bowlers nicknames. Want to hear?'

Mohan Kumar had taught his sons to do this, to establish psychological dominance over the bowlers. Manju had given the leg-spinner the name 'Taibu', because he was small and dark, like the Zimbabwean; one tall fast-bowler started off as 'Akram', because he was left-handed, and turned into 'Nehra', as his deliveries were smashed to the boundary. And this chubby round-arm spinner who was preparing to bowl, this spinner who had been hit to the fence and over it so many times, how else could Manju refer to this spinner but as 'Loser'?

'Don't call him a loser,' Javed said.

'Why not?'

'His father died the other day. His name is Jamshed. I heard the boys talking.'

'So what if his father died?' Manju asked. 'I'll call him what I want.'

Pudgy little 'Loser' – Jamshed Cutleriwala, the world's worst off-spinner – took five fat steps to his bowling mark; he wiped his forehead and got ready to bowl.

Manju examined the spinner's body. All that jiggling fat.

'Wait,' he said. 'Everyone wait.'

Manju walked to square leg, removed his chest-guard, and threw it at his feet; then threw his helmet at his chest-guard, and then, reaching into his trousers, pulled out the triangular box from around his underwear and threw it at his helmet.

Before he could get back to the crease, he heard a voice: 'Put your helmet back on. Then put your centre pad back on.'

He turned around to see Javed right behind him.

'Why?' Manju asked. 'When a real bowler comes to bowl, I'll wear a helmet and centre pad. Not till then.'

'Put the helmet back on. I *told* you his father died. Don't insult him.'

'I told *you*, I don't care.'

Javed's forehead expanded: a large vein stood out.

'You and your brother still didn't say sorry for what you wrote on *my* chest-guard,' he whispered, gritting his teeth.

'And we won't *ever* say sorry for that,' Manju replied. 'And we'll do it again after this match.'

He drove 'Loser's' next ball to the extra-cover boundary, hitting it so hard it reached the adjacent field where another match was being played, and scored a four there too.

When it was 'Loser's' turn to bowl again, Javed was on strike.

The first delivery was a full toss, but Javed did something strange with his bat that puzzled everyone, and the ball dropped dead. Even the umpire whistled. Manju licked his upper lip from this side to that, and from that side to this. Javed Ansari, nephew of a Ranji Trophy player, sophisticated newspaper interviewee, suddenly can't hit a full toss.

Fat 'Loser' was walking to the top of his run-up; and though no one spoke, Manju thought he could hear a voice inside his head say, quite distinctly, 'I'm going to get out now. Watch me, Manju.'

The next ball was a long hop.

Javed Ansari took a step back, his long white sleeves rippling as the bat's edge struck the ball. Jamshed 'Loser' Cutleriwala stared at the ball's arc, open-mouthed, before screaming:

'Catch it!'

The fielder at mid-wicket, who for two days had been watching so many balls fly over his head, realized that this one was coming straight to him; he raised a pair of trembling hands. And then everyone was running up to him, except for 'Loser' Cutleriwala, who turned to the Ali Weinberg tent and made an obscene gesture.

Under the bougainvilleas, a voice grew ecstatic – *I told you boys Jamshed could do it! Chauhan, hug the bowler for me! – Hug hug hug. Let's get them all out in the next twenty minutes – Do it for your coach, boys. I've been sitting in the sun for two days.*

Third day: morning

257–350 runs

A half-naked man, swinging a mallet, pounds a wooden cot to pieces near the Cross Maidan. Up goes the hammer: there it stops. He has heard a louder noise than the one he is making: it is coming from inside the maidan.

Setting down the mallet, he joins the spectators.

'What's going on?'

'That little fellow has batted for two full days. This is the third morning. Still batting. He had a partner but that boy got out. This one goes on.'

'What stamina. Imagine when he grows up.'

'He already has a double century. He's going to make 300.'

'300? No, he's already made 300.'

'The short ones are always better. "Small frame, big fame." It's an ancient saying in our language.'

'Which language is that?'

'I'm from here, boss. Born and brought up in Mumbai like you. Or were you?'

'Can we just watch the cricket, please? Can we just watch the cricket for once?'

More spectators gather. Contracting his sweat-oiled muscles, the labourer continues smashing the wooden frame; pausing only when his blows are again drowned out by those produced by the little man with the cricket bat.

THIRD DAY: TEATIME

351–450 RUNS

Tommy Sir was trembling. Not because of anything so crude as the fact that Manju, having broken his brother's record for the highest score in Mumbai school cricket, was now all but certain to become the first under-18 in the city's history to go past 500 runs in a single innings. No. He was trembling because to watch young Manjunath was to observe a remarkable fusion. See: in the old days of cricket there used to be good technique and bad technique. There was such a thing as proper footwork, playing within the 'V'. But then the new cricket, twenty-twenty, American-style, came along. Bad technique became good. Batsmen withdrew their front foot. They lofted the ball in the air. They reverse-swept; they switch-hit. Now a batsman had to have two techniques, good and bad, and two cricketing personalities, traditional and maverick, and produce the right one on the right occasion: and this confusion undoes even the best batsmen – who loft when they should block and block when they should loft. But as Tommy Sir observed the continuing evolution of Manju's batting, it occurred to him that this boy, who was switching at will between classical and contemporary footwork, between 'good' technique and 'bad', was fusing his two cricketing personalities into something new and flawless – and unprecedented in the history of Bombay cricket.

CLOSE OF THIRD DAY

FINAL SCORE: 497

At the close of the third day's play, the *Mumbai Sun* had sent a reporter over to the Cross Maidan with a camera crew. Holding a mike to Manju's face she asked:

'What happened when you reached the 497-run mark, Manju? Why didn't you go on?'

The boy's gear was off him. His shirt was soiled; his hair was wet; but his body was dark and radiant with victory. Behind him his father stood with folded arms; and his lips were puckered as he listened to his son say, 'I made 300, and then 400, and then 450. But I don't know why I got out at 497.'

The reporter turned to the camera:

'Manjunath Kumar just missed becoming the first school batsman in a hundred and fifty years of Mumbai school cricket to score 500.'

She turned back to the champion:

'Manju, how do you feel?'

'Satisfied. Happy.'

'Happy that you missed the global record of 500 by just three runs?'

'Unhappy about that.'

'Do you want to play for Mumbai?'

'I dream of that every day.'

'Do you also dream about playing in the World Cup?'

'Yes I dream about that every day too.'

'Your brother is also a record-breaking batsman. Which of you is better?'

'He has a secret contract with God, and I do not.'

•

Now she interviewed the father, on crutches (the victim of a tumble down stairs), who gazed into the camera, and said:

'Manjunath, my second child, is more complex. As a boy he used to eat stones and glass and other strange things. Chappals too. I had to work hard to make him a normal person. Shall I explain with examples?'

As Mohan Kumar informed the world about his methods in nutrition and pharmacology, Tommy Sir came and sat down by Manju, who was looking at the sky. Tommy Sir scraped the side of the boy's face with his fingernail:

'Shave.'

It had happened to Tommy Sir before: the boys he was mentoring became men on his watch.

'Looks bad on television, otherwise.'

Manju scratched the back of his neck and asked: 'Where is Javed?'

'Forget him. Everyone knows you're better than Javed. The way he got out, it was ridiculous.'

'Javed got out on purpose. The way he was batting, he would have made 500 first.'

'Forget that Javed. Posh creatures like him will never make the team, too delicate. You know he writes poems and gives them to the other boys, and they all laugh. But *you*. You are almost as good as Radha now. Manju: listen. Do you know how much you improve every single time I see you bat? Now listen: you are going to play for Mumbai, I know it. *Marathi kathin nahin. Tu lavkar shikshi.* You must learn Marathi. Good for the back foot. Manju, are you listening?'

This was not all Narayanrao Sadashivrao Kulkarni wanted to tell the boy, but it was time for a photo shoot with the *Mumbai Sun*.

'I don't want to do it,' the boy said.

Tommy Sir stared.

Manju stared back. The dark groove in his forehead, the one that tilted left, flickered to life.

'It's twilight,' he said, looking up at the sky. 'It was my mother's ...'

'Go, you duffer: go.' Tommy Sir slapped the tired boy on the back, harder than he meant to.

Then he watched, his arms folded, as the photographer for the *Mumbai Sun* made the virtually quintuple-centurion sit on a stone-roller, the victorious bat over his shoulder like Hercules' club, and asked him for a Young Sachin smile.

After complying with a series of big smiles, and after the cameras were done with him, Manjunath Kumar, everyone's darling, no doubt overcome by fatigue and attention, raised the bat which had made 497 runs and swung it down on the stone-roller. As all of them watched, he raised and swung it four more times until it broke down the middle.

•

On Sunday – three days after Manju's 497 – visitors were still arriving at the Tattvamasi Building. The latest were two strangers, husband and wife, who had come by taxi (taxi!) all the way from Colaba. They had a son of their own, a cricketer, naturally – would the father of Manjunath Kumar kindly offer a few tips? No, Mohan Kumar wagged a finger at them, no, he won't, he will not. Because are *you*, as parents, prepared to earn the lifelong hatred of your children while doing what is, scientifically speaking, necessary for greatness? Just this morning, for instance, Radha, his own eldest son, had accused him of needlessly extracting his tonsils through minor surgery at JJ Hospital – when everyone knows that tonsils attract infections which have to be treated by expensive Azithromycin, once a day, or even more expensive Amoxycillin plus Potassium Clavulanate, three times a day. Dangers of all kinds lie in the paths of young men today: do you know how many new cases of male VDs are reported daily from JJ Hospital? Devilish thing, the male urinary system, the father of two boys said (demonstrating with his fingers) – excellent internal flushing, tough for bacteria to get into, but if they *do* sneak in, with all that tubing and piping around the bladder … Finished! Maybe Cipromycin can clean it up, maybe not. Remember my words: a young man, a healthy young man, is always being stalked by parasites with big hungry eyes. You *haven't* come to see Radha? Oh, the young one. Manjoooooo! Mohan Kumar, followed by the Colaba couple who were eager to pose for a 'selfie' with the cricketing superstar, strode into the boys' room shouting: Manjoooooo! Stop being shy like a girl! Come out and meet new people!

•

With a copy of the *Mumbai Sun* that showed him sitting victorious on the stone-roller, the boy had walked all the way from Pedder Road to Kemps Corner and then up Nepeansea Road into Priyadarshini Park.

In one corner of the park, under the trees, a group of old men and women were inhaling and exhaling together – *Hu! Ha! Hu!* Hiding behind a tree, Manju spied on the other corner of the park, where, inside the oval loop of a jogging track, a dark beak-nosed boy, wearing knee-high orange socks trimmed with red, was playing football by himself.

Behind him, an ocean smashed into the park's edge.

It was Sunday. Javed Ansari, exactly as he had described in his newspaper interview, was practising football in Priyadarshini Park.

Hu! Ha! Hu! Though he was hidden, something told Manju that Javed, out there on the football field, knew he was being watched, and that he also knew by *whom* he was being watched. *Hu!* – Manju's body trembled: as they raised and lowered their arms, the senior citizens directed wicked grins at him.

Manju's intuition proved right, because Javed suddenly stopped playing. Abandoning the football, he came running over to the trees to investigate. Hitching his orange socks up with his free hand, he looked this way, and that way, but – *Hu! Ha! Hu!* – found nothing hidden behind the trees but vigorous retirees.

•

On Tuesday, at last, the two boys met.

After passing so many black sewers, so many concrete towers, so many patches of grassy wasteland onto which slums encroach, you finally reach, somewhere within Kandivali West, a little Eden: a green field where boys practise cricket inside blue nets propped up on bamboo canes. Beside the green field is an old shed with a metal staircase leading up to its terrace; an awning supported by wooden poles is covered by blue tarpaulin in the manner of slum huts. This shed, legendary in Bombay cricket, birthplace of many a Ranji Trophy batsman, bears the sign *Payyade Sports Club*.

As Manju approached the club grounds, a black Honda City stopped behind him. A door opened and 'J.A.' stepped out.

One look at him and Manju knew that they had both arrived at the club early for the exact same reason: to see if the other would also be there.

It was the day after Lakshmi Puja. A mess of firecracker wrappers, extinguished sparklers, charred rockets and mounds of ash covered the cricket ground. A bonfire burnt outside the compound wall.

Maintaining a good distance between them, the boys unpacked their gear. Javed began stretching, alternately touching his toes.

As he had rehearsed all morning, Manju put his hands on his hips, and expressed himself in English:

'Are you Mahatma Gandhi?'

Javed, still touching his toes, regarded Manju curiously.

Who continued: 'You didn't hear me just now? Why did you get out to the fat boy? To make me look bad, no?'

'I heard, Captain, I heard you.'

Straightening himself, Javed shook his body loose, and asked:

'What is it you want? Why are you here, little Manju?'

His temples flexed and moved back; his eyes, unlike Manju's, became narrower when he was angry.

Manju responded by looking Mr 'J.A's' body up and down, with his tongue sticking out, the way the boys did when starting a fight in the slum.

'Just say you think you are as great as Mahatma Gandhi, then I'll go. That's all I want.'

U-ha, U-ha, U-ha. Javed chuckled. Passing his cricket bat from hand to hand, he chopped the air and drove it towards Manju's face.

Manju felt the skin tighten over his forehead, while the base of his neck turned warm. He left Javed and walked to where the other boys had gathered: *You were born in '94, idiot. You're not going to make the under-17. Shut up, you homo. My birthday is 3 July, so do I make the cut for this year's Selection Day or next year's?*

In the pavilion, the coach of the Payyade Sports Club was on the phone: *Ten thousand rupees. It's for your own son, after all. He'll learn from retired Ranji players. And we'll put in a word on Selection Day, we'll godfather him, don't worry about that ...*

Manju walked around the pavilion, turned, came back, and stood in front of Javed, who, done with his stretches, was changing for the game.

'Why *did* you get out on purpose?'

'Don't be such a slave.' Javed grinned, exposing his sickle-shaped dimples, and making Manju's ears expand with shame. 'I heard you smashed your bat after the interview. Is that true?'

'Yes.'

Javed grinned again. 'You're a cricket terrorist, boy. I like it.'

'No,' Manju said.

'What does your father do?' Javed asked, as he strapped on his pads.

Manju, apparently doing a bit of pre-game stretching himself, turned his neck to one side.

'Business,' he said, as he turned his neck to the other side. 'What does *your* father do?'

'Textbooks, scientific textbooks. He imports them from Canada and sells them here. But the truth is,' Javed said, '*I'm* his business. He wants to make me captain of India. Another question for you. Can you swim?'

Manju looked at Javed.

'No.'

'Drive?'

'No.'

'Hm.'

Javed smiled. He turned the rubber handle of his bat round and round to tighten it.

Manju looked down at Javed's huge white shoes; in his mind they disappeared, revealing a giant's pair of naked feet.

'Stop looking at my shoes. Stop looking at me. Go away. You want to know why Javed Ansari got out on purpose to that boy you called "Loser"? You won't. Because I don't like you. I never liked you. You stare at me too much.'

Manju stared. Javed resumed his warm-up exercises with his bat.

'Where is your mother?' Javed asked, freezing his bat in mid-air. 'I see only your father. Mine's living in Bangalore. She gave my father divorce. Same story with yours?'

Slap! Slap! Javed struck the bat against the sides of his shoes.

'You know you have the world's biggest eyes? Seriously.' Manju moved his head. Javed continued, 'Do you drive? I've got my car here. I can teach you to drive. Right now if you want.'

'My father will teach me.'

U-ha, U-ha, U-ha. Again. Manju begged his shoes to take him away.

A small man in a startlingly white uniform approached them, holding up a red BlackBerry for his master. Javed looked at it, frowned, and gave it back to the man in uniform, who wiped it clean with a corner of his shirt, and said something in a low voice.

'My driver says something funny is going on over there.'

Manju followed Javed to the barbed-wire fence that separated them from the next compound. A gang of street boys were playing something. One of them wore a very large and strange brown glove; another was throwing a white ball at the glove.

'This is what they play in America?' Manju asked.

Javed nodded. He too had forgotten what it was called. In a state of wonder, the two boys watched the throwing and catching on the other side of the fence. How silken the movements of that oversized brown glove, how prehensile the catcher's forearm, rotating to the left to intercept the hard white ball.

Javed broke the spell.

'Softball, this is?' he shouted at the boys.

'Base-o-ball, uncle! Base-o-ball!'

The two cricketers put their hands on the fence and leaned forward.

'Who teaches you this game?'

'We have a coach, uncle. He's from the YMCA, he'll be here soon. Now watch me, uncle. Can you cricketers do this?'

The boy now threw the white ball with a brute force they had never seen in cricket. The pitcher turned to the two boys in white and showed his teeth.

'Better than cricket, no? Come over, uncle, we'll convert both of you to base-o-ball.'

Javed climbed over the fence. Manju placed a hand on his shoulder.

'Shouldn't we go back?'

'No.' Javed called to him from the other side of the fence. He winked.

'Come over this side, play baseball – since you're so bad at cricket.'

Manju climbed over too.

The cricketers stepped through wild grass; dragonflies flew around them. Soon Manju and Javed were running circles around the baseball players, throwing gloves and stones and handfuls of grass at each other: 'Kambli! You're Kambliiiii!' Behind them, as they chased each other, they heard the hard white baseball smacking into the glove.

Laughing wildly, they fell down into the grass.

'What is the story with your father, man? Does he ... ?' Javed pantomimed a man having a drink.

'Shut up. What is the story with *your* father?' Manju asked. 'He wants you to *leave* cricket. In every interview he says this.'

'He just wants to look good on TV. Don't you know fathers by now?'

Manju was still thinking this over when he felt someone take hold of him by the chin; trained by his father's touch, Manju froze, and let the alien hand turn his face from side to side.

'U-ha. Someone needs to shave. U-ha.'

Still offering no resistance, Manju said: 'My father won't let us.'

Javed let him go.

'So? Do it anyway.'

Manju shook his head.

'Not brave enough?' Hands rubbed through Manju's spiky hair. 'Not brave-rave-shave enough? See, I made another poem about you.'

Waiting for Javed to remove his fingers from his hair, Manju – horrified beyond words, Manju – thrilled beyond words – demanded:

'Yours never hit you? *Never?*'

'No one hits their sons in the city, Captain. Only a chutney salesman from the village does that.'

'Don't talk about my father like that.'

Javed shrugged.

'What do you want to study in junior college?'

'I don't know,' Manju said, and added at once, 'I want to do science.'

'Too much work. Go for commerce.'

'I want to be a forensic scientist.'

Javed's lips parted.

'*CSI*?'

Manju nodded.

'You want to cut open dead bodies? I think you have a problem. Mental problem.'

Happy for no good reason he could tell, Manju bent and

drummed his hands on his knees. I have a mental problem, he thought, and, sucking in his lower lip, gave a final flourish to his drum roll.

'Your mother's what, divorced or dead?'

Manju lay still and let Javed's shadow cover a part of his face; he did nothing as Javed took his arm, and rolled up the short sleeve, exposing his arm all the way to the top of the bicep.

'As I thought,' Javed said. 'You're not really dark.' Biting his lip, Javed forced the shirt all the way back to the top of Manju's shoulder, where the skin had the pallor of something rarely exposed to the sun.

'See?'

Manju saw his naked arm, smiled, and said: 'My brother is better than you at cricket.'

It worked: Javed let his arm go. The shirt again covered the pale flesh.

'Your brother won't make the team, Manju. He's got a weight-transfer problem.'

Manju tried to pull his short sleeve further down his arm.

'Fuck off. My brother has *what*?'

'Sorry, Manju. Sorry.' Javed shrugged. 'Your brother is the best cricketer in the whole world, and he *will* make it onto the team. Happy? Which college will *you* go to?'

Manju closed his eyes and frowned: he could still sense that Javed was watching him, watching the left-slanting, rather stylish, furrow in between his eyes. He smiled.

'I'll never get into science.'

'Who told you that?' Javed sat down beside him. 'Your father?'

Manju swallowed. His heart beat hard against his ribs. 'You need 80 per cent for science admissions.'

'Wake up!' Javed clapped right before his eyes. 'Wake up! You never heard of the sports quota in admission?' Javed was almost shouting now. 'You don't even need that. I see you answering all of Tommy Sir's questions. What was Sobers's batting average against left-arm orthodox spin, all that *Wisden* bumshit. You know what I read? Have you heard of George Orwell?'

'Which college should I go for?'

'Go to Ruia. Best for science. Do you know of *The Animal Farm*? And by the way, what happened to your mother? I'm asking you a second time.'

Manju took Javed's palm in his hand and said, 'Twilight is my mother's favourite hour.'

'What?' Javed asked.

So Manju kept talking.

'She had this thing in her right hand' – he traced his finger down the webbing on Javed's palm, describing a groove. 'Nitric acid fell on her hand at the goldsmith's shop when they were working on the old jewellery. Where the acid went, it left a deep mark, and that mark was how I knew that it was my mother and not a fake when she came home after she'd been gone for a long time. Before I let her touch me I would say: "Show me your hand, woman," and I would check for the nitric acid mark.'

Looking at his hand, held tight in Manju's, Javed asked: 'Your mother disappeared and came back?'

Manju dropped Javed's hand and covered his mouth with his fingers. He was appalled by what he had just done. Even more scary was the thought that maybe he had babbled about the secret groove in her palm, something he had not told even Radha, only because Javed had asked twice about his mother. Manju had a horrible premonition about intimacy: it could be this simple, this could be how something starts – just because he asks you twice to tell him your story.

'My brother can squeeze his cock into seven colours. He says he can do twenty-four but it's really just seven,' Manju said. He looked at Javed. Both laughed, and Manju, helpless to stop, continued:

'Even if I get the marks, my father won't let me go to junior college.'

Javed, with a smile, placed a finger on his lips. They had been found.

'You two!' Coach Pramod Sawant stood with both his hands on the fence, panting. 'You two!'

'They were supposed to play base-o-ball with us, uncle,' the boy with the big glove shouted. 'But then they started to play with each other!'

•

The next morning, Mumbai's interschool cricket schedule brought them together again, at the P.J. Hindu Gymkhana.

Manju woke up that day and found that he could not get out of bed. He yawned; he stretched, he turned from side to side. Raising his head, he saw that his legs were trembling.

At midday the tall boy wearing a blue cap with the initials 'J.A.' stood fielding at long leg. When the wind blew, the dust rose around him: and in that dust, Manju saw a boy sprint, attack, gather and throw the ball back without breaking stride. Manju searched Javed Ansari's long body, half expecting to find an 'H' branded on his shirt or trousers.

In the drinks break, Javed stood in the tent, near the twenty-litre bottle of mineral water; he was talking to someone on his red BlackBerry. Manju went up to the big bottle and poured himself a plastic cup.

Javed put down his BlackBerry, turned to Manju and asked:

'Do you actually *like* cricket?'

Manju thought he had either heard the question wrong, or that he was being mocked, shamefully.

'Wasn't that baseball much better? I've been reading about baseball on the Internet. Do you know of Baby Ruth? He's like their Bradman: but better. Do you want to go back with me and play baseball with those slum boys one day?'

Manju thought: *Is that how he sees me, too? As a slum boy?*

'We live in Chembur,' Manju said. 'In a housing society. We have air-conditioning.'

'Chembur?' Javed looked at him sideways. 'Chembur smells. Too many factories there.'

Manju felt his ears turning hot.

After that they did not talk again until Ali Weinberg played Fatima at the Oval. In the afternoon, watching his team bat from the dark players' tent, Manju was conscious of a presence on a plastic chair next to him – someone who had just stripped off his white shirt, and was sucking a bottle of water. Manju got up from his chair, and was about to leave the tent, when a voice from behind him said, 'I wrote a poem about you, Manju. Do you want to hear it?'

'Shut up.'

'If you don't to want to hear it, see it. Turn around.'

'No. I won't,' Manju said.

'Turn around and see the poem I wrote for you,' the voice said again. There was no one else in the tent. Manju could hear someone removing his clothes.

When he finally turned around, Javed had stripped off his trousers, revealing his white underwear.

And Manju watched a poem.

Beyond the tent, sunlight and cricket continued, and the world kept turning; here, in the darkness, 'J.A.', stripped to his briefs, down on all fours, lifted himself up on his wrists and the tips of his toes. Slowly he turned his wrists around till they faced Manju. He grunted, awakening a giant vein on the side of his arm, and raised his toes off the earth. He was supported only by his wrists now. 'Watch me,' he said. Manju's lips parted. 'Watch me.' Inside the dark tent, his near-naked adversary, cheeks puffed out and forehead swollen up, was parallel to the earth.

Moving back, step by step, until his back was pressed against the taut fabric of the tent, Manju stood still, as if someone had held a knife to his throat.

•

That Saturday (Ali Weinberg v. Rizvi Springfield), as Javed batted in Shivaji Park, someone in the crowd – Mumbai's most discerning cricketing audience – shouted: '*Makad.*' Monkey. In the argot of Shivaji Park, 'makad' was a term of honour: it meant Javed could bat, bowl, field, run, he could do anything.

The nickname brought a smile to Manju's lips.

The next day he went to a paan shop by Chembur station, gave an old man a rupee, wiped the receiver of the shop's yellow payphone against his shirt, as his father had taught him to, and dialled a number.

When the phone was answered, without introducing himself, Manju asked: 'I don't know what my father will do, and what your father will do if they find out, but do you want to practise together with me from now on?'

There was a pause, and the voice of the makad said, 'Why not, man?'

•

Being both an atheist and a cricketer, Tommy Sir was twice as superstitious as other men, and when he felt something fall on his hair from a tree on the seaside promenade at Carter Road, and move down his forehead and nose like quicksilver, his immediate thought was that it was a sign from heaven.

This was reconfirmed when Tommy Sir discovered that what had fallen on him was a caterpillar, a little green dynamo, by this time going down his chin towards his neck.

The old scout had just come from a meeting where he had given Anand Mehta tremendous news: Radha Krishna Kumar was about to go to England for six weeks … 'No, he is not!' shouted the investor, who had not yet heard the key word.

'On a scholarship?' Tommy Sir finally got through.

Someone else was paying? Delighted.

'Founder Ali called me. He complimented me, as no one in the Mumbai Cricket Association has ever done, on my excellent work, and then he said he would personally come to the school today to give "My son, young Master Kumar" his scholarship and plane ticket to England. His own words. He called Radha his son.'

Tommy Sir picked the caterpillar off his neck, and examined it. Look at its legs go, he thought; look at the brio in this fellow. Like a worm drawn by Van Gogh. He raised it up with care to observe it against the elemental backdrop of the Arabian Sea.

His viewing pleasure was interrupted by the passing of a group of bearded young men in loose white cotton clothing. Forgetting about the caterpillar, he watched the men in white intently. Muslims probably from Uttar Pradesh, the nation's barely governable heartland. Behind them followed half a dozen women, dressed from head-to-toe in black burka. There was visual evidence of it every day: the biggest change in India, happening right in front of everyone's eyes. The Muslim population was growing. In number and in religious fervour. Not that the increase in their number, due to an exponentially higher birth rate, was in itself a problem for Tommy Sir, who had no issues with either Christians or Muslims – point one, a universalized misanthropy protected him from such petty resentments (*all* men smell, after all), and point two, who are the most passionate cricketers in the whole wide world? Muslims! Yet Tommy Sir, watching the young women in all black follow the young men in all white, worried. He worried that the fecundity and the fundamentalism *together* were going to bake a nice big Christmas cake for India in about twenty years. Burka here, fatwa there. Sharia for all. Personally, of course, Tommy Sir didn't approve of buggery – normal sex was filthy enough, and the thought of men doing *that* to each other was nearly enough to make him faint – but this is a free country, let the chaps do what they want in the shadows. The Taliban, however, used to bury men behind brick walls simply because they were gays. What will happen to fellows like Pramod Sawant if the Fundos take over here too? Lots of people worry, about this and other things, but no one dares say it out loud. Because they'll surround you at once and call you a name: racist! In *nothing* can we Indians find the right balance, not even in tolerance.

Suddenly remembering the caterpillar, Tommy Sir looked all around him.

Didn't matter that he couldn't find it now: it *had* been a sign.

See, right now, at the Kalanagar Signal, there was a big bank advertisement that said: 'When Sachin Tendulkar dreamed of becoming the world's greatest batsman, so did Ajit Tendulkar.' But if Tommy Sir looked hard enough, it changed before his eyes and became: 'When Radha (and/or Manju Kumar) dreamed of becoming the world's greatest batsman (and/or batsmen), so did Narayanrao Sadashivaro Kulkarni, known to all as Tommy Sir.'

Fear intruded on his fantasy. The UP Muslims, turning around, were heading back towards him. With his instinctive courtesy, he stepped aside to let them pass, then sat down on the wall of the promenade, and looked at the wilderness of rock, rubbish and dead trees that kept the ocean a few yards away from Carter Road.

He laughed.

Near the water's edge, a pipe sputtered slow black water, and in the sewage that trickled to the ocean he spotted a crab hunting for its food – emerald-backed, slime-coated, iridescent, with many moving red arms, many moving plans. 'Anand Mehta,' said Tommy Sir, and looked around for someone to share the joke with, but saw only UP Muslims everywhere.

•

Manjunath Kumar was changing. The fat was leaving his face, but the pimples were larger. His eyes were more heavily lidded than they had been in childhood. His voice had not yet broken, but his gaze, like an adolescent's, seemed always to be recoiling from something that had just noticed it. He had developed a sly grin, and an annoying new way of chuckling. While he still spoke Kannada to his father and Hindi to his brother, now he uttered entire sentences in English. He wore a baseball cap all the time, possibly to make himself look taller than his five foot two inches. He was more brazen, and at the same time, more secretive. The moment he realized that he was being observed, by his father, by his brother, by the neighbour, Mrs Shastri, or sometimes, when no one else was around, even by 'B.B. Balasubramaniam', the landlord's nameplate hammered into the door, he withdrew his new mannerisms and hid them behind a dark face and scowl: as if this thing, his new personality, were one of those secret science experiments of his boyhood.

In the morning, standing half-naked before the mirror, he puffed out his cheeks, and flexed his arms, gritting his teeth. Nothing. Manju turned his head from left to right to check. Absolutely nothing. Though his forearms were thick, he had none of those sexy veins that should bulge from a man's biceps when he made a muscle. He moved closer to the mirror, until his breath fogged it. His tongue extended and touched itself. This is what he had always assumed he tasted like: cold glass.

Then his tongue disappeared.

Scraping her way on her knees as she mopped the floor with a wet rag, the maidservant had entered the boys' bedroom; in the mirror, her narrow eyes found his.

Buttoning himself up, Manju went to the living room, where his father was talking to Mrs Shastri, the most star-struck of their neighbours, who was visiting, as usual, with her eight-year-old son Rahul, a prospective batsman.

'No: it is not enough to start thinking when they are six or seven. You start before that. You start from the moment the sperm enters the egg, and creates the zygote.'

Manju went to the window with a view of the brick-wall courtyard where they had once practised cricket, and which Radha had nowadays turned into a darbar-hall where he held court, bat in hand, to a gang of local admirers.

'You know what I like best about being with a girl? When she's just washed her hair, and you're holding her, and the wind blows right over her head, bringing all the shampoo into your nose, and you go … Ummmm.'

High above his brother, closing his eyes and inhaling deeply from a phantom head of shampooed hair, Manju whispered, 'Ummmmmmm.'

'What is this thing you did to your eyes, Aryan?'

He opened his eyes to see Radha now touching one of his friend's eyebrows.

The boy, Aryan, explained he had gone to a barber to 'weave' his eyebrows: sleeking them into a stylish line arching over his eyes. 'My father would kill me,' Radha said, as he traced a finger over the arch. 'Once I go to England, *then*.'

Glancing up, Radha saw Manju, but pretended not to.

People had begun to say that Radha Kumar had his father's face, but that inverted triangle formed by his grey eyes and his strong nose belonged entirely to their mother.

Watching his brother show off, Manju picked up the tennis ball they used for practice, and squeezed it in his right hand until it was warm and angry:

'*Behenchod!* It's late!'

Throwing the hot ball down at Radha, he made his admirers scatter.

Dressed, and with their cricket bags slung over their shoulders, the boys came to the living room to see Mrs Shastri, her hands folded on her son's head, staring at their father.

On the sofa, Mohan Kumar sat without a word, looking at the blue wall above the television set.

'He was telling me how I should give the boy regular check-ups and then he just –' Mrs Shastri said. 'He just …'

Mohan Kumar had let thick grey stubble overrun his face: but it was not a beard, it was a 'statement' – it was a 'protest', he said, against Tommy Sir's step-by-step encroachment upon his paternal rights. He couldn't even speak his mind these days: but when he stroked his beard, when he bit his lip, the boys knew what he wanted to say.

Manju had noticed that his father would sometimes stop speaking in mid-sentence, apparently to scratch his beard, and then he would look at the clock; sometimes he might even forget an ancient proverb. For two or three hours at a stretch they found him slumped on the sofa, or with his pen in his hand, alternately looking at the clock and attempting to make a mark on a blank sheet of paper.

Manju seized his inert father by the shoulder, and shook. 'Appa. You're doing it again. Doing it again. Stop.'

Emerging from his daydream, Mohan Kumar smiled at his son as one might at a headmaster, then looked at Mrs Shastri and her eight-year-old Rahul, and resumed his lecture on why only Cipromycin, bloodhound among antibiotics, can be trusted to sniff out, locate and exterminate even the most cunning of bacteria hiding inside an infected prostate gland.

•

On their way to class, students of the Ali Weinberg International School would occasionally hear residents of nearby buildings shout that their founder was a 'thug' before slamming down their windows. Depending on whom you spoke to, Karim Ali had either created this corner of Bandra or destroyed it, or done that peculiar thing to it, involving in equal parts creation and destruction, that happens sooner or later to every suburb in Mumbai. They said there was no room in this end of Bandra to build skyscrapers: Karim Ali found room. Had he threatened Catholic widowers to do so? Had he violated city zoning laws? Catholics are rich, they will survive, and this city's laws were written to be broken. Karim Ali was now Founder Ali, patron of the new enlightenment, proprietor of Ali's Educational Empire, comprising medical, dental, journalism, and many other colleges, to whose number more were being added year by year, but the Jewel in whose Crown would always be the Ali Weinberg International School (run in partnership with the Joseph P. Weinberg Memorial Institute of Lafayette, Mississippi), known for its headline-capturing cricket team, into which boys were recruited, with financial aid, if necessary, and from deep within the slums, if necessary.

Today, the Unseen Power and Guiding Genius of the Ali Weinberg School was paying his cricketers an extraordinary visit.

All sixty-five members of the junior, senior and standby teams, along with Coach Sawant, marched into the auditorium to find a bald, bantamweight man waiting for them on the stage. The ceiling lights shone off his smooth skull.

'Remember what you promised me?' Manju whispered. Radha, his features taut and expectant, smiled sardonically. Oh, he remembered. For Radha to visit a real morgue in England and take photos of the bodies under dissection: that was the only gift Manju wanted.

'My dear batters and bowlers,' declaimed the Founder's ringing voice. 'Your attention.'

His eyebrows, thick, salt-and-pepper, rose defiantly, and though his voice was calm, he examined the boys with a hint of anger in his set jaw.

'My dear batters and bowlers. Only two problems exist in this country.'

He made a 'V' with his fingers.

'Fundamentalism, terrorism, nutritional poverty, so on and so forth are not really problems, or more precisely, stem from two underlying and rarely discussed factors. First is anti-intellectualism.' The anger in the Founder's face rose palpably. 'My dear batters and bowlers: we as Indians are becoming dumber and dumber with each generation until our children are now not even half as smart as Chinese children in standardized learning tests. I tell you there are people in this country who do not know whether Delhi is north or south of the Vindhyas. I am not making this up. The pressing need to fight anti-intellectualism in India persuaded me, after many years as a champion of multipurpose construction in the city of Mumbai, to set up the Karim Ali Foundation for Academic Excellence. You are all members of this great Academy, my dear batters and bowlers.

Intellectualism and a calm mind are what we teach here. How does cricket fit in? For that we must understand the second problem facing India today. Sensationalism. In other words, our Indian media, which is the joke of the world.'

The Founder looked around.

'My dear batters and bowlers, consider the following facts. One, our country is named for a river called the Indus. Two: The river Ganga has six times the volumetric capacity of the river Indus – and three – yet it is still shallower than the Grand Amazon, which is the most powerful river in the whole world by volume of water transported from end-point to end-point. These are hard, solid facts. Why do I keep these and other such facts at my fingertips? Because facts are the only known remedy for the evil of sensation. I have created the best school in Mumbai, with the best facilities, the best faculty, the best resources. And yet the media ignore us, and choose instead to talk only about the Cathedral School. Campion School. Ambani School. The journalists of Mumbai ignore us until we feed them what they live and die for. Sensation. And the biggest sensation we have in this country is called cricket.'

The Founder closed his eyes, and opened them, and continued.

'My dear batters and bowlers, last year we lost twice to Fatima School. We lost by fourteen runs in Giles Trophy, by eight wickets in Harris Shield. My dear batters and bowlers, you cannot lose again this year: you must win for me. When you win the wonderful Harris Shield for me, everyone in Mumbai, including press, papers, radio and TV, will applaud our new but already sensationally prestigious school.'

Founder Ali stood silent; his lips showed just the hint of a smile; he allowed anticipation to grow.

'To bring us glory in the Harris Shield, I have decided to groom a new captain for this school's team. Having watched all my sons at play for many months now, I decided that this future captain, who will go to England on my scholarship, is ...'

The boys clapped, and started a chant: 'Ra-dha. Ra-dha.'

Manju searched for Javed's face in the crowd. You said Radha was not going to make the team!

'No, not *that* Kumar,' said the bald man on the stage, motioning for the boys to quieten down. 'Not *that* one.'

Manju was still searching for Javed; but all at once everyone seemed to be looking at him. Why? His heart began to beat against his ribcage. His mouth open, Manju turned to the stage to see Founder Ali pointing a finger straight at him.

'*This* Kumar will go to England.'

Looking back, Manjunath could never recollect what he said to Radha at that point, or whether he did say anything: because the next thing he remembered, he was up on the stage, beside Founder Ali; and when he gazed down, he saw, in the vortex below him, Javed Ansari's face, smiling, and his brother's face, not smiling.

Then he heard someone say, 'My dear humble young son,' and felt a fatherly hand on his shoulder.

'My dear batters and bowlers, I've watched this humble young son of mine bat many times before this. He didn't see me, but I saw him at Shivaji Park when he scored a superlative 237 not out against Anjuman-i-Islam, and he didn't see me, but I saw his magniloquent 163 in 120 balls against the Ambani School. That was a *most* satisfying knock. This young son of mine can bat like an angel, and he can bat like a devil. What I love most about this humble young son is his *heart*, which is as capacious as an African lion's. My son is khadoos: when he's given out leg before or caught behind, he controverts the umpire and refuses to leave the crease. That's the spirit. That's the rage. Now I command him, humble young son Kumar, go to England, learn on their classical green lawns the subtle secrets of cricket and come back to India a super sensation!'

And with that the Founder drew the cricketer to his bosom and held him tight, while the boys cheered and chanted the name of the correct Kumar, who continued to look thoroughly appalled.

•

The truth was, he *had* known that Karim Ali was watching him for weeks before the announcement of the scholarship. Other boys told him the Founder was coming to cricket matches – they had thought that he was spying on Radha Krishna. But Javed had whispered: '*You're* the one he's come to watch, Manju.' Javed wasn't going to get the scholarship: he had written a poem about Karim Ali, pasted it on the noticeboard, and had been suspended from school for a week.

'Bat *better* than your best today,' Javed urged, during the match against Ambani when Manju scored his big century. Manju knew he was becoming good: frighteningly good. It was like running downhill – like cycling downhill – when some force much greater than you urges, "Faster, faster." He was a Natural. High above Javed's head, he saw the golden fruit – England – and stood on his shoulders to pluck it: Founder Ali had approved. In the Founder's office, Manju was hugged, offered chai, and told many important details about the military, moral, and economic disposition of England – most of them dealing with the year 1066, a key date in that remarkable little island's history – before being sent home with a wealth of hard, factual information about the United Kingdom in his head and a warm press release in his hands:

Young 'Braggado of the Bat' takes on Great Britain

Press Contact: J. Satish

Corporate Relations, Karim Ali Group (022) 2390-3468

•

England!

It fell on him like crimson dye on a dry leaf in Chem Lab, exposing a network of nerves and sensitive ends: a secret life.

England! *Six weeks* in England! Without his father!

•

'There was a magician who came to our village with an elephant, one day, boys. An elephant in chains. You just couldn't see the chains. We are all elephants in chains too, we three Kumars. And the magician's name is Karim Ali. He's playing with us. He's setting one of us against the other.'

Mohan Kumar scratched his left ankle. As was usual in the evenings, his breath smelled of a paternal mix of Hercules rum and Limca.

The wrong young Kumar, bent over at the sink, was splashing water on his cheeks.

'You should have spat in the face of Karim Ali and given the scholarship back right away!' Mohan shouted at Manju. 'You should not have taken what is rightfully your elder brother's!'

Radha, who had been sitting at the dinner table without a word, picked up his bat and left for the door.

'Radha,' his father pleaded. 'Radha, come back, we'll work out a plan together. We'll make Manju return what he stole—'

At this Radha stopped, and kicked over a little table.

When his father whimpered, 'The landlord will keep our deposit if you do things like this. He expects us to keep the flat clean,' Radha came back from the hallway, bent, picked up the table, and flung it at the wall of the living room.

That was what he thought of the landlord's deposit.

•

From the window came the noise of a rubber ball hitting a brick wall. But Mohan Kumar was locked in the toilet.

'Javed,' Manju whispered into the landline phone in the living room, twirling the black wire around his fingers, and looking at the toilet door, 'they are making me give the England scholarship back.'

'You idiot,' Javed said, 'if I am not going to England, fine, but you should go. You're the only one on my wavelength. Don't let your father fuck with you. Do you want me to come over and bash him up?'

Manju laughed, but his laughter died away.

'Javed, but the scholarship is my brother's. I stole it.'

'Bullshit,' Javed said. 'You are much better than your brother.'

'What should I do, Javed?'

'Do? Do? You've already done it. You've got your scholarship. I'm going to send you a letter when you are in England, and it will say: "Manju, my little one, are you actually having fun?" Because you need to relax, man.'

Javed laughed, and Manju already felt himself relax.

'Just tell your father, if you give back the scholarship, Founder Ali will award it to Javed Ansari. Because they're both Muslims. He'll believe that. You're not alone, Manju: remember that. You're never going to be alone ever again.'

•

England! A drop of my semen is going to England for six weeks! Mohan Kumar closed his eyes. He dreamed of the laterite arch built by the unknown king, the starry skies above, and the croaking bullfrogs on the forest floor. Tears of vindication entered his eyes – England, on a fully paid scholarship, my little drop, my baby boy! – and he wanted to hug his little Manju.

But from the backyard he heard the sound of a rubber ball on a brick wall, and he had to open his eyes.

Towards the end of the previous year, Mohan Kumar had decided to slap Radha a few times, after his batting average fell below 40, but Tommy Sir had intervened, explaining that it was not Radha's fault. The elder Kumar had developed a 'weight-transfer problem'. Tommy Sir had seen it before. The body grows so suddenly that it is no longer used to its own new momentum. Radha had shot up; he was becoming a handsome young man, and this was ruining him as a cricketer. Because his body now made him hop when he went on the back foot, the same bowlers whom until recently he had been thrashing around the park were now getting him out clean bowled.

But Manju: now *he* had stayed compact. The voice was breaking but the body was not growing. The centre of gravity stayed low. Think of Lara. Gavaskar. Tendulkar.

But a father has a plan, and a contract with God, and the offspring had to follow this plan and this contract, and it was not Manjunath who was meant to go to England this year. Down his right arm Mohan Kumar felt a nerve twitch. Let me fix it, Mohan, it said: let me hammer the scholarship out of the wrong son and into the right one.

•

A brick wall stands in Bowral, New South Wales. Once upon a time, a boy appeared before the wall and threw a tennis ball at it. It bounced back; so he hit it with his wooden bat. He kept on doing this and kept on doing this until he became Sir Donald Bradman, the world's greatest batsman.

A brick wall stands behind the Tattvamasi Building in Chembur, Mumbai. A boy has thrown a tennis ball at the wall, but he has no wooden bat in his hands. It bounces, and hits him on the side of his neck. He tosses it back at the wall. This time, he wants it to hit him on the face.

'Radha,' said his younger brother. 'Radha.'

Radha threw the ball at the brick wall again, but this time Manju extended his foot like a football defender and kicked it out of their compound.

Raising his bat, Radha looked at his brother.

And Manju knew he should not have stopped his brother from hurting himself: for now he would hurt others.

'When we played Fatima in Ghatkopar,' Radha said, 'you were out. LBW. Plumb. That umpire let you go on batting.'

With a hunch and a goblin face, Radha showed his younger brother how he had looked as he stood at the crease.

A window opened above them. From the fourth floor, a moustached man with a raised eyebrow looked to his left and looked to his right, and hissed:

'They're all listening to you, boys. The neighbours have a high opinion of me.'

At the window, Mohan Kumar reached inside his banian and scratched at his chest hair.

'No, they don't!' Radha shouted at his father. 'You know what they call you around here? Mad antibiotic uncle. Go inside and drink some more Hercules rum.'

Mohan Kumar stared at one son, and then at the other, nodded, and shut the window.

An hour later, Manjunath stood shirtless in front of the mirror in his bedroom, which was lit by the tube-light in the living room; from down below, he could hear the ball hitting the brick wall. He turned from side to side, looking at his naked torso in the mirror, and made his muscles bigger.

Maybe the veins would emerge in England.

As he stood half-naked before the mirror, a creature three parts Hercules rum and one part his father sat on his bed.

'It's all because Radha kicked me that day in Ballard Estate. Because he tried to murder me. God has punished him. I think he has started shaving, don't you? But a contract is a contract, and Radha was the chosen one. Manju, if you love your father, you must tell Principal Patricia that it is all a mistake and she must phone Founder Ali. First thing in the morning.'

Manju thought 'England': in his mind's eye, he saw a plane flying over the silver ocean, flying direct to a British dissecting table where Grissom and Nick were waiting for Agent Manjunath to join them in their next autopsy.

Sitting upright on the bed in one motion without using his hands, Manju shouted at his father: 'I am not alone!' He turned his face to the ceiling and shouted: 'I am *never* again going to be alone!'

'Manju …' his father whimpered. 'Is that a no?'

•

In the morning, Manjunath woke to the sound of the tennis ball bouncing off the brick wall in the backyard.

As he brushed his teeth, he smelled sweat. Radha, wet from practice, came to the door of the bathroom and stood watching him brush.

Suddenly, Manju felt someone pinching his left arm tight: and holding on to it.

'Maybe if I keep pinching you like this, I will destroy your batting arm, Manju.'

Manju did not move his left arm; toothpaste oozed from his mouth as he stared at the flowing water.

'Did you call Javed last night? Did he tell you not to return the scholarship to me?'

Through the corners of his eyes, he could see his elder brother scraping his fingernail against a canine tooth.

Radha pinched even harder: the pain in Manju's left arm became maddening. Still offering no resistance, Manju leaned forward, and splashed himself with his right hand: he felt faint, he felt he could fly. If Radha pinched his nerve until his arm was damaged, he could tell them in England, I can't play cricket anymore, but I can study forensic science and I want to join your London CSI team, please, and suddenly Manju laughed, and, as the cold water struck his face, he laughed again.

•

One morning, over 100 million years ago, India left Eden and went looking for Tibet. Tearing itself off from Gondwana, a primeval continent covered in rainforests and teeming with dinosaurs, a 'V'-shaped chunk of land called India (accompanied at first by Madagascar) decided it wanted to join, for some godforsaken reason, South Asia.

For that 'V'-shaped piece of land, the next 120–140 million years, needless to say, have been mostly a catastrophe.

Tommy Sir – after the death of his wife, he had allocated Saturday evenings to the enhancement of his draughtsmanship and colouring skills – now stood by an easel, painting the geological history of the Indian subcontinent. That history was, in his eyes, a tragic one. Eight panels had been completed, and were drying in a corner of the room; now he was filling in details of the giant volcanic eruptions that started sixty-five million years ago in the Deccan Plateau – releasing so much gas and smoke that the sky was darkened, the earth shuddered, and an Ice Age began, killing all the dinosaurs. Mexicans say it was their Yucatan meteor that did it – bullshit: our Deccan Plateau murdered the Tyrannosaurus. Fire and brimstone. You can still see the evidence of all that volcanic rage when you hike around Mahabaleshwar, as Tommy Sir did each year, by himself. The mountains, ridged and layered, consist of millions of tons of congealed lava; here and there you may see a jagged peak, carved like a stegosaurus's spine, like a trophy kept by the Deccan Plateau of its most famous victim. Inside a giant amphitheatre formed by concave red cliffs, Tommy Sir had stood, observing the cataract of plastic bottles and cellophane rubbish left behind in the mountains by tourists – educated, English-speaking, middle-class tourists – and had wondered aloud: What happened to you, Mother India? Where are your fountains of fire now? How did we become this pathetic people?

We should *never* have joined Asia, never. Should have remained an island off Africa, super-Madagascar, inviolate: Atlantis!

Blowing on the easel to cool the paint on his volcanoes, he went to the window and looked down on Kalanagar.

'It's a moonlit night, Lata,' he called to his daughter, who was in the kitchen. 'You know what the Christians do on a night like this?'

He did not wait for her to answer.

'Out there in the Bandstand, they are going mad. Boys and girls run out into the water and sit on rocks kissing and cuddling and godknowswhat-ing, and then the tide covers the rocks and they can't come back – have to call the ambulance to rescue them! Are you listening to me, Lata?'

Lata, Tommy Sir's daughter, worked at a bank in the Bandra-Kurla Financial Centre. A Maharashtra state-level volleyball player, she had dropped out of the sport after just missing the cut for the national team (because even if she had made the team, her father had told her, what future for a woman in sport?), and now managed Tommy Sir's little Kalanagar flat, a role that she appeared content to play for the rest of her life, though her father still harangued her once a month to find a boy, a salaried boy of any religion or looks – even a Gujarati boy if all else failed – as long as hands, eyes, ears, nose, legs, and everything in between functioned. For what more can a girl want?

Incomprehensible Youth!

In the background, the radio played old film songs.

Lata, in the kitchen, hummed along and did the dishes.

From his desk Tommy Sir removed a packet of cigarettes and a manila folder full of sketches, war maps, and notes made in Marathi, Urdu and English. It bore the title: '1761: The soul breaks out of its encirclement. Notes for a proposed true history of the third battle of Panipat'. Looking over the elegant handwriting of his youth – how beautifully we Indians wrote in those days – Tommy Sir smiled, remembering that this project had once been a passion greater than cricket for him. For the Emperor Shivaji, the Peshwa Baji Rao and other successful Marathas, Tommy Sir cared nothing: in history, as in geology, failure excited and aroused him. Because only failure – the right kind of failure – has tragic grandeur. Plus, didn't his blood boil at the thought that students across India were still learning about Panipat by reading Sir Jadunath Sarkar, that inveterate Maratha-basher? No one knew how close the Marathas had come to winning – after five hundred years of effeminately surrendering to invasions from Central Asia, an Indian army almost triumphed at Panipat. It was *that* close. No more than the space between Tommy Sir's fingers. After being foxed and fooled by the Afghan king Abdali for months, after losing ally after ally to him, after running out of money and food, and then sitting passively within a trench for weeks while the enemy encircled and taunted them – in other words, after doing nearly everything humanly possible to ensure their own defeat – the Marathas, just before dawn on 14 January 1761, finally decided to fight. And *how* they fought. In this, one notes a resemblance to the way Indians once played Test cricket. By noon on the day of battle, Abdali, stunned by the ferocity of the Maratha charge, told his soldiers to get his wives away to safety. Man's soul, which is bogged down in a monkey's body, and Mother India, bogged down in some lesser nation's history, were both about to break free. *That* close.

Holding a cigarette in between his thumb and index figure, Tommy Sir put away the old manila folder. One of these days, one of these days. But for now – he lit the cigarette, and switched on the lamp over his computer – it was time to start his next column for the newspaper: 'Some Boys Rise, Some Boys Fall: Legends of Bombay Cricket and My Role in Shaping Them Part 24'.

He stopped writing as soon as he began. The headache was starting again.

Biting on his cigarette, he used both index fingers to massage his forehead. Into this thin tense forehead had been crammed the entire history of Bombay cricket. Vijay Merchant's technique, Ravi Shastri's tenacity, Sunny Gavaskar's craftiness. You can believe in the future, but you must worship the past. Tommy Sir worshipped all hundred and fifty years of Bombay cricket, but his forehead, of late, had begun to hurt.

Mean blood sugar had reached 141 in the last report. You have to control your stress, the young doctor at Lilavati Hospital had said. Control my—? Are you *crazy*?

After forty-one point five years of service to cricket, didn't the men who ran cricket in Mumbai show more respect to one of those homeless girls that sell yellow balloons and blue wigs outside Wankhede stadium before an IPL game than they did to Tommy Sir? And why? Because Tommy Sir knew many things, but he did not know how to lie – and especially did not know how to utter the one big lie required today of everyone involved in the game of cricket, a lie that is dragged out over ten excruciating hours every match day by our chipmunk TV commentators, but which really boils down to a single deceitful statement: 'Cricket in India still smells good.'

The old scout winced: oh, my forehead. My fore ...

It must be the pollution, he thought, smoking his cigarette by the window. Or perhaps it was what he had read in the papers that morning. Out in Chembur, a man named 'Metro' Mahesh had been arrested by the police, for running a racket of illegal betting on international cricket matches. Of course he'd be walking free by evening. The politician to whom he sent up his betting money would call from New Delhi – or Dubai. The police would be promised a bigger cut next time. 'Metro' Mahesh. What a name. Just one of thousands doing the same work, all the way from Mumbai to the smallest villages in India, collecting bets from every bar, hotel, recreational club and police station. The worst part is the public know this – they know exactly what's happening with the betting and the fixing – and they don't care, they keep watching, they keep coming to the IPL matches.

Oh, my Darling, my Cricket. Phixed and Phucked. Tommy Sir wanted to cry.

How *did* this thing, our shield and chivalry, our Roncesvalles and Excalibur, go over to the other side, and become part of the great nastiness?

He put both his hands on the windowsill for support, and leaned forward. You could hear it already, the whispering and the bargaining, the lies and corruption: it has just begun, and before the sun rises again, India will be sold and India will be bought, many, many times over. Tommy Sir smelled shit on the night air.

'Manjunath Kumar,' he said, and drew on his cigarette. As he exhaled, he saw the boy as though in one of Van Gogh's paintings, smiling, backlit, meteors and shooting stars and falling stars behind him, the whole whirling universe, waiting for the boy to turn around and *see*. When you are that age you can go anywhere, become anything. 'Manjunath Kumar,' the old scout said again.

But when he raised his eyes from the street to the sky, Tommy Sir saw the full moon and thought of the Bandstand. Foam and spume washed over the young half-naked bodies, and in the dark he saw three digits, like a price put on all he had missed out on in life.

604.

Tommy Sir looked at the glowing tip of his cigarette. He dispersed, with a quick movement of the cigarette, the stars and galaxies behind Manju's head.

I've waited more than forty years to paint you, and now I'll paint you better than Van Gogh himself, my little cricketer.

604.

Return from England and set a new batting record for me.

Turning away from the window, Tommy Sir shouted:

'I'm coming to the kitchen, Lata, I'm warning you. If you've done the dishes, I don't want to see any lights left on in there. What was the electricity bill last month, can you please tell me the exact figure?'

With a final look at the full moon, he extinguished his cigarette on the windowsill.

•

A month passed before Radha asked:

'How is Manju?'

'In England,' Mohan Kumar said, yawning on the bed.

'I know that, Father,' Radha said, as he picked up his cricket bag. 'What is he doing there? You talk to him on the phone, don't you?'

'You said you didn't want to talk to him. I brought the phone to your ear and said, here is your brother, talk, ask him for batting tips from English county cricket, and you said, no.'

Radha said nothing as his father got up and began talking about Manju's life in the home of the game. Seizing one of the bats from near the fridge, Mohan Kumar demonstrated: See – see that fiendish Duke ball, keeps low, wobbles in the air, does things that it never does in India – but see how my Manju's wrists have tamed the red ball, disciplined and broken its Britisher pride.

Letting his father make a fool of himself, Radha took a bat and left for practice.

The front door of his home, all of Radha Krishna Kumar's life, had opened into a tunnel, which had led, via a fast train, straight to a cricket maidan or a practice net.

But today he took a left turn on his way to the train station and wandered to the compound of a Ganapati temple that also housed a cybercafe, with a black glass door, outside which lay a pile of men's slippers.

Removing his shoes, pushing open the black glass door, Radha went into the cybercafe and discovered what it was that all the other boys in the world had been doing in *their* spare time.

While he had been fending off hard red balls thrown at his face by his father, they had been playing a video game that involved open-hatched cars, athletic women in skirts, and lots of shotguns. It was apparently called *Grand Theft Auto (San Andreas)*.

Closing the door behind him, Radha put on his shoes and picked up his bag to return to cricket practice, when all at once, the temple bells rang.

Six weeks in England. Six weeks *alone* in England.

Radha Kumar shivered. Dropping his bag and pushing his way back into the dark cybercafe, he asked the boys:

'Will you teach me to play this game?'

One year to Selection Day

TENTH STANDARD BEGINS

MANJUNATH KUMAR IS BACK FROM THE UK

After spending one and a half months at the J.F. Browns International School, Manchester, playing cricket and attending classes, Manju Kumar has just returned to Mumbai. To give you the correct perspective on the activities of Manju in the UK, here are his observations as narrated orally to Shri Pramod Sawant, his school cricket coach.

'In just six weeks I can say with the utmost confidence that I adapted superlatively to England. The scorecard speaks for itself. 1446 runs at an average of 45 is very respectable. Beyond the cricket field, I also attended classes at the school, where I showed a particular relish for science and mathematics, and made an effort to read the British newspapers every day. I visited a planetarium and two science museums. I most humbly thank Mr Karim Ali for giving me this exquisite opportunity to experience first-hand the uplifting culture of the United Kingdom.'

Members of the media may see Master Manjunath Kumar at the Cricket Club of India, where he will hold a press conference.

Contact:
Shri Pramod Sawant, 'Head Coach'
Shri N.S. Kulkarni, 'Designated Mentor'

'Day-to-day life in England: your conclusions?'

'It rains all day not just in the monsoons like here.'

'What was the food like?'

'The cheese is smelly.'

'It sounds like you were homesick and eager to return to Amchi Mumbai.'

'Every single day I missed my father and brother. Every single day I prayed to God to bring glory to my school even in the UK.'

'What are your observations on the differences between India and England in terms of cricket?'

'For them, it is just a game.'

(Well said.)

'Will you go again to the UK?'

'Certainly. As part of the Indian cricket team.'

(Bravo!)

'Did you chase any English girls when you were there, Manju?'

'Some things are best left private.'

(Ha ha!)

•

'Press conference?'

'He was brilliant, I say. A natural. Told them exactly what they wanted to hear. And all in a strange British accent. It's called Mancunian. He said this in the press con. And furthermore: "I am looking forward to playing in the Kanga League. It will be a huge challenge to bat again in tropical conditions." Tropical conditions! Boy from a slum says all this in English!'

'Press con? You should have told me, Tommy Sir. I am now the brand ambassador for South Australian red wines in India. Remember the time I took a planeload of children from Mumbai to Bowral? It did wonders for my profile in that part of the world. I could have arrived, dramatically, at this press con, like the Santa Claus of South Australian Red Wine if only you had communicated.'

'Next time. Because guess who wants Manju to be their mascot? Kolkata. In the IPL.'

'Great. He can start paying me off right now.'

'No, no, I won't allow it.' Tommy Sir wagged a finger. 'That boy should not be exposed to the IPL at this age. He'll pick up bad habit after bad habit. All those foreign cheerleaders. Too much sex in cricket these days. He's just a boy.'

'Cricket, cricket, cricket.' Anand Mehta yawned indulgently. '… what a circus, anyway.'

'A what?' Tommy Sir inquired.

'The slum kids beg you for money, you beg me, I beg my classmates, it's just a big circus. Cricket.'

Tommy Sir left without saying goodbye.

Anand Mehta smoothed his moustache with a finger, and smiled. You had to feel sorry for that old man – so easy to hurt him, just say something bad about a game invented by medieval shepherds in Essex or Doublesex or some other such sex. Ridiculous creature, this Mister Tommy: all the insights and follies of a child, never traded in for the insights and follies of an adult. Anand Mehta yawned again.

For a soothing half an hour he read online about the twists and turns of the Battle of the Bulge, 1944, and then emailed an old girlfriend in New York, and then browsed on Twitter for Nietzsche quotations. He closed the laptop and returned it to his desk, next to the bottles of liquor, and then went and stood by the window.

The ocean, rolling in towards Nariman Point, struck a shore of black rocks in front of the National Centre for the Performing Arts – and then, moving again, the foaming water rolled past the low white Mediterranean wall of the NCPA, past the blue-glass building of the Indian Overseas Bank, past the Arcadia building (the very ugly Corporation Bank building behind it) and past Dalamal Chambers. And this, Anand Mehta thought – this citadel of brain-dead wealth, fortress of the world's least educated elite, a place with ten thousand ways to mispronounce 'swanky' and 'entrepreneur' – this is what won't let me in. Moving past Nariman Point, the surf subsided near the blue-tarpaulin-covered shanties. The exact spot where Ajmal Kasab came with the jihadis to kill us on 26/11. If only he'd done a better job.

I gave up Central Park for you, he yelled down at the city, *you piece of shit!*

Anand Mehta's mind was now like a stanza from the Bhagavad Geeta in reverse: from brooding too much on what had gone wrong in his life, he became angry; from this anger was born frustration; from this frustration was born a round glass of drink; from this one glass was born an entire bottle of 90-proof liquor.

The day darkened; he sat with a goblet of red wine, sipped, spat, then ransacked his cupboards, searching for scotch – not single malt, not Blue Label, not Black Label. Just give me Indian scotch, honest Indian scotch.

'Press conference,' he said out loud. Press conference, at the age of fifteen. Anand Mehta felt again the thrill of having bet on that grandest of investments: a growing human being.

Young Manjunath Kumar.

One minute, slum; next minute, Angleterre. Mehta had a vision of a great milky waterfall, a cataract of free sex, whose sheer descent had fathered many rainbows. That slum boy must have humped like crazy in England. 'Asha,' he shouted, 'let us go congratulate that boy, that English gentleman of ours.' But then he remembered that she was away with her friends at a kitty party. He kept drinking.

Later in the night, he dialled Tommy Sir's number, getting it right at the second attempt.

'I want to see my investment.'

'What?'

'My Man-cas-ter boy. Where ... ?'

'You've gone mad?' Tommy Sir asked. 'Do you know the time?'

'I know they're in Chembur. Where in Chem ... I went there once but I forgot the way now. You shut up and don't tell me my bloody business, mate. Where is my Man-caster?'

'Go in the morning. I'll tell you, but go in the morning – promise?'

Minutes later, Mehta was driving towards Chembur, squinting at signs, shouting out for directions, trying to remember how he had made it there once – but that was in daylight! – while the road played games with him, becoming muddy and narrow, and then opening up into the highway, while train tracks kept appearing and disappearing by its side.

'I can't believe you're doing this,' he told himself, and he burst out laughing. He kept talking to himself. Look at all these buildings, stuffy with seventies' concrete and nineteenth-century morality. Hollow, hollow, the concrete buildings are all hollow. The fat middle class is hollow. So let us get rid of the farce that Indians are a most moral race, that only married people should live in good buildings, girls should be virgins and homos should be in jail, let us rid ourselves of the Victorian Hindu Penal Code, declare a republic of cunt & cock and a sovereign secular socialism of cock & cunt and force everyone here to live in the twenty-first bloody American c&c century, please. God, he wished he had brought some scotch, some honest Indian scotch, for the drive.

Slowing down, he squinted at the names of the passing buildings, until – 'Tattvamasi. That's it.'

Anand Mehta got out of his car, tripped over a stone, recovered himself gleefully, and reached the entranceway of the building. He pressed the bell and went up the stairs. After a while, he became aware that he was relieving himself in a corner, as a dark face watched him from a higher floor. 'Relaaaaaax,' he whispered, zipped himself up, and continued up the stairs.

'This way, sir, this way,' the dark face said. It wore a banian and lungi and stood before an opened door.

'It's an honour to see you, Benefactor. I recognized your car. It is an honour to have you visit us again.'

'Benefactor.' Anand Mehta laughed. 'You know how to speak to your benefactor, good man, good man ... where is my Mancaster?'

'Sleeping. I'll wake him up? And his brother, Radha?'

Mohan Kumar showed the guest into another room, where the boys were in bed. Anand Mehta stripped the bedsheets off the sleeping boys – one rubbing his eyes, the other squinting at the light – and stared at them.

'Which one went to England? That one? Or this one?'

'Get out of bed, Manju. Do you want to see them bat now?'

Anand Mehta clapped at the boy who was struggling to his feet.

'Say something with full fucking British accent.'

Manju, who was wearing only a pair of shorts, covered his nakedness with his arms and blinked. When the investor shouted at him a second time he said, 'Hello, sir,' in a small voice.

'Louder,' the investor said, cupping an ear. 'With the full accent. Sound like Mancaster, Mancaster! Isn't that funny? This boy is a little superman, I tell you. Superman. Is that what you are, Mancaster?'

Radha, also naked to the waist, looked around for his bat.

'Sir, you have honoured our home at just the right time. Radha has changed his backlift and stance. We worked on it all summer. Radha – demonstrate, demonstrate.'

Anand Mehta wiped his lips.

'No bloody cricket demonstration. I asked to hear this one talk British to me. I talk New York, and you talk British, you little fucker. Talk. Talk.'

He sat down on the sofa and gaped at Manju, who stood with his arms making an 'X' across his naked chest.

'Relaaaaax.' Anand Mehta laughed. 'At your age, you have nothing to be shy about, not a thing. After all, what is a cock, I ask you?' He turned to the father and grinned. 'A cock is this: when you're a boy, it's your manhood. When you're a man, it's your boyhood.'

Both men laughed, but Mehta caught the expression on the boy's face.

'Why is Mancaster staring at me like that?' He pointed at Manju. 'Talk, little fuck. Don't think you're too good for me and my money. Talk British *now*.'

•

Even after the door was bolted, even after his father assured him that Anand Mehta would not return, Manju dreamed. He found himself in a forest: one without paths, but where everything glowed in the moonlight, and every illuminated branch guided him to the spot near a lake. This was the dream that he had had again and again in England. In the darkness, as promised, a woman's hand reached out for him. He checked between the thumb and the index finger, and there it was: the nitric-acid scar from the goldsmith's. And though he could not see his mother's face, Manju was happy, for he knew she was beside him in the night. Until a bird flew overhead, silhouetting itself against the moon, and his mother withdrew her hand; his heart pounded. He could not see a single star in the sky. This was *Kattale*, the old darkness. It was back, and would keep coming back, now that it knew how to reach him: *Stay here. You don't have to go out and face that man, Mehta: stay here, Captain. Stay within*. The cold water of the lake lapped his feet, and his ankles: and soon his lips were wet, and he was hard. Manju awoke, turned from Radha, and, licking his forearms quickly, masturbated, taking care that his come did not stain his bedsheet, which his father might notice.

•

After breakfast, when Manju insisted, 'The police know we're cricket stars. They will listen to us,' all Radha did, once again, was to shake his head from side to side. The two brothers left home and walked to the train station, but only one of them had brought a cricket kitbag with him.

'That man can't treat us like that. He can't wake us up in the middle of the night.'

'Just because you've gone to England and speak with an accent, doesn't mean you're special, Manju. He's paying us.'

Manju saw that the red handle of his brother's bat, sticking out over his shoulder, was rubbing against the back of his neck as they walked.

'What do you want to do anyway, Manju?'

'Go to the police. Tell them.'

Radha had stopped.

'Police? Englishman wants to go to the police. Give me your hand. Give me your foreign hand.'

Manju held his hand out to his brother, who squeezed it in his.

'Come, Manju, let's go to the police together.'

Hand in hand they walked like that. As they passed a streetside barber's stall, Manju leaned back, reflexively, to check himself in the mirror in between two men being lathered for a shave. And this was too much for Radha: *My brother*, he thought, *is such a little bugger.*

'Manju,' he said. 'I like police stories. Do you like police stories? Good. Manju, Sofia's friend's father, the ACP, was telling me a story. Listen. This ACP was telling Sofia and me the Mumbai police now go on the Internet, and they go onto these chat sites, right. They go on to gay chat sites, Manju. Gay chat sites.'

Radha squeezed his younger brother's hand.

'First they make friends with the gays, Manju, and they say, you want to exchange videos? Blue videos? Let's meet outside Dadar station. Fine, the gay brings his blue video, he comes to Dadar, he meets the ACP, who has come with another blue video, they exchange the videos, and then the gay is walking home when the ACP does *this* (Radha seized Manju), and says,' (holding his brother's shoulder, Radha curled his own tongue to touch his upper lip like a bull) 'and says, that isn't a blue video in your hands, is it? That isn't a *gay* blue video, is it? Let's go to the station, fag boy, let's go. Then the ACP and his police friends take the homo to jail and say they will lock him up for ten years and tell his mummy and wife he's not a real man, just a fag boy, till he sweats and begs and pays the policemen lots of money. Isn't that funny, Manju? I asked, Englishman, isn't that funny? Hey, Manju, where are you running? The police station is *this* way. This way.'

'Fuck off,' Manju told his brother. He walked a few steps, then turned around and shouted: 'I took it from you, Radha. Remember that every night before you go to sleep. And if there's a new scholarship, I'll take it from you again.'

•

It was virtually an instinct now, to call Javed whenever he was in trouble. After leaving his brother, Manju found a pay-phone near the Chembur train station. He told Javed everything. 'I knew that investor was no good the first time I saw him,' Javed replied. 'Which man with self-respect would wear a red Manchester United T-shirt? Listen to me, little Manju. Take the train to Navi Mumbai. I've been waiting for you. You can tell me about England, too.' 'Alright,' Manju said, and put the phone down, and paid the shopkeeper a rupee for its use.

Then the strange thing happened. As he was crossing the road, a traffic policeman, in his white shirt and khaki trousers and topi, raised his left hand; with his right hand he pointed a wooden lathi straight at Manju. He took a step towards the boy. Manju's throat had contracted. He stood in the middle of the road, his heart beating, until the cold glass of a passing autorickshaw's rear-view mirror touched his back, and he started. The traffic policeman walked right past him and began talking to the rider of a motorcycle; now the rider was remonstrating and pleading with the policeman. Ah, Manju thought – the fellow has forgotten to wear his helmet. The policeman has caught him for that. Hunter and prey would now start negotiating the size of the bribe that the motorcyclist had to fork out for his offence.

That lathi was never pointed at *me*, Manju understood. Yet his heart still thumped against his ribs.

Drops of water fell on his nose. He looked up at the dark sky. Deciding not to meet Javed, he instead ran home for his cricket gear: he would go join a match in the Kanga League. He was going to be the best in Mumbai today.

For Manju was now batting to protect himself.

TENTH STANDARD CONTINUES: THE KANGA LEAGUE STARTS

Even in mid-May, even in early June, they keep playing cricket: right through the heat, and through the terrible days when all-India strikes are called and buses are burned. Right through till the sixth or seventh of June, when the rains say: 'Stop.' Then the nets are taken away, and the stone-rollers are smothered in yellow tarpaulin. At the Oval, bare-chested workers scoop out mounds of dark earth from what used to be the cricket pitch, as if excavating a mass grave.

It rains and it pours, and the semi-naked bodies dig deeper and deeper into Mumbai.

But barely a month later, the cricketers have come back from the dead: the Kanga League has begun.

Standing in a multitude of circles they hear the same pep-talk from a multitude of coaches. Crows are rising and swooping in front of the Bombay Gymkhana. Dozens of matches are in progress on one maidan. The rain grows heavier each minute. The grass is mad and the human beings are mad. Young men are skidding, falling, and resurrecting themselves out of the mud. It is as though the life-force of Mumbai city were flowing from the street into the middle class: well-fed school kids, dressed in Victorian white, are hustling like homeless children. *Strong is the thunder, and strong is the lightning-bolt: but we are stronger.*

•

Beyond Mankhurd, the Harbour Line went past slum after slum, slums that were gloomy and hopeless in a way that Manju couldn't remember the old place in Dahisar ever being, past the clustered buildings of a Slum Redevelopment Authority project, and into green wilderness.

Then came a bridge, and glowing water, and in the distance, a new city: Navi Mumbai – New Mumbai.

•

In the men's toilet at Vashi station, Manju looked at himself in a mirror and washed his face with soap, twice, and checked his hair.

Right outside the station, he found a shopping mall made of glass. A foot away from the entrance, where security guards waited with metal detectors, a boy stood admiring himself in the glass wall. His powerful neck was shaved clean below the hairline, and his shoulders were exposed by his low-cut T-shirt.

From the reflection in the glass Manju could see that the boy was wearing Aviator sunglasses, and had a gold ring in his right ear.

He began to run towards him.

But Javed had seen his reflection in the glass: waiting till Manju was almost upon his back, he turned around and caught him and for a long moment they held on to each other.

•

Knowing that Javed's first question would be: What is England like? Manju thought, I will tell him about the forest bird. There was a garden behind the school, and there were deer in the garden. Deer? Yes. In England you have deer everywhere. On the way to cricket, Manju would stop to watch the deer in the garden, and one day, he heard a sound from the bushes. Parting open the leaves of a big dark bush, he found a forest bird, motionless and curled-up in a wet nest, like an ebony foetus. Indian boy and British bird stared at each other, for a full minute, each asking the other, What are *you* doing here? Then, with a beating of wings, the bird made Manju's heart stop as it rose right over his head, as if it meant to seize him, like the roc that lifted Sindbad over the seven seas.

But Javed had seen a roc of his own: and he had caught his. Because while Manju was away on his grand Manchester scholarship, Javed Ansari, without leaving India, had also visited a foreign country. He had celebrated his sixteenth birthday a fortnight ago. Around midnight, in Colaba, alone, walking past the open-air mutton and chicken kebab grill of Bademiya's, seeing a young man smile in a certain way, a young man with blond streaks in his hair, Javed had smiled back at that young man, to feel a finger scrape diagonally down the back of his jeans, and turned around in surprise to see the young man now standing behind him, no longer smiling, but with his nostrils tense, his eyes candid, and realized that all of these formed a closed door: and that the door could be opened, and would reveal something – something as big as an ocean, and as turbulent – behind it. And Javed, right there, went up to the blond man, negotiated a deal without saying a word, and with a beating heart followed him up wooden stairs to a room on the third floor of a private hotel behind the Taj, where the blond man inserted a key into a door, and said, 'Go in,' and when Javed entered the room, trembling, he smelled the ocean for the first time in his life, early in the morning after his sixteenth birthday.

•

And now Javed walked alongside Manju, hand on his shoulder. He smiled condescendingly, and asked: 'So what was England like, Superstar? What is England's food like?' The two of them rode the escalator up into the mall. Manju said: 'The Britishers eat cheese all the time.'

Javed removed his Aviator glasses and put them in his pocket to get a better look at the superstar.

'Manju. Please.'

'I'm telling you, the white people eat cheese for breakfast and smell of it all day.'

Javed laughed, just once, but so hard the Aviator glasses fell and he had to grab them with both hands.

'Manju. Did you *really* go to England?'

The boy looked the same as he had before leaving for England, just a bit fairer, a bit broader. He was also definitely wearing some sort of deodorant.

'Pass me the hammer, Miss Moneypenny' – Manju spread his arms wide, and lowered his voice an octave – 'I'm a young Sean Connery!'

Javed stared.

'There were workers on the roof of the school, and they would bang their hammers and sing that all day.'

Javed tried it out himself. Pass me the hammer, Ms Money …

'Who is Sean Connery?'

A whistle blew. Short women in blue uniforms stood by the sides of the escalators, making sure no young ruffian ran up or down the metal steps or did anything else to set off a panic among the crowd, many of whom were using an escalator for the first time in their lives.

Keeping his eye on the blue-uniformed guards, Manju said: 'You didn't come to Kanga League the other day.'

'Fuck cricket. Why didn't you come to see me till now?'

'At the press conference they complimented my accent.' Manju beamed. 'It's called a Mancunian. It's got *glottalstop*. Do you know what *glottalstop* is?'

'It's sexy,' Javed said.

He said the word as casually as he could, but he saw it wiping the grin off Manju's face, and stopping his breath: *It's sexy*.

Javed tapped on his gold earring and looked at Manju.

'Did you go to the police yet? And tell them about the investor, how he invaded your home? That's what they call what he did. Home invasion. Did you tell—'

'No.'

'No?'

Javed felt his ears move on their own, as they always did when he gritted his teeth. Look at Manju go to England, spend six weeks there, eat the cheese, breathe the scented air, and come back and still behave like a *slave*!

The escalator had now reached the highest level of the mall. There was a bowling alley up there, in what was called the Play Park, where they could talk.

'What was the point of going to England, Manju?'

'I went to the Science Museum and read the *Daily Telegraph* newspaper.'

'Bullshit.' Javed touched Manju's left cheek with the back of his palm. 'You went to a *CSI* morgue. To see dead bodies.'

The whites of Manju's eyes expanded, and he looked to this side and that, and then grinned. Wanted to, sure, but he had been too shy to ask the white people for directions to the morgue in Manchester.

'Thank God. Otherwise they would think all Indians are mad like you.'

At the entrance to the Play Park they found a machine with illuminated numbers on it; a boy swung a mallet – *thud!* – and the numbers began to light up, one by one.

'To see how strong you are,' Javed said. 'Want to try, Captain?'

'No.'

Javed took him on a tour of the video games. *Ghost Squad* ('No'), *Police Squad 3* ('No') and *Formula One* ('No') until Javed said, '*Relax*, Captain. I'm paying. Is *that* what you're worried about?'

Air hockey: a group of boys standing on either side of a table were smashing away at something small. Saying 'Yes,' Manju went closer, inspected the boys at the table, and then said, 'No.'

'Man. You keep changing your mind. They sent you to England and you became an English lady.'

They stood by the side of the Play Park, watching others try their luck or skill at the machines.

'Did you think of your family when you were over in England?'

Looking Javed in the eye, Manju said: 'Not once.'

'And did you really play cricket?'

Manjunath Kumar betrayed the slightest of smiles.

'Only when they were watching.'

Javed grinned. 'Maybe you are on my wavelength at last. By the way,' he asked, 'how is Radha? And which junior college is he going to?'

'He's not going to any.' Manju turned to Javed, and, to pre-empt any criticism of his father, added: 'He can't be running after girls in college. He has to practise every day.'

'And if your brother doesn't make it in cricket?'

Manju looked up at the glass ceiling of the mall, which was in the shape of a lozenge, with a metal grid supporting it.

'My father knows what he is doing.'

'Manju, Manju, Manju ...' Javed shook his head. 'Seriously. Stop acting like a villager. It was my birthday the other day. I'm sixteen. Do you know what I did on my birthday?'

A vein bulged in Javed's forehead; he decided to tell Manju everything. But wait. Since he had no idea how Manju would respond – whether he would just run back home, shouting, Daddy, Daddy, that fellow is a homo – Javed said, instead:

'Close your eyes.'

Manju, unable to disobey, did so.

Javed touched him. Manju, blind, held his breath, as a fingernail scraped against the beard on his cheek.

'You need to shave.'

Manju shook his head.

'Your father? Still?'

Manju said nothing, but Javed heard the answer anyway. So when Manju, predictably, tried to run away, Javed, in a fury of compassion for this poor, exploited boy, who had gone to England, but was still too scared to shave by himself, caught him by the wrist, and said:

'Let's shave you now.'

He took Manju to the supermarket below the Food Court, bought a disposable Gillette razor, and an eighteen-rupee tube of shaving cream. Then they went to the men's room on the first floor.

The attendant from the Dosa-and-Idli stall at the Food Court was washing his hands. He stared at the boys.

Standing before the mirror, safety razor in hand, Javed demonstrated. Down up, down up. Downward stroke first, see? Javed took the safety razor out of its plastic cover.

Leaning against the door of a toilet stall, the Dosa-and-Idli attendant began offering the first-timer additional tips.

Manju turned around to have a word, but Javed guided his face back to the mirror. Let's get this thing done. Squeezing Manju's cheek with his left hand, he moved the razor over the beard. Downward stroke first, then up, then down. Stroke by stroke, Javed removed Manju's fuzzy mask to reveal a shining new face.

Then, fogging the glass with his breath, and wetting his finger, Javed wrote on it:

Roses r red
violets r blu
u r a giant
or u r a tool

'You know what this poem means, or shall I explain?' he asked.

Javed saw Mr Glottalstop gaping at the mirror and moving a finger toward his reflection.

'What are you doing? Don't touch the glass. You'll make a mess of my poem.'

But Manju touched Javed's reflection, and drew a line on its forehead.

'Javed.'

'What?'

'You're losing your hair.'

•

On the way back to Mumbai, Manju leaned out of the open door, his left hand touching his smooth right cheek. Another train was passing by. In the women's compartment, the passengers squatted on the floor; one of the women had her back turned to Manju, and he could see the nuggets of her spine, each demarcated and bulging like a taunt, and he wanted to reach out and touch. Down her back, one bone after the other, reach and touch. In the next compartment, two schoolboys stood in their all-white uniforms, looking back at him; their shirts dazzled as the train gathered speed. Cut for the first time, Manju's face stung when the wind hit it. Stepping back from the open door, he endured it for as long as he could, and slapped his raw cheeks again and again. Suddenly he found himself hard, and pressed his cock against the steel wall of the train and screamed at the schoolboys and the fat bones in the woman's back as he exploded into a million little ribbons of hormone.

•

'When you got home, what happened? I told you, Javed Ansari expects a full situation report.'

'I got home, and went up the stairs, and the door was open. I went in, and he was sitting on the sofa and reading the newspaper.'

'What did he say? Details.'

'Nothing. He just looked at me.'

'When you go to war, first you must have a map. How many chairs did you see around the flat?'

'There are three chairs at the dining table. I got ready to do like you said, I was ready to lift one of them high high up, and say, *Don't you dare touch me*. But guess what, Javed? He looked at me and saw I had shaved, but he didn't say a word.'

'And then?'

'Then Radha came in with his cricket bag and we sat together and ate.'

'And no one said a thing?'

'Javed, this morning I shaved again, and I can't believe it, the way my father looks at me now. He's *scared*.'

There was a pause and then Javed announced, quietly, 'Mine is scared of me too. *All* of them are. I told you, read *The Animal Farm*, Manju. This is just the start of my plan. Next thing is you come to Navi Mumbai to see my career counsellor. Agreed?'

'Agreed. And one more thing. I went to the bathroom and I wrote a poem. You want to hear it?'

•

The square root of 181, multiplied by 11.1?

Present capital of France?

Draw an accurate isosceles triangle, please?

On the wall behind the plump-faced man with the weak chin, a framed photograph showed two white mice peeping out of their wicker basket to examine the caption: *My life is not limited by* your *imagination.* A cold glass slab covered the table between them. Manju slid the piece of paper across it. The plump man nodded as he read Manju's answers.

'And what do you want to do with your life?'

In his fingers Manju held a business card, the first he had ever been given –'Jignesh Seth, Guidance Chief, Best Choice Educators' – while across the glass-faced table Mr Seth adjusted his glasses with an index finger and waited for the boy's answer.

'Be a cricketer. And represent my country in the World Cup of cricket.'

'You said that very fast.'

Manju, in response, began twirling a lock of hair with his index finger.

The counsellor asked: 'Are you ambitious?' Manju shook his head.

'Do you want to be famous? Is that why you go for cricket?'

'No.' Manju thought about it, and said: 'I want to be the fellow at the back.'

'Have you ever been the fellow at the back?'

'My father never let me be. But I like it when I'm there.'

The counsellor nodded. 'You don't know what you do want. Fifty per cent of this country, that is half a billion people, are under the age of twenty-five, and we older Indians have no idea how to listen to them. Javed told me about your case, and I said at once, bring the boy here. I'll listen. I want to be the Mother Teresa of listening to your generation.'

Silence.

'Do you know who Mother Teresa is?'

Manju looked at the white mice in the photo.

'Let me try this, Mr Manjunath, as a way around your inhibition. Let me talk about myself.'

The counsellor smiled.

'This office, this job, is not what my father did. We're Gujaratis. You know what we do? We cut diamonds for a living. That's what I should be doing right now, in a shop in Opera House: but one day I heard a voice inside my head saying, Jignesh Seth, you're cutting the wrong diamonds. Your vocation in life is to guide young people – like Mother Teresa. I listened to this voice. This job doesn't pay, but I'm happy and I don't drink anymore. Now, let me help you find your inner voice. Follow me?'

Manju nodded.

'For now, I want you to repeat something aloud. When anyone says, you must do this, you must make money, must play cricket, just say in response: "My life is not limited by your imagination." It is our motto here. Repeat it, please. Excellent. Now the second thing I want you to do is a mental exercise. Please close your eyes, and imagine a future in which you play cricket for the next twenty or thirty years. Tell me if you like what you see.'

The moment he closed his eyes, for some reason Manju thought of something he had seen on *India's Got Talent* the previous evening, a slim young woman with a ponytail and layers upon layers of abdominal muscles – and a silver ring piercing her belly-button.

The boy started: across the table, the career counsellor was striking his knuckles on the glass, and Manjunath Kumar had been returned from the distant planet where he suffered his erections, to this one, our earth.

'Did you like what you saw, Manju? A life as a cricketer?'

Keeping his eyes on his shoe, Manju said, 'Yes, yes.'

But then he gazed over Mr Seth's head at the photograph of the white mice, and read the slogan again, and this time he felt the same strange exhilaration as he had when he'd seen Javed nearly naked in the dark tent, and so raised a finger to catch the counsellor's attention and asked if he could please change his answer.

•

An hour later, Javed and Manju were back at the big mall in Vashi, playing air hockey on the top floor, until Manju asked:

'Are you in a *gang*?'

'How do you know?'

'Your counsellor told me. He said it's called Mad Max Gang. He told me not to join it.'

'I knew he was a spy for my father,' Javed said, concentrating on the game. 'That son of a bitch.'

'*Can* I join it?'

'No. Mad Max Gang is for experienced boys only. Not for you.'

'I am shaving every day now. I am experienced.'

U-ha, U-ha. Running across the table, Javed caught Manju by the forearm, but he freed himself, and kicked back.

The two raced from the mall to Vashi station, and when he realized he was going to lose, Javed stopped running, and began playing air-guitar, forcing Manju to turn around and come back – and *beg* to be allowed to join in the guitar concert.

•

Waaaaaaaaaaaaaa ... Wah, Wah, Wah Waaaaaaaaaaa ...

He concentrated on the Sea Link bridge: the white mesh of wires over the central pier throbbing in the sunlight like plucked string, until he could almost hear it buzzing across the water. He felt Javed touch him on the forearm, recoiled, and moved away.

Slices of coconut flesh clustered by the shore at Dadar beach; marigold petals and plastic garbage floated further away. Immersed to his waist, a bull-necked brahmin turned round and round in the water, scattering the coconut and petals each time he dipped.

Right behind the praying brahmin, jumping on the wet stones for special effects, 'J.A.' was demonstrating a dance done by Freddie Mercury, who was a poet, and a Parsi, and a gay. He had just downloaded the video on his new cell phone. He kept going, *Waaaaaaaa, Waaaaaaa, Waaaaaa*, until he stopped and shouted, 'Hey, Glottalstop, is this a boycott?'

But Manju had already left the beach.

'Yesterday in Vashi train station you were like Tarzan, and today you're boycotting me? Why?'

Four pale legs with claws stuck out from beneath a black taxi, as Manju left the beach and walked to Shivaji Park.

'I'm not doing any boycott.'

The benches at the park's entrance reeked of molasses; a man lay in a puddle.

'Don't lie to me,' he heard Javed say.

But the previous night, lying in bed, smelling the sweat and cricket practice from his elder brother's tired body, hearing the breathing from his open mouth, Manju's mind had been penetrated by doubt.

Why is he being so nice to me? Maybe, Manju thought, because this Muslim boy had always been greedy for that thing around which this dark enterprise of cricket sponsorship revolved, Manjunath Kumar's forearms – these Bradmanesque, Tendulkaresque forearms – and maybe he wanted to snap them like a pair of kebabs and chew on them. And post a photo on Facebook.

As he walked he saw a condom on the ground, and stopped. He turned around to see Javed, waiting by one of the stone obelisks near the park's entrance, tap meaningfully on the stone, and go into the park.

Manju turned and walked back to the sign taped to the obelisk:

Professor Joshi's Tutorials
ICSE, IB, SSC (English Medium)
Limited number of students (max 10 per class)

Another notice was stuck to the bottom of this notice:

Swiddish Massage
Experienced Male Masseur
Home Service Only
Call 9811799289

And at the bottom of *that* notice, in Javed's handwriting, was written:

YOU ARE SLAVE

In the shade of the trees at one end of the maidan, the cricketers sat on plastic chairs, their pads and gloves spilling out of their bags and getting mixed up. Manju stripped off his shirt, and put on his chest-guard, and then his forearm guard. Beside him, Javed, stripped to the waist, was doing the same.

Fully dressed, the two batsmen walked towards the green cricket pitch, when Manju stopped, held up his bat, as if he were talking to it, and shouted:

'I am not *slave*, okay?'

'U-ha, U-ha.'

Manju looked at Javed.

'Did you take me to see Mr Seth and tell him to say all those things because you want me to give up cricket?'

Again: 'U-ha. U-ha.'

'So you can take my place on the team?'

Now Javed stopped laughing and looked at him – before he threw his bat on the ground.

'Manju, this is the last season for me.'

'Last season?'

'I told my father. No more cricket.'

So Manju also dropped his bat.

The number of open middle-order batting slots in the Mumbai Ranji team had just increased by one. He had to tell Radha the news.

Bending to pick up his own bat, Manju also handed Javed his. A woman wearing an ochre sari walked between them.

'Why?'

The umpire clapped.

'Whatever it is, discuss in the tent, not on the pitch.'

'I don't believe you,' Manju said, loud enough for all to hear.

'Time them out, Umpire – time them out!'

'Look,' Javed told Manju. 'Do you think I'd lie to you? About *anything*?'

'No,' Manju said, and then tried to understand.

'But if you don't play cricket, what will you do?'

Javed gave Manju his answer, and then shouted at the fielders, silencing them.

At the non-striker's end, Manju stood with an open mouth. Behind him, he heard the fast-bowler's feet pound into the earth. Beyond the park, a saffron pennant fluttered from the top of the Veer Savarkar monument. Three urchins had enriched the slips cordon; as the wicket-keeper scared them away, their mother tried to sell oranges to the umpire. A young man with kajol around his eyes sang in falsetto as he loped around Shivaji Park. Manju had never seen these things before in a game of cricket.

And when Javed Ansari, who for so many years had been the most elegant young left-handed batsman in Mumbai, took a crude swipe at a wide ball and missed it, drawing chuckles from the fielders and a remark from the umpire, Manju knew for sure that he had not been lying (and would never lie to Manju); as he raised his head to hide his smile from the rest of the world, he saw the saffron pennant beating in the wind like Javed's answer to his last question:

Everything.

•

'That Mohammedan boy is the one telling Manju, give up cricket and go to college. Science! 2,500 rupees for lab fees; 1,500 rupees for a dissection box. To cut open cockroaches! You know he is in trouble with the police, this Mohammedan. He has a gang and they smoked ganja one day and drove their bikes full speed through Navi Mumbai. Without a driving licence. Through red lights. His father is a rich man and paid the police to let him go. Big thief walks free.'

Back home in Chheda Nagar, Mohan Kumar was delivering a full report on the evil named Javed Ansari to his neighbour, Mrs Shastri, who had again ventured into the Kumars' home with her boy, Rahul, the would-be cricketing star.

Collating reports from Tommy Sir and Radha, Mohan Kumar had created a full mental picture of Javed: now, as he looked about the home he had made for his sons, his rich imagination searched for metaphor and symbol. Got it! One summer many years ago, in his village near the Ghats, standing outside the biggest bungalow for miles around, the official residence of the criminal court judge, Mohan had seen the bushes by the gate shaking. Out came a brown furry thing that leapt up on the compound wall: a mongoose. With his instinctive dislike of rodents, Mohan took a step back, but could not stop watching: for this little fellow was almost human in the way he studied the judge's compound this way and that, all the time flicking his enormous tail this way and that. Behind him, another, more timid mongoose waited, until the gangleader turned and gave him a nod; then the timid one leapt up on the gate, and the two of them raided and raped the criminal court judge's garden.

'Yes, this Ansari boy is a mongoose – a cunning furry mongoose – and only a snake can save my family now – a snake,' he said, as Mrs Shastri, her hands folded on the top of her son's head, nodded.

•

After their cricket match ended, Javed took Manju in a taxi all the way to Horniman Circle in the city. He did not tell Manju where they were going, but instead kept explaining his reasons for giving up the game.

'It's all pro-puh-gun-duh these days.'

'What is that?' Manju asked.

'Pro-puh-gun-duh,' Javed said. 'It's all corporate propuhgunduh. Tatas batting, Reliance bowling. Cricket is just brain-control; and no one is going to brain-control Javed Ansari. You went to England, but I was the one who was thinking for six weeks.'

After they descended from the taxi, the little wheels on Javed's cricket kitbag rattled along the street; Manju, his own cricket bag slung across his shoulders, followed a yard behind him. They had reached one of the crowded by-lanes of Fort. The rattling stopped: Javed had lit a cigarette.

He turned around and smiled, blowing smoke from the side of his mouth. 'I had a brother once. A big brother.'

'Was he a cricketer too?'

'No! He was too smart for that. Usman was five years older than me. One day he went up to the top of our building and jumped.'

Manju cringed, and avoided the smoke.

'Jumped?'

'Jumped. Usman was a great guy, fun guy. He wanted to have fun but they wouldn't let him. My father built a shrine to him in the backside of our building. Hurry up, now.'

KAJARIA CEMENTS said the sign above a dark door that led into a stairway. Manju could already hear Javed's shoes booming up the stairs.

He followed.

Below a framed sign that said

Drugs and Alcohol have no place in society

sat a woman wearing half-moon glasses. She put her elbows down on the pages of her book and looked over her glasses at Manju. Her look said: don't do anything silly in here.

Behind the woman, another corridor began; Manju could see the first three of a series of blue doors. One of the doors was open; and when he looked inside that door Manju had his first glimpse of the pile of human debris that was growing under Mumbai cricket.

A tall bony man with a goatee stood at a window, looking down on Horniman Circle. 'Got anything for me, buddy?' he asked, and at first Manju thought the question was directed at him.

In another corner of the little room, Javed shook a packet of cigarettes teasingly, and tossed it into the air. As soon as the bony man caught the packet, he slapped both hands back on the windowsill, as if he were in constant danger of falling over.

'Manju,' Javed said, 'this is Shenoy.'

'Which Shenoy?' Manju asked, and then his mouth opened.

... Fastest ball ... ?

Javed nodded.

Some Boys Rise, Some Boys Fall: Legends of Bombay Cricket and My Role in Shaping Them
Part 21

> Date: 4 September 1996. Place: Bombay Gymkhana, Selection Day. A young man comes thundering down to the stumps, turns his arms over, and bowls a ball. No speedometer was possessed that day – but it is believed by every single observer that it was the fastest ball delivered in our city. Who was this boy? T.O. Shenoy. And who discovered his talent?

Ex-Speed Demon Shenoy struck a match and glanced sideways at Manju, who recognized the look: fatigue, the fatigue of meeting people all day, every day, who want more from you than you want from them.

Waaan-waan-waaan! Javed began showing off his Freddie Mercury dance-number; Shenoy walked over to a bed in the corner of the room, lay down, smoked, and spied on them through the corners of his eyes.

The blue door creaked. The woman came in, holding her glasses in one hand, and waving the cigarette smoke away from her nose with the other. 'Who brought cigarettes? Who? This boy is a recovering alcoholic.'

Behind her, his back pressed to the wall, Javed, smiling a guilty little smile, put a finger to his lips. He looked as if he had suddenly shrunk in size, and turned into a small, scared rodent-like creature.

'I brought the cigarettes,' Manju said.

'You should be ashamed – get out. I told you: this boy is a recovering alcoholic.'

Saying nothing till they were safe in the street, Javed laughed.

'What a bitch. Right?'

Manju looked Javed up and down. Now he wished he hadn't lied to protect this grinning, insufferable show-off.

They were walking through the humid garden in the centre of Horniman Circle which was full of flowers and dark leaves and crows grown as fat as eagles, while straight ahead of them, a row of classical Greek pillars glistened between thickets of bamboo: the Asiatic Society's Public Reading Room, standing beyond the garden above a broad flight of steps.

'How did Shenoy end up there?' Manju asked as he followed Javed up the steps, to a black door.

'Same way you'll end up, unless you leave cricket. Then that fat woman will come in and shout at *you* every day. Get out of it *now*, Manju.'

At the top of the steps, one cricketer sat down, and the other remained standing.

'*Me?*' Manju gaped. 'You were the one who told me to bat well and go to England.'

'I've become more advanced now, Manju. You've fallen behind. Cricketer.'

'Shut up,' Manju said.

'Tatas batting, Reliance bowling. That's all it is,' Javed grumbled.

And now Manju thought he could read Javed's mind at last: where others saw a game called Test match, or one-day, or twenty-twenty, Javed saw only a circle of fat rich men, like the ring of glossy black birds that sit in the middle of the Bandra *talao*.

Javed yawned.

'I come here to the library to write poems. Do you want a write a poem with me?'

Manju bit his lip. He sat down.

'Can you make magic with a poem?'

'I don't write that kind of poem. I make brain-waves with poetry.' Javed winked. 'But first you have to be on the right wavelength. First you have to learn the rhetoric.'

'The what?' Manju asked.

Amidst the cricket gloves and centre pad in his kitbag, Javed had hidden a long green notebook: he took the book out of the bag, and, as Manju spied over his shoulder, flipped through the pages – sketches of their teachers and fellow students from Ali Weinberg, handwritten couplets – until he reached a particular page, which he snapped with his fingers before turning to the other boy: 'Read.'

Leaning over, Manju did so.

> *My rhetoric*
>
> *Javed Ansari*
>
> *Analogy: As the tiger is brave in the jungle, the king was brave in battle.*
>
> *Comparison: The king was as brave in battle as the tiger is brave in the jungle.*

Simile: The king was like a tiger in battle.

Metaphor: The king was a tiger in battle.

Epithet: The Tiger-King.

Apostrophe: O thou Tiger-King!

'I don't understand,' Manju said.

'That's because you have no brain-waves, man.' Javed closed his notebook and returned it to his cricket bag.

'Give me that book one more time,' Manju retorted. 'I have brain-waves.'

'No. No. I don't feel any brain-waves around you.'

Manju showed Javed his middle finger. 'You're full of shit. You talk big but you're scared of a woman who wears half-moon glasses. Listen. Enough of this poetry of yours. I have a serious question. Do you know a cure for pimples? They became worse in Manchester. I think it was the cheese.'

'I never had pimples. Though I get worms when I eat bhelpuri.'

They watched the garden, and the taxis going around the curved colonnade of Horniman Circle.

'Have you been to Las Vegas?'

'No. Have you?'

'No. Where do *you* want to go?'

'There is a lighthouse all the way at the end of Mumbai, did you know?' Javed asked. 'It's true. It's the last thing in the city. Beyond Navy Nagar. You can see it as you come in a taxi from Babulnath: there are these little dots, and then a white tower. The lighthouse. Actually, it's white, red and black. You can walk to it over the rocks and mud at low tide. I tried it once, but the police chased me away. Fuck them. They're always after Javed Ansari. But I *will* do it, I will climb to the top of the lighthouse and scream to all of Mumbai, "Here is Javed Ansari! Here is Javed Ansari!" I have my birthday parties at the Taj or near the Taj. Where do you have yours?'

Manju jabbed Javed in the ribs.

'How many times have I told you? Don't talk about my father.'

'Who talked about your ...? I asked where you have your birthday parties. Wait. He *never* threw one for you?'

'I know what you're thinking, that my father is a bad father. I don't like that.'

'Bullshit. You know what I'm thinking? *You*?'

'Yes. I know what everyone's thinking,' Manju stated, proudly.

Nostrils flaring, Javed prodded the mind-reader in the ribs.

'Okay. Tell me what I am thinking about you right now.'

At which the back of Manju's head tingled and his feet began to tremble, even though he couldn't say why. He saw that Javed had gone quiet. His jaw was set, and he was holding his breath. Manju followed his eyes and spotted a man in a sailor's white cap and uniform walking past the library. Strong, thick, hairy arms; and his bell-bottom trousers fitted him snugly around the waist. The sailor now stopped, as if he could sense something, and turned his head.

'He saw you,' Javed whispered. 'Manju, he's coming here! He's going to beat you and rape you!'

But Manju had long ago disappeared.

•

He got back to Chheda Nagar, climbed up to the fourth floor of the Tattvamasi Building, and at once something was wrong.

Mohan Kumar turned up the volume on the TV when he saw his son. 'You just missed the news. Sit.'

As Manju obeyed his father, the newsreader announced that two more ministers in Madhya Pradesh had stated that the increasingly fashionable practice of homosexuality, sanctioned neither by the Indian Penal Code nor by four thousand years of Hindu civilization, should be curbed at once and that nationwide 'rehabilitation centres' should be established, incorporating a daily regimen of cold showers and group exercises for young deviants, so they could learn the value of physical hygiene and family life.

Wiping his face with the back of his palm, Manju turned his eyes towards his father, who did not move.

Next, the newsreader announced that the record for the highest cricket score by a Mumbai schoolboy, only recently held by Radha Kumar (388 runs), and surpassed by his own brother Manjunath (497), had now been super-surpassed.

A fifteen-year-old left-hander named T.E. Sarfraz Khan, batting at number four for IES Sule Guruji, in a Harris Cup match at the Fort Vijay Cricket Club, had broken Manju's record by scoring 603 not out. He had flicked, cut and pulled for two days; and at the end of the match, he had gone in a car to Bandra to see Shah Rukh Khan, who had called him a teenage human skyscraper.

Mohan Kumar turned to his son. So *this* was the news. *I am not the best anymore.* Manju's heart beat with guilt. He looked at his father's shrunken face, and he felt his own face change. This was what came of spending too much time with that makad.

He went and stood by the fridge, looking at the stack of expensive cricket bats next to it. He felt unworthy of touching any of them. Robusta!

That night, as he lay down to sleep, Manju saw the numerals '603' burning in fire on the wall of his bedroom; he got out of bed and, forging a bat from the darkness, he took guard.

He lay down again, telling himself it was time to rest, so his chest could expand and his forearms strengthen, but could not sleep. Now he saw words in fire – on the inside of his eyelids.

Simile: The king was like a tiger in battle.

Metaphor: The king was a tiger in battle.

Epithet: The Tiger-King.

Apostrophe: O thou Tiger-King!

The two words ('Tiger' and 'King') drew together, tighter and tighter: until they fused and became something new, blacker than the darkness and brighter than fire.

Then it was as if a midnight sun split open his room: because Manjunath Kumar had understood the rhetoric.

In the morning he called Javed from a pay-phone, without wiping the receiver, and said he wanted to know more about the rhetoric. And about poetry.

And about *everything*.

•

The Gateway of India had vanished. The Taj Mahal Hotel was no more. The entire Indian Ocean? Boiled and evaporated.

'Is that Ricky Pointing?'

And all because a middle-aged white man with greying hair, wearing a plain T-shirt and blue shorts, was standing in front of the Gateway, signing autographs. Hundreds were gathering.

'No. Are you mad? And it's Pon-ting anyway.'

'I hate cricket, dude. How will I know who that is?'

'It's Steven Waugh.'

'Who?'

'Steven Waugh?'

'I've never heard of him. Now go get his autograph.'

'No way. Waugh will want *my* autograph next year. Just you wait.'

Sofia laughed. 'Sure.'

Avoiding the crowds around Steve Waugh, the two went down the steps to the boat docked at Jetty Number Two. It was getting ready to leave, and Radha had to help Sofia on board just before the trembling plank was pulled away. They found her 'crew' waiting on the upper deck of the boat – a girl with blonde streaks in her hair, and two boys, each of whom had big curly hair and wore horn-rimmed glasses. One of them, so Sofia said, was the son of a policeman.

The water began to seethe; a milky wave slapped the stone wall that stands around the Gateway of India, returning to the tourists some of the rubbish they and their predecessors had tossed into the sea.

Burning diesel generously, the ferry was heading away from the city.

'That's the RC Church. In Cuffe Parade. It's too gorgeous.'

'She's just learnt this word, so she's using it everywhere. Too, too gorgeous.'

'Fuck off.'

'Have you noticed how girls these days use dirtier language than boys?'

'Shut off.'

'You said "Shut off". Everyone, did you hear?'

Their chit-chat was interrupted by a dark, sweat-covered man, climbing onto the upper deck and asking for tickets.

'That ... ?' The conductor pointed at Radha's bag, '... is goods. Means you have to pay extra.'

'It's not goods,' Radha said.

He removed an object from the bag to substantiate his claim. It was a shining slice of true wood: a Sunny Tonny Genuine English Willow bat with brand-new leather handle. All the noise was knocked out of the ticket-collector: hadn't he too once hoped to play for Mumbai? He opened his mouth and left.

Radha had grown his hair long and tied it in a ponytail; with his powerful chest and arms and the contrasting delicacy of his eyes, he had fulfilled his boyish promise of film-star looks. Sofia slid a foot from her chappals, and touched Radha's cricket bat with her toes. Then one of his feet came to the bat's defence.

The ferry passed near oil tankers anchored in mid-ocean; garbage and seagulls bobbed up and down on the waves.

The girl with blonde streaks in her hair had been studying Radha.

'You were on TV, yes or no?' she asked, when the foot wrestling had ended. 'You scored that 300. Shah Rukh Khan met you, yes or no?'

Radha gave her his television smile. 'I scored 388. Yes. I met Shah Rukh Khan. He called me a human skyscraper. On Selection Day I will be picked for Mumbai.'

The blonde girl looked impressed.

'Here's a quiz for you: What does the term KKK stand for in modern cricket?' Radha asked her.

'No. What does it mean?'

'Kiss, Kock and Kuddle. KKK. Isn't that funny?' Radha grinned. 'Hey, Sofia, I made that up myself.'

Perhaps he could score with Sofia *and* this one with the blonde streaks. Anything goes on Alibagh, right?

'His brother scored 600 or something and broke his record,' Sofia said. 'Why don't you ever bring Manju along?'

In the distance, Alibagh just about made itself visible. Radha persisted with his TV smile.

'Your brother has big eyes, so cute. The girls are going to go crazy for him.'

Still smiling, Radha narrowed his eyes and lowered his voice: 'For your information: one, he didn't score 600, and two, *he's* not going crazy for the girls.'

But no one had heard him: because the policeman's son, rummaging about in his backpack, had produced a pack of condoms.

'Hey, cricketer,' the other boy shouted. 'You know what this is? KKK. Kondom, Kondom, Kondom.' The girls laughed.

'I have many more inside my bag. The *real* KKK.'

'He's so funny,' Sofia said.

He stole *my* joke, Radha thought. To hell with these rich kids. Big thief walks free. He knew that Sofia was the only one here who was different – for the others, I'm just the boy from the slum, he thought, and looked down at his dirty shoes.

Then he closed his eyes and tightened his grip on his cricket bat: when the moment comes, when Radha Krishna Kumar scores his double century for India in the World Cup, when his name will be applauded in far-off and wonderful places like Cape Town and Christchurch and Trinidad, we'll see who is laughing.

When he opened his eyes, Radha saw small white birds skimming the waves. The euphoria faded; his smile disappeared; he remembered his younger brother.

The boat docked; people shrieked; the girls held on to the seats for support and almost knocked Radha into the water.

When they reached Alibagh, the blonde and the boys walked down a grey beach. Radha kept his eyes on the water's edge, where indistinct birds left deep black prints on the sand.

Sofia said, 'You were saying something about Manju? I didn't hear.'

Radha had seen something dark moving within the white surf – a turtle, or something like a turtle. He gnawed at his fingernails, and spat.

'I said *nothing* about Manju.'

With his cricket bat in hand, he walked into the water, and the ocean swelled, mockingly, around his feet.

Two nights ago the TV had been on, and Radha, seeing Manju sitting on the ground and watching with narrowed eyes, had thought, *CSI Las Vegas*. But no: not *CSI*. It was a programme about the gays in America: they could now marry each other. He had stood behind his younger brother, watching him watch the programme. Manju heard his breathing, and jumped, and turned the television off: it was that leap, more than anything else, that had made Radha's heart pound.

Now he smashed his bat into the Arabian Sea.

Is the world's second-best batsman a homo? And is the world's best batsman, the one with a secret contract, not going to be selected for Mumbai? Radha waded deeper into the ocean. He bashed at the waves with his SG Sunny Tonny. 'Weight-transfer issue.' The phrase was as heavy as a death-sentence. His jeans were now wet above the ankles, and he felt their soaking mass pulling him down. Weight-transfer. What I wouldn't give you, ocean, to make this problem go away. The water had risen to his knees. See, sometimes I have to drink a beer to go to sleep. And when I wake up, the eyelids do not want to open, and a voice in my head says, 'What does the morning have to do with a man like you, who can't even *hold* a bat?' And then the voice says, 'Your little brother is a homo, and *you* can't hold a bat anymore.'

Why? Why? Why?

Someone up there was rewriting the promised contract, and Radha Kumar, who could do nothing to undo the changes to the script, who had learnt – as his father had – what it meant to be only a man before he had learnt what it meant to be fully a man, bludgeoned the waves around him with his bat.

'Radha!' Someone was shouting at him. 'Come back, are you crazy?'

The water rose above his knees now. Wading deeper into the sea, Radha Kumar raised his bat and looked around for that turtle.

•

While Manju slept in Mumbai, someone was thinking about him on the mainland.

A white moon moved over Navi Mumbai, and Javed Ansari had slipped from his bedroom, passed the couch on which his father snored, the cricket magazines his father had left on the dinner table in a pathetic attempt to revive his fading interest in cricket, opened a door, and walked, a free man, into the night. Vashi was deserted. Javed walked past a government school: *click, click*, he heard a rolled-up flag knocking against the metal pole in the school compound. A bike had toppled over outside the school; a policeman slept at a traffic light. Javed walked down the centre of the road, knowing that all the gates of the night were open to him. He could just kick at a door, go into someone's flat and rob it, he thought, and half considered the idea before laughing into the darkness: U-ha, U-ha. Money was for idiots. Money *and* cricket were for idiots. He grabbed at the night air as if it were black, physical material, coal that his strong fist could crush into diamond.

Poetry.

Wiping the sweat off his forehead, Javed looked up: the moon waited white and immense over the earth, like a mandate to dream and create.

'Sean Connery,' he said out loud. Yeah, he had looked him up on the Internet. Very handsome man, Manju: but seriously old, too.

With a grin, Javed directed a giant brain-wave right at the Tattvamasi Building in Chheda Nagar, Chembur.

Pass me the hammer, Miss Moneypenny. I'm a young Javed Ansari!

•

Over the next few weeks, Manju became aware that two parties were in open conflict for possession of something precious and hidden inside him: his future.

First, his father took Manju to the local Subramanya temple and made him put ten rupees into the collection box before reminding him to keep his end of the contract with God and drop out of education, as he had long ago promised his father he would (and as the great Sachin himself did, remember), to concentrate full-time on cricket. 'Yes, Appa, I'll do it,' Manju said.

He went straight to a pay-phone near the train station, wiped the receiver clean with his shirt, and called Javed, who listened and said: 'Unless you want to be a slave, you must never drop out of college.'

Manju, in principle, agreed.

He gave Javed his word, no matter what manipulation his father and Tommy Sir tried, he *would* study all day and all night for the exams, and *would* get into Ruia College.

But the next morning, he went to JJ Hospital morgue. The boys were practising cricket at Azad Maidan, and he, still in his cricket whites, just slipped down the road, and took the bus. He found the morgue and told the guard, 'Let me in, please.' The old man in khaki squinted at him: 'Only doctors, interns or medical students are let in.'

'But I play *cricket*,' Manju said.

'Fine,' the guard said. 'Go on in.'

So at last Agent Grissom of the CSI Team (Las Vegas) walked into the JJ Hospital morgue (Mumbai) and suddenly shivered in the cold, and couldn't go on.

'Why not?' Javed asked, when Manju, almost in tears, called him from a one-rupee pay-phone.

'It smelled.'

'Dead bodies smell. Didn't you know?'

'But Javed, it *smelled.*'

Finished. Manju could never again imagine himself Agent Grissom. He couldn't even eat his food; his gorge felt full of all that was awful and real, and it came out of his eyes as tears.

How Javed laughed at the other end of the line.

'Maybe I can go back to Manchester.'

'Why? You think dead bodies don't stink in Manchester? Idiot.'

Manju was so angry he announced he wouldn't go to Ruia College. Or any college.

Two minutes later he dropped another rupee into the pay-phone, wiped the receiver clean again, and called Javed back to say, 'Don't tell anyone what I told you, okay? About the morgue?'

'I won't. But did you mean what you said, Manju, are you really not going to college?'

'I mean it.'

'You really *are* a slave. You think Javed Ansari wants to talk to slaves on the phone? I thought you were on my wavelength.'

Then, ten minutes later, Manju wiped the receiver clean a third time, and called Javed to inform him he *was* on the same wavelength.

•

August was almost over when one morning Manju tiptoed out of the boys' bedroom, turned the tap in the sink, and ran three wet fingers through his hair.

'Manju, don't think I didn't see you. Are you going to JJ Hospital morgue again? To look at naked dead women? Foreign naked dead women?'

Mohan Kumar followed the boy out of their flat; he leaned over the edge of the stairwell, hearing the boy's quick footsteps, and boomed into the echoing airshaft: 'Are you going to meet that Mohammedan cricketer at the morgue?'

From down below in the stairwell, Manju stopped and turned his face up to his father's.

'Why *do* you see that Javed Ansari so often?' Mohan Kumar asked.

They stared. Then Manju stuck his tongue out at his father, and showed him his middle finger.

'Mongoose has got to you, my little Manju ...' his father whimpered. 'Mongoose, Mongoose, Mon—'

'Don't call him that again!' Manju shouted from below. 'He's my friend.'

He went out of the building, turned around, came back in, and this time shouted:

'He's my *real* father.'

Free! Manju steadied his bag on his shoulder and walked fast. The door of the Subramanya temple was open. Chanting in Sanskrit the priest exalted the dark deity with a flaming brass vessel. Manju bowed before the fire-garlanded idol and asked the God of Cricket for a big favour:

'Please don't let my father stop me from going to college.'

Done praying, he walked to the train station, stopped, remembered, and ran back to the temple to ask for another thing.

'*And* please let Javed stop losing his hair.'

Half an hour later, Manju got off at the Matunga station and stood, in a crowd of teenagers, outside the gates of Ruia College.

The third list of admissions had been pasted to a bulletin board on the other side of the college gate.

Manju had known already from the email and the letter, but he wanted to touch the admissions list. Touch it.

The gates were closed, so he walked back towards the station. They were playing tennis at the Matunga Gymkhana; someone threw a ball high up, and the act seemed to say 'freedom' in a way nothing in cricket could.

When Manju walked back to Ruia, the gates had just opened. The crowd rushed in.

Jostling against the others, he stood in front of the noticeboard where the admissions list was posted; his heart began to pound.

Even as elbows and fingers poked him, glancing over his shoulder to where he imagined Navi Mumbai would be, he fired, high over land and creek, a giant brain-wave of his own.

Javed. Javed. We did it. I got into Ruia.

Three months to Selection Day

First year of junior college

The Banganga tank, in Walkeshwar, high above south Mumbai, late in the evening. This is one of the oldest parts of the city, and even now, with its temple bells and wandering cows and narrow streets, it retains the look of a village tucked inside the metropolis.

White tubelights shone around the enormous open tank, and ducks floated on the black water, as two young men walked down the old stone steps that led to the water. One of them was in stained cricket whites; the other wore a leather jacket over blue jeans.

'Do you ever miss it?'

'It, Sir Manju, being?'

'Cricket.'

'Only you would ask a question like that, Sir Manju.'

Just a fortnight into junior college, and Javed had reinvented his image. His long-sleeved white shirts had given way to T-shirts and a leather jacket; the gold earring was gone, and his wavy hair was now streaked with copper highlights. It was receding, so dyeing it was the right decision, Manju felt.

'*Never*? You never miss it?'

'Why ... why ... Sir Manju ... why ... would I miss that pro-puh-gun-duh and manipulation and mind-depopulation? I am no slave, Sir Manju.'

This was a new mannerism Javed had picked up ever since he'd started junior college in Navi Mumbai: a pout of his lips, an exaggerated emphasis on a random word in a sentence, followed by a spitfire burst of syllables, all delivered with a lopsided grin and an unstable head, a confounding mannerism which reminded Manju of the cricket commentator Harsha Bhogle.

'By the way, you *like* this place? I now come here sometimes on the weekend,' Javed said. 'There is some energy-*wenergy* here, isn't there?'

On the final step above the water, the two boys sat down.

'The monkeys are terrible around here,' Javed said. 'Watch out for your phone and wallet.'

Javed gestured at the vast black water and the searing reflections of the white tubelights. 'Isn't it beautiful, Manju? Isn't it gorgeous?'

'Gorgeous,' Manju repeated. '*This* is gorgeous.' He pinched Javed's jacket between his fingers, and squeezed the rich dark leather.

Javed chuckled. 'Don't rape my jacket, man.' He snapped his fingers at Manju, who reluctantly let go of the leather.

'The jacket isn't gorgeous, anyway. I am. Yes or no?' Manju smirked.

'Give me an answer, Manju.'

Javed thrashed his legs about when he did not get an answer.

Gorgeous.

From the figure of Javed, who was now spreadeagled on the steps in his leather jacket and tight blue jeans, Manju's gaze moved to the tank and its skin of glossy black water. *Gorgeous.* It turned into a milky-white cloud: he remembered a morning when thick fog covered the Western Ghats as their bus climbed up the road, and the only things piercing through the fog were giant roses – no, not a rose, a mountain flower larger than the largest red rose on earth – and Manju felt he was flying high over the earth. When the sun finally pierced through the fog, the first thing he saw, seated on a low mountain wall, its enormous wings folded and its eyes intent on the bus, was a vulture.

Manju smiled with pleasure, and leaned back in stages until his neck touched a damp stone step. He shivered. Stretching out his hand, he pinched Javed's leather jacket again.

'Let go of my jacket, man. You're crazy.'

I'm crazy? Manju thought. That was what people called Javed. Your rich crazy Muslim friend. Radha had told Manju, with much glee, about a rumour circulating among the cricketers that Javed Ansari (though now an ex-cricketer, still very much the focus of gossip) had been caught by the police a second time. On Independence Day. He and his friends had been driving about Powai without a licence: caught, taken to the station, and then bailed out – once again – by his father. Manju had been waiting for Javed to say something about the whole affair.

'Don't call *me* names. I don't get arrested by the police.'

'Who told you?' Javed looked at him.

'Everyone in cricket knows. Mad Max Gang. You guys must be idiots. No one else in all of Mumbai gets caught by the police for driving without a licence. Just your gang.'

'Fuck cricket.' Javed spat out the words at Manju, staining his face with saliva. 'Fuck them all. They have no right to talk about me. It's all pro-puh-gun-duh.'

'I know, I know. Tatas Batting, McDonald's Bowling. If you think cricket is for idiots, why are you imitating the biggest idiot in cricket, Harsha Bhogle?'

When Javed became furious these days, his scalp went back several inches, and this hint of premature baldness highlighted the vein in his forehead even more prominently: how Manju loved the sight of that face – volatile, vicious, glowing with dark blood.

'Fuck you,' Javed said. 'Stay here and rot here.'

And there were footsteps. Should I make the effort to run, Manju, tired from cricket practice, asked himself, or just wait till he comes back?

He waited: and sure enough Javed came back, and stood over him with folded arms.

'I do *not* sound like Harsha Bhogle. Just say that, and I'll go. And I'll never see you again.'

'It's not that easy to leave cricket behind, is it, Sir Harsha Bhogle Ansari?' Manju winked at him.

Javed nodded, as if agreeing with Manju.

'You want to hear a poem, Manju? A Bhogle poem?'

'Tell me.'

'Listen:

> '"*Twilight is my mother's favourite hour.*
> *When I stand in it I am in her power.*"'

Manju couldn't breathe. He stood up at once and climbed two steps to bring his face level with Javed's.

'That's *my* mother! You bastard! You unwrite that poem at once. At once.'

'Sorry, sorry, sorry, Sir Manju.'

Disdain, as Javed smiled, seemed to exude out of him like a musk, a secretion of his endocrinal glands, like something – Manju thought – you could milk out of his body and sell in small glass bottles in Bandra. ('Contempt: A New Fragrance for Men.') Plunging his face into his black leather jacket he laughed into it. U-ha, U-ha, U-ha. By now Manju was familiar with Javed's gruff cackle, both mocking and self-mocking – at once taunt, defiance, confession and plea. It was his way of saying, Yeah, I stole it, sorry, I shouldn't have done it, fuck you.

They were even: friends with each other again. As they left Banganga village, and went through Walkeshwar, the lower part of Malabar Hill, they could see the lights of south Mumbai below them.

'Come over to Navi Mumbai this weekend. Tell your father you have a cricket camp in Pune or shit.'

'What about *your* father? What will he say if I come and stay with you?' Manju asked.

'He *wants* to see you. You know what my father calls me at home? The Nurse. Javed the nurse. It's true. After my mother left him, I've been taking care of him.' Javed stretched his neck from side to side; his voice softened. 'When he falls ill, I put four Disprin tablets in a glass of water and bring it to him. Now my father says, Javed has forgotten me and is only a nurse to this Manjunath, so I want to see my competitor. Come this weekend.'

He reached over and touched Manju's face, and the boy's body warmed at his touch.

Someone blew a sharp horn; right behind them, traffic was moving down Malabar Hill.

When Javed lowered his hand, Manju picked up a stone and threw it at the city.

'Can't come. I have *Young Lions*. They're doing a new television programme.'

'You?' Javed turned. 'Wasn't it Radha?'

'This time it's me.' Manju tried to throw another stone, but Javed held his arm:

'Are you happy to be on television? Tell me the truth.'

'No. I'm stealing from Radha again.'

'Don't lie.'

'I'm not a thief. Radha is the Young Lion.'

'I said don't lie to Javed. Are you happy to be on TV?' Freeing his arm, Manju threw the second stone at Mumbai.

'Yes!'

•

> The thunderous opening chords of Richard Strauss's '*Also sprach Zarathustra*' fill the darkness. A single stump stands in the middle of a pitch.
>
> We hear footsteps, as a boy in cricket whites comes running with a red ball in his hand. Leaping high with the red ball he rolls his arms over. The inspirational music reaches its crescendo as the stump is knocked over.

VOICE-OVER:

Three years after the original groundbreaking *Young Lions* programme, we revisit the boys on whom we were the first to cast a spotlight. Will the pace of Deennawaz Shah triumph over the quicksilver footwork of T.E. Sarfraz, and can either of them match the mighty forearms of Manjunath Kumar?

YOUNG LIONS: THE NEXT GENERATION BURGEONING LEGENDS

MONDAY 6.30 P.M. REPEATED ON WEDNESDAY

We discovered our first Young Lion this evening three years ago in a slum in Dahisar. Today, he lives in a good neighbourhood in Chembur: proof of the magical power of cricket to uplift lives in today's India.

In this clip, taken at the Catholic Gymkhana, 23 April this year, Manjunath Kumar shows us why he is so special: the ball, pitched short, moves into him at 110 kilometres per hour. Observe how the Young Lion's first movement is across the line, 'I intend to pull this,' but then he braces his ribs, 'I will let this go by,' only to turn his wrists at the final instant, and send it flying down to the fine leg boundary: 'Fooled all of you.' Cricketing experts describe young Manju as cunning, deceptive and brutal. Before we talk to him about his practice methods and cricketing secrets, let us see him handling the full-length delivery. This next clip is from MCA, 14 February, Valentine's Day…

A Portrait in Numbers: Manjunath Kumar

Young Lions Expert Panel Ranking: 2nd

Height: 5'2"

Weight: (no data)

Average (within India): 46.70

Average (outside India): 45.00

Strike rate (per 100 balls): 91.40

Highest score (within India): 497

Off-side to leg-side scoring ratio: 38:62

Coach ranking (city-wide survey of school coaches): 2

Peer ranking (city-wide survey of school cricketers): 19

How angry my brother must be after seeing that programme.

•

The net is held aloft by bamboo poles; inside the net stands Radha Kumar. Blue helmet, trembling bat. The net makes a box around him, as a draughtsman makes cubing for a study of his model. Now a red ball comes at Radha, who lifts his shoulders and lets it go. All around the net, people take a step back. The ball hits the net, it vibrates; the onlookers draw closer again. The batsman shuffles his centre pad, his pads, and then, after sweeping the ground with his bat, suddenly removes his helmet, throws it to the ground, and waits. Now the spinner bowls at him. Down the pitch, cover-driven.

Standing behind the net, Manju feels his big brother's familiar timing. *That* remains. What is gone is the power that accompanied the timing.

To Manju's left, a girl in a grey T-shirt stood watching him: her thick hair, freshly shampooed, parted down the middle, was drawn over her shoulder in a neat, glossy swoop, like an eagle's folded wing.

Like all celebrity sportsmen, Radha Kumar was allowed the luxury of a pitch-side girlfriend, even if there was some ambiguity about the status of their relationship. Running her fingers now and then through her glistening, geometrically perfect length of hair,

Sofia kept watching the younger Kumar, oblivious to the handful of male spectators who were watching her.

'I'm going to pitch it short, Radha. Helmet.'

As Radha bent down and reached for a blue helmet, his eyes met his younger brother's.

Radha Krishna Kumar: now a former Young Lion.

Manju smelled fear. He could smell his brother's sweat: and of the seven types of sweat, this was the one signifying fear. Yes, *fear*: Manju smelled every fear in the world coming from his brother's face; and smelled every fear in the world coming from his brother's bat.

'Duffer! Duffer! What have you done to your batting?' Tommy Sir had come to the nets yelling at the top of his voice.

'You changed your grip! You cut your backlift!'

'My father. Coach Sawant,' Radha explained. It had been a decision taken jointly by Sawant and his father, based on computer analysis of Radha's recent dismissals, the backlift should be sacrificed for a longer stay at the crease.

Tommy Sir placed his hands on the netting and shouted at the boy inside.

'You're now batting like a girl. Congratulations.'

Radha removed his helmet; he wiped his face with his shoulder; he tried to deny the charge.

Tommy Sir's voice softened when he saw the boy's face inside the helmet.

'You should ask me about these things, son. But don't worry: you are lean, mean and magnificent. He reached over and patted Radha's shoulder. We'll fix your problems, don't worry. Now it's time for your brother to bat. Manju, pad up.'

When she heard this, Sofia turned with a smile towards the younger Kumar, letting him see all the dark spots on her neck. At once Manju glowed with pleasure: for he knew that he was the only boy in all of Mumbai who was *truly* lean, mean and magnificent with a cricket bat.

•

After sixteen days apart, the two friends were meeting again, at a table in the Golden Punjab Hotel, not far from the Vashi train station.

Javed was still grinning and wobbling his head like Harsha Bhogle. He had gone with his father to Aligarh, and from there they had taken a taxi around Uttar Pradesh. It was the first time he was seeing his home state. From the Taj in Agra, they went to Benaras, and then to Kanpur. UP was one big fucking brain-wave, man. *Amazing*. Near Agra, Javed and his father went to this dargah – 'You know what that means, Manju? – and there was this marble slab inside, and there was this long groove in the marble, and you know what my father told me, Manju? That in the old days a Persian poet used to sit on that marble slab and write with a peacock feather, and that when he grew tired, the poet would set his peacock feather down in that groove in the stone. I touched that groove, Manju: look!'

Javed showed his fingertip, brought it nearer, and touched it to Manju's forehead: Manju smiled, as if thrilled, but then began to cry.

As he sat curling a lock of hair over and over again around a finger, he could see, through his wet eyes, grey tubes of chicken seekh kebab in a rich red sauce lying on a plate in front of him. Using three fingers, Javed picked one up, squeezed the kebab in two with his thumb, and rolled the longer half towards his friend. Manju shook his head; he kept working at the lock of hair on his forehead.

'And what are you crying over *this* time, my little Sachin?'

'You don't know what happened to me. You were gone for so long and you don't know what happened. You didn't even call me from Aligarh,' Manju said, and the tears came out freely.

'Sorry. Tell me what happened.' Javed left his food. He came and sat by his friend and listened.

Chemistry Practicals Lab made him nervous, Manju confessed, so he had misread the level of the hydrochloric acid in the long test tube during titration. He kept taking the upper meniscus reading –

he showed Javed how the liquid sticks to glass and gives you a false reading. After that even his litmus tests were screwed. Screwed. He was going to fail and they were all going to mock him, and then throw him out of college, and he would never become a scientist in America.

'*That's* all? No one's going to throw you out of college. Before the year end you will be the best student in chemistry. I promise you. Does Javed ever lie?'

'No,' Manju said, still curling the lock of hair on his forehead. 'Have you made new friends in college, Javed? Even before you went to Aligarh I didn't hear from you for two days.'

For once Javed spoke slowly and clearly. 'I'm here, you're there, how can we *meet* every day?'

It made sense to Manju, and yet it was unfair. He thought it had been a deal; he would study hard and get into science at college and in return he would see Javed every day.

'What about *you*, Sir Manju?' Javed asked. 'Other day I called, and you didn't pick up the phone.'

'The pictures.'

'You saw a picture? With who?'

'Alone.'

'Only mental patients go to the movies ... *alone*,' Javed said. 'Come to Navi Mumbai and watch movies with me.'

Manju felt a sense of elation. 'Really?' he asked, hoping that Javed would say more good things about him. He moved closer.

Only the sound of the laughing warned Manju that Javed's mood had changed, and that he had turned into the other 'J.A.' – the nasty one.

'U-ha, U-ha. Hey, Tendulkar. Find a new mirror.'

'Find a new mirror?' Manju asked. 'What does that mean?'

'It means you're not that good-looking. And you're always looking at yourself in the mirror. Even in the cinema hall I bet you were looking at yourself in any glass surface. Right? U-ha, U-ha.'

Manju had to contract the muscles in his throat to avoid replying to that. He felt the same numbness in his face and neck that he did when his father slapped him.

They walked, at first in silence, towards the train station. But suddenly Javed's face and mood changed, and he became playful again.

'Are you going to *practise*, Captain? Are you?'

Manju said nothing.

'Are you?'

'Yes.'

'No. You're not, Captain.'

'I'll find a way to study chemistry *and* practise cricket.'

'No. There is another reason, Captain,' Javed said, 'that I had to leave cricket, and it's the same reason you too will have to leave, sooner or later.'

Javed tickled him in the ribs.

'When we were in Uttar Pradesh, my father asked me if I wasn't interested in girls.'

As they crossed the road, an autorickshaw came between them; Manju hurried to catch up with Javed.

'And you said?'

'And I said, if I'm not, what is your problem, Daddy?'

'And he said?'

'Do whatever you want, as long as it doesn't cost me any money. Man, I love my father sometimes.'

Javed laughed: Manju could smell fat and meat and freedom.

'One time the wicket-keeper from that Dadar school asked me, you're a gay or what? Manju, has no one yet asked *you*?'

The question burned away the sun and the day; now Manju felt small and dark and as though a litre of pink disinfectant had invaded his stomach.

'Why … they would … me?'

He wished he had said it louder. He wished that Radha were here, by his side. But the only one here was Javed, grinning.

'Manju, stop being a slave. What's your problem if someone calls you a gay?'

Manju felt the sweat on his forehead.

'I know you're scared of everything, so I don't even talk about anything to do with sex when you're near me. But why just *look* at everything? It's not normal. Do something.'

'Fuck you.'

Now run.

'I'm asking you, what are you scared of? It's all normal, man. Don't let them brain-control you.'

But Manju stood frozen: Javed, as if he had read his mind, was laughing at him. U-ha. U-ha. In the coarseness of Javed's croak, in the length of pink gum that showed above his canines, Manju saw nothing but the contempt of one who knew more about the animal truths of sex and life.

'Fuck you.'

Without looking back, Manju ran to Vashi station, boarded a train and sat still all the way to Chembur. At dinner he looked at his father, and said, 'I'm going to cricket practice every evening from now till Selection Day.'

Mohan Kumar sighed.

'And will you un-shave? But I forgive you, Manju. Just promise me one thing, son. Promise me and Lord Subramanya you won't learn to drive a car, but from now on will stay pure and think only of cricket.'

Manju promised everything.

•

He *loved* playing tricks on her, her father. One morning every April he filled the house with green mangoes and then led her in, blindfolded, while the scent of raw fruit drove her mad. As his hand moved down his stomach, on which he could feel the downy hair that was growing up from his groin, Manju thought again of her childhood. Not his – *hers*. His mother's. Lying in bed with his eyes closed, he thought of the stories his mother had told her sons about her life in her father's home, and through which Manju understood what a childhood must be like for everyone else. His mother had loved her father more than anyone else on earth. He was tall, fair, handsome – people in the village used to call him their 'European uncle', because he was so light-skinned – and he loved her back. Each time he went to the market he returned with toys for her, but would say nothing to her, just leave them, as if by accident, on the dining table, or lying on the floor: and how she screamed with joy when she discovered them. One day, her father and she – just the two of them, no sisters or mother with them – took a bus and went up a mountain and all the way to the great temple of Tirupati. Yes! Just the two of them. Still rubbing his stomach hair, Manju nuzzled against his cotton pillow. This was the only place he had ever felt entirely safe: his mother's childhood.

•

Sitting at a terminal in the computer lab at Ruia College, he had been googling morgues in Manchester in a bid to revive the attractions of forensic science, until the noise from outside made it impossible.

It was the day of Durga Puja: the festival of the Mother Goddess.

Carrying his three textbooks, he came out of the college, and headed towards the source of the noise – the makeshift wooden pandals, each adorned with its twelve-foot idol of Ma Durga slaying the pitch-black buffalo-demon, in front of which devotees beat drums and burnt incense.

He stopped in front of the Matunga Gymkhana to watch the girls in white playing tennis. He looked at the legs of one of the girls, pale brown, glossy, with strong diamond-shaped calf muscles, and then up at her tight T-shirt, from which a golden necklace dangled.

'Wrong game, Tendulkar.'

A Honda City had stopped beside him, and a girl held a door open for Manju.

'Don't act as if you don't know me now,' Sofia said, as Manju looked about. 'Get in.'

'Is Radha here with you?'

'Why should he be? I was just going to Ram Ashraya to meet a friend. Get in. Manju, don't worry. Your father isn't here. That man tried to kill me in Ballard Estate. I feel sorry for you. Get in.'

The door was still open and the car was holding up traffic; so, Manju got in, closed the door behind him with one hand, and sat with the textbooks pressed against his chest.

Sofia smiled. He tried to read her mind.

'Tomorrow is your big Selectors' Day, isn't it? Everyone is so nervous right now. Are you nervous?'

As the car moved, Manju felt his stomach starting to churn.

'Hey. I asked, are you freaked out by Selectors' Day? I know that they asked you to come even though you're one year younger than everyone else.'

He wanted to raise his palm and just block Sofia out.

'No. I'm not nervous.'

'Salim,' the girl told her driver, 'this boy has no blood pressure. Look how cool he is the day before Selectors' Day.' Leaning in to him she whispered: 'Manju, be honest with me. I'm on *your* side, understand?'

'Yes,' Manju said.

The traffic was bad; a colossal image of Durga, seated on the back of a lorry, was approaching, surrounded by chanting and singing devotees, some of whom carried their own smaller idols of the Mother Goddess.

'Salim.' Sofia touched her driver's shoulder with her BlackBerry. 'You know who this is, Salim? He's Radha's brother. But he doesn't look like Radha, does he?'

'No, ma'am.'

An idol of Durga with a red tongue scraped past the windscreen as devotees transferred the goddess from one side of the car to the other.

'By the way, I'm participating in a paid marketing brand survey for Amaze cars versus Polo. Which do you prefer? Sorry. You can't drive. Your father won't let you.'

Manju concentrated on the image of the Goddess Durga, still in the distance, to calm himself.

'Radha has taught himself to drive. He'll teach me one day.'

Sofia clicked her tongue: sure, sure.

'You know Radha and I broke up, right? One day he hit me, and I said, Don't dare do that again. It's abuse. Get out of my life. But we're still friends. Do you approve of friendship after a relationship?'

'Yes,' Manju said.

Her magenta T-shirt had a gold-rimmed hole around her navel, and big letters above it said: POW. How silly he would look, Manju thought, wearing something like this; how silly *anyone* would look in it. Not Sofia, though. She pulled it off, she could pull anything off: she knew her prerogative as a rich girl in Mumbai, which was to be one step ahead of the city she lived in.

Sofia helped him understand Javed. The same note of irritation sounded in her voice even the first time she asked for something; and the same carelessness when probing the personal life of one not of her class.

'Salim,' Sofia said suddenly to her driver, 'Salim, be careful, we're going to hit and kill someone. Look at all these mad people doing this puja. All these *Hindus*! Did they walk out of a film set? Now, Manju, I'm on your side. We're all on your side. No one likes what your brother is saying about you, okay?'

Manju felt that churning in his stomach grow stronger and stronger. Ask her what your brother says about you, he told himself. Ask her. She knew this; Sofia, like his mother, like most women, could read minds.

'Are you scared of me, Manju? Don't be.'

She had rehearsed for this encounter: it was not by chance she had driven up just as he had stepped out of the college.

'People discuss you a lot, do you know this, Manju?' Sofia said at last. 'But we're *all* on your side. I told Racha, stop talking of your brother like this. I mean, it's Manju's choice, Manju's lifestyle, let him be whatever he wants. I defended you.'

That he was being talked about, analysed, and gossiped about, came as a shock; and as Manju sat with Sofia, he felt a net falling over him. Frenzied devotees of Goddess Durga pressed against the windows of the car.

'What does my brother say about me?'

'I just want to be your friend, Manju,' Sofia said, and bit her lip, and told herself she sounded exactly like one of the men who creep closer and closer but claim they are only looking for 'friendship'. But talking to Manju was so much harder than talking to his brother, who was a simple soul, after all.

Enough. She leaned forward and yelled at the driver's shoulder:

'Salim, stop the car at Ram Ashraya. Tendulkar,' she touched his shoulder, 'relax, okay? This is the twenty-first century and you are in junior college. Be who you are. Look at me, dude. The other day I told my father, I've grown up. I told him, Dad, I'm on the college committee to protect turtles and birds. We go to Crawford Market every Sunday to free them from cages. I'll protect you too, Manju.'

'Protect me?'

Fine. To make it clear to one and all that she was not behaving with Manju the way boys sometimes behaved with her, but out of a genuine and sincere interest to protect him, Sofia just cut through the bullshit and told Manju it was normal, perfectly normal, 100 per cent normal, lots of people these days were homosexuals, it was no big deal anymore, there was even a gay and lesbian club in Xavier's for chrissakes, so why make a fuss over the fact that his brother was going around telling everyone he was a—

The next thing Sofia knew, cymbals and drum-beats were deafening her and her driver had had to brake hard; because a door had opened in the moving car and a body had leapt out and run. Sofia reached over and shut the door at once.

•

Off stump line pakado, bhai. Kaise bowling kar rahe ho? New ball hain, waste mat karo!

Waiting, waiting. Now bowling.

Lavkar daud – Ramesh!

From the Fort Vijay Club, Manju had gone counter-clockwise around Azad Maidan, past the Lord Northbrook Cricket Club, the Times of India Sports Club, and the Bohra Cricketers Club until he was just outside the Young Hindu Cricket Club. Cloud and wind and unbearable sun; the smell of woodsmoke in the breeze; spike-marks in red mud; the sounds of balls being struck and bodies colliding from one match and another.

And at last he found what he had been searching for.

Radha Kumar, his brother, fielding in the covers, fingers spread out, eyes on the wicket.

There was a loud cry: a fielder, running after a ball from his own match, had been hit in the shin by a ball flying from another match, and had fallen with a cry. Now there were spots of blood on the mud. As he stood up, with torn trouser and bloody knee, the fielder grimaced at Manjunath.

At the far end of the maidan stood two traffic policemen.

Manju watched them.

When at last the match was over, Radha returned with the other boys, tossing the red ball from hand to hand with a big grin. Reaching his tent, he stopped.

He dropped the ball, and looked at his younger brother.

'Radha,' Manju said. 'What have you been telling people about me?'

Looking at the earth, Radha bit at his right thumbnail, tore away a part of it and let it fall.

'Radha. What have you been telling people about me?'

He did the same thing with his right index fingernail, and then looked at the ring finger as if he were considering whether to bite it;

instead, he turned and began to run. In his cricket whites Radha ran – and in T-shirt and jeans Manju ran after him – all the way down Azad Maidan and past Xavier's College, past the soccer ground from behind whose wall and barbed-wire fence came the noise of a marching band, and then to Metro Cinema, and through Dhobi Talao, before taking a left at Alfred, the dance bar he had visited only that weekend with his friends, and further past the blue Parsi Dairy Farm, and up the bridge, past a basket of peeled pineapples carried on a coolie's head, and down past the flyover, and out into Marine Drive and all the way to where the pigeons had huddled in the noisy kabootarkhana, the metal enclosure designed for them to gather and feed. A man in white pajamas, having just emptied a sack of grain for the birds, stood with his palms folded before their auspicious gluttony.

Radha stopped, panting: from here he could see a game of cricket being played in the Gymkhana beyond the pigeon-stand; and another game of cricket in the Gymkhana beyond that one; and another game of cricket beyond that one too. There was nowhere to escape.

He turned around to see Manju slowing down.

Sounding its long horn, a train drew into Marine Lines station.

Folding his arms across his chest, Radha braced himself for a blow, as Manju came running up to him. He kept his eyes on the feeding mass of birds, the rippling crowd of emerald necks and grey pulsing bodies, which paid attention only to their free grain, and waited.

Nothing. Absolutely nothing.

Manju had moved a pace to his right. There was something new in his face: there was malice in his smile. As Radha watched, he climbed over into the kabootarkhana, lifted his shoe over one of the feeding pigeons, which kept clucking at the grain, oblivious to the danger over its head; he kept his shoe like this, and then, very deliberately, brought it down on the bird.

'Manju!'

Everything else flew away at once.

The bird was still alive. Alone in the kabotaarkhana, it thrashed about the grain bed in mad, helpless circles.

Radha slapped his brother.

In the train to Chembur they stood side by side, looking at each other.

Even before the train had come to a stop, Manju leapt out and ran; Radha followed, trying to hit him from behind, all the way past the Subramanya temple, and to Tattvamasi Building, where they went to the backyard and slapped and punched each other by the brick wall, even as the neighbours watched, slapped and punched each other until they were simply too tired. They walked up the stairs to the fourth floor, drank water that their father poured into glasses for them, ate dinner, washed their faces, went to bed, and turned off the lights.

Manju opened his eyes and saw the figure standing by his bed. He averted his face and clenched his jaw.

And waited for it to start all over again.

But no blow came; and the body fell back onto Radha's bed. Manju heard sobbing in the dark.

'Manju, I'm sorry I said those things about you. Sofia kept asking about you and kept asking and kept asking and I got angry and … Manju, you always win, you are the golden boy, what about me? Do you want me to carry your cricket bag for you?'

The sobbing grew louder.

'… he said I was lean, mean and … Manju …'

It comes slowly to some: they sink by degrees, over years, into paranoia – and to some the estrangement from reality occurs in a single shearing instant. For Radha it had occurred at the nets: it was the moment Tommy Sir touched his shoulder and said, 'You are lean, mean and magnificent, son.'

Because Tommy Sir had never praised him when he was good.

'… he said … lean, mean and …'

With a single exertion, Manju had moved his brother's moist, pathetic body away from his bed.

'You should have practised.'

Practised? Manju observed that the word went to Radha uninsulated. His body trembled.

My big brother must be thinking, what else have I done in my life until now other than *practise cricket*?

Jumping from the bed, Radha stood over his younger brother and made a fist: Manju grinned as his brother mimed a blow right at his neck.

'Hey. Homo. Listen. You have to throw your wicket tomorrow. Get out early. Tomorrow is my day. If you don't get out early I'll kill you. You hear me?'

Manju just thrashed his feet about.

Radha tightened his fist, and then let it go, and sagged, and sobbed.

'I'm sorry, Manju. You're not a gay.'

Manju ordered: 'Say it once more.'

'You're not a gay.'

After making him say it a third time, Manju sighed: for the fighting was over.

'Now don't cry like a girl. Go to sleep.'

'Yes, Manju,' Radha said.

Though he could hear his brother, next to him, sobbing, though his own face was bruised and his neck oily with sweat, Manju was exultant: he was thinking only of the moment when he had stepped, knowingly, on the fat body of that pigeon and held it under his shoe. Something new was starting in Manjunath's life; he had tasted power.

•

From Metro Cinema to Victoria Terminus the black avenue is deserted beneath a series of pulsing red traffic lights. The Municipal Building is lit up, but VT station is just a white circle inside a rim of gold: just a clock that says '5.45 a.m.' People are sleeping, entire clans are asleep on the footpath, but in a blue stall near the station, the first cups of tea are ready, served by a young man who is so fresh from the village that he does not know what you mean when you ask him for 'takeaway', or 'parcel', or even 'just give it to me in a plastic cup, will you?' Now a policeman blows a whistle: the traffic moves. The sky is a faint violet, and the great mass of the Gothic train station, like a dreadnought that has lain in wait all night, emerges into view. Pigeons cluster on rooftops, landing and taking off, flying in loops and returning, as if rehearsing their movements for the whole day. Outside Azad Maidan, a boy wearing a black eyepatch sleeps on his mother's stomach, his mouth open, as a blue-masked municipal worker advances towards them with her broom. In this chaos of rubble, raw earth and dust, an articulate sound announces that it is morning: a cricket bat is tapping the earth. Beyond the fence at Azad Maidan, a wilderness of waste paper and abandoned plastic appears to have risen up and taken human form: hundreds of young men in whites are bowling and batting, and more join them every minute.

This is, at last, Selection Day.

Selection Day

Mohan Kumar woke to find that Manju was missing from his bed, but he was relieved that his bat and his cricket gear were also missing. The father of champions went to the kitchen, turned on the lights, and looked about for the earthen pot filled with boiled water that the maid left by the fridge every night.

From the kitchen, he could see Radha, sleeping on his bed like a cat, all his white teeth showing.

Mohan sat down next to his older son and sipped his water.

Radha opened his eyes, but did not move.

'I wondered all night: did Lord Subramanya mix things up? Give one boy the talent and the other the desire? But no, such things don't happen to those who have trusted God, Radha. You *will* be selected today.'

With a kick of his legs, Radha rose from the bed.

From a drawer in his room, he took out a plastic envelope, placed it on his table, and withdrew a sacred cricket glove. He raised it to his face, touching it to his right eye, and then to his left.

At the Subramanya temple, the doors were opening for the morning, and it took a few minutes for the priest to chant the necessary Sanskrit and circle the dark image with the sacred fire, the aarthi. Because everyone in the neighbourhood knew it was Selection Day, the priest revived a South Indian tradition; raising a silver crown, God's own crown, he placed it three times on the cricketer's head. The third time it touched his skull, Radha had the hallucination that the God of Cricket, Subramanya, was standing before him, mounted on his sacred serpent Vasuki, and saying, in a voice familiar from a thousand television advertisements, in Sachin Tendulkar's own voice:

'My son, you were not born to fail: believe in me, today of all days.'

An hour later, at the Azad Maidan, Radha Kumar was heading to the crease; a sacred glove, Sachin's own, bulged from his pocket. He stood at the crease, taking guard with his SG Sunny Tonny bat, genuine English willow.

Bad luck can take a million forms at the start of an innings. A feather touch on an outswinger; a French cut onto the stumps; a deflection off the pads into the hands of forward short leg. Survive till you reach 20, and you are settled in. When you cross 50, the selector's brain will say: 'This boy is special.'

Radha batted as many of them had not seen him bat in over a year. The bowlers pitched it short at him, and then they pitched it full. He cut; he drove.

When he reached 20, he took guard again. *Subramanya, God of Cricket, it's only thirty runs from here to safety.*

A ball had rolled onto his pitch from another game. With the natural cricketing grace he had first revealed at the age of four, Radha, one hand on his bat, scooped up the ball just as a fielder came running for it, and hit it into his hands. 'Thanks, man!' shouted the other boy.

Waving at him, Radha again took guard.

The sun shone on the Municipal Building; a drum-beat rose from a distant part of the ground. Radha saw white sandbags piled up to his right and wondered why they had been placed there. A crow swooped low.

Deennawaz Shah had started his run-up.

•

Ninety seconds later –

Though the boy's head is between his knees, and though thick hands cover his ears: the words still penetrate.

'You hopped. A weight-transfer issue. After so many years of my coaching, you did it again. On Selection Day.'

Radha opened his eyes and saw Tommy Sir standing over him. He was back in the tent at the far end of the maidan.

His brother, Manju, was now taking guard at the wicket.

'I practised for months, Tommy Sir. Even in the rains. I stood in the nets every day from seven thirty to eleven o'clock and from three to five thirty.'

It was all over now. Deennawaz Shah had smelled out Radha's weakness: his first ball had pitched short, and jagged back into the batsman. It hit Radha on the right thigh pad and fell on his foot, and as he watched through the corner of his eye it found its way through his prayers and fifteen years of early mornings and late evenings at the nets. Mohan Kumar's first son saw the bails fall.

'Your brother listened to me, Radha. Manju always listened to me, but you …'

Radha opened his eyes.

'My brother's talent comes from God, old man. You had *nothing* to do with it.'

Extracting Sachin Tendulkar's glove from his pocket, Radha held it high in the air. Had everyone seen it? Good. He tried to rip it with his hands – then he tore at it with his teeth, and spat it out to the ground.

Tommy Sir stared at the departing boy.

Tommy Sir always has a short speech for when it is over: the speech he delivers when there is no further hope of selection. When the kid is angry, when he wants to scream at his own mentor: *Why did you make me play cricket, old man?* At such a moment, hand on the boy's shoulder, Tommy Sir will respond: *We had no choice, son. But if you have learnt how to give this absurd game everything, you will have learnt how to do the same in business or medicine or anything else, and you will be a king in that life.*

But this Radha – look at him go, look at him go – what could you tell a creature like this? Finding his throat dry, he drank half a bottle of Bisleri, gargled the last of the water, and discharged it into the red mud.

Some boys fall.

•

In a teashop near Azad Maidan – low ceiling – Radha sat with his palms over his face, and sweat running down his forehead onto his nose. When he opened his eyes, a man had materialized at the table in front of his, silver polyester shirt, big paunch, hennaed hair, and parted, panting lips. Radha observed the man's paunch, which jiggled constantly, as if it were a battery-operated toy. He gaped at that tummy, until its owner, leaning forward, whispered:

'Are you a sportsman, son? A sportsman?'

Four small fans turned on simultaneously: hot air hit everyone in the restaurant.

Radha lifted his eyes from the paunch, which continued to jiggle on its own behind the silver shirt, to the man's face, anxious and avid beneath his red hair.

'You look tired, son. You played hard, no?'

The man held up his teacup, whose sides were coated with thick brown liquid.

'Want a taste of my tea? My nice tea?' With a grimace, he reached over his paunch, and placed his cup on Radha's table, then nudged it forward with a finger.

Tears filled Radha's eyes. He bit his fingernails as he watched the cup of tea being nudged closer and closer to him.

Leaning against the wall, an old waiter sucked his cheeks and scraped at the peeling plaster with his left foot. One by one, three more barefoot waiters joined him to watch the fun.

'Don't worry about fat uncle here,' said the waiter who was scratching the wall with a foot. 'He's harmless. Uncle, stop giving your tea to young boys.'

'Why can't the sportsman have some of my chai?' the fat man whined. 'Such a nice thing to have, chai.'

Banging his fist on the table, spilling the tea, Radha said something to the fat man. His paunch no longer jiggled. And the waiters told the crazy adolescent to get out at once.

•

Small green typewriters hammered all along the edges of Azad Maidan: men with thick glasses struck the keys, filling out legal forms for their clients. Smoking a beedi, an old man spread himself on the footpath behind a painted sign.

PALM / FACE READING
ON THE SPOT SOLUTIONS
FOR ANY 5 LIFE PROBLEMS: Rs 150
FOR FULL LIFE PROBLEMS: Rs 500

'Five of your problems solved for seventy-five rupees.' He squinted at Radha, who was inspecting the sign. 'I like your eyes, son.'

Radha stepped back. *You too?* He looked at the grinning old palmist. *You too?*

In the slums along the edge of the maidan, aluminium pots were on the boil. It was lunch hour. At the triangular wedge of grass at the end of the park, Radha saw red flags tucked into the fencing. Something behind the trees blared:

'Kohinoor Mills. Swan Mills. Sreeram Mills. India United Mills Number One. Where is our compensation, where is our justice, where is our share in Mumbai?'

Radha ran. Past the clattering typewriters. Past the men smashing wood. Back to Azad Maidan, where Manju was showing off with the bat for the selectors.

Radha came near the tent with all the other cricketers but remained outside: he could not go in and face them again.

Two homeless men squatted nearby, watching the cricket. A black hen, after clucking around them, came to peck at the earth at Radha's feet, making him shiver.

'Sorry I got you out, man. No hard feelings, no?'

Having slipped during the game, Deennawaz Shah, the young Pace Terror, was limping over to the tent, rolling up his white trousers to expose the red wound on his shin.

He smiled at Radha, in a docile, even ingratiating way, and said: 'Give me some water, man.'

Deennawaz turned back towards the cricket. From behind him, Radha observed the boy's small neck.

Whack! The sound of the ball striking the meat of the bat made Deennawaz look up with an open mouth.

'Your brother is on fire today. He's pulling good-length balls. Fast balls. And off the front foot. Give me some water, dude.'

His jaw clenched, Radha thought of Javed Ansari: he was the one to blame for everything. Everyone knew *he* was the homo. When he thought of 'J.A.', he saw a boiling pot of steam behind which his baby brother's face was hidden.

Radha was now right behind Deennawaz: close enough to see where the bone thickened on the boy's neck and the downy hair started to climb down his back. One Muslim would do as well as another.

His tongue curled up like a bull's to touch his upper lip: and the right hand that was no longer good for cricket turned into a fist.

Deennawaz was about to turn around to ask again for water, when he felt something hit him at the top of his neck, pounding him like a sledgehammer, compressing the length of his backbone, until the tip of his spine almost pierced through skin.

The cricket stopped when the players heard the scream.

•

Instructing his father to stand still for a moment, Manju signed the guard's register for both of them. The lift waited behind a collapsible lattice gate. There was no lift-boy inside: just a cold wooden stool. Getting in, Manju held the lattice gate open for his father.

Then the lift rose.

'The moment we get home, there will be news of Radha, just you see. He'll call and tell me where he is.'

A small sickly figure, coughing from its diaphragm, opened the door of Anand Mehta's flat on the thirteenth floor. Manju could see that the room behind him was dark, except for a table-lamp, where Mr Mehta sat holding a glass filled with a golden liquid.

'They're here, Anand,' the man with the coughing fit said hoarsely.

'Come in. Rakesh, you sit right here. I'll handle these people.'

Manju pushed against his father, to force him to enter the room.

Anand Mehta got up and walked about the dark room with the glass in his hand, sipping from it as he glanced at Manju and his father; the coughing man who had opened the door sat on the beige sofa and ran his fingers up and down its leather arms.

Manju and his father stood.

'Where is this famous thug and terrorist of yours, Radha Krishna? The police haven't found him yet. Rakesh, this is the younger boy in the sponsorship. He must be a criminal too. You watch out for your wallet.'

'Sir, I come to you shamed and publicly humiliated that my son has attacked his fellow cricketer. There is a saying in our language, he who steals an elephant is a thief. He who steals a peanut is also a—'

'Shut up!'

Anand Mehta pointed a finger at father and at son. He put his glass down on the silent television. A cloth-covered object sat on the

TV; unwrapping it, Anand Mehta picked up his cell phone, which he read, and then covered it again in the white cloth.

'I took your idea, you fuck. I covered my phone in a hankie. Keeps the germs away, you said. What about the big fat germ known as Mohan Kumar? Do you know what this Deennawaz Shah's uncle wanted from me? 75,000 rupees in compensation. 75,000. Tommy Sir brings that man here and tells me, please pay him. Otherwise he's going to file an FIR against Radha for assaulting his nephew. They had to put Deennawaz Shah in hospital, your boy hit him so hard. After which, still crazy, he tried to strangulate him right there, and would have done so, if the others hadn't … I've been paying and paying and paying you people for years.'

Joining his palms together, Mohan Kumar tried to bend down and touch Anand Mehta's shoes.

'Don't touch me. Go back. Go back. I'm sick of being fucked and fooled around by you. Bloody Mexican bartender thinks he owns the whole fucking bar.'

The sickly man on the sofa cracked his knuckles.

Now Mohan turned, and reached for the shoes of the man with the loud knuckles.

'Don't bow to him, bow to *me*,' Anand Mehta shouted. 'I own this bar.'

'Don't shout at my father.'

'What?' Mehta looked at the boy.

'My father is not very strong these days. It's not his fault, what Radha did today. It's not Radha's fault, either.'

'You talking to *me*?'

Anand Mehta put his hand on Manju's head, and rubbed the boy's hair. He kept his hand there.

'Say what you said again. Say what you just said, a second time.'

Manju looked at the dark carpet. A violent coughing from the sofa dragged the carpet back and forth.

'You listen to me, golden boy. I'm dealing with the mafia in Dhanbad. Do you understand? Rakesh here is an IAS officer's son.

He's helping me handle mafia there. I don't even want to think about cricket, I don't even want to think about Mumbai anymore. Why? We've got a power plant near Dhanbad and we're turning it around. Do you know the operating capacity? Four hundred thousand units of electricity a month, and current operating output zilch. When we turn it around, we make six crores a month. Do you know how much money that is, you fuck? And you make me waste my time here? Of course there are problems. Of course. Everyone in the district has lined up for a bribe. Instant the plant starts working, it gets worse. The phone will ring every hour. Hello, I am your Member of Parliament. I'm sending fifteen men from my village. Employ them or I'll murder you and fuck your wife. You understand what this means? If I say jump, you jump. And right now I'm saying, you and your brother have fucked me over enough. Where is that criminal boy now?'

Manju said, 'I think he is on his way to our village, sir. They will hide him from the police.'

'Fuck.'

Anand Mehta's face had become darker and older, and made Manju remember the night he had invaded their home.

'Sir' Manju could smell, all the way in the pit of his stomach, the liquor on Anand Mehta's breath. He had to speak or retch. 'Sir. Sir. Sir. I don't want to play cricket anymore after today.'

The air-conditioning was working strongly, and Manju rubbed his forearms up and down.

'I did this thing to my brother today. I won't play after this. I want to stop and study forensic—'

'Shut up!' the two men said together, and then Anand Mehta informed Mohan Kumar: 'I'm the one who says shut up in this room.'

The sickly man coughed a bit; Anand Mehta pointed a finger at Manju.

'Golden Boy: in one minute I'm going to tell you, do something, and you will bloody well do exactly that.'

He opened a cabinet and took out a bottle and poured two full glasses.

Mohan took one glass, emptied it and put it down. Anand Mehta's finger pointed at Manju, and then at the second glass.

But Manju said, 'No.'

'Do you want me to tell the police where your brother has gone?'

Manju picked up the glass, closed his eyes, and drank. His small body convulsed.

Anand Mehta smiled.

'And there's a bill to pay. For this scotch. Good Indian scotch. Nothing is free for you people anymore. It's my bar. Start paying me.'

Mohan Kumar took out his wallet, and held it out, and Anand Mehta removed the only large note, a hundred-rupee bill, from it.

•

When they finally made it outside the building, Mohan saw his Manju bend over, stick out his tongue like a happy jackass, and vomit on the pavement.

The gates had closed behind them.

'Let's go to the police, Appa. Let's both go to the police right now,' Manju said, as he wiped his lips clean. 'He made me drink that. Right in front of you. And you did nothing.'

Mohan Kumar said nothing; his shirt stuck to his body.

Manju came close and examined his immobile father. He saw no eyes, no lips, no features; and he realized that for all these years, his father had not had a face. All these years, there had been no secret contract with God, no scientific method, no antibiotics and no ancient wisdom: just Fear.

Manju turned and observed: not one adult walking around him in the night had a face.

•

'The first point we have to establish is this. Did Javed tell you, or did he not tell you that exactly this kind of thing would happen to you if you kept playing cricket?'

Leaving his father before the gates of Anand Mehta's housing society, Manju had crossed the road to a grocery store with a yellow pay-phone. The store-owner had a black tear-like birthmark running from his eye to his nose, giving him the look of one born to sorrow; he flicked through a copy of the *Mumbai Sun*, entirely indifferent to Manju, who stood beside him sobbing on the phone.

'… don't be a bastard. Tell me what I should do, Javed. Just tell me.'

'Bastard? You're calling me a bastard? I shouldn't even talk to you. I told you, you keep playing cricket, I'll stop talking to you. And I keep my word.'

'Javed, everything bad that happened today, what Radha did, this is all my fault. You don't know the story. You don't know half the story.'

'Manju: it's nobody's fault. Your father is fucking you in the head again. Leave him *now*.'

'Leave and go where, Javed?'

'Come to Navi Mumbai. I have my own flat now. You'll be safe here.'

Manju heard, on the other end of the line, the sound of Javed's jaws moving and crushing darkness.

He *would* be safe there. Javed would protect him.

The store-owner kept turning the pages of his *Mumbai Sun*.

'Come stay with me, Manju. How many times do I have to say it?'

There was a pause.

'But one thing: don't call me till you're ready to give up cricket and come here. Javed Ansari won't break his word again. No more calls from you will be taken. Everyone in my house has received instructions. Because I worry you will come to Navi Mumbai, say "Fuck cricket, I am here for good," and next morning decide to go back to Daddy.'

The phone went dead. Manju replaced the receiver; the store-owner folded his newspaper, placed it on his desk, and smiled. This act of kindness refreshed Manju, but then he saw the story on the last page of the newspaper:

Woman Kills Husband, But Not Without A Reason, Police Say

> The 32-year-old wife of a building contractor who murdered her husband yesterday in horrifying circumstances, as reported in this paper, did so only after discovering that he had been having an affair – with another man, the police have disclosed. The full story of this lurid act of revenge, the police say, forces us to reconsider …

'Everything alright?' the store-owner asked.

'Everything is perfectly alright, sir,' Manju replied.

And then added a smile to his statement.

•

Perched upside down on the telephone wires along the road, parakeets screeched at the passengers in the bus.

Radha Krishna Kumar licked his lips to rid them of the coating of metal. He had slept with his face against the bars, and now, when he moved his head, there was pain, as if a wrench had been left behind in his neck.

Radha saw hills in the distance, and day breaking over them. The bus had come to a stop, and the passengers had descended to line up in front of a man pouring tea from a stainless-steel kettle.

He had caught the bus from Crawford Market the night before, as his brother had suspected he would. He was on his way to his village, to his uncle Revanna's house, where he would be safer than at home: his uncle would never hand him over to the Mumbai police.

When the engine restarted, a baby whimpered; Radha saw a black sobbing face, raw, wet, rising in front of him, like something just lifted out of the primeval pond: and then rising further, towards the ceiling of the bus. Its father was lifting the baby high up, so it could see there was nothing to fear from the noise: the child saw, and squealed. But to Radha's ears it had roared like a lion in the jungle. He turned to the iron bars of the window in tears. My father never did that for me; never held me up like that so I could roar over the noise of the world. He watched the inverted parakeets. He wanted to bite the rusting bars of the window; yes, *bite* and *break* them, one by one: how else was he to tell God what he thought of having been given a man like Mohan Kumar for a father?

When he looked up at the sky, the light of the new day seemed unbearable: for what did the morning have to do with a man like him, a man who was no longer good for cricket?

'Close your eyes, Radha,' a voice whispered; he obeyed. Fingers snapped in the dark; and then he saw, beneath a rusty grille, black water, which foamed and parted to reveal a domed creature with quick limbs rising up into the light.

A small soft voice said: 'Radha Krishna Kumar, elder brother of Manjunath Kumar, the morning will *always* have something to do with a man like you.' Then the turtle sank back into the deep. Radha's soiled and tensed body relaxed; though the light now struck his face directly, he slept.

•

To call, after you have been told not to call; to press the redial button after the dial tone has been silenced; to sleep with the phone next to your pillow in the hope that it will wake you up in the middle of the night; these are new experiences for a sixteen-year-old.

Not a word in twenty days. Three weeks tomorrow.

You can't even pick up the phone when you know it's me, Javed?

Sitting in the last seat of a bus, Manju wore his ear-phones as he scrolled down the songs on his cell phone to find Eminem. Around him were Mumbai's most promising under-19 players, selected by the Cricket Association; they were on their way to the P.J. Hindu Gymkhana for a 'Friendly'.

Manju had made a round wall of music surround him: yet in its centre, he sat, exposed, naked to any pair of eyes that knew of the pain that one boy could inflict on another.

Someone turned to look at him, and at once the wall was breached: so Manju hid his deepest troubles behind others. There was only bad news of Radha from the village: their relatives complained that he sat in a corner and said nothing but 'Punish me'. And every day, as soon as Manju opened his eyes, the first thing he saw was Anand Mehta Sir ordering him to suck his whisky. There? Happy? He glared at the boy who was looking at him.

Happy that I have troubles that someone like you can understand as troubles?

Now he closed his eyes and thought of how Javed was treating him, just because he hadn't left everything and gone to Navi Mumbai.

I am not slave, he had texted him six times. *You are not nice to me*. Four times. *I am coming but I can't come right now*. Twice.

No reply.

Now he wanted Javed's hair to fall. Let it be eaten up, in widening bays of bald skin. Let that Muslim boy become ugly. Let him wish he had never met Manjunath Kumar.

Slowing as it passed Chowpatty beach, the white bus stopped in front of the P.J. Hindu Gymkhana. When Manju opened his eyes he saw Tommy Sir standing outside.

He clutched his cricket bag, pushed his way out of the bus, stopped and realized that the old scout had been waiting for him.

Tommy Sir started to say something but Manju walked right past him.

Tommy Sir found him in the dressing room of the pavilion, apart from all the other boys, earphones still plugged in to his cell phone.

Tommy Sir removed one of the boy's earphones, put it into his own ear, and indicated his approval.

'English music? Good. I too like English music.' He relinquished the earphones but placed a hand on the boy's thigh. 'Manju. We have to talk. Look at me, I say, look at me. How is Radha doing? Is he okay?'

The boy looked at him as if he failed to understand. Then Manju's features changed.

'I don't *know*.'

'Manju. Look at me. Answer my question.'

'*I* don't know,' the boy said.

So Tommy Sir asked the question again, and for the third time, Manju, in the voice of one who was unmistakably enjoying himself, replied:

'I *don't* know.'

Tommy Sir took a while to understand what was happening.

All the other boys left the dressing room.

Tommy Sir reached out to seize Manju's shoulder to shake some sense into him, but his hand stopped in mid-air.

Staring back at Tommy Sir, Manjunath Kumar looked like a Doberman barely restrained by a metal fence. Remembering what his elder brother had done to Deennawaz Shah, the violence in the blood of this family, Tommy Sir checked himself. But he hadn't been scared of anything his whole life – and he certainly wasn't going to be scared in a boys' changing room.

'Manju,' he said, 'because the selection match the other day was disrupted by your brother, everyone's a bit nervous about the two Kumars, and the selectors just want to make sure you're okay, so you have to come to Shivaji Park tomorrow and show—'

Tommy Sir stopped breathing, for Manju's face had turned darker and even more vicious.

'You crazy, bloody ...' Tommy Sir first considered giving the boy a good slap on the head, but changed his mind, and then considered retreating from the room gracefully, but finally just turned and fled.

•

Posed like a hero in the old Hollywood movies, his right foot on the sea wall of Marine Drive, his head erect and scanning the ocean, white hair trembling in the breeze, Tommy Sir thought, 'If I don't have a cigarette, my brain will burst open.' Having left the gymkhana, he had crossed the road for safety (glancing over his shoulder to make sure Manju wasn't following), then continued to the other side of Marine Drive, and gone a distance for further safety, before stopping at the sight of an ocean liner that had entered into Back Bay. Though it was a lifelong rule never to do this thing in the open, where some young impressionable boy might spot him, Tommy Sir now took out his packet of cigarettes and tapped on it.

First Radha blames him, now Manju blames him. After all he had done for them. He lit a cigarette.

Exhaling, relaxing a little, Tommy Sir observed the pleasure ship on the horizon, the foreign ship. Chock-full of lovebirds. Around the world they go, these little lovebirds: Italy, Scotland, Russia, maybe even to those Pacific Islands where there are still smoking volcanoes. At such moments, Tommy Sir remembered his late lamented wife, in whose company he had never been able to enjoy such pleasures.

Can you believe it? He wanted to shout to the young lovebirds on the cruise liner: You find the new Tendulkar and he doesn't want to play cricket!

Half an hour later, as he retraced his route, recrossing Marine Drive and returning to the gymkhana, he saw two urchins playing cricket near the parked cars. One ran up and bowled an imaginary ball. The other swung at it with an imaginary bat.

'Do it like Manju, yaar!' the bowler shouted. Tommy Sir stopped.

'Do what like ...?'

He sprinted the rest of the way to the P.J. Hindu Gymkhana.

Men had gathered by the boundary wall. Men who had been working all through the night, and who still had an hour-long trip to Govandi or Thane ahead of them, and had come to watch a few overs first; two Indian couples; and a European couple in floppy caps, sitting, backs against the sight-screen, to consult their guide book. Now four pale legs move with a single shriek; for a hard red ball is heading straight at the sight-screen.

'This fellow, they say his name is Kumar, he can bat, can't he?'

'He's going to play for Mumbai.'

'India! The World Cup!'

Two trains were passing each other in Marine Lines station; their metal roofs overlapping.

For the first time in four decades, Tommy Sir allowed the Mumbai cricketing public to see him smoking. Cigarette in hand, he watched Manju. Because this was the best the boy had ever been. Earlier, if he had cut and flicked the ball out of a love of batting, now he did so out of hate. His strokes had become crisp, his footwork precise. The story of the past few days was there, in every ball he played. Every flick of his wrist said, do you know how much I hate you, Anand Mehta? Do you know how much I hate you, Mohan Kumar? And do you, Narayanrao Sadashivrao Kulkarni, really want to know what I think about *you*?

This is what I have not understood in all of forty-two years, Tommy Sir told himself. The shroud has parted: this is the one thing the boy needed to make him a great batsman. He needed to hate the game.

When the *Mumbai Sun* sends a reporter to interview Manju on my seventy-fifth birthday, let him say Tommy Sir was a Monster. He destroyed my life, he sucked my blood. And if they ask me, I'll say, a great sportsman is a kind of monster. This was the final discovery of my career as a Talent Scout.

•

'Why won't you talk about the match, son? A reporter for the paper called me and told me you were great.'

Mohan perched on the bed, bird-like, beneath the fast old-fashioned fan. His hair was wet. He turned his head from side to side.

Manju sat with his organic chemistry tutorial notes. Pads and bat had been stacked up in a corner of the room.

'They've put him to work in the fields. A son of Mohan Kumar, a big-city boy, and they treat him like this, in the village.'

Turning the fan off, Mohan got down from the bed, bent his head, and rubbed his hair with a thick white cloth.

Now Manju looked up.

'So why don't you do something? Write to Revanna Uncle to bring Radha back to Mumbai.'

Mohan had stopped rubbing his hair; he looked about the floor, as if the words he needed were lying down there waiting to be picked up.

It has been a long time, Manju thought, since this small man has tried to hit me. He had to strain to catch his father's muffled words.

'The winnowing has begun in the villages. I heard from Revanna just an hour ago. It's the work I used to do. Breaks the back. Imagine if they found out in Dahisar, in the old neighbourhood. Ramnath, he'll laugh so hard he'll forget to press clothes for a day. And then he'll give us four rupees which we'll have to take as charity.'

Putting his hands on either side of the cot, Mohan Kumar pressed, as if trying to squash his own bed.

Manju sat facing the kitchen. The maid was making chapatis, stacking them up on a tin plate. He imagined her doing this for years and years, the pile growing higher and higher.

Mohan Kumar was still trying to compress his bed. '"On its way into town, the king's white horse turned into a donkey." A golden proverb. I had illusions about my sons, and all of us suffered because of them. If you make it onto the Ranji team, that'll do. One point five lakhs a month will be your salary; first we have to give Anand Mehta his 75,000 rupees for saving your brother from the police. Then we have to give him back his 50,000 rupee house loan. In two or three years, he'll go away, don't you think?'

'What if I fail? Tommy Sir said Radha would make it, now he says I will make it. Who can believe a thing he says?'

'Who, Manju? Who fails in cricket? Everyone becomes happy in cricket. And you're the best.'

'I'm not the best. I don't want to be the best the way T.E. Sarfraz does, and if you make me stay in cricket I'll be just a ...'

Mohan Kumar sighed and scratched himself.

'If you are a fraud, you are still my son. You can go to Bangladesh to play. They have IPL there too. You send me the money by mail. They must have a post office over there? And whatever you earn, we'll give half to Anand Mehta Sir. I signed *this* on the name of our family god, and let them never say at Deepa Bar that I am the sort of man to break my word.'

Closing his eyes, he recited from memory what he remembered of the contract:

'*... will be the legal property of Shri Mehta, in return for his commitment to ... May God fill our mouths with worms if either—*'

'Have some self-respect, Father. Please stop.'

When he opened his eyes, Mohan Kumar saw Manju looking darker and smaller, as though he had lost his essential oils. He clapped his hands.

'... Oh, I completely forgot, Manju. Completely forgot. A man came from the MIG club and gave you this. It's a gift from Tommy Sir. To inspire you to bat well tomorrow at Shivaji Park. Here, read it and feel better. You were always a big reader.'

It was an old black-and-white magazine, *Classics of Modern Indian Cricket*, a photograph of the Nawab of Pataudi on the cover.

A yellow note was pinned to it, bearing the handwritten words: 'For Manju Sir. You will be joining them one day.'

Manju stared at the magazine, but thought instead of a BBC science documentary that showed how an amoeba reacts to a drop of dilute hydrochloric acid: by contorting itself in an almost human grimace, and moving away. 'One of the distinctive traits of any life-form is irritability,' the British voice-over had observed. That is how *he* felt right now: like a colourless amoeba irritated at everyone and everyfuckingthing around. He grit his teeth, and turned the pages of the magazine.

Mohan Kumar went to the sink and let the water run. Bending forward, he submerged his hair in the fast-flowing water. When he emerged with his head wrapped in a towel, he found Manju speed-reading the magazine, until he stopped at one page, and ripped it out. It was another photograph of the Nawab of Pataudi. Throwing the rest of the magazine in the waste-bin, Manju pushed his father aside and went into the toilet.

'Why are you taking that photograph in *there*?' his father asked.

From behind the closed toilet door, the boy roared: 'Why do you *think*?'

And his father put his hands on the toilet door and whimpered like a dog. 'Manju, this is immoral, he was our greatest captain, don't ... don't ... do immoral things in there, Manju, with the Nawab of Pataudi. What will the neighbours think of your father?'

'Shut up!' the boy shouted from inside. 'It's like batting. I need to concentrate. Don't disturb me for the next three minutes.'

•

Towards morning, Mohan Kumar dreamed of the laterite arch in the jungle, set against its backdrop of stars, with the bullfrogs croaking all around it ...

... then he raised his neck off the pillow and the arch and the stars and the frogs suddenly disappeared: it was morning in Mumbai.

When he went to Manju's bed, it was empty. Mohan touched the bed, up and down.

Without breakfast or a bath, he left the flat and went to the temple. It was not yet open, so he sat under a nearby banyan tree and looked at the dark little leaves. Suddenly all the leaves lit up: Mohan Kumar remembered that the Deepa Bar was open early in the mornings.

He took an autorickshaw to the train station, and found himself, an hour later, entering the bar, where the manager, Mr Shetty, recognized him and smiled.

He sat down at a table. The only other customer, a villager with a close-cropped grey beard and shrewd rustic eyes, a man who looked like he'd fuck his own daughter-in-law any day, chewed aniseed, while Mr Shetty, the bar manager, arms folded over his white shirt, talked to him about real estate.

'Things are mad enough in Udupi. My uncle's small plot was bought for five lakhs. And Mangalore – forget it. Real money is out there nowadays, not here.'

Mohan Kumar began drinking.

After a while, he had a pleasant surprise. His old neighbour, Ramnath the ironing man, had come to the bar with a carton of sweets and great news.

'My daughter has done it,' he said, handing the entire box over to Mohan Kumar.

She had been accepted into the Illinois Institute of Advanced Technology, a famous college in America. A teacher had filled out her forms; she had studied for two years for the entrance exams. The best part was that this Illinois Institute of Advanced Technology was paying for her to study there. Even the plane ticket.

'Wonderful, wonderful. But, no thank you, no sweets for me. Just another whisky.'

All his life Mohan Kumar had warned his sons about the danger from other talented boys: he had forgotten that the real threat was from the normal and the average, like this smug shirt-ironer from the Shastrinagar slum. These were the people who had destroyed Radha: they and their normal sons, who had tempted him with drugs, shaving kits, and sexual materials.

When he unwrapped his phone from its white cotton handkerchief, he saw that Tommy Sir was calling.

'Good morning,' Mohan Kumar said with the phone held in front of his mouth, and then moved it to his ear to listen.

'Where is he?' Tommy Sir asked. 'At this very minute, where exactly is he? Your second son.'

'At the cricket. Isn't he?'

Tommy Sir's voice was hotter this time:

'No. He's not in Shivaji Park. I told him, he had to come show himself to the selectors or they'll think he's crazy like his brother.'

Mohan Kumar hung up on him. The sunlight was harsh; he did not want to leave Deepa Bar.

The phone rang again. Mohan Kumar picked it up again: 'Yes,' he said, and held it to his ear.

'The boy's phone is switched off.' Tommy Sir's voice was thin, tense. 'The match is starting now.'

Mohan Kumar moved the phone from one ear to the other.

'... eh ... um ... mmm ... mmmm ... eh ...' he said. There was a pause and then Tommy Sir's voice hissed at him: 'Congratulations. This boy has also run away.'

Tommy Sir swore, and the phone line went dead.

Mohan Kumar re-wrapped his cell phone in his handkerchief. He remained in the bar for several hours. Late afternoon is when the sunlight hits the tables, and the germs and the slime begin to shine. Darkness will clean the bar, but right now nothing is concealed. The life you have made for yourself – and have hidden from yourself – is on full display.

He began to play with the menu card on his table. The back of the laminated card bore a cyclostyled advertisement, something that looked decades and decades old.

'Improves memory, inner strength, and character.'

Learn Chess! Play Chess! Love Chess!!!

Game of Kings and King of Games!

The fascinating game of international renown.

1. Chess develops methodical precise and logical thinking.
2. Chess promotes creativity and true imagination.
3. Chess shows there is no substitute for hard work. A study was carried out to determine the contribution of hard work to success. It concludes that hard work alone contributes 75% of success, the rest made

up together by such other qualities as intelligence, tenacity, determination, 'grit' etc.

4. Chess develops memory.

Chess. Today's Preparation is Tomorrow's Achievement.

Don't let your child's brain be wasted.
Let him play with it and use it.
P.T.O. (continued)

Mohan flipped the menu card over and over. Why *chess* – on the back of a bar's menu? Maybe because of the remarkable convergence in the benefits of chess and long-term alcoholism, he told himself, and laughed a little. Or maybe because there is no 'Because' in Bombay anymore. Things just happen to people like Mohan Kumar and his sons. No reason. No meaning. No 'Because'.

Complimenting him on his remarkable menu cards, Mohan Kumar paid the manager, and left the bar.

While he waited for the train on the platform, his hand rose, his palm rotated to the left and vibrated. In the old days you solved a problem like that. Come here, Manju. Come here, Radha. He stopped swiping his palm through the air, and looked at it with disgust, wondering how many millions of Gram-Negative Bacteria had accumulated on its flesh during his stay in that filthy bar.

In these seas of septicity where you have cast your sons, O Father, how do you expect any man to stay sane, to stay safe?

It was over an hour before Mohan Kumar, his hands washed, could lie down in his own bed.

Closing his eyes, he thought of that moment, years ago, when his wife had left him alone in the slum in Dahisar with two boys to raise; when he stretched himself on the bed and thought, I am mocked by all other men, my life is over. But how simple it was back then to hear the fingers of his destiny snap and command: 'Get up, Mohan. Get to work.' Back when failure still had its innocence. On his way out of Deepa Bar, something had touched Mohan Kumar on the shoulder: it was a senile creature, pale and trembling, every known species of broken Indian male in one ancient wrapping, exhaling beer and trying to escape from the bar two inches at a time. 'That is going to be me,' Mohan told himself. 'I am going to die mad and alone.' No: he curled up both his fists, breathed in, and invited Yama, the God of Death, to tighten the noose around his throat while he was yet a man.

Minutes passed, and he was still alive, so he decided to approach a more familiar god. Wallet in hand, he went to the prayer room with the image of Lord Subramanya in its small oil-coated stainless-steel altar.

Mohan Kumar moved coins, into a line, till they made six rupees, and pushed them before Lord Subramanya. It was an offering: a new secret contract he was proposing to God. Mohan Kumar was reinstating 'Because'. Because I am giving you this money, God, you must make my sons cricketers, God.

Looking at the coins, Mohan re-counted them subaudibly, and slipped three back into his pocket.

Only one son this time.

One week after Selection Day

'Wake up.'

'Hm.'

'Get out of the car. We're home.'

All through the early-morning train ride Manju had stayed awake; but the moment he saw Navi Mumbai shining beyond the Thane Creek, his eyes began to close. A dark station with giant columns; an anonymous crowd; and then, detaching itself from everyone else, as his heart beat faster, Javed's dark face. With his powerful arm around Manju, Javed led him out into the car park. They got into a car, and Manju slept at once.

'We're home, man. Wake up,' Javed said, shaking him by the shoulder.

Getting out of the car, Manju followed Javed into a building where a man in khaki saluted them both. An old woman opened the door of Javed's flat: and they walked into a sunny room smelling of fresh red sofa. Manju sat on a hard chair opposite the sofa to remove his shoes.

'Who else is here?' he asked.

'This is my place, I told you. If a cousin is visiting, Dad sends him here. Otherwise it's only me.'

Leading Manju into a room with a bed, Javed opened a wardrobe and showed him what was inside: a stack of shirts.

'These are mine. You can wear them all.'

Then Javed pointed to the bed. It was covered in a golden bedsheet.

'Yours.' And then he went into the bathroom and closed the door behind him. 'I have to brush my teeth. It'll only take a minute. You can go to sleep now.'

Afraid he'd crumple the immaculate bedsheet, Manju lay down slowly and stretched his legs.

'Javed,' he shouted. 'Are you going to sleep here too?'

'No,' the voice boomed back from the bathroom. 'My father said you could stay here, but only if I slept at night in the other place. My family flat. He doesn't want me to become gay. Changes his mind on the subject from day to day. Once, he even went to a store and bought condoms and left them on the table. Other times he threatens to send me back to Aligarh. Like there's no gays there. Ha!'

Javed came out of the bathroom, combing his fingers through his wet hair.

'One day I'll take you to meet a gay mullah, Manju. You should see these fellows in UP. They're just ... *fantastic*.' Javed bit his lower lip; sickle-shaped dimples winked from his cheeks. 'Half the mullahs there are gay. *Half*. You go into any madrassah and the man with the big beard makes the boys sit on the floor right next to him, and calls them nearer, nearer, and then tells the girls, you go sit *far* away.'

Manju, for the first time in his life, seriously considered conversion to Islam.

'Do they all look like the Nawab of Pataudi, these gay mullahs?'

'No, only I do. Idiot.'

Javed sat by the bed, smelling of wet hair and a light musk cologne; Manju smiled and closed his eyes. Without opening them,

Manju drew nearer to Javed, nearer the cologne. His finger ran down his friend's neck to his chest.

'Stop doing that.'

Pushing him away, Javed stood up; he clacked his tongue. 'You're going to change your mind in two minutes. I know you.'

Manju opened his eyes. 'I won't change my mind.' Javed regarded him with a frown, and then looked away.

'Anyway, the first thing is to say goodbye to cricket. I have a plan.'

Manju sighed. 'What is this plan?'

Simple: Manju was not going to leave Navi Mumbai today under any circumstances. The cricket people were not going to get their hands on him.

Before he let him sleep, Javed asked Manju to surrender his cell phone. Sixteen missed calls. And twelve text messages.

'Is this Tommy Sir's number?'

Manju said nothing.

'You can't talk to Tommy Sir, or he'll spin your head and make you go back.'

'I'll kill Tommy Sir if I ever see him again. Seriously.'

'Cool it, dude. You're tired and confused. You're talking crazy.'

Unable to sleep, the young cricketer thrashed his legs on the golden bed, till he heard Javed say, 'There's something underneath it. Put your hand down there.'

Manju's hands searched – and came out with a comic book.

As he lay in bed and read about the Fantastic Four, a sparrow flew into the room to sit on the blades of the ceiling fan. The stumpy fan trembled as the bird hopped from one blade to another. Watching that old fan, which seemed so familiar, Manju felt as if he had been living in that room for years and years.

Covering his face with the comic book, he breathed in and out, his eyes still open. He was so tired of batting out of, breathing out of, living out of, going to *sleep* out of rage.

•

Around eleven, wrapped in a golden bedsheet, Manjunath awoke.

Javed was sitting by the bed, examining his cell phone with a grin.

'Tommy Sir has called you two hundred and forty-two times since you got here.' He chuckled. 'He's still calling you. You can still go back.' Javed offered him the phone, which was ringing again.

Manju shook his head. The sparrow was still up there on the ceiling fan.

'Sure?'

'Yes,' Manju said. He let Javed keep his cell phone, and said, 'I finished Fantastic Four. You have X-Men?'

•

The next day was Friday. While he was brushing his teeth, Javed said, sure, it was okay for him to go to Mumbai: no danger from cricket now.

He took the train to Matunga station. At Ruia, he was called to the principal's office; Tommy Sir had informed them that he had run away.

'I am not living with my father, sir. I am sixteen and a half years old.'

The principal pinched together the wings of his nose and shook his head.

'My father is a violent man, who has beaten me in the past,' Manju told him. 'He may try to do so again. Being also an unintelligent man, he is unaware that I am now stronger than he is, and I might accidentally hurt him, or even kill him. In which case my only regret would be wasting the rest of my life in jail over a man like my father.'

His fingers still pinching his nostrils, the principal's mouth opened.

Manju took the train back to Vashi, and walked down the road, past the Golden Punjab Hotel, to Javed's flat, to give him the good news: the college had agreed he need not live with his father.

But when he returned to Javed's flat there was another teenager sitting on the bed with the golden bedsheet, and sharing a cigarette with Javed.

'Manju, this is my friend Ranjith,' Javed said, putting a hand on the newcomer. 'My dear Big Boss, *that* is Manju.'

'Look at this chap,' Ranjith said. 'Where *did* you find this fellow, Javed?'

'Cricket,' Javed said.

Manju and the boy on the bed examined each other. A tuft of blonde hair grew under Ranjith's lower lip. He wore braces on his teeth, but had blue tattoos on each of his smooth arms, and smelled one part tobacco or pot, other part superior cologne.

Manju's nostrils suddenly longed for home. He waved away the cigarette smoke.

Ranjith took a final drag at the cigarette, and then flicked it out of the window.

'That must be the best place to find them, no? All that dressing up in white, so romantic.'

Manju had never seen Javed like this before: he nodded demurely at everything Ranjith said, and hunched forward, arms folded across his chest, lips pursed tight, looking almost scared of the boy with the blond tuft.

Ranjith slapped him on the back: Javed shook.

'Buddy,' Ranjith said, 'we must all go to Mad Max racing in Powai. Have you told the little cricketer about the bike racing? Dude, Cricketer, you know that each of us takes his bike – you do have a bike, right? – and goes from Powai all the way to Bandra without stopping. Let the police shout, let them chase, we keep going. Because we aren't frightened of the police, or anyone else, are we, Javed?'

'No, we're not frightened,' Javed said, and laughed, almost painfully.

Manju got it now: his own lies were deflating Javed. He *was* scared of the police. He was also scared of this boy, Ranjith.

So when Ranjith asked, 'Javed, are you ready for the challenge on Tuesday?', Manju sat on the bed between the two.

'Javed is not coming for Mad Max anymore,' Manju declared. '*You* get caught by the police this time. Don't get us into trouble.'

Ranjith gaped. Manju heard Javed's voice behind him.

'Don't talk to him like that. He's my friend.'

Ranjith smiled over Manju's head. 'Mad Max on Tuesday, Javed?' He stood up.

'Yes.'

'Don't bring any inexperienced types along with you.'

'I won't.'

The door slammed shut.

Manju's face had gone numb, like it did after his father slapped him: tears filled the corners of his eyes as he looked at the golden bedsheet, where Ranjith's arse had left an impression. Maybe Javed had brought him to Navi Mumbai only to show him off to Ranjith and the rest of the Mad Max gang. Here is the boy who I took away from cricket. Here is my catch. And in a day or two, his cricket career finished, the maidservant would open the door, and say, 'Get out.'

Manju could feel Javed sitting right by him on the bed.

Was he going to gloat now? Was he going to tease Manju for being a virgin? He looked at Javed: but he could not see into him. The only mind in the whole world he could not read was Javed's: for what we discover, when we think we are discovering someone else's thoughts, is our own diminished expectations of them. And the one person Manju could not create a diminished version of was this beak-nosed boy.

'What? What are you angry about *this* time?'

Each second that Ranjith was gone, Javed visibly reverted, sat more upright, and seemed more like himself.

'I'm not going to Mad Max. Are you happy, Sir Manju? I just said I was going, to keep Ranjith quiet. Who wants to go to Powai anyway? This is where I want to go. Look up.'

Javed sketched a 'V' in the air.

He had it all planned out. As soon as the holidays came, Manju and he were going to rent a motorbike, and drive from Bangalore to Alur to see Radha, and from there to Mangalore, and then – Javed sketched that magic 'V' a third time, signifying the entire coast of India – drive *top*-speed all the way down to Kanyakumari, tip of the subcontinent, and there they were going to find that black rock that Swami Vivekananda had stood on with folded arms and they were going to adopt the same macho posture and take selfies of each other and become very enlightened, and smoke a *shit* load of ganja. Manju *had* done ganja, right?

'What motorbike are we going on?' Manju had to ask.

So Javed showed him, parked against the compound wall of his housing society: a black Royal Enfield bike, formerly his father's.

'Can I sit on it, Javed?'

'Yes! Of course! Captain – don't be such an ass!'

So Manju got to sit on a motorbike for the first time, touched its metal surface, gripped its handles, and smiled. When he got down, uncertain how to use the foot-stand, he leaned the bike against the compound wall; and then, with an elbow, he rammed into Javed, driving the taller boy back.

'Don't call me Captain. Don't ever call me Captain again.'

Javed chuckled.

They played with the bike for three hours, and Javed showed Manju how to take it for a ride around the compound. Tomorrow they could start driving on the road.

•

'O, I *do* read Indian novels sometimes. But you know, Ms Rupinder, what we Indians want in literature, at least the kind written in English, is not literature at all, but flattery. We want to see ourselves depicted as soulful, sensitive, profound, valorous, wounded, tolerant and funny beings. All that Jhumpa Lahiri stuff. But the truth is, we are absolutely nothing of that kind. What *are* we, then, Ms Rupinder? We are animals of the jungle, who will eat our neighbour's children in five minutes, and our own in ten. Keep this in mind before you do any business in this country.'

And Anand Mehta sipped some more Diet Coke.

Dressed in a grey business suit, holding a glass of sparkling water in her hand, young Ms Rupinder controlled her smile, and asked: 'Has it been a bad day for you, then?'

'You could say that.' Anand Mehta smiled at his interlocutor. 'I've been meeting hipsters all day. The sons of my classmates. All of them are stockbrokers like Daddy, but they've also become hipsters.'

The young Punjabi–American businesswoman struggled again with laughter. 'Hipsters? Here in India?'

'O, yes, Ms Rupinder. Our trains aren't running, our roads are full of potholes, but our cities *are* bounteous with hipsters. Without understanding what capitalism means, we've vaulted' – Mehta made an aeroplane with his palm – 'straight to post-capitalist decadence. What is an Indian, after all? Picture today's young man from Mumbai or Delhi as a vulture above the nations, scavenging for his identity. He sees a pretty thing in Dubai, and he brings it home; he sees a pretty thing in Williamsburg, Brooklyn, and he brings it home. One day he looks at his life, finds that it makes no sense at all, and then he turns to religion. Now, Ms Rupinder, I *would* like to give my portfolio folder, which has information about my two visionary ventures ...'

A Paradoxography is a book illuminated by monks in the Middle Ages, and in his New York years, Anand Mehta had once seen a whole bunch of Paradoxographies lying under a panel of glass at the Morgan Library: each page glistening with impossible creatures, centaurs, unicorns, half-man half-fish, fanged things tamed by the touch of a saint, that sort of thing. Right now, standing in this glittering hall of the Grand Hyatt Hotel, Mehta felt he was living inside a Paradoxography, surrounded by a bestiary of financial analysts, brokers and bankers who had been transformed, from the waist down, into Mother Teresa. Officially, it was a gathering of social entrepreneurs from around the world, looking for business in India. One man, a former Lehman banker, was now running a corporate social responsibility consultancy, and this chap, who had worked with Bill Miller at Legg Mason, had developed software that increased corporate donations to primary education by 25 per cent, and that white guy, once in junk bonds, was now in windmills. Mehta discovered from him that the big game in Indian bio-renewables was no longer Rice Husks. 'It's all about Elephant Grass these days. We have three fields in Assam already. What's your big idea?'

And young Ms Rupinder here, to whom he had just explained all about hipsters – authentic stockbroking Gujarati hipsters – represented a venture fund in Iowa City that apparently wanted to 'both do well *and* do good in India'. Right up my alley, dear lady: Anand Mehta sipped more Diet Coke, as the young Punjabi–American woman, who reminded him in some ways of his own wife Asha, before she put on weight, examined the brochures in his folder.

'This doesn't interest me much,' the American snapped her fingers at one brochure, 'the old power plants. But *this*,' she snapped at another, 'tell me more about *this*.'

'Modelled closely on the US college athletic scholarship programmes,' Mehta added, as he told her all about young Manjunath Kumar, his fully sponsored little superman.

'Except,' Ms Rupinder said, as she returned the folder, 'isn't it illegal, what you're doing? I mean, it would be in America: you can't bribe boys to play football or basketball until they're eighteen. Very strictly enforced. They send college coaches to prison all the time over this.'

'*Nothing's* illegal in India,' Anand Mehta replied with a smile. 'Because, technically, *everything's* illegal in India. You see how it works, Ms Rupinder?' He had not been wrong: this woman really *did* remind him of Asha.

He gave her his card anyway.

An hour later, done with the paradox-people and their bullshit, a little bit tipsy from all that free Indian champagne (he had promised Asha, who worried he was turning 'psychotic', that he wouldn't drink for a month – but not that he wouldn't reject *free* drinks),

Mehta walked out of the hotel, and into an autorickshaw, and said, 'Bandra Kurla Complex.' Well before they came to the financial centre, he told the auto to stop at a bridge with a view of the Mithi river, and got down. Some shade of colour between grey and black, tinged with the dark green of the brave trees growing on its banks, the ravaged Mithi river, into which all the city's effluent and shit flowed untreated, moved towards the ocean slowly, sluggishly, and indecisively – so human-like in its movement, Anand thought. In the middle of the river, an old man, shirtless above his blue lungi, rowed a boat with a single oar, as he searched for something in the murky water. What the fuck are you fishing for? Nothing lives in this toxic river of Mumbai. As if agreeing with Mehta's assessment, the old man turned his boat around, and began moving back to shore. Now Anand Mehta's sense of scale changed. He watched the old man struggle, with his thin tough arms, to take his little boat against the current. Pitted against a human's strength, the dying river had become a powerful thing. 'Do well *and* do good,' Mehta said aloud and smiled. A decade ago, when he returned to India, Anand had imagined that matters would be as simple as floating along a river. Yes, he would lead the good life – servants, a big flat, a wife, home-cooked food, weekend fucks in air-conditioned hotels near technical colleges – but he would also do *good things* for his motherland. It would be simple enough, he had imagined. There would be Rotary Clubs and Blood Banks on every street – a man would just have to sign up and show his face on Sunday mornings; moral glow would be one of the ancillary benefits of living in India. Now, watching that old man strain his muscles to row his boat, Anand Mehta wondered: what if doing good in India was like going *against* the current? You can barely make a buck here, and in earning it, what if you end up screwing the poor, the people you imagined you would help a bit in your spare time? The boat struggled to reach dry land; Anand Mehta dreamed of New York.

When the smell from the river became overpowering, he took an autorickshaw to Bandra, and from there a taxi over the Sea

Link bridge and all the way to the Cricket Club where he settled down into his favourite veranda table for tea and toast – which was precisely when the bombshell landed.

Tommy Sir called and told.

Manju was gone. After three years and two months, the cricket sponsorship programme was over. A table shook; breadcrumbs scattered and tea spilled on the tablecloth.

'Gone?' Mehta asked Tommy Sir. 'Gone where? Gone why? What the fuck are you talking about? I could be on the verge of getting some woman from a venture fund in Iowa City to take this boy from me, how can he be gone now?'

'Goldenboy is gone,' Tommy Sir said quietly. 'He ran away. He didn't come to the selection match in Shivaji Park. His career is over.'

'Where is he now? With his brother? That other criminal?'

'No. He's in Navi Mumbai.'

'Why has he gone to Navi Mumbai?'

But Tommy Sir hung up.

In the next few minutes, Anand Mehta came up with the following observations about cricket: that it was a fraud, and at the most fundamental level. Only ten countries play this game, and only five of them play it well. If we had any self-respect, we'd finally grow up as a people and play football. No: let's not expose ourselves to real competition, much safer to be in a 'world cup' against St Kitts and Bangladesh. Self-obsession without self-belief: the very definition of the Indian middle class, which is why it loves this fraud sport.

Poised to offer the world more deep thoughts about the gentleman's game, Mehta heard:

Shot! Bloody Good Shot!

A blue screen on the veranda of the Cricket Club protected club members from the matches played in the Brabourne stadium; it rippled, and two boys in white rushed towards the dark red ball rolling about the base of the screen.

Confronted by the sound and smell of an instant of real cricket, Mehta felt all his mighty observations turn to ashes.

In the evening, after a tele-con with Rakesh, the IAS officer's son, (whose cough, thank God, had improved), Mehta booked another flight to Delhi, to meet a political connection before taking the train to Dhanbad to work on his distressed power plant. He seemed to be in high spirits.

'We'll have to do battle out there for our power plant, Rakesh,' he declared, 'so let's do battle.'

But in truth, the end of his cricket sponsorship programme had shaken Anand Mehta more than he admitted even to himself, and he was going to need a long holiday when he returned to Mumbai.

For this too is hell: knowing you are not – and can *never* be – as good as you want to be.

•

Across a shining creek, in Navi Mumbai, Manjunath was waking up. Yawning and slapping his cheeks, he got out of bed and saw that familiar sparrow sitting on the fan. Can this really be my new home, he wondered. Can this really be my new bed?

Some part of him was starting to believe it.

It was his third morning in Javed's flat, and he was growing used to waking up like this, a comic book under the cot, and a bird hopping about the blades of the fan. With each new morning, a life without cricket seemed to become more real.

Except this morning when the doorbell rang, and Manju opened the door; expecting to find Javed and breakfast, he found a strange man staring him up and down.

'Javed is not here – he went to the mall to buy some film tickets. So I thought, it is time for me to come and see you.' Bald and moustached, luminous in cotton clothes, Mr Ansari had the family's trademark beak nose; but his slit-like hooded eyes reminded Manju of an Uzbek warrior he had once seen in a programme on the History Channel.

As the maid came in, and prepared the table for breakfast, Manju felt that pair of Uzbek eyes inspect him very thoroughly.

'Mr Manjunath. My son is always talking of this Mr Manjunath. Now at last I see this Manju, and his famous forearms.'

They were served curry and pieces of warm bread, which the Ansaris, family of eccentrics, ate every morning in preference to parathas.

'You know I am a cricketer myself?' Mr Ansari spun a few imaginary balls towards Manju. 'I got into Aligarh on the cricket quota, in 1976. Left-arm spinner, right-hand batsman. Cricket is every Indian boy's dream; but not my Javed's. Cricket and corruption: an old song, and not one that you two boys invented. Javed's uncle Imtiaz said the same thing when they didn't select him for India. It *can* happen. A selector can push his son into the team, yes: but when he stands at the crease, all three stumps fly. Not the best game, not the beautiful game: just the honest game, in the end. Have you ever heard me on the BBC Hindi service, by the way? I have some old tapes here. But eat now. Eat well. We'll talk later.'

When they were done, Mr Ansari summoned him into his car, and they drove to an office, where they descended into a basement hall past a sign saying 'Bulk Science Textbooks'.

'You know left-handers are all brilliant people, like Leonardo da Vinci?' Mr Ansari spoke suddenly.

'Yes, sir.'

'My Javed is a genius, if he fails at cricket – by the way, I hope you know he failed only because he *wanted* to – he will start a big company like Mister Steven Jobs. So I don't blame *you* for anything, Mr Manjunath. That I don't.'

Opening a door, Mr Ansari, importer of scientific textbooks, ushered Manju into his empire, an underground hall filled with textbooks, some still lying inside half-opened cartons, others arranged in bright piles which rose two or three feet tall. Men were lowering more cartons into the basement.

Manju counted the cartons and decided he would never again have to worry about the cost of college textbooks.

'You know what I call my son Javed?'

'The Nurse,' Manju said.

Mr Ansari looked up sharply.

'He tells you everything. Yes, you go to the hospital and you'll see all the nurses are from Kerala. My Javed has a nurse inside him – he has a big fat Malayalee nurse inside him. That's the only way he can take care of himself: if he's taking care of someone else. It's not charity. It's the only way he can preserve himself. By falling in love. First he loved me. Now he loves you. But I don't blame you for anything.'

You *do* blame me, Manju thought. You blame me for everything. But you've been too scared, ever since your other son killed himself, to tell Javed what to do or whom to see.

Now Manju understood why Javed had aborted his cricketing career – to prove a point to this sweetly manipulative father: and in Javed's mind this raised him higher than everyone else he knew. But soon he would have to do this again, destroy himself again and stand even higher on that wreck (maybe the next discarded self would be labelled 'College Student who talked like Harsha Bhogle', and the one after that 'Guitar Player who sounded like Freddie Mercury the Rock Star', and the one after that ...), until he was entirely isolated from other people by an enormous pile of his own dead selves. And when he got there, to that high and arrogant place, he would be lost to everyone else. Except me, Manju thought. I will always be able to get to him.

Mr Ansari turned to shout at the men delivering more cardboard cartons of books, and then turned back to Manju.

'You think I don't know Javed wants to run away with you and go to Kanyakumari and whatnot? Look at me as I talk, Mr Manjunath. That boy *is* mad sometimes. But another part of me says, he is seventeen, he is young, now is the time for him to run away with a friend. This is the most important time of your lives ...

seventeen and eighteen is when the world can still be saved, do you follow? Once the door closes … are you actually listening to me, Mr Manjunath?'

The workers had left: the two of them were alone in the room. Manju folded his arms; his eyes on the textbooks, Mr Ansari picked his way in silence through cartons and boxes to the far end of the room. Manju wondered if he could leave.

The textbook businessman scratched his jaw.

'Look at me when I talk, Manju. Good. Now I told Javed, please be careful what you do, I don't want the neighbours or the relations talking. Be quiet. Be careful. That's all I ask for.'

Getting down on one knee, he ripped a carton of books open, and kept talking, even as he gasped from the exertion.

'He has no discipline. No discipline or self-control. The only discipline he has is that he loves people very honestly and sincerely …'

Rising to his feet, wiping his palms against his trousers, Mr Ansari penetrated deeper into the labyrinth of textbooks, looking among the cartons as though for some lost codex.

Manju was no longer sure he could mind-read Mr Ansari, no longer certain that this bald man with the sly eyes was just a subtler version of a familiar figure.

Out there, Manju thought, with regret – a regret he would feel so keenly for the rest of his life – there must be fellows who are actually *proud* of their fathers.

•

Coca-Cola in his right hand, Javed Ansari sat at a table in the highest level of a mall in Vashi, and turned the pages of a legal textbook. *Mastering the Indian Penal Code for Competitive Examinations*. A cheap paperback edition, probably pirated, that an old man had been selling on the footpath outside the mall. Javed had bought the book while waiting for Manju, and now, pen in hand, he flipped through it while glancing at his cell phone.

He turned to a blank page at the end of the textbook, and, with only his finger for a pen, wrote:

What is it we search for, in drink and in the depths?

The sentence had occurred to him two nights ago, as he watched inebriated men staggering through Vashi. Why did they do this, night after night?

Producing a ball-point pen from his leather jacket, he completed the poem:

What is it we search for, in drink and in the depths? asks Javed.
A star fell to the earth, and we hunt for it in the world's rubbish.
The name of the star is love.

He sucked his teeth. No. The poem didn't click. He crossed out the three lines, and dropped his pen: *nothing* he wrote these days clicked. Maybe he should give up poetry and stick to guitar. Try to start a band with Ranjith and the others.

He continued reading randomly through the legal code.

'Section 120-B: Possessing assets disproportionate to known sources of income.' He amended it with his pen.

'Section 120-B applied to Poets: Possessing goals and ambitions in life disproportionate to known sources of talent.'

He closed the textbook.

Manju, where the *fuck* are you? Sipping on his can of Coke, Javed checked his cell phone again. Nothing. Not even 'Sorry Javed I'll be late'. Don't tell me the boy is *still* thinking of going back to cricket. Yes, he is – obviously. Javed grit his teeth. Because Javed Ansari knew this Manju by now: knew this Manju's tactic of exposing vulnerability, which drew others – boys and girls alike – to him, and then withdrawing from them, leaving those boys and girls angry, because they did not know he had read their minds and had been vulnerable in a way *calculated* to lure them in, and that this unselfconscious drawing-you-in-and-then withdrawing-from-you was the flaw in the alloy, the necessary element of perversion in Manju's character, which gave this boy who grew up in a slum the inner strength of steel.

Opening the legal textbook again, he turned to the last page once more and wrote: 'Thoughts are like politicians that get between our bodies.'

Did *that* make sense? Catching himself about to burp, Javed stuck his hand into his jacket to rub his chest. Nasty stuff, this Coca-Cola. It must be fucking with his brain. Maybe it was also making his hair fall out, he thought, and ran his fingers over his forehead.

Stretching his arms over his head, he glanced up at the ceiling, wondering whether to call Manju – or whether instead to call Ranjith and talk to him about starting a rock band. Let's wait another five minutes for Manju to turn up.

Stirring the Coca-Cola can with his right hand, he kept turning the pages of the lawbook until he reached 'Section 377. "Unnatural offences."'

'Whoever voluntarily has carnal intercourse against the order of nature with any man, woman or animal shall be punished with imprisonment for life, or with imprisonment of either description for term which may extend to ten years, and shall also be liable to fine.'

Picking up his pen, Javed drew a giant penis over the page, before embellishing it with appropriately sized balls and pubic hair.

•

Fear: how it enters your world again, like the cool, dark, delicious current that ripples beneath the sun-warmed surface of a mountain stream.

Are you *sure* you're done with cricket, Manju? Don't you remember your innings against Fatima School, and that even better one against Ambani School … are you *absolutely* sure you want to leave cricket and stay here in Navi Mumbai?

Rather than meet Javed at the mall after leaving Mr Ansari, Manju had returned to the flat, opened the door with his spare key, and gone to the bedroom with its golden bed. After a long time, he was thinking about cricket, and at first he pretended that this was the result of Mr Ansari's speech to him. But deep down, he knew it was not cricket that was making his heart thump: no, not cricket. It was the other thing.

Fear.

Opening the wardrobe, Manju ran his fingers through the pile of Javed's shirts, and drew his nose closer to them. Sniffing through the cool beautiful shirts, his mouth filling up with saliva, he found a blue-bordered handkerchief doused with the scent of citrus, and put it across his face.

All that was warm in Javed's heart touched his own heart and chilled it. Now that he had come to Javed's home and slept on his golden bed, Radha would call him a gay. *All* the boys would call him that. Sofia would smile and say, 'I'll protect you, my friend. My *gay* friend.'

Then the phone began ringing, startling him.

Recognizing the number as Sofia's, he did not answer.

It kept ringing. It kept ringing.

Manju kept hunting through Javed's wardrobe. He looked over the bright shirts, and then at the rows of size-twelve shoes and sneakers and rubber chappals that were even larger than size twelve, until he saw, nearly buried under the footwear, an old blue cricket helmet, embossed with golden initials that said 'J.A.' Raising the helmet with both hands he brought it closer and closer, until the initials touched his forehead. Manju shivered from the cold touch of the grille that protected the batsman's mouth.

With the helmet pressed against his forehead, he sat down on the floor.

Leave Javed? No, he could not just leave Javed now. If he went back to cricket, Javed would follow. He would write poems for him. The other boys would talk.

Getting out of Navi Mumbai, he thought, as he put the helmet back into the wardrobe, would take just as much preparation as getting in.

The phone began ringing again.

Hiding behind the curtain, Manju stood at the window, turning every now and then to the glowing phone on the bed. Down below on the street, a teenager on a canary-yellow bike zipped through the busy road. Behind the curtain, Manjunath Kumar watched: the silliest thing on a scooter was freer than he would ever be.

•

City bread is not served in the villages around the Western Ghats; nor is raita, pulao, biryani, basmati rice, or whatever else you've been fed in the city. Sit on the floor and be served *raagi mudde* like everyone else. Once a week you'll get chicken, and once a week you'll get mutton.

Eat, son.

Radha Kumar had still not grown used to the dark violet ball of *raagi*, which sat amidst a dark brown soup of sliced onion and cabbage.

He dreamed of white rice.

He talked to himself.

From eight in the morning, he had been sweeping the fields where wheat was being winnowed, cursing and mumbling and delivering long, bitter soliloquies that amused his cousins. He did not *have* to work in the fields. His uncle had made that clear, for they remembered their cricket hero Radha, and for people in this village he would always have a film-star's eyes. But Radha *wanted* to work: and did not want to chit-chat or play cards or go to the movies.

He made them work him for eight, eight and a half, nine hours a day.

In the evening he washed himself with cold water and went to the dining hall, where his cousins, sitting cross-legged on the dining room floor, were eating their *raagi mudde* while his uncle Revanna talked on the cell phone, fixing the price of wheat or corn or something else that grew on fertilizer.

'Phone for you.'

His uncle Revanna rubbed the Nokia against his shirt, and held it out to him.

'Phone for you. From Mumbai. He called in the morning as well.'

Radha leapt up and grabbed the cell phone, and without pausing to confirm there was someone at the other end of the line, shouted:

'Manju. Manju. Why *does* the boiling water turn into ice first?'

There was a long pause, and Radha brought his right thumb towards his teeth; but he heard his brother's voice break into a laugh, the way it did in the bedroom, in the dark, when he made a joke about their father.

'Manju. Manju,' he said, pressing the phone so hard to his body that his earlobe grew hot. 'How is Navi Mumbai, tell me everything. Tell me, tell me.'

Closing his eyes, Radha sensed from the words, from their tentativeness, that Manju was looking around to make sure Javed was not listening in.

'Manju, you're mad. Don't think about doing it. Don't think about going back to that man in Chembur. Stay with Javed in Navi Mumbai. Stay there for two or three years. Listen to your older brother for once.'

Silence on the other end of the phone; down on the floor, Radha's cousins kept licking *raagi* from their fingers. Blocking them out, Radha concentrated on what he had to tell his brother.

'Manju, I've been thinking about you every day, every day. Manju, I know what your problem is. Manju: you always liked pain and thought you had to bear it for our sake. Remember when you broke your thumb and kept batting? Don't do it again.'

He was aware that Manju was now talking about their father, about his health, so Radha shouted:

'His health? I hope his balls fall off, I hope his fingers fall off, I hope he goes blind, I hope he has cancer on his tongue, I hope he is sent to some mental hospital where they beat him once a day.'

Radha was aware that on the other end of the line, his brother was asking him if he had gone mad, and so he shouted again:

'No. No. I won't go mad if I talk like this about that man, I will go mad if I do *not* talk like this about that man.'

Radha looked at his cousins, gorging themselves with the messy raagi, their lips stained, their eyes dazed by country carbohydrates, and he said:

'Manju, Revanna Uncle here says he knows where our mother is. He says she's alive. She's still in Mumbai, Manju. Ten years ago she sent Revanna Uncle a letter asking how you and I were – he showed it to me. There's an address on it in Virar She could still be alive. Maybe I can go to her and ask her for some money? No. She never wrote after that. No? Why not? You're right, Manju, you're right. Either she's dead, or if she's alive, she doesn't want us, and we don't want her, either. But I *do* want to go back to cricket, Manju. It's all I'm good for. Listen: I think I know what is wrong with my backlift. I've been practising here in the fields. We have to reimburse Anand Mehta his 75,000 rupees, and then he'll let me play again. If you do go back, will you tell them all to give me another chance to play for Mumbai?'

•

A coconut palm grew right outside Tommy Sir's building in Kalanagar: it was time for it to be culled of its fruit before they fell on passers-by, and the man from South India who did the work each year was at it again. Stripped to the waist, secured to the tree by a cord around his middle and another around his legs, he had climbed up with a curved knife to hack at the nuts, which rained down on the footpath like artillery. Done with his work, the man wiped his face and glistening torso with a cloth, and rewarded himself: slashing open the final coconut on the tree, he threw his head back, raised the coconut high, and drank its shining water. It was like a tableau of triumphant completion.

Tommy Sir sighed, let the curtain cover his window, and went back to his desk.

A waste-basket next to the desk was stuffed with what remained of a torn manila folder; now he continued the business of tearing up his unfinished notes on the third battle of Panipat. The geological watercolours had already been taken away by the trash collector this morning. He remembered that he had to call the Jehangir Art Gallery to cancel his show.

Manjunath Kumar was gone, and his life's work as a cricket scout was finished. He had emailed his editors at the *Mumbai Sun* asking that his column be terminated. They said that 'Some Boys Rise, Some Boys Fall' would continue, with or without him – they owned the rights. Pramod Sawant would write it from now on.

Manjunath Kumar was gone. And he would never find another boy like that.

Six Point Two.

Tommy Sir had to go to Lilavati Hospital for another round of tests for his blood sugar, B.P. and cholesterol. He smoked a cigarette on the way.

Near the Kalanagar Signal, he stopped, and looked up at the billboard that had once said, 'When Sachin Tendulkar dreamed of becoming the world's best batsman, so did …' Now it featured an advertisement for Coca-Cola. From the advertisement, his eyes moved up to the skywalk, the zig-zagging metal bridge that connected various locations in the neighbourhood to the Bandra train station. Behind the metal grid, men moved back and forth. Tommy Sir's eyes grew tired. He felt that up there, on that seemingly never-ending bridge, shadowy figures were moving towards obscure destinations, possibly only to return to their point of origin, like in an architectural sketch of infinity by M.C. Escher. Hell is a choice, made daily and by millions, and breathing slowly and watching this aerial cage, Tommy Sir saw Mumbai, minute by minute, unbecome and become hell.

•

They were in an autorickshaw that was moving slowly through crowded streets towards the train station. Next to him Manju felt Javed's powerful body, his thick shoulders.

'I know you must be worried about Radha,' Javed said, 'but don't do anything rash.'

Javed's forehead had darkened, and the two veins bulged: a sight so impressively real that it drained the life from the hapless crowd around the autorickshaw. Ordinary people, bloodless people. If Manju went back to Mumbai, he would become one of them. If he stayed here, he would become whatever Javed was. These were his choices.

'Manju, when you phoned and said you were coming to Navi Mumbai, you know how happy I was? In the station I looked into each and every train to see if you were there.'

The autorickshaw hit bumps and potholes in the road, and Javed said, 'Fuck,' each time.

'What do you like about me?' Manju asked. 'The only thing I'm good at is cricket.'

Javed turned his face as he spoke. 'I'm not going to sing your praises, Captain. Javed is not that kind of man. Manju, c'mon. Don't believe all that shit your father has put in your head. Think.' Now Javed turned to show that he was tapping his forehead. 'What *would* someone like about you? *Think*.'

Manju tried.

•

Before a background of luminous green mountains, a succession of ponds and wet paddyfields fled past the train tracks, solitary egrets stalking in them, and the bushes sparkling with wild flowers close enough to pluck. Then came the towns, shining and white and set in geometrical grids against the green hills. For Manju's benefit, Javed pronounced the name of each place where the train stopped.

Belapur.

Man-a-sa-saro-var.

Now and then the sun disappeared, and when it shone down on them again Manju again noticed how fast Javed's hair was receding.

Soon he would have a bald spot on his crown. Manju raised his right hand to block the sun from scorching Javed's scalp.

'I'm really happy your brother said you could do whatever you want,' Javed said. 'Now you're free.'

They stood apart from everyone else that morning, two boys older than their years, older and wiser than anyone else on that slow-moving train.

A man in a grey bush-shirt lit a cigarette and smoked; in between puffs, when he cleared his chest, the mucus made a noise like five hundred years of human history. The light in Javed's eyes shone playfully on Manju. Then a passenger heaved his luggage to the door and stood between them, and they had to talk around his sweating body, until the train pulled in to Panvel station.

Once there, they ran. They had been in that train so long. They ran to the end of the platform and up the stairs, and then Manju leant over a bridge to see a train down below. 'Read what's written on its side. Nethravati Express.'

Javed pressed against him and looked down at the train.

'And?'

'This is the train. This is the train we take every summer to see our village.'

Javed pinched his collar.

'What is your shirt size? We'll buy you a shirt.'

'Why? I don't want any.'

'If you have clothes here, you won't leave.'

Manju nodded. He moved alongside Javed among the clothes sellers, pretending to look for a shirt, till he found what he wanted: a baseball cap.

A gift for Javed. He fitted it on his friend's head, and thought that it covered the receding hairline pretty well.

Javed slapped the cap off his head.

'I'm *not* going bald. It's just the Coca-Cola I was drinking. And even if I *was* going bald, Javed Ansari is not the kind of man to hide anything. Do you understand?'

They were at the edge of a flight of steps that led out of the station; Javed ran down the steps. Oranges and chikoos were being sold from cane baskets at the edges of the steps, and four Muslim beggars, each missing a different body part, sat on four of the steps, one above the other. Manju followed Javed, avoiding the beggars. The edges of the stairs, smoothed from wear, were covered with straw, and Javed's feet were size twelve. Manju knew it was going to happen, but before he could shout a warning he saw Javed lose his footing, and, arms flailing, drop straight down three steps. Manju leapt to steady his friend, who had held on to the bannister just in time to prevent a major accident. Both looked down at the steps; Javed winced and stretched his right foot. 'Man,' Manju said. 'It must hurt. Man.' Now, for a moment, they could hold each other in the open, safely and without worry, as poor boys could with impunity, and as people of their class could not.

Hand in hand, the two continued down the stairs.

But the moment they reached the foot of the stairs, Javed found himself alone again. Amidst stacks of cargo jeans, shoes, and T-shirts, Manju had seen a man who was selling green mechanical frogs that crawled over the floor. Javed watched as Manju turned the noisy frog toy over and over with his shoe. 'Complex boy,' Javed said.

Manju let go of the frog, which crawled in circles until the vendor of clothes repossessed it.

'If you go back, your father will marry you off, Manju. That simple.'

'No,' Manju said, and with greater emphasis each time, 'No. No. No.'

'Yes. And one more thing, Manju: you'll have to marry your father, too, and look after him like a wife. You know all this, and you're still thinking of going back?'

Manju shrugged, as if he didn't care.

'My life is not limited by *your* imagination,' Manju said.

'Good,' Javed said. 'Good. Tell *them* that.'

Instead, moving away from Javed, Manju narrowed his eyes and searched again for the Nethravati Express, which he spied among the trains behind him. But when he turned around to view it better, he found that the roof of the train had suddenly turned into glass; and Manju saw its compartments filled with familiar faces of relatives, cousins, and neighbours from his village: all of them, like his uncle Revanna, dressed in their cotton shirts and white dhotis, chit-chatting in their loud dialect, and smelling of rural curry, as if the entire village had arrived in Mumbai. Now everyone sitting in the glass train went quiet and gazed at Manju, as if they had come here just to ask him a question.

The hallucination ended – the roof of the train turned into metal again; something was tickling Manju's ankle. He looked down to find that another of the noisy mechanical frogs had found him out, and had propped itself against his shoe, as if it meant to crawl up his leg; turning it round with his shoe, he kicked it back in the direction of its vendor.

'Javed,' he said. 'Javed.'

But when he looked around, Javed had disappeared.

Manju ran into the crowd looking for him. He ran up and down steps, and came out of the station, yelling, 'I'm not going to leave you! I'm not going back to them!'

'Manju.'

He turned around to see Javed waving at him.

'You're mad. I just came outside to get a coconut. You are completely mad. You know this?'

'I thought you had left me.'

Javed shook his head. 'Why would *I* leave you?'

The coconut-seller was watching, but Manju put his arm around Javed.

They took turns drinking from the tender coconut.

Before Javed was done, Manju knocked the nut out of his hand. 'Kambli!'

'*You're* Kambli!'

'*You! You!*'

The two chased each other down the road.

From behind, they heard the coconut-seller yelling; the boys stopped.

'Shit. We didn't pay.'

'We should go back, no?'

'No! Just run. He can't come after us.'

'He *is* coming after us! He *is* coming!'

Manju held on to Javed's shirt, and they ran, and then he went ahead and Javed held on to *his* shirt; in this way, one holding on to the other, shrieking and laughing, they charged down the mud road that led into Panvel city.

•

One morning when she was about ten years old, Manju's mother had discovered that the man she loved more than anyone else in the world, her father, had left a toy on her younger sister Prema's bed. He had never placed anything there for *her*. She went out to the courtyard, and found the rusty saw that her mother used to cut jackfruit: tiptoeing back in, she went to the bedroom, and slapped Prema awake. Twice. Thrice. When her younger sister woke up, she held the saw right at her throat. 'If you take his love away from me … if you even *think* of taking his love away from me …' Her sister Prema wailed at the top of her voice and her father came running into the bedroom: dropping the saw at once, she tried to explain, but that was the only time he had ever struck her in the face.

•

Manju opened his eyes: someone had clapped his hands right in front of them.

'How much *do* you dream every day?'

Manju took stock of his situation; he was lying on the golden bed and had been dreaming once again of his mother's childhood.

Showered and fragrant and back from the hot day's running around, Javed stood wiping his hair with a thin cotton towel.

'Your turn now.' Javed threw the wet cotton towel at him.

Manju tied the wet cotton across his face, tucking it behind his ears like an armed robber's mask, making his friend laugh. Inhaling the scent of freshly shampooed hair, Manju spoke through the mask.

'Javed, when do you have to go back to your father's place?'

Javed shrugged. 'Before it's dark. That's when my father thinks I might get up to something with you.'

Tearing away the wet towel from his face, throwing it to the bed, Manju pursed his lips, licking them from inside his mouth, before he said: 'Javed.'

'Yes?'

'Go down and get some condoms,' he said. 'We have three hours left.'

Javed looked at him with a frown.

'What? Condoms?'

'Yes. Go get some. It's time,' Manju said. 'I'll take a shower while you're gone.'

'You want *me* to go get condoms?' Javed asked, trying to figure this out.

'Yes. I'm shy. You go down and get them from the chemist's shop,' Manju said.

This was it: it was going to happen now.

When Javed left, to make sure of his resolution, Manju went to the wardrobe and opened it again. The helmet was there, waiting for him. Then he leaned forward, picked up the helmet, and brought it, with its metal visor, to his eye-level; he peeped into the three round holes that had been bored into the top to make it lighter, before turning the helmet over. He smelled Javed's head-sweat, and recognized the indentations made in the foam padding by Javed's skull; from the padding, his eye was led down into the black bowl of the helmet; and that curved darkness, along with the cold touch of the metal visor, reminded him of the well with the rusty grille in Dahisar, where the turtles with glints of gold swam, and as he brought his nose closer and closer to the smell of Javed's head, he felt himself fall through the rusty grid and down through the well's darkness into something deeper – into fear, all the fear that had ever been born on earth, his brother's fears, his runaway mother's fears, Mohan Kumar's fears, the fears of his village, fears of the time before he was born – and then, instead of turtles, Manju saw the faces of Mohan Kumar, Radha, Tommy Sir and Anand Mehta merge into one collective animal – and this animal bellowed at him: 'Do you know what name we'll give you if you stay with Javed?'

Yes. I know.

Manju was sick in the stomach; he dropped the helmet, and kicked the wardrobe door shut.

He was sweating: it had begun, and it would recur throughout his life. Confusion in Manjunath would lead to fury in Manjunath: and this fury – against the way things are – would grow and grow until it destroyed every single alternative to the way things were.

Back in the living room he sat on the floor. Curling his hair with one forefinger, he sketched 'V's in the air with the other. The 'V's burned, and disappeared, and he saw darkness. He gave it its oldest name: *Kattale*.

He stood up. Step by step he returned to the wardrobe; and as he did so, he could see already that years from now, he might look back at this moment and these steps, and think of them as the last moment and the last steps when he still had a choice; but he would know in his heart that there had been no choice and no selection to make.

He opened the wardrobe. The helmet was waiting – *of all the masks you will have to choose from*, it asked, *why not take me as your own?*

As he strapped the helmet on, from behind him he heard the door open, and Javed come in.

'Manju.'

When he turned, helmeted and with his lips pressed tight, Javed gaped at him. Something in a brown paper bag fell to the floor, and Manju saw the packet of condoms.

'Why are you wearing my helmet?'

'You have the condoms?' Manju asked. Javed nodded.

'Good.' Manju pointed at the thing lying on the floor. Then he looked Javed in the eye: 'Why don't you pick one, put it on, and then fuck yourself.'

Unstrapping the helmet, he threw it to the floor so hard it bounced once, and then smacked against the wall.

Javed just stood. This was his other face – the small, scared one.

Walking around him to the open door, Manju stopped, and just to make absolutely sure that this had all not been a waste, that this would be final, and he would not see this pathetic face again in the morning at cricket practice, he whispered, as he went past, the word that he and his brother had written three years ago on Javed Ansari's chest-guard.

'You *homo.*'

With that he left, and walked as fast as possible to the train station.

•

The flight landed at 11.45 a.m., disgorging, in addition to the usual mob of men and women shuffling between Delhi and Mumbai, a businessman who had been forced to discover, yet again, how fucking fully this atavism among nations, this Republic (so-called) of India, was filled to the brim with the repressed, depressed, and dangerous.

Anand Mehta had returned two days later than scheduled. Another failure – after all the money he had put into turning around the power plant, into developing his relationship with Rakesh the IAS officer's son, what does it all come down to in the end? Rakesh the IAS officer's son turns out to be a very inhibited character, their local lawyer was incompetent, and this nexus of second-rateness ensures, even after they have paid the politicians and bureaucrats, that some other IAS officer's son (the very opposite of inhibited), who is in tandem with some other Mumbai entrepreneur, coolly occupies the power plant one morning; and the moment those guys are inside, and have *their* lock on the compound, the police – as always in India, Constitutional Defender of the first and fastest to encroach – take their side, and tell Anand Mehta *he* is in the wrong, and he should think himself lucky he's leaving Dhanbad a free man. On his way home from the airport, observing a dark Victorian Gothic building with its complicated white windows, Mehta felt as if all that nineteenth-century tracery had been knotted across his chest.

You're back to begging your classmates for money now, mate.

'Beer.' He touched his driver's shoulder.

He got out of the car by the yellow awning of Café Ideal on Chowpatty.

'Tuborg,' he told the waiter as he sat at the window with the view of the ocean and the beach, and then checked: 'Costs the same as Indian beer?'

One big green Tuborg down, and half of another.

Sea breeze streamed in through the open windows. So here I sit, in strong sunshine, and my imperishable mistakes. Well done, son. Well done. One more flop. Anand Mehta wiped away his tears. Ah, fuck it. The whole world is a Failure, anyway. America is ten trillion billion dollars in debt. They're fucked. Everything is fucked. Which is why, Anand Mehta decided right there, that his next move should be to short-sell the entire S&P 500 index, plus the FTSE, plus European equities and bonds. 'I'm betting against every-fucking-thing out there. If the stock market crashes,' Mehta said, summoning the waiter over, 'I make a *lot* of money. If the world ends,' he winked, '…I make a *killing*.'

'One more Tuborg, sir?'

•

Six beers! Enough, enough. Mehta left the cafe, and with some effort climbed the bridge that led to Chowpatty beach. His stomach churned, and he wondered if he should find a toilet. Don't worry about me, I'll be fine, sir. My liver is a freak of nature, sir: my liver is bigger than Pfizer. Don't worry about me, don't, sir, don't. A stray copy of the *Mumbai Sun* was fluttering around; bending down with care, he picked it up. He began looking for that page in the middle with all the stuff about which actress was … and with who …

He stopped turning when he reached the sports page.

Two each from Ruia and Jai Hind in
Mumbai Under-19 squad.
T.E. Sarfraz, record holder, is Captain.

Five boys had been captured in a photograph below the article. There. Mehta put his finger on the lower right hand of the photo. *That* boy. The one with the bat slung on his shoulder like a hero, sitting with a big smile on top of the stone-roller. That boy. I know you, I know you. Anand Mehta turned the paper over, and read it again, and then took out his cell phone and went down the speed dial address book until he got to 'T'.

'Who is this?' the gruff voice asked.

'Anand. Anand Mehta. Don't remember me?'

After an almost audible hesitation, Tommy Sir said:

'Yes. Remember.'

'Our boy has made it. I saw the article in the paper. He's made the Mumbai Under-19s. Our boy. Manjunath Kumar.'

To which Tommy Sir said: 'Leave him alone.'

Anand Mehta, suddenly transported to the Hernshead lake in Central Park for a brief second or two, returned to Mumbai and said, '… leave him alone … ? Who are you to tell me what to do?'

There was a sigh, and Tommy Sir, accepting the inevitable, said, 'He made it, yes. But what a drama. There was too much tension,

I tell you. Too much. So the boy runs away at the last minute to Navi Mumbai.'

'Yes, I know that, Tommy Sir. But he came back?'

'Yes, Mr Anand. See: out of the blue, my daughter Lata, this morning, tells me, she will turn off the lights in the kitchen every night, so half my life's worries are solved there. It's like a Van Gogh scenario; I want to take a canvas and paint a sunrise. Why? Because the other half of my worries were solved four days ago. What happened four days ago? Four days ago, Sofia, formerly Radha's girlfriend, phones me and says, cool as ice, "He is back. And I'm his new girlfriend." Gives the phone to Manju and Manju says, "Tommy Sir, I'll never run away again. I'll never go to Navi Mumbai again." Did you hear all that, Mr Anand Mehta? And he has a *girl*-friend now.'

Mehta took his time to say: 'I knew it.'

'Personally I spoke to Srinivasan Sir. Personally I spoke to each of the other selectors. Personally told them lies, that the boy had a family health issue. Nine times in ten they would tell me go to hell. But this Manju is a golden boy, born to shine, never knows what it is to lose. I got him in the team for the Policeman's Invitation Cup. Selectors turn up to see him. He batted brilliantly, I tell you. Best he's ever been. Now Manju is in the Mumbai Under-19s. As I've always said: some boys rise.'

'So they *do* have character in the slums, Tommy Sir. They still do. And my money? What about the sponsorship?'

'Manju has promised, you will get your 75,000 rupees, Mr Anand. From the first cheque the boy makes, he will pay you back. But you must let his brother return to Mumbai and play here. Don't go to the police or make trouble.'

'Has the boy left college? You always said that was important.'

'Yes, he has. I told him, there is no other way. And he went to the principal and dropped out yesterday.'

With his left hand, Anand Mehta slapped both his cheeks and pulled at his moustache.

'Fantastic. By the way, Tommy Sir, you're fired. I'll take things over from here. I'll deal directly with Goldenboy.'

Before the old man could reply, Anand Mehta hung up. The newspaper had flown back to the floor of the bridge. Bending down, Mehta outlined the boy's grinning photograph with his thumbnail … No: not a *boy* anymore.

Manjunath Kumar

Said to be 'one of our brightest young prospects'

Anand Mehta stood up tall.

He thought he was ready to cry. Had 'Jo-Jo' Mistry ever done something like this? O, this was big. Bigger than Barbarossa. Remember where that cricketer and his brother and their father had been living when all of this began? Dahisar. Slum, absolute slum, rats *this* big running on his roof. And now: the cars, lifestyle, flat, stars and starlets chasing after him, everything he wants. (We should tell Pepsi and Adidas at once.) In return, little fellow with the big forearms is asked to do what for next twenty years? Something he loves, something everyone loves, cric … cri …

He staggered down to Chowpatty beach.

He had to call his wife and tell her. Asha. Asha! It worked. My plan worked!

Anand Mehta walked towards the water, watching it recede, watching the city become bigger with every step he took.

I have set a man free, he shouted at the waves.

In *Bombay* I have set a man free.

PART TWO

Eleven years after Selection Day

His eyes were growing smaller each year. He was certain of this when he examined his face on his birthday. Full of all those changes that are supposed to happen to *women* with age: the nose becomes big, and the eyes …

He was twenty-seven years old today.

Sitting astride a bench in the toilet of the Cricket Club of India, he was reading the newspaper. In his pocket was a white envelope with his severance cheque in it.

A man called Karan from SwadeshSymphony, the public relations firm that ran the Celebrity Cricket League in partnership with the Cricket Board, had given him the envelope, and the good news.

Two months. And they had a new job for him, starting right away.

Humming a film song, Manjunath turned the pages of the newspaper until something made him smile:

12 May

The Prime Minister's Office has stated that a person by name of V.V. Cherrinathan frequenting Mumbai under the pretext

> of being 'the prime minister's special adviser on marine biology' is not employed by the PMO in this capacity, or in any other. He is not an accredited expert on marine biology, meteorology, plate tectonics, political theory or personal finance. If approached by this person for money, the public is urged to report the matter to the police. *(Press Trust of India)*

Tearing the article out of the newspaper, he added it to the white envelope in his pocket. This was the kind of thing he liked to bring Radha from the outside world – it would be good for a laugh, and would defer the moment when he had to give his brother the bad news.

He looked around, and realized he was alone in the men's toilet.

So he bent over and licked his forearms like a cat, again and again. What if someone came in? Let them come in and scream. Call security, and throw me out. This would be the last time he was in the Cricket Club. No more wearing the armour – the pads, chest-guard, arm guard, the 'box' tucked in, thigh pads, forearm guards – no more of that second body of foam and plastic covering his own. He was free.

what happen?

His phone beeped six times in a row with the same message.

what happen?

Of course it was his father.

What happened is they dropped me, he texted back.

On the way out, two schoolboys in cricket whites stood pressed together, watching something on their cell phone. One of the boys glanced up: and said, at once, 'Can I have your autograph?' He held a little notepad towards Manju. 'And a selfie?'

'Do you know who I am?' Manju asked.

The boy smiled.

'Cricketer.'

Must have been a lean day for the two autograph hunters.

Manju, still only five foot four inches, observed that the two schoolboys were nearly as tall as he was. But he knew that for a cricketer, shortness of stature only adds to his mystique.

With an ironic smile, exactly like he'd seen Ravi Shastri affect for female admirers, he asked: 'What's my name?'

The boys looked at each other.

Manju said, 'I played for India Under-19, and for Mumbai, three seasons in the Ranji. Maybe you saw me in the Celebrity Superstar Cricket League? I was one of the non-celebrities, the real batsmen. I batted with Sanjay Khanna once: the actor? I have the record for the longest six hit by a non-celebrity in the history of the Celebrity Cricket League. Do you know how many metres the ball went?'

He seized the autograph book, before the boy could change his mind, and wrote his name on it.

Manjunath Kumar

Batter

He could read the question forming in the boy's eyes.

You really hit the biggest six in the Celebrity League?

You?

No one ever believed it.

'Yes, it was me,' he said, even before the boy asked.

Outside the club, he pushed past the grimy white clothes of cricket-playing teenagers and the immaculate white uniforms of their adult servants (chauffeurs, delivery men, peons). Manju looked quickly at his own T-shirt: he was wearing, appropriately enough, beige.

The two teenagers had followed him, perhaps for another autograph, but the moment they saw him sit down on Marine Drive, they turned back. No boy wants to see a cricketer enjoying solitude: it is not how he imagines his heroes.

A clear summer's evening. Looking to the south, Manju could see the skyscrapers of Nariman Point give way to a line of nearly identical low-rise buildings, Navy Nagar, and beyond them, and before the Arabian Sea, a final twinkling, a dot … the lighthouse at the end of Mumbai.

To his right, a pair of little slippers, each studded with glass gemstones, lay next to two warm black shoes; from somewhere down below, among the concrete rocks that buffered the city from the ocean, he heard a woman's laughter. When he looked at the slippers again, the sunlight shining in the cheap glass stones was suddenly too much to bear.

Twilight had set in by the time he got off the train at Santa Cruz station and walked through a congested market to a place called the Mafia Bar, which he visited each year on his birthday.

No connection whatsoever between name and decor (but then, this *is* Mumbai). The low wooden ceiling of the bar was ribbed like a Buddhist cave in Ajanta, and the red velvet covering the eight empty tables was so ancient that its decomposition could be smelled on the air-conditioned air, and after a few hours, would coat the tongue and render everything slightly acrid.

A black beam divided the bar; four tables on this side, four on that. Someone was sitting right behind the beam.

That was the spot Radha always chose, because whoever sat behind the black beam had an interrupted view of the small television fixed into a corner of the ceiling. Radha said he did not want cricket to poison even his drink.

Leaning around the black beam to smile at his brother, Radha held up a glass of rum: 'You're on TV. Turn around.' And though Manju knew this was just mischief – almost malice, on this of all days – he turned, in real hope, to the TV screen.

Of course he wasn't on TV. It was Ashvin Trivedi batting in a one-day match. Maybe from the recent India versus Namibia series? No: it was a replay of an older series against Puerto Rico. 'Legendary Encounters in Indian Cricket.' So Ashvin Trivedi, who had joined the Mumbai team after Manju had been dropped from it, was already a modern legend.

When the waiter came, Manju ordered a Coca-Cola.

'It's your birthday,' said his brother. 'Experiment.'

Radha had the fastidious good looks of the perennially

unemployed rake: his long black hair was gelled and brushed back until it curled up around his neck, he wore a silver ring in his left ear, and looked like a prince out of Sanskrit Romance. His beautiful irises, those 'film-star eyes', were now battered in by drink, but Manju could still see their colour.

'Alright, stick to your Coke. But happy birthday.'

Manju raised a glass of water to his brother's rum.

Still noticeably shorter than Radha, though better built, his hirsute forearms striped with veins, Manju's close-cropped hair was already turning grey, and he was starting to look the older of the two.

In the manner of such little bars, a door opened, three men came in, and then three more, and now the place was packed.

Mafia Bar was one of what Manju referred to as the Quarter Bars that filled the eastern side of the Santa Cruz station: as a stencilled logo on the wall indicated ('Quater System Available Here'), patrons were served liquor in nothing smaller than 180 ml 'quarters' (although 60 ml refills were permitted) while they gazed blankly at a TV screen showing cricket, either Indian or international, classic or instant, live or canned: quarter men, quarter sport.

They had started coming here three years ago, on Sofia's suggestion. ('Why don't you two meet on your birthdays like normal people?')

Behind the manager's desk stood a grandfather clock, with a dully moving pendulum. A lampshade hanging from a long cord glowed down on the bespectacled manager, who was hard at his accounts, like a Victorian allegory of Diligence in a den of vice. He had a silver pen in his shirt pocket.

'Look, Papa just walked in.'

'Papa' was an old man who visited the bar every night. Along with his whisky he ordered a plate of French fries which he ate one at a time. He had been doing this for nine years at this bar, according to Radha, and before that for eighteen years at the bar that had previously stood here.

'The waiters say he came in for a drink even during the Babri Masjid riots, Manju. But I see you're looking at your people again, aren't you?'

His people. Five middle-aged gay men, whom Manju remembered from the previous year, sat at a table in a corner, discussing the new Shah Rukh Khan film. First all five delivered their verdict together, 'Fantastic!' 'Amazing!' and then, after clearing his throat, and pronouncing his individual verdict to be 'very different', each man at the table analysed the film in turn, concluding that it was in fact either 'Fantastic', or 'Amazing'.

Now one of them said:

'Enough about films. This is my topic of discussion for today. Have you noticed how every young boy in Mumbai is now called Aryan?'

'So what's your worry?'

'My worry is, these boys called Aryan will go abroad to study, and the Americans will think all Indians are now Nazis.'

Laughter.

'*Aren't* we all Nazis now?'

Much more laughter.

The lights went out in the bar: at once, total silence. Radha and Manju felt themselves caught out – five dark silhouettes, turning in tandem, looked over at the brothers.

The lights returned, and everyone was happy and heterosexual again. The TV came back to life on a different channel: a chameleon was unrolling its tongue in slow motion. 'Papa', who had been eating French fries and gazing at the TV all through the blackout, did not seem to mind.

Radha ordered another quarter bottle of rum.

'Javed was in the papers today,' he said.

'I don't want to know.'

'Why not?' Radha asked.

Manju said: 'I haven't seen Javed in eleven years. I don't want to know.'

But Radha insisted on telling him why Javed had been in the papers, and Manju looked at the floor of the bar and bit his lip.

'You need to find a job, brother. A steady pay cheque. My contract was terminated today,' Manju said, abruptly, to get even with Radha. 'They said it was nothing personal. My form hasn't been bad. They just have too many other dropouts from the IPL who want a job in the Celebrity League.'

His brother reached over and took the white envelope out of Manju's pocket.

'How many months did you get?'

'Two.'

'Congratulations,' Radha said, as he patted the white envelope, which was now in *his* pocket. 'So it really is your birthday. No more cricket. You should have left years ago, before they kicked you out.'

He nudged his glass towards Manju, who said: 'No.'

With a grin, Radha whispered: 'You don't drink, you don't fuck. You're a monster, you know that? Go to that table and introduce yourself to those men. Show them your forearms, little brother.'

'Give me back the envelope,' Manju said.

But it was only to take out the newspaper clipping about the scientist. Reading it along with sips of rum, Radha burst out laughing, spraying Manju with liquor.

'V.V. Cherrinathan: what a name – what a fraud. Telling women he's the prime minister's scientist, asking them for cash. A bit like you, Manju, eh? I have a gift for you, too,' Radha said, reaching into his trouser pocket. 'Birthday gift. A man gave it to me in Versova two nights ago.'

Manju looked at an actor's résumé, which featured a black-and-white snapshot of a brooding chubby-faced man with 1990s hair:

ASIF K. JAMAL

Cintaa (Life member)

Actor by Birth: Thespien by Nature: International by Choice

D.O.B: 23-10-1982

Age of: 28 Yrs

Height of: 5'2

Languages: Hindi, English, Bhojpuri, Urdu, Marathi (plus all known Southern and also Sri Lanka)

Most recent role: Eunch character in latest Shah Rukh Khan film *Dance Baby Dance!*

Notices and Mentions: *Times of India*, *Mumbai Times*, *Mumbai Sun*, *Hollywood Reporter* of US

KINDLY NOTE: I have done 18 very challaging roles including

Female

Mentally Challenged

Epileptic Patient

Gay

Eununch

Zombie

Blind Man

Blind and Handicapped Man

Dumb-Deaf-Blind-Handicap (All in one Character)

Hunchback Notre Dame Type whose body is deformed in nine unique parts (first time in India)

Fustratred Impotant Man

'Why the fuck did he give this to you?'

'He asked me to "push" his career along.'

Manju got all his revenge with a look and a word. He glanced at his brother's leg, and said: 'You?'

'Yes, me. Because I told him I had a brother who was a professional cricketer.'

Touché. Manju studied the résumé.

'He must be from a village. I-m-p-o-t-a-n-t. Like you, Manju. Just like you.' Radha winked. 'Sofia would marry you in two minutes. You treated her badly, but you know she'd leave her husband for you. How much money has she given you by now? She's your new sponsor. You should be nice to her, jump up and down for her, the way you did for the old sponsor. And she's not the only one, is she? You don't screw them, but they just keep doing whatever you want.'

Before Manju could say 'Shut up', a glass broke.

A waiter brought a broom and swept the shards towards the black beam. 'We don't want all that glass here,' Manju protested.

Suddenly smoke filled the bar. The manager, performing a ritual that was either religious or fumigational, circulated a black pot filled with burning coals around his table, and then proceeded to walk with the smoking pot from table to table, starting with Manju and Radha's. Once a Quarter Bar decided to be obnoxious to its patrons, there was no end to it.

The western side of Santa Cruz railway station led towards good residential areas in well-planned blocks; the eastern side was a sea of people.

Coming out of the bar, and re-entering the sea, the brothers were confronted by a beggar. A woman without legs sat on a wooden platform; she began pleading for money, but stopped when she saw how Radha was walking, and sighed.

After all these years, Manju could not get used to the sight of his handsome brother limping, his grotesque left foot in its custom-made shoe. As they left the bar, he turned his eyes away from Radha and pretended to look at the skywalk. The pedestrian bridge, which stood on giant columns down the centre of the road, had a glossy metal frame covered by a glowing blue canopy, and looked like a giant UFO, stretched, partly dismantled, and abandoned over Santa Cruz. The lights of the traffic illuminated the underside of the bridge, and Manju could read the posters stuck to the columns: 'One call can change your life. Phone Rita Mam or Sanjay Sir. Rs

25,000–40,000 per month. Guaranteed.' At least half of the posters were upside down.

Making their way through beggars, drunks, commuters and vendors, the brothers turned towards the Milan Subway, one of the underpasses that led into the western side of Santa Cruz.

Now they passed by an open blacksmith's workshop, the men in masks cutting metal with oxyacetylene flames, raw sparks flying out at passers-by. Manju seized his brother to shield him from the sparks. He was only five foot four inches tall, but he still had the strongest forearms in all of Bombay. He wanted to protect Radha from all of it: the pavements filled with craters, the cars driven by drunks, the cars without headlights, the unpruned tree with the sharp branches ready to fall, the maiming carelessness of life in Mumbai ... but the sparks flew too thick. The autorickshaw driver had been on his cell phone, eight years ago, as he turned his vehicle over Radha Krishna's left foot.

'Manju.'

'What?'

Radha thumped him on the back with his fist.

'Scientist. My little scientist.'

Manju winced: he knew what was coming next. Radha would tease him for still being a virgin.

'Little brother, have you ever tried ... *group* sex? Just wondering.'

'Yes, big brother,' Manju replied. 'I once used *both* hands.'

Radha Krishna Kumar resisted; but then gave up, and howled with laughter.

'Everything was wasted, Manju. Your balls *and* your brains.'

They walked and limped as one body, Manju with his arm around Radha, beige holding on to blue.

They were now right beside the Western Expressway. The cars sped up a ramp towards the airport, giving the brothers the impression that they, in contrast, were descending into a nether-city. Honest work continued around them: shops that sold gravestones engraved in Urdu and Arabic emitted the high-pitched noise of drilling and a fine marble mist that enveloped the brothers. Manju knew that Radha lived somewhere nearby, because he had once asked for a loan to start his own marble-cutting shop. Radha had not met their father in a decade.

When they came out of the Milan Subway, an old man in a suit and tie shouted at them from the other side of the road.

'You!' he said. 'You two – Egypt shall slobber about like a drunk with vomit on his shirt. It is written.'

Radha had apparently seen the old man before

'He's a Telugu Christian from Dharavi. He preaches near the pipeline in Vakola, even when there's no one there. Maybe he wants to convert the petrol.'

Manju frowned.

'Who is Egypt?'

'Egypt,' said Radha, who had gone to a church for a year after his accident, 'means someone rich and powerful.'

'So why is he yelling at *us*?'

The old man kept shouting; a passing bike-rider slowed and said something to him; then a breeze wafted the smell of shit everywhere: the uninterpretable madness of the urban night surrounded the brothers Kumar.

Listening to the crazy preacher across the road, Manju began to laugh. 'Though I am not at home in the world,' he thought, 'I am at home in the street.' A proverb – a new one. He felt he could walk through Mumbai like this forever.

But when he turned he saw Radha biting his fingernails.

Suddenly he found he couldn't bear Radha's company – he wished he hadn't come.

'I am *not* normal people.' He should just tell Sofia that the next time she asked him to meet Radha. 'I want to be alone on my birthday, as I want to be alone every single day.' His excellence, his uniqueness, was not in cricket, not in batting, he had discovered –

but in withdrawing. He could pull back from human beings like the ocean. *That* was his contract with God: Manjunath Kumar would never have to compromise with another person – man *or* woman – would never again have to do for him *or* her the things he had done for his father. Never. If the whole world vanished tomorrow, Manjunath Kumar would barely notice. Didn't Sofia know all this already? Hadn't she said, more than once – 'You are the Einstein of being alone?' So let me retain my one excellence: let me *be* alone!

But when he looked up at the sky, he saw a white moon, as bright and powerful as a man's fist, over Mumbai.

It took his breath away: a sight to remind one of a poet.

'*Kattale*,' Manju said, and held his palm over his right eye, as if to block the sound and smell of his city. Yet behind his mask, he began smiling, thinking of the surprise he had in store for Radha.

Lowering and raising his palm, Manju teased his brother, as if they were playing a children's game, and now Radha permitted himself a smile; for in each of the Kumars had been renewed, by this rare proximity to the other's body, the belief that their shared destiny had not yet been stolen from them.

'This is what I brought you to see,' Manju told his brother.

Behind a ten-foot-tall steel-ringed fence, a floodlit asphalt courtyard was criss-crossed with yellow lines, the kind of place where you saw American children playing basketball in the movies, except here, under the white lights, boys were practising cricket. Dozens of teenagers, padded and helmeted: either sitting on the benches, or standing in the nets while grown men pitched tennis balls at them.

Radha and Manju pressed their faces to the steel-ringed fence.

'This is what I'm going to do from now on. It's part of the severance package.'

'Looks like a cricket factory.'

'They've just opened it. SwadeshSymphony owns it. You come here after school, and train for the IPL. It's open till eleven. You pay this much for three months, then you work with coaches on your batting or bowling.' Manju put his fingers through the steel rings and tried to shake the fence. 'They're paying me eighty-five thousand, and bonuses for finding new talent.'

Manju's eyes reacted with excitement, as always, to the white glare and dark shadows of floodlights: he wanted to get out there and hold a bat. And hit a six, the biggest ever hit in history.

Radha turned to his brother.

'You're going to become a coach? You're going to end up as Tommy Sir?'

'Don't mock him,' Manju said. 'He's dead.'

But Radha was no longer mocking anyone; there was emotion in his voice. He put his fingers through the metal rings of the fence.

'*Why* don't you get married?' he said.

Radha saw that furrow on Manju's brow, the flame-like mark that inclined left, and which indicated that his younger brother was either angry or ashamed or (once upon a time) thinking.

'No,' Manju said. 'Whatever I am, I'm not a *fraud*.'

'What the fuck are you then? Are you *sure* you don't like women? You'll die and go to heaven and even God won't know if you were a homo or not. When we're walking, do you know that if you see any two people holding hands you stare? If two *donkeys* are happy together you stop and watch. I don't know what you really want, but I know it all seems a big mystery to you: two things of any kind being together. It's not a mystery, it's very simple. Get married. There are always women chasing you. Why, I don't know. Even better: you know what you *should* do? Catch a train right now and go to Navi Mumbai. That's what you'd do, if you ever got drunk, and that's why you don't have the guts to drink.'

There was a loud sound of wood cracking: one of the boys at the practice nets had broken his bat.

'You really sound like him now,' Manju said.

'He still talks?' Radha asked. 'I thought he was a vegetable.'

'He's stronger as a vegetable than you and I are as men. He still tries to hit me sometimes, would you believe? Texted me ten times today. "How much did they give you as severance, how much?" Ten times, though he can barely move his hand now.'

A son's true opinion of his parents is written on the back of his teeth. Radha, who had gnashed his just thinking about Mohan Kumar so often that his upper incisors had moved from the pressure, opening up a gap between them and ruining his once perfect smile (one *more* thing he blamed his father for), bit his teeth.

'Why are you here, then?' he shouted at Manju, when he could again talk. 'Why do you meet me once a year? Stay with the vegetable on your birthday.'

Radha could see there was no hope for his brother, who seemed to desire men at one moment and women at another, and lived in between his two desires, like a hunted animal – an animal which had finally run to their father for protection.

'Why *are* you here?' Radha asked again. 'Why?'

'I'm not here,' Manju said, gripping the fence. 'You're not here.'

But he thought of what his brother had said a few minutes ago: take the train and go to Navi Mumbai and meet Javed. Was it still that simple?

Repression may be a red-hot distortion of the truth, but what follows it, acceptance, when a man finally examines his heart and says, 'This is what I must have been, partly or in whole,' is hardly liberation. Nothing much changes because you have stopped lying to yourself. A moment of relief, yes, the sense of shedding some terrible weight – but it passes. Manju had long ago accepted – it had occurred to him one evening in the changing room of the Wankhede stadium, after a particularly fine innings – that what he had known for Javed must have been what the film songs called love, and that his fear of this fact had driven him away from Navi Mumbai and back to cricket. After he wet his hair in front of the mirror and combed it with his fingers, Manju stretched his neck first to the right and then to the left, and accepted that he had been, and was still, attracted to men as much as to women: but knowing and accepting all of this had meant, in the end, not much. The fire of denial had set into the ice of acknowledgement. For himself, for his lies and cowardice, Manju had scorn – (although what else *could* he have done back then?) – but he had much more scorn for a world that had never shown him a clear path to love or to security.

This was enough, he sometimes felt, this anger was enough. A man could feed on it for the rest of his life.

Except that sometimes he saw the moon, and sometimes he heard this laughter in his head: U-ha. U-ha. Even now, he remembered that first morning when he really noticed Javed – was it a morning, or an afternoon? – sitting in that circle of stupid cricketers, the only one unenslaved and unmastered, with his beak nose and his black-panther limbs and the sickle-shaped dimples emerging when he grinned, like the most gorgeous thing created.

O thou Tiger-King!

Manju controlled his breathing. He steadied his pulse. He did all the things he had learnt to do as a professional sportsman, and yet his heart beat fast. Still, with every step he took he was more in control of himself – he remembered that Javed was in the newspaper again – and now it seemed eleven more years might easily flow before they met. If they ever met again.

Standing by his side, Radha tried to read his brother's mind. Why *did* this fellow leave Javed to return to cricket – did he imagine he would save everyone by coming back? Radha remembered what his father used to say: a snake would have to rescue his family from Javed Ansari. But the snake that bit Manjunath had come from within his own heart. He was meant to be the hero of the story, and look what he has become.

Coward!

A whistle blew from the court: cricket practice was over for the day. The boys in white were already leaving with their gear, and workers went about the field, picking up rubbish. One carried a plastic bucket with him, and he splashed the asphalt floor with water.

'I told you to throw your wicket on Selection Day.' Radha raised his voice. 'I *told* you. If you had done that, I wouldn't have got mad, I wouldn't have hit Deennawaz, and they would have given me a second chance to play cricket. And you could have become an engineer, a scientist, you could have gone to America by now. You could have sent me money from there, instead of—'

He threw Manju's envelope to the ground.

'You're drunk, Radha. Eleven years ago, I had no choice. How many times have I told you?'

'Then have children. And make sure *they* have a choice. You know I can't.'

Children? While Radha bent down unsteadily to pick up the envelope, Manju saw in his mind's eye, as he had so many times over the years, an old image from science television: a strand of red-and-blue human DNA, turning nonstop, like a strip of unwinding plastic, the twisted strip of DNA that we inherit from our fathers. And on this red-and-blue helix was inscribed the message from Mohan Kumar to his sons and their sons: that life, if it is to be lived, is to be lived but badly; is to be, if it is to be *anything*, but an agreement with hell; and can have for fire and light, if it is to have either, but rage and remorse. Joining a thumb and index finger through a steel ring of the fence, Manju caught the strand of DNA in his fingers and stopped it from turning: no more cricketers.

'No.'

'Tommy Sir.' Radha laughed. 'Have some self-respect, little brother. Do anything else. Beg. But don't go back into cricket. Don't become Tommy Sir.'

Manju took a deep breath.

'I *told* you, don't mock him. He's gone. Tommy Sir had his stroke right after they picked me for Mumbai. He was hiking in the mountains, they say, and when they carried him to hospital he kept saying, I have to live till I see that boy bat for Mumbai. That would have been my one satisfaction: for him to watch me fail with his own eyes.

Stepping back from the metal fence, Manju cupped his palms, as if he were holding an invisible bowl. He looked straight down into it.

Radha still held on to the fence.

'But he was not the one, Manju. Not Tommy Sir. *He* was never the one to blame.'

Manju stood frozen in his strange gesture. Radha guessed that his younger brother, excited by the sound and smell of live cricket, was imagining himself holding a cricket helmet again. Radha ground his teeth. The boy had just been fired – and here he was dreaming of getting back into the game. Every man must martyr himself to something: but we have martyred ourselves to this mediocrity.

Freeing one hand from the metal rings, Radha pinched Manju in the right shoulder and said:

'I want to fight you again. Till one of us falls. Right here.'

'No.'

Radha pinched harder.

'No.'

And harder and harder: until Manju, at last, shouted – 'Yes!'

Acknowledgements

Over a period of five years, my friend Ramin Bahrani read and edited several drafts of this novel. In the jungle of my life, he has been the white tiger – the only one who ever believed.

Makarand Waingankar, the dean of Bombay cricket writers, shared his knowledge of the game with me over several months in 2011 and 2012. Thank you, Mac.

Ramachandra Guha, Jason Zweig, Malcolm Knox and Jeremy Kirk read early versions of this book and encouraged me to persist with it, as did my editors, Ravi Mirchandani, V.K. Karthika and Andrea Canobbio, and my wonderful agent, Karolina Sutton. I am grateful to each one of them – but above all to Dr Guha, who always found the time to write back.

Girish Shahane, Naresh Fernandes and Jehangir Sorabjee (in Mumbai), Vikas Swarup and Sudeep Paul (in New Delhi), Shalini Perera and James Payten (in Sydney) have helped me more than I deserved to be helped.

Over the oceans that separate us, I send my thanks to an old friend, Mark Greif – and to a new one: two-year-old Simone Greif, who will surely grow up to be every bit as compassionate and intelligent as her father. Some families, I am forced to conclude, work.

When I finished Selection Day, *I knew for whom I had written it – my mother, Usha Mohan Rau, who died on 20 January 1990.*

25 HarperCollins India Pvt. Ltd

Celebrating 25 Years of Great Publishing

HarperCollins India celebrates its twenty-fifth anniversary in 2017. Twenty-five years of publishing India's finest writers and some of its most memorable books – those you cannot put down; ones you want to finish reading yet don't want to end; works you can read over and over again only to fall deeper in love with.

Through the years, we have published writers from the Indian subcontinent, and across the globe, including Aravind Adiga, Kiran Nagarkar, Amitav Ghosh, Jhumpa Lahiri, Manu Joseph, Anuja Chauhan, Upamanyu Chatterjee, A.P.J. Abdul Kalam, Shekhar Gupta, M.J. Akbar, Tavleen Singh, Satyajit Ray, Gulzar, Surender Mohan Pathak and Anita Nair, amongst others, with approximately 200 new books every year and an active print and digital catalogue of more than 1,000 titles, across ten imprints. Publishing works of various genres including literary fiction, poetry, mind body spirit, commercial fiction, journalism, business, self-help, cinema, biographies – all with attention to quality, of the manuscript and the finished product – it comes as no surprise that we have won every major literary award including the Man Booker Prize, the Sahitya Akademi Award, the DSC Prize, the Hindu Literary Prize, the MAMI Award for Best Writing on Cinema, the National Award for Best Book on Cinema, the Crossword Book Award, and the Publisher of the Year, twice, at Publishing Next in Goa and, in 2016, at Tata Literature Live, Mumbai.

We credit our success to the people who make us who we are, and will be celebrating this anniversary with: our authors, retailers, partners, readers and colleagues at HarperCollins India. Over the years, a firm belief in our promise and our passion to deliver only the very best of the printed word has helped us become one of India's finest in publishing. Every day we endeavour to deliver bigger and better – for you.

Thank you for your continued support and patronage.

HarperCollins*Publishers*India

@HarperCollinsIN

@HarperCollinsIN

@HarperCollinsIN

HarperCollins Publishers India

www.harpercollins.co.in

Harper Broadcast

Showcasing celebrated authors, book reviews, plot trailers, cover reveals, launches and interviews, Harper Broadcast is live and available for free subscription on the brand's social media channels through a new newsletter. Hosted by renowned TV anchor and author Amrita Tripathi, Broadcast is a snapshot of all that is news, views, extracts, sneak peeks and opinions on books. Tune in to conversations with authors, where we get up close and personal about their books, why they write and what's coming up.

Harper Broadcast is the first of its kind in India, a publisher-hosted news channel for all things publishing within HarperCollins. Follow us on Twitter and YouTube.

Subscribe to the monthly newsletter here: https://harpercollins.co.in/newsletter/

Harper Broadcast

@harperbroadcast

www.harperbroadcast.com

Address

HarperCollins Publishers India Pvt. Ltd
A-75, Sector 57, Noida, UP 201301, India

Phone
+91-120-4044800